SINGER OF NORGONDY

Susan Shell Winston

The Blazing Star

Threatening the world with
Famine, Plague, and War:
To Princes, Death!..
To Sailors, Storms
To Cities, Civil Treasons!

–De cometis
John Gadbury, London, 1665

ISBN-13: 978-1492225904

ISBN-10: 1492225908

LCCN 2013915628

in acknowledgement

I dedicate this novel to my husband Tom for all his years of inspiration, and encouragement, and understanding me, and for always and 4ever being my first reader.

To Jennifer -- for always being a first reader too, for being a most patient critiquer through numerous revisions, and for telling me Ailil lied.

To Steven -- for long hours discussing ideas and possibilities, and for making the Iceman and the "computering" work.

To Janis -- for her insight into people and personalities that helped me create and understand my characters more and for walking to school one day while I was still at home writing. And to her Bob and Rob, new readers someday too, I hope.

To Karen and Tom for being a first reader and a great supporter, and for always being 29 at heart.

To Jeanne Cavelos for starting Odyssey, encouraging me and so many other new writers into going forth down our roads less traveled, stuffing our backpacks full of the skills, suggestions, and helpful criticisms we need to endure those unexpected plot turns our characters keep making. And for a beloved picture of a bear her husband drew.

To Odfellows who've helped improve this novel with their comments and suggestions, especially to the members of the first Odyssey class of 96 who were the first writers to tell me that perhaps I could write fantasy -- Patricia Jackson, Aly Parsons, Judi Hardin, David Schwartz, JoAnn Forgit Cox, Mark Stafford, Lee Smith, Lynda Rucker, and Derek Hill.

To Odfellows of later tneos who read and commented on Singer, suggesting new directions and spotting false turns, and most importantly, giving me encouragement to keep writing it.. Special thanks to Rita Oakes, Ellen Denham, Jim Hall, David Corwell, Geoffrey Jacoby, Jennifer Brinn,

Barbara Campbell, Dan Fitzgerald, Larry Taylor, Susan Sielinski, Bob Cutchin, Joe Berwanger, Hannah Strom-Martin, Roger Bagwell, and especially to the Western Odyssey group members Abby Goldsmith, Laurie Lemieux, Jennifer Weideman, Rebecca Shelley and her daughter Kimberly, and to the Clarion spy, Candy Byrne for wading through the whole thing!

And finally to Houston writers who helped me to learn to write and critique long years ago-- Sandra Worth, Dick Lemmon, and Carlos Valrand.

And to Erica Aguilar for a last minute edit. And to Arielle Rohan-Newsome, fantasy artist extrodinaire.

I thank you all. And Jesser does too.

For maps of Norgondy, visit holdenstone.com.

SINGER OF NORGONDY

Chapter 1
Dreamwalker

Smoke teared Horl's eyes and stung through his chest. He added two hands of numbstool to the fire in the giant clam shell, chanting as he worked. The new moon was entering the year's window and would soon stretch from base stone to top stone, and the Naming would begin.

He waved the thick yellow smoke into his face four times, humming and swaying to stay awake, to keep his concentration.

The ancient cypress door creaked open. The glow from the lighthouse below flooded the stone hut, brightening the smoke to lemon haze and blurring the silhouette of the first dreamer.

"Enter, boy, and return a man," cawed the Pelican, standing guard outside the door. Beneath the bird's heavy mask and feathers was Jornal, the village cooper, but this was a secret a nameless boy was not man enough yet to know.

The door closed and the boy stood alone before Horl. His newly made man's tunic, much too long for a seven-year old, still dripped from the initiation dunking.

Horl sat unblinking as the boy--it was Orul's son, Yaris, it looked like--stared at him. It was the first time Yaris would've seen Horl's head unturbaned. The web of circles, waves and spirals tattooed into his shaven skull, each line a dangerous thread into the whale's dream from which true men had sprung, was highlighted tonight by vicious black and gold god-paint on his face. Horl had stained his teeth with blood, and he bared them as he lifted a bony finger and pointed to the dreaming mat.

Yaris lay face up, his hands clenched at his sides, his breath raspy. It would not be long before the smoke overtook him, as young as he was, and as scared.

Horl waved the smoke into his face and closed his eyes.

Then, through dark and icy cold he walked, unbodied, unskinned. The air was smoke that stung him, lifted him, passed through him. Seeking, he found the one tiny flicker of flame. He held it up in his hand and stepped into it. And he saw with Yaris his dream.

The stark shape of a great black iron hood against soot-grey bricks. Sweat-stained arms glistening red with forge fire. Hammering, the constant sharp sound of hammering.

The great sigh of bellows; and a scythe blade being tempered. Its curved blade, brought bright red from the fire, lay hissing in water. The blade was refired until the colors graded down, light straw to blue to brown to a bee's-wing color. When the long blade was held up with tongs in front of the forge, its hammered edge sparked war-blood red.

Horl walked out of Yaris's dream.

"Awaken, young man of the village. You shall be called Yarisol. True brother of the whale. True son of the blacksmith. Walk in his path."

Excitement and relief shone in Yarisol's face. He had inherited his father's soul and would become a smith as his father was before him. Horl nodded and allowed a smile.

"Send in your year-mates," he said kindly.

Stal's twins came in together. Their mother had died seven years ago giving them birth. It was a rare, blessed thing for an Islander village to have twins. The village had paid for them dearly with her death.

The twins lay down together. One, young Cray, would paddle his goat-hide coracle out into the bay as their father had before him, throwing his nets and emptying baskettrap after baskettrap of salmon into his small bobbing

6

boat to feed the village. The other, young Cree, whom Horl's wife had suckled at his hearth along with their own infant son, dreamed of pots, and tins, and tinkering, and of a small tinker wagon rattling down the road from town to town, and of...

sharpening a scythe blade. Wiping it clean of war-blood. Swinging it like an axe at a guardsman on an ice-covered river. The guardsman struck back. His sword, long and bright, flashed an instant in Cree's face. Then it cleaved into Cree's side.

The dream vision swirled into a whirlpool of black, and blood, and smoke.

Horl snapped open his eyes and stared at the lad. What ever would a fisher's son have to do with fighting a guardsman of the mainland?

He called the twins awake.

"Rise, Crayl, true son of the fisher. And Crel..." The lad stood up in the smoke-filled hut looking across at him with a solemnity in his dark amber eyes beyond his years, looking as if he too could remember the dream. Horl's throat constricted over the taste of thick smoke. "You shall walk the path of a tinker."

Horl's head pounded by the time his own son stood in the doorway of the stone hut. The sickle moon had long passed beyond the year's window and was entering the small smoke hole overhead. His son was the last of the only six boys who had lived through the week of ordeals; and the timing of the moon was propitious.

"Enter, Ver, and return, a man," cawed the Pelican.

As the door closed behind him, Ver stood in the smoke in his still-dripping tunic and watched Horl with clear blue eyes, noting every flick of movement he made. There was no fear in the boy; he had seen his father unturbaned and god-painted before, although he would have never spoken of it to his year-mates.

As Horl tossed another hand of numbstool into the fire, Ver studied the weaving of his fingers. Ver had already shown much talent in the making of the small magics, starting a fire with a song on his stick, clouding the vision of his year-mates and hiding as he stood in front of

7

them, casting his voice into the leaves of a tree behind them as he laughed at them spinning around to search for him.

Horl pointed to the dreaming mat, careful to control his own emotions. He had high expectations his son would become a great Village Father after him.

Horl closed his eyes to step into Ver's dream. As soon as he found the small white flame, Ver's presence stood inside it, waiting for him. His son plunged with him into the dream.

...Fingers, long and skilled, shaped smoke into circles. Fire under the smoke rose through the circles into a flower bud; its seven pointed petals bloomed into a golden starflower. The smoke thickened, began smelling of lemon and meadowlands.

The fingers closed through the smoke upon the glistening strings of a lute, and rippled through them fast, certain, gentle. Its music rose like fire into flowers. Golden starflowers showered down upon the uplifted faces of a sea of listeners. One face--

One face, entranced, melted everything into it. Pained and bloodied, a deep wound opening his side, a farmer's scythe blade lay on the ice beside him. Ver's long gentle fingers lifted his friend up, crying. The grown-up face of Crel lay in his arms, dying.

Horl stepped out of the dream. Ver, awakening on his own, stood up in the smoke-filled hut. His eyes, too young for what he had seen, beseeched his father for an explanation.

It took all of Horl's training to stay calm. "You shall be called Verl. You shall be a healer and a great harpist someday."

The boy stood waiting for him to say more. When he did not, the boy's face fell. He would not become his father's heir.

"It is not a dream to be ashamed of," Horl said, hiding his own disappointment. "Your music shall fall like flowers to us on that day."

The boy's eyes lit with the brightest vision of the dream, of the golden starflowers falling upon a sea of listeners; and one of those rare, quick, unguarded smiles, still full of his son's innocence and youth, broke toothily across his face.

The smile vanished when Horl added, "Go tell your mother that you shall leave on the merchant ship tomorrow. You'll be sold into apprenticeship to Singerhalle in Norgarth by week's end. It's the only place left to learn to walk the path of such a dream."

Horl closed his eyes and listened until the door was pulled shut.

Then, slowly, he gathered his bags of numbstool and reeds, and, chanting, quenched the fire. But his hands paused when he heard a loud sharp wail of grief coming from the longhouse in the village below. His wife had heard his son's news. Horl had hoped to give his village an heir in Verl. Instead, by this time tomorrow, Verl's name would be struck from the village records and never be spoken again.

Horl closed the dreaming hut behind him and walked down the hill. Before the sun rose, he would have to take a new wife into his house tonight, and this time, make for his village a true son.

Chapter 2
Singerhalle

Twelve years later

By the light of the fire, Verl scratched charcoal across the rough surface of a hearthstone. Paper was a luxury no apprentice at Singerhalle could afford. At least not to waste on idle drawings.

Some of the circles and spiral paths he remembered vividly. The web of guilt, the song of gifts, the edge of sorrow, the path of hope were etched into four of the five corners on the pentagon he had drawn, but Verl could never remember seeing the spiral of forgetfulness tattooed among the twenty-five mysteries on his father's skull. If he had seen it, it was only as one of the many intricate spirals he had never learned to recognize in his short failed life as his father's heir.

Many times since, he had filled in the empty corner with a spiral of his own design, hoping he knew the path to forgetfulness without knowing he did. It would be bliss, he often thought, to forget.

But tonight, he left the fifth corner empty and began scrawling the dream inside the pentagon, well aware that, unbounded, he'd more easily let the dream escape.

It mattered little. His dreams always escaped him.

First, the gull, his own device, no more than oval wings, an open beak, and a circle for a head. It was the one sign he had never changed from his first crude drawings in his childhood. This time, tonight, for pure malice perhaps, or in grim hopefulness, he etched a meadow starflower hanging from its beak. He took great care to make each detail of the flower right. The seven petals opened half-way up. The long slender leaves escaped in a cluster from the gull's beak. Verl took a fresh, harder piece of charcoal from the fire's edge and drew in the tiny twelve tendrils of the stamen in the flower's center. He counted and named the path of each tendril, then he stepped towards their spiral

10

and saw them clearly. He smelled the crowd of lemony flowers in the meadow around him, he heard the wind blowing--

"More witchdoctoring?"

Verl tensed, then he pulled back into himself, out of the dream. He stumbled a second over his first quick reaction to fight or run before he could control his old embarrassment at being caught practicing his father's forbidden arts. When he was younger, he had been called before the masters daily, it seemed, for striking out at the other apprentices who'd called him 'the witchdoctor.' But most of those apprentices, his old friends he had once drilled with, had long since earned their chains of mastery and had gone off journeying on their own. None of the newer apprentices, the oldest one, three years younger than he, dared tease him to his face for what few Islander beliefs he still held.

The voice above him, though, was not someone Verl had heard speak to him in the last two years. The corner of his lips pulled upwards into a faint smile.

He rose and dropped a slight bow, then he sat back down on the hearth, covering his scrawlings with his hand. "I did not hear you come in, Eleidice, forgive me."

She looked down at him. Her stiff black curls tumbled from both sides of her white cowled hood, framing her dark brown face. She wore the sable-trimmed azure robe of a Singer, and on her chest, the gold links of a master's chain reflected the firelight. She had matured considerably in the last two years, filling out and curving in. She was taller too, as statuesque as everyone in the countess-side of her family. He remembered when she had first come to Singerhalle when he was ten. Two years younger than he, she had been put in his care then, to teach her the first five fingerings. She had earned her master's chain two years ago, and he had only seen her from a distance since.

She sat down on the hearth and lifted his hand from his drawings. She tilted her head at them, trying to understand them. The charcoal had smudged and little detail was left.

11

"You promised once you'd show me what these meant."

He crooked a smile. It felt odd to acknowledge his drawings, especially to someone who was not teasing him for doing them. "Years ago, Lady." He met her eyes. "We were younger then."

Her black eyes caught the spark of the fire behind him. "And have your drawings lost their meaning since then?"

Verl dropped his hand back over them. "I did not think anyone would be coming to the Hall tonight."

She glanced around the dark recesses of the vast room. No candle or lantern was left burning, aside from the candle she herself had brought in. "I saw the fire was still high. You don't sleep among the cinders in here these days, do you?" There was a tease in her voice.

"I finished everything in here an hour or so ago," he admitted. "But I haven't quenched the fire yet." Truth be known, he had fed it. Wood was expensive to keep more than one log in all of Singerhalle burning throughout the night. And that one log was in the masters' private wing.

Eleidice darted her eyes back at him. "You're not still on the scrunging team, are you?"

He shrugged. "Pays my keep still." His father, he remembered suddenly, and oddly--having just been thinking of him and that night, he guessed--his father had expected to be paid for selling his son into apprenticeship. But Singerhalle didn't work that way. And when neither envoy nor collector could convince his village to pay for his training or else take him back, Verl had spent as many hours during his long years here hand-scrubbing the flagstone floors and polishing the silver wine trays of the masters, as he had learning to play the lute. Few apprentices past twelve stayed on the scrunge team. But then, far fewer apprentices were still apprentices at Verl's age.

"Is everything in here polished down to the last leaf and curl for tomorrow?" she asked, wickedly. The silver barrel of the telescope in the bay window was notorious among the apprentices for its ornate engravings.

12

Verl tightened when she mentioned tomorrow. He switched back to the safer subject. "My father, my Lady, would have been insulted that you had dared to look at my drawings."

"Your father?"

"You," he explained. "It'd be taboo. You're a woman... Now."

Her lips parted slightly. "Ah. And in the Eller Islands, women have no rights?"

"Different rights. The women own all the land and wealth, but the men own all rights to knowledge and dreams of the soul–" She cocked her high brows at him. "Or so the men believe," he amended softly. "Will you be judging me tomorrow--?" He kicked himself. He had not wanted to blurt that out.

She lifted his hand off the drawing, spread open his long slender fingers. "You always had more talent than any of us."

He stared off into the dark merciful room. Talent had taken him nowhere.

She went on in his silence. Singerhalle training kept her voice soothing. "Three masters from Abirne, Sherd, and Dallet shall sit in tomorrow as your guest judges, plus all six of our high masters at the Hall, of course. As for the journeymasters--" he turned to her, and she met his look, "Edex and Juliard shall sit in for us. Everyone else left the city when the war began. But…if I can, I will be here in the Hall too, watching and counting on you, Verl. You can be sure of that."

Verl shifted his eyes away again, said nothing.

Eleidice rose and went to the far corner of the fireplace. There, half in shadow, a velvet pouch leaned against the wall. She took it back to Verl and pulled his lute out of its pouch.

"Have you named her yet?" she asked as she handed the lute down to him.

He took it, then quirked a grin up at her. "Leidel."

She gave a start, recognizing Leidel to be what her name would be in the far-away Eller Islands.

He motioned her to sit back down. "Perhaps it will inspire her to sing as well as her namesake can someday."

Eleidice traced a leaf carving on the lute's soundboard. "You did beautiful work on her," she said.

He lay his arm over his lute protectively and settled it across his lap, hiding the soundboard. "Perhaps I should have apprenticed to a woodcutter instead."

"Verl--"

He shook his head at himself. "Do you see this?" He pointed down to his smudged drawing. "It's supposed to be a seagull. One of the many I saw as a boy, back when I believed in omens. I had a puppy. You could see his whole life in his eyes, and in his excited stubby tail. I climbed a cliff above the sea. My puppy didn't make it, he slipped on the loose rocks, fell, and broke his neck. Before I got down to him, a gull stood on his head, pecking his eyes out."

"--Verl!"

He gripped the neck of his lute tightly. "I've drawn a gull eating my dreams ever since."

Her dark gentle hand closed over his stiffened fingers. "You could pass easily tomorrow. You could play anything else--"

"No! " He stood up, quieted his voice. "No. There is only one song I was sent here to play. The song I swore out loud I would play when I first came here. The song that ended who I was to become."

"Verl! No one expects you to play a song that can actually make people see flowers--"

"I do." He met her eyes. "I have to."

~

Pulling a peasant shawl around her baby's face and her own, the Capsen tellerwoman Ailil shoved through the crowd to the king's execution. Perhaps she should have walked unseen, it would be safer now. But she'd always promised Henrik she would never create an illusion here, not in his city, not against his people. And her baby Eris deserved to see his father look down on him one last time.

Ailil pushed through to the front of the crowd just in time. Henrik lifted his head a fraction of an inch and met her eyes; then not saying a word to reveal their presence, he lowered his head to the stone. One last testament to his honor and courage she had always loved in him.

Queen Felain stood on the dais in the sunlight. No shawl covered her head. Her son Laird, Eris's half-brother, hid his face in his mother's skirt as the executioner raised the axe. Felain gripped the boy's shoulder and turned him back around to watch his father be beheaded in the public street.

Ailil uncovered Eris's face a moment to let him see too, and remember, always.

To cheers, Felain's high priest circled Henrik's decapitated body, shaking his belled staff over him. He bent down and lifted up Henrik's head by blood-soaked blond hair and shouted, "Glory to the Winged One!" The priest tossed the head into a waiting cauldron to be boiled and preserved for later display.

As Henrik was being quartered, arms from shoulders, legs from hips, Ailil sank back into the crowd. Her hands trembled; she kept biting her lip to keep herself from screaming out loud. Little Eris closed his hand around her finger.

Ailil looked down at him, then touched his cheek softly, grimly, and wiped a speck of blood off his eyelash. She covered the shawl back over them both.

Shaking his belled staff, the priest approached the boy on the dais and bowed before him. He placed Henrik's crown on the boy's head. "Long live King Laird!" he shouted to the people.

All around Ailil, the crowd threw up holy feathers, hats, and roses. "Long live the King!" they shouted, as riverlets of kingly blood flowed beneath their feet.

Felain's face glowed triumphant in the sun.

Hidden behind her shawl, Ailil sputtered a few words at her in Capsen. The queen blanched suddenly and glanced behind her.

Ailil walked away from the square with her head held high, her vengeance begun. Someday she and Eris would return. Until that day came, let Felain go mad hearing Henrik's voice call her name in every crowd.

"And," she whispered to Eris, kissing his forehead with the promise, "come their dreams by night, may Felain and Laird both fear shadows far worse than just hearing your father's voice." The baby gurgled and batted his fists in the air.

She had not broken her promise to Henrik. Not yet. …Not on a large scale yet at least.

~

Light from the three high stained-glass windows in Singers' Hall splashed across the polished flagstones. Verl listened as young Kirt played before the masters. It always seemed to him that the different colors of the lights falling on the floor brightened and faded in time to the changing notes.

From outside in the distant streets, a crowd started cheering. Verl kept his head lowered, determined to hear only Kirt play.

Like watching colored harp strings vibrate, he saw streaks of yellow shimmer into gold on the stones in front of his left boot. The music softened, and Verl saw instead quivering streaks of green and blue grow brighter. Then red splashed discordantly back onto the next stone as Kirt played the first strident calls of the war horns ripping the peace of the countryside in Aarik's *Shepherd's War*.

Then undertone, Verl heard the crowd shouting louder. He tried still to ignore it.

Despite the commotion, Kirt didn't falter. Any other day of the year, all the Master Singers would have left the hall immediately, gone outside, to record in song and story whatever was happening.

They would still have to send someone to record it, Verl knew. Even today. He glanced around. Eleidice was gone.

Of course she was. Verl quirked his lip in a twinge of disappointment. She was the only Master Singer left in Singerhalle, she had said, who would not be sitting as a judge today. She was the only one who could go.

16

The cheering came again. It was the prince's birthday this week, everyone knew that. Laird was turning seven.

But the crowd sounded closer than the palace.

Perhaps the people were celebrating an end finally to the war. Verl hoped so. He'd heard a week ago that the old king had been captured. He'd heard nothing since, third stage apprentices had been kept in seclusion over the past week to prepare for today— *Counting on you, she had said last night*. The words twisted. He wondered if Eleidice had known then she would be gone today. He stiffened, and acknowledged the likelihood.

Then he lowered his head to the lights again and listened only to Kirt . Within a minute, there was no sound left coming in from outside.

Throughout it all, the lad had kept playing his required piece well. *Shepherd's War* was a song noted for quick scales and sudden changes of chords and tempo. Yet after long afternoons of Verl's tutoring, Kirt was skillful enough to be sure of his fingering. He was concentrating instead on playing with emotion, a true talent of the lad that would set him above the other apprentices in the room today, in Verl's proud estimation.

Verl listened to the crescendo of the battle scene: red, purple, blue streaks of light on the floor, red, red, blue -- <u>orange</u>. Verl's breath stopped. Then he closed his eyes and gripped the lute at his side.   He prayed that the masters seated in judgment would not count the one slipped fingering too much against the lad.

But Kirt had noted his error as well, and his playing from then on grew hesitant. That was a worse mistake.

Six new chains of mastery had already been awarded this morning. But Kirt, failing this year, returned to the apprentice circle beside Verl. Bravely, the lad gave Verl an encouraging nod when the Lord Master called Verl's name.

The lights on the floor went with him. Blue, yellow, softly blurred splashes of rose spread around him and moved before him, as rainbows in the waves moved when he was a child on the beach trying to catch them.

17

Verl stopped in the center of Singer's Hall, in the center of the fall of lights from the highest rose window, and bowed before the masters.

He played the scales, the studies, the required pieces expertly, with a surety and feeling many masters twice his age would never achieve. With the lute in his hand, his Leidel, it was music that played him, he always felt. The music and the lights. He was music's conduit only, he took no credit for it. The lights, the colors on the stones welled up through him, from the tight tingling in his toes, through the tense strained feeling in his legs, up through the swelling in his chest, and then stretched out into his fingers onto the strings. He translated light into song, until each shining string became a note, a shimmering color of light on the floor before him.

"And now," the Lord Master said, "your masterpiece."

Verl looked up at the Lord Master, at the high withered cheekbones sharpened by age. At the wisps of white hair, at the stern cracked lips that still sung evening chants like a deep-throated loon. At the kindness in the Lord Master's eyes, and at the sad smile in them.

Verl glanced at the other masters seated with the Lord Master. He saw the rapture on the faces of the three guest masters who had never heard him play before. *You could pass easily*, Eleidice had said last night. *You could play anything else.*

Verl flexed his fingers, then bowed to the Lord Master. "'The Song of the Meadowflowers' by Dellet the Younger," he announced. "My own variation," he added softly, knowing it would happen to him again.

He entered the song well, controlling the music, quelling the lights inside him, playing the notes precisely as they were written. Then, softly, he let his fingers play the wind blowing across the meadow, and the sun shining on the golden flowers. On one golden starflower. He closed his eyes to the music, saw the lights shining on the flower, outlining it petal by petal, redrawing it in his mind as he had with the charcoal last night. Each stamen, each petal and leaf, precise, exact, forming a flower out of song and light to rise and shower down upon him in the light from the rose window, as his music someday, his father had promised, would fall like flowers upon his listeners.

But this flower was in his mind only, his fingers were making music, touching strings only. He had to make the vision *true*. Had to make others see the flower, see the music as he saw it. He felt the power, the rapture within him from his father's blood flowing through him to make the flower real, the need to translate the song back into light.

He played, he forced the music louder, stronger, note after note, petal after petal, redrawing the flower, making it *form* out of the shimmering lights.

Then he snapped his eyes open to see.

His Leidel, his lute was in his hands only. No flower, no music was a shining substance in the air before him. No flower was there for anyone else to see.

He had done it to himself again, lied to himself again.

Lights shone down from the rose windows above him, broke apart into colors, their circle of light trapping him back into reality, into his inadequacy to make a flower. Mocking him for believing he and his music could be more than he was, for believing he could still one day be his father's heir.

There was no note left for him to play now that could come from within. His song was unfinished, and there was no easy way to slide back into the notes of Dellet's 'Song of the Meadowflowers' as it was written.

Verl ended the song as he had begun it, precise, exact, fluid notes, the music controlled, and inadequate. Unfinished, and sounding unfinished, after what he had done to it.

He lowered his head a moment, then he stiffened his shoulders and looked up, awaiting the judgment of the masters.

"You play beautifully," said one of the guest masters.

"With the touch of a great artist," said another.

"But your song was not ready to be played yet, was it?" challenged the third.

"What is your answer to that, Verl?" asked the Lord Master.

Verl met his eyes, then spoke the truth. "It is not finished yet, lord."

The sad smile pulled at the corners of the old man's lips. "A masterpiece cannot be judged as a masterpiece until it is ready to be heard. You have been told this in years past, Verl. Too many years past. You've been apprentice here longer than anyone, twelve years as I recall. We've kept you because you have the talent to be better than any of us someday. But talent alone can never earn you a chain of mastery from our guild. You must learn to control your music first. In twelve years, you have not. It is beautiful, but it is wild--not finished yet, as you say."

Verl's fingers closed around the neck of his lute. He nodded mutely and started to turn back to the apprentice circle.

"Wait," said the Lord Master.

Verl looked back up at him.

"As I said, you have been apprentice here longer than anyone. You will be twenty within the next year, is that not so?... Then, Verl, we have discussed this and decided. Today was your last chance."

Verl froze. He heard the master's words fall to him one by one like dark notes echoing around him in a well.

"You can no longer be an apprentice here...you are too old...I'm sorry...You will come to me tomorrow...I will have your papers made ready for you to go."

Numbly, as the words echoed around him, Verl stood motionless in the circle of lights falling around him from the rose windows above. Then, his lips twitching with irony, he bowed to the judgment of the masters. His hand clenched around his lute.

"This is not the end, Verl," the lord master went on. "This is not the last we hope to see of you." Bowing in the light, dark words falling to him, Verl barely heard them. "You must go, but you may come back to try again someday. However long it takes you to play your song,

20

you will play it for us, Verl. You must," the old man said,
looking down at him sadly. "You can just never,
apparently, learn to play it sheltered here."

Chapter 3
Tinker

"Damn you, Jesser, move it!"

In slow, serene motion, Jesserlinellian turned her head and looked past her black snout at Crel with small, disinterested bear eyes.

"Do you see this?" Crel drew his knife. The blade caught the orange glow of the setting sun. It was a long fisherman's blade, his one prized possession from the Eller Islands, the one gift his father had ever given him before selling him off to become a tinker, seven years ago, when he was still just a lad of twelve. His father had bequeathed everything else, his nets, boats, and soul, to Crel's twin brother.

The dancing bear lifted a heavy, dainty paw off the ground to lean her head closer to the blade. Her black nostrils widened as she whuffed at it. Then deciding it was no carrot, perhaps, or long apple, she gave Crel a disdainful grunt and swung back around to face the corner of the two boulders she had wedged herself into. She sat on her haunches, her back turned to him, nine hundred talenweights of stubbornness and arrogance.

"You don't believe I'd use it, do you?" With one hand still holding the chain he'd already attached to her collar, Crel stepped closer to her, touched his knife blade against the back of her neck, and slid it up through her short wiry fur to the soft spot behind her ear. "I'd loved to, you know," he whispered. "Just one nip off your ear perhaps, just to teach you a lesson."

Jesserlinellian arched her neck back closer to his hand, making it easier for him to reach the soft spot where she loved to be scratched.

In spite of himself, Crel chuckled at her, then used the back of the knife blade to lightly rub her behind her ear. The bear grunted again, this time, in satisfaction.

"Damn you, Jesser. I don't want to be late again tonight!" A good stiff kick in the rump would be awarded with no more than another grunt. A hard switching with willow branches would have no greater effect. At least once or twice a month, Jesserlinellian would wedge herself between two trees or rocks like this and be unmovable for hours, just to remind Crel who was in charge. There was a softer spot beside her tailbone where a knife prick might truly get her moving. Tonight, the urge to try something so desperate was tempting. Otherwise, Crel knew, she was waiting for him to beg. To say out loud--five times!--he was sorry. Old Wiss, master tinker and off-time bear trainer, had taught her to count.

Old Wiss swore that Jesserlinellian understood every word they said. Unlike, he added, any of his last three wives he had named her after.

"I warn you, Jesser. I'll take you to town myself tonight, and *sell* you for a bag of silver! Enough to buy my own wagon. And Wiss would never know. I'd tell him you were stolen." Not true of course, but if Wiss's bear understood every word he said, Crel could make use of every word.

The bear snapped her head around. Perhaps she had understood after all. She growled deep in her throat, her rumble growing.

Crel wrapped her chain around his arm, ready for her to move. The last thing he wanted to do, though, was to pull on her chain. That, she never allowed, and he valued his fingers too much when he fed her. As well as his ankles when he slept--

The bear growled louder, but not at him. It still was loud enough, close enough to make the hair on the back of his neck rise. She lumbered up onto her hind legs and whuffed the air. Crel gripped the chain.

The next instant, she was bounding away on all fours through the woods towards their camp, Crel running as hard as he could to keep up with her.

She was running faster than usual, though. Wiss must have returned to camp already. He was the only thing that could make her run this fast.

The bear kept bounding away faster, pulling Crel along behind her with her chain, until she was going faster than he could run. He held onto the chain, but he stumbled; then he was dragged across hard roots and stones, yelling at her to stop. It took torturous long seconds before he could free his arm from her chain and let her go.

"Damn you, Jesser!" he yelled after her as she bounded out of sight.

He rose stiffly, testing the elbow that had hit the roots the hardest. He cursed after her, brushing the twigs and forest litter off his hair and black woolen half-coat. His tinker hat must have been left somewhere behind. While that damn bear was probably hugging Old Wiss by now, or doing a dance for him, as if nothing had happened.

"Nothing but porridge and beans for a week for you, Jesser!" he shouted. His leg was stiff. His black woolen tradesman pants that hung wide and loose from the waist buttons were torn open on the right knee, and he could already see blood. Through the trees ahead, he could hear the bear snarling. "And you can forget about the beans too!"

He retrieved his hat and started walking back to camp.

But the growling kept growing louder.

Crel listened, then began to run.

When he reached the meadow, he pulled himself up short, grabbing a branch at the last second to keep from entering the clearing.

Their camp was in shambles. Pots, tins, stools, everything tumbled out of the wagon. The snake and squirrel meat he had hung to dry were gone, and the barrel of salt pork was pulled down from the wagonside and broken open. Esra the delta mare and her mule colt must have bolted. And Saris, notably the most dim-witted of all tarney oxen, was on the other side of the clearing confronted by trees, splayed-legged in front of them, bellowing at them, not knowing which way to go.

Closer to the wagon, Old Wiss was up a tree, hanging on for his life.

Below him, stretching its massive arms up the wide trunk, its sharp claws reaching just below Wiss's heels, stood the largest crested bear Crel had ever seen.

And growling, pacing back and forth behind it, was Jesserlinellian, half the crested bear's size.

No way in the Goron was Crel going to enter that clearing and get between those two bears. Not so long as Old Wiss was safely up a tree, at least. Unlike the smaller, more agile black bears, crested bears did not climb trees.

Still Crel needed to do whatever he could to get Jesser away from that bear too. For Wiss's sake.

Crel glanced up at the tree next to him, calculating his own escape route just in case. Then he took out his sling and opened the pouch of stones at his side.

So far, the crested bear was still ignoring Jesser's challenge.

But that little bear, damn her, never one to like being ignored, ruffed up the back of her neck and growled louder. Crel fitted his largest, smoothest stone into the pit of his sling and waited for the crested bear to turn around. If he had any chance at all to scare it away, he'd have to hit it between the eyes.

Then everything happened at once.

Wiss's left foot slipped a few inches down the tree.

The bear below him swatted sharp claws at his foot as the old man scrambled to pull his leg back up.

And Jesser chose that moment to swat the other bear on its rump.

The crested bear growled and snapped its jaws back around at her; then it swatted at Wiss's foot again, madder now, more dangerous than before.

Jesser rose up on her hind legs behind it, growling louder, ready to cuff it on its shoulder.

"*Jesser - Linel - Lian!*" Old Wiss called down to her, warning her. He always called her by her full name, saying each name of his three wives distinctly. "Cage, Jesser-Linel-Lian! *Cage!*" Normally Wiss's order would have been enough to send her loping happily into her cage wagon.

But tonight, that bear was in no mood to obey anyone.

She growled as fiercely as she could and cuffed the crested bear's shoulder.

25

"No! *Cage!*" Wiss yelled. His foot slipped again in his urgency.

In slow, dreadful motion, the crested bear stretched one lazy paw up closer to Wiss's foot. Then, not quite reaching it yet before Wiss scrambled his leg up higher, the bear dropped lumberously down to face the pest behind him.

Jesser stood up on her hind legs in dance position, her forepaws raised like a boxer's. Her white diamond patch from her chin to her belly was fully visible as she and the crested bear circled each other, the crested bear padding around her on all fours.

Crel could not get a clear shot with his sling.

Jesser swatted a paw out in the air above the crested bear's head.

The crested bear growled, then it lifted itself up to full height until it towered its massive brown head above her. It swatted down at her and growled louder. A growl that started as a deep rumble in its throat that crescendoed into a fierce, loud snarl as it pulled back its jaws and showed its teeth. It raised its head skyward. Saliva frothed in the air as it shook its head back and forth above her. Then it lowered its head to Jesserlinellian and thundered at her in a roar that still shook through Crel after it ended.

He stood paralyzed by the roar. Then, recovering, he gasped in a breath. The bear was still standing up, facing him.

Crel stepped into the clearing and whirled his sling.

The crested bear's roar and impressive display should have been enough to warn any bear --Jesserlinellian included--to leave it alone.

But as Crel launched the stone aimed between the big bear's eyes, the dancing bear charged. Jaws opened, foreclaws striking, she lunged head-long into its furry brown chest, tearing into its shoulder as high as her teeth could reach.

The two bears tumbled to the ground and rolled over each other, a vicious mass of shaggy brown fur and short black-and-white fur. Crel's stone thunked into Wiss's tree above them, embedding itself there.

Crel made ready another stone to send as soon as he could. Other than that, he could only watch as the bears twisted and snarled and rolled over each other, then broke away, circled again, and attacked again--

Then his breath stopped. Old Wiss had climbed down the tree.

Crel lowered his sling arm, incredulous. The old man crept behind the fighting bears, bent down, picked up two large copper pots.

Crel rammed his sling into his pouch and drew his knife instead and started running to Old Wiss. The sentimental old fool. He'd get himself killed trying to save his pet bear.

He barely reached Wiss's side before the old man slammed the back of one of the heavy pots squarely on top of the crested bear's head as it circled past him.

Crel yanked the old man away as the crested bear snapped around and snarled at him.

Jesser rushed in from the other side and buried her teeth into its exposed neck, diverting its attention just in time. The crested bear twisted back on her, clawing at her. It spun its massive neck back and forth, yanking her with it, swatting her down. Larger, swifter, it tore in after her.

Wiss turned silently to Crel, stared at him with crazed expectations.

The bears were circling each other again, Jesser losing, still growling.

Wiss held out one of his pots to his journeyman.

Crel swallowed air. He clenched his fist, glanced down at the pot. Then with a thin line of recklessness pulling at his lips, he took it.

Substituting himself into the fight for the old man was the only thing he could do, he had seen in his expression, that would keep Old Wiss out of it. He had no delusion he himself would live through it.

Crel approached the circling bears, shouting, banging on the back of the pot with the hilt of his knife, trying to make the clangor as loud as he could. Frighten it to death? As good a hope as any. His shouting became a hysterical laugh.

But then, the old man rushed in beside him, and slammed the heavy pot on top of the crested bear's head again, and kicked in at its side as it passed.

Crel could barely pull Wiss away this time. The look in the old man's eyes had become feverish. He meant to single-handedly fight for his bear if Crel would not.

Crel shoved the old man back behind him. Then, with his own recklessness grown intent, hard-edged, he dropped the pot from his one hand, tightened his grip on his long knife with the other, and watched the bears circle closer. He would have one chance only.

As the crested bear passed him, Crel leapt onto its back, flung his left arm around its massive neck, ripped his knife hand hard around it, slashing deep into the furry throat as he pulled the blade back to him. Then he tried to jump free.

But Jesser was attacking again, rushing in, clawing at the diverted bear. One of her claws in the twisting flurry flew higher up, raked into Crel's side as he jumped free.

He clutched at his side, stumbled to his feet. He had tried slashing deep cuts in the crested bear's neck, but had done little damage, never drawing blood as far as he could see--

His breath started coming in painful starts. Damn Jesser's clawing that had ripped his side open. He swayed. It was getting hard to see. He held in his side, saw black fur for brown, white for black, mixing up the fighting blur of bears in front of him.

He focused again, forcing himself to, saw Jesser attacking again. She was wounded. Crel stumbled forward, slashed at the back of the big brown giant as its claws raked into the smaller bear's back and crushed her forward. Crel's knife missed sometimes, connected sometimes. He swayed with them, slashed harder, faster.

Somewhere in the flurry of brown, black-white twisting furs before him, the giant bear roared, swung around, lashed out sharp claws at Crel instead, freeing Jesser from its hug.

Crel fell backwards to the ground, saw black, brown, white fur above him, yelled one last order. "To Wiss, Jesser! *To Wiss!*"

Black, white, red fur lifted away as Crel scrambled up. Brown long shaggy fur rose up enormous before him.

"To Wiss, Jesser!" Crel shouted again. He could not tell if that was what she was doing; he prayed for once she'd obey. With Jesser going to Old Wiss, protecting him, if that was what she was doing, the old man would save himself. The crested bear swayed as it lumbered towards Crel.

Disoriented, his side gashed, bleeding more than he'd realized, Crel stepped back, one step, two steps, three, tried to focus on the bear as it came. He bumped into a hard mass of fur behind him--Jesser! still there, damn her!-- and Old Wiss beside her.

"Hold him off, lad. We're not finished yet."

"Run!" Crel shouted back at his master. "Go!"

Then Crel stepped forward again, shouting, waving his arms.

The brown mass halted in front of him.

"Go on!" he shouted again to Wiss. The wagon was only ten yards away, the tree Wiss had climbed less than that. Wiss was not moving. Crel swayed.

The bear whuffed at the air in front of him, scenting all three of them together. It rumbled in its throat, dropped down to its feet, started to circle them.

Crel tried following it with his knife. Maybe... standing there together, all three of them, it would leave them alone. If he...could keep standing on his feet, not moving, he clutched his side, sucked in a painful breath, saw again. Crested bears, he knew, could be unpredictable. When they paused in an attack like this, they might charge, deciding their prey was easy enough, presenting no problem, or they might leave, deciding the effort no longer worth it. This bear had already had an unfruitful fight. Now all three standing together--

Then from behind Crel, Jesser growled. All the crested bear needed--

29

In the next instant, Crel saw a flurry of brown mass charging at him, swiping him up high through the air across the meadow. As he landed face-down, his second side ripped open, he heard Old Wiss shouting "<u>Nooo!</u>"--then growling--then silence.

~

When Crel felt pain again, he was encased in blackness. His eyes, if they were open, saw nothing. Hot breath whuffed along the back of his neck. His sides were in agony. The back of his right leg--he didn't remember a bear wound there--stung worse. He blacked out again.

Then the whuffing was in his ear, hot breath whuffing in his hair, and something licked at him. A wide, flat tongue.

Being eaten alive. Mauled by a bear.

A bear claw turned him over by his shoulder.

He saw blackness still. White... Stars. Or a moon. A long, long diamond of white in black fur.

It was Jesserlinellian who whuffed at him.

"Jesser... *Jesser!*" He could recognize her now, focus on her now, the long white diamond starting at her chin down to her belly over him, rumbling in her throat at him.

He tried to sit up. He collapsed with the effort.

"Wiss?" he said.

Jesser rumbled urgently at him, prodded his arm up gently with her claw.

Crel winced. "Thanks to you," he gritted through his teeth, "--and that claw--that side's in as bad a shape as the other."

He lifted himself up slowly. His sides were both scratched and bloodied, and there was more blood near his feet. He looked down. A full moon shining above him, he saw in its silvery light that the back of his lower right leg had a ring of bear teeth marks on it, larger than Jesser's.

If he had not passed out, if he had not landed lying face down in the dirt, if he had moved or tried to fight back when the crested bear must have come back and tested him, he would have been mauled to death by now. And might

30

still have been mauled--unless the crested bear had come
back to him no longer hungry--

"<u>Wiss</u>?" he asked Jesser more urgently.

$$\sim$$

As slow as Crel walked, his hand on
Jesserlinellian's back for support, it took him almost an
hour to find what was left of Old Wiss.

Chapter 4
Spring Tree

There are times, Crel thought numbly, when the rest of the world is all background. On the road, the trees, the hills, the whimsy of the weather. Or in the villages, the sea of faces, the rows upon rows of houses, some brick and half-timbered, some limed white and painted with legends, the town squares built inside them one after another. All unnoticed that passes you by.

Or at night, the black silhouettes of the Norgol Ridge pressed flat against the dark horizon, the unquestioning stars, the silent moon that demands nothing of you. That is when the world you know is close in, comfortable. When nothing counts beyond the fire's glow, the hoot of an owl, your friend's good laughter. ...Old Wiss's good laughter.

Or in the day when your world gets smaller still, when there is no circle of firelight to include inside your awareness more than just the two of you, or the three, or the crowd of you in a tavern where all become quickly the best of friends. Or, perhaps, the one girl out of the many, drawing a cup of water for you at the fountain, with a smile on her face that stays in your mind longer than her words, longer than the quick press of her body under yours behind her father's shed. She could become, in soft, remembered moments, part of your world too.

Then there are times, like today instead, once a month, maybe once a year, when the world widens, when the world beyond comes into focus and starts watching you. When each tree separates from the forest and becomes your judge, staring down upon you, whispering after you. When the hills, stones, villages, stand in relief, expecting your explanation to them. When you become small, unwelcomed; the world large and unforgiving.

Crel halted Esra in front of the gates of the Capsen city of Drespin and stared up at the chopped-off arm and hand skewered onto a post. The skin was shriveled, parchment-dry, covered by flies. Dried blood streaked the sign hung beneath it, words in the high language of the realm.

> The king is dead.
> Death to all traitors and heretics who supported him.
> Warning to all townsmen who aided him.
>
> In the name of the Nameless One,
> Long live King Laird.

Crel stared at the hand. He'd heard half a year ago that Old King Henrik had been quartered and sent in piecemeal warnings across the realm. It'd be wise to turn around, not enter this city. The dead king's stubbed fingers curled forward from where the hand exited the post. One of the fingers pointed straight at him. As if it knew too, like the rest of the world pressing down upon him, that he was bringing Wiss home dead in the hutwagon behind him.

Crel geed the delta mare and drove her through the gates.

~

With its long ears twitching madly, Esra's mule colt hugged as close to its mother as the traces allowed. Crel pitied the little fellow. New to a city, it looked everywhere at once, frightened by the din of the carts, the dogs, the horses, the honking geese. Above it, perhaps more startling to the little mule, the wind flapped through a confusion of colors, snapping at bright clan flags and banners hanging from every window. On many of the balconies below the flags, women in yellow kerchiefs shook feather quilts and did last minute decorating for the festival week ahead.

Festival week. Crel frowned in confusion. Nowhere did he note anyone around him concerned by the dead hand at the gate. Half a year. Too long to remember the warning?

Or perhaps the Capsens counted on being the ones forgotten by now. He spotted no Norgon guardsman patrolling the streets.

As he approached the town square, long murals colored the stone walls of the large clan inns. Wiss had told him once these murals boasted the trek of the Capsen caravans from wastelands to warlands to here in the Tessern Valley, where the Capsens had settled two hundred years ago. Above the hostel of the bear clan, the great warleader and visionary of Wiss's tribe loomed larger than life in the front of the historic march he had inspired. The warleader, Alred, Wiss had called him, stood glowering down upon the street; his stern unmoving eyes boring straight into Crel--blaming him too.

Crel urged Esra through the crowd. Nothing would stop him now. He had a delivery to make first, while Wiss was still in the wagon; then he would come back to the hostel and deliver Wiss and his hutwagon to his clan. And after that... After that, Crel couldn't care what happened.

The hutwagon jerked over the cobblestones. Crel felt each jerk ripping at his sides, and his breath came in short, punishing gasps. He'd lost a lot of blood from the two bear wounds, he knew; but he'd bound in his sides tight with the shreds of Wiss's chemise and jacket before redressing what was left of the old man in his last new set of clothes. Now Crel had to keep going for only a few minutes more.

When he reached the count's palace across the square, he drove straight into the park to where the young craftsmen of the city were finishing painting yellow and green stripes on the long pole that would become this year's Spring Tree. Many of the craftsmen were standing around waiting for the tinker's hutwagon, bottles of honey-sweetened festival wine swinging from their hands.

"Ho! There you are, tinker!" greeted a young cobbler swaggering forward in his leather apron.

"Where's the old man?" said another, as they crowded around the wagon.

"We've been waiting since first bell!" a young tile maker accused. He spoke too loudly and swayed on his

34

feet, then grabbed hold of Esra's reins to steady himself. Capsen men drank heartily, but rarely to excess. Except on this one week each year when all sanctions were off. Still, Crel knew, by nightfall these young craftsmen would separate themselves into teams, one to stay here, sobered up, guarding their city's Spring Tree after they had erected it, other teams forming bands of marauders whose duty it was to sneak into the neighboring villages and pull down their Spring Trees first, before invading village teams could pull down Drespin's tree. The one tree left standing at the end of the week would become the Spring Tree for the county, and veiled Capsen maidens from leagues away would come 'dance the spring in' around it. Afterwards, that night, one of the craftsmen from the winning town would be chosen by a maiden to perform the rites of spring publicly on the ground with her, to insure the year's fertility.

Without saying a word to the craftsmen, Crel reached back stiffly into the hutwagon behind him and pulled out the leather sack filled with tin signs to hang on the Tree. Wiss had spent his last month making the signs, one for each craft hall active in Drespin, and several larger, more intricately painted signs for each clan animal of the Capsen tribes. Crel handed the signs out to the craftsmen, remembering the long nights he had helped Wiss hammer and shape each one of them.

Last, he held in his hand the tinker's sign, a grey tin watering can, chained, and ready to be hung.

Three of the young men were standing by watching as others attached their signs to the tree-like frame atop the pole, above the ring where the long dance ribbons would be tied.

"You..." Crel tried calling to one of the craftsmen. Then he held in his side and forced his words out louder. "You there...would you hang this up...for Wiss?"

He heard a clattering beside him, then a gruff, laughing voice.

"Come down, hang it up yourself, lad!"

Crel turned, saw the constable of Drespin standing by the front wheel of his wagon. The constable's grey beard and hanging mustache reminded Crel of Wiss.

"Where's Wiss?" the constable said. "When he came in yesterday to pay his fees on the wagon, he said you two'd be sure to come in early this morning. The lads here have been getting rowdy, waiting for you."

The constable held out his hand for Wiss's passport.

What happened next, Crel barely remembered. He started shifting on his seat, reaching for Wiss's felt pouch he'd tied to his side, taking out the papers, saying, "Wiss is..." His breath choked, his sides squeezed in, punishing hard. The constable said, "What is it, lad?" Then Crel doubled over.

~

Crel woke to rafters overhead. The dark oak beams were low enough to see the cracks in them, their lines running nowhere. He remembered an arm nailed onto an oak post, its dead finger pointing at him. And a face painted on a wall, its stern eyes staring straight through him. A fly was on the rafter overhead, rubbing its two hind legs together, cleaning itself before flying away. Crel could feel nothing, neither his sides nor his leg.

There were voices whispering nearby.

"When can he go? They'll be here in three days. If he's trapped with us, he'll have no papers."

"He can't go. Not yet, at least." The second voice was not a whisper, but it was still soft.

Crel turned his head. The voices stopped.

"Crel, is it, lad?"

Crel looked up at the rough face of the constable. His long sea lion mustache, so much like Old Wiss's, framed his grin.

"Wiss..." he started to say.

"We buried him yesterday. You've been here two days, lad."

Crel turned his head back, stared up at the rafters.

36

The constable went on. "He lies there where you brought him, under the Spring Tree. The count himself chose the spot."

Crel frowned, turned back.

"Ah Wiss," the old constable chuckled. "I thought so! He never told you, did he, lad? The count is his brother. Wiss was the youngest son of the great bear clan."

Meaning Wiss was a direct descendent of the hero he had so often told Crel about, the warleader Alred who had led his people to freedom. Crel felt hollow, a sudden dull hole inside him. Wiss had apprenticed him at twelve, been more of a father to him than his own father ever had. Crel thought he had known everything about him.

"He never told me," he said, as if that explained why.

The constable shook his head. "Perhaps he never thought he needed to yet. He would never come back here to stay. He chose a wandering trade. It's in the blood of all of us clansmen."

Crel stared up at him blankly, not knowing what to say, what to think.

"He fought a great one?" the constable asked.

Crel nodded. "A crested bear."

"He died nobly then. He will be remembered in our songs."

Crel's mouth felt dry. He could not feel his lips. "I couldn't save him," he said.

"Ah, lad!" The old constable's voice was a gruff, sad laugh. "You fought at his side. And you have the mark of the great bear and the lesser bear both, one on each side. You're a hero among our clans already!"

Crel's mouth opened slightly, noncomprehendingly. *No!* he wanted to shout. *It's my fault the crested bear came, I left the jerked meat out, when I went to get Jesser--* He shook his head back and forth, in shock of what the old man said. In shock of what he'd just realized himself. *It is my fault Wiss is dead!*

"The mark of the leader," the constable went on with a nod. "And the protector both. One on each side!

37

Not since the coming of Alred has it been so. You're the recoming of our savior, the lads say."

Still protesting, still in horror, Crel pressed his lips closed and stared up at the constable, but not seeing him, seeing a dead king's shriveled finger pointed at him.

One thought did come to him finally, one question left, discontinuous, but as urgent. Or, more likely, just passingly curious. "Jesser?"

A hand touched his brow. The voice that was softer but not a whisper spoke. "She is being fed well. All of Wiss's friends are."

Crel strained his neck higher to see the speaker. And saw...only eyes, grey-flecked, oval like Wiss's, long, black lashes. The rest of the face was hidden behind the yellow silk veil of a Capsen dancer. Or rather, witchwoman, as some of the more superstitious villagers outside the Tessern Valley called the old tellerwomen of the Capsen tribes.

The veil over the woman's lips moved slightly, into a smile maybe, when she saw him recognize her for what she was. She stepped closer into his view.

"Orist," she said to the constable, but never taking her eyes off Crel, "leave him now. He needs sleep."

~

Crel woke hours later, or so it must be. A small shuttered window had been opened and the light that was streaming in was tinted the orange of a spring sunset, and the rafters above were making more shadows. A soft breeze cooled him. The air smelled of the mustard-like mix of burning sandalwood and numbstool.

Crel dared not move. His cover was off him. He lay naked--at least from the waist up, as far down himself as he could see without lifting his head. The witchwoman was bending over him changing his bandages on his sides. Her hands were swift and gentle. Her veil was dropped from one side, but Crel could not see her face.

He smiled crookedly at an odd thought, thinking that he might feel less exposed if the witchwoman were wearing her veil.

38

She finished bandaging him, glanced up, saw him watching her. Her hand moved swiftly to fasten the veil, then, holding her head higher, she dropped it again. She smiled what on other women might be a real smile, and raised her brow at him, daring him to comment.

Crel stared. She was younger than he had imagined, not much older than he, if that much. Her features were soft, oval, delicate, not sharp as he'd somehow expected. The steel in her grey eyes glinted.

Crel swallowed. He was the one feeling exposed as she stared down at him, waiting. Wiss had told him that Capsen tellerwomen never dropped their veils to anyone but their husbands. And Crel had never paid for a younger silk dancer to see if it'd be true of them too.

He opened his hands at his sides, palms upward, into as apologetic a shrug as he could manage in his position. "I'm afraid I'd be quite harmless to you now," he said.

Her smile widened, and her whole face softened into a sudden laugh. "More so than you can imagine," she said.

Crel stared up at her, suddenly entranced. She was beautiful, smiling like that, truly beautiful. And then and there, Crel made a vow to do whatever he could to keep her smiling like that, again and again, every time he saw her.

"You have Wiss's eyes," he said, as if that were his best compliment. Then he grimaced. It was not something he would have thought to say to any other girl at a time like this.

She raised her veil and pulled the blanket back over him before she spoke. "He was my uncle," she said.

~

Over the next two days, Crel tried to make the witchwoman smile again. He joked, he laughed, he spoke the lines that had worked with every other girl; he babbled, he told her stories Wiss had told him, then stories of himself and Wiss. Then his dreams, stories he had never told anyone else.

It never affected her. She worked swiftly and gently over him, never speaking, never raising her eyes to him again. Her veil was always on whenever she was in the room with him, and also, when he woke and found her there. And he could never tell again if she smiled behind it.

Then, on the third morning, Crel woke to a pungent lemony smell instead of burnt incense. A wide vase of yellow and blue and white starflowers was on his window sill, the morning breeze blowing over them. Wiss had always said there was no more welcome sign of spring than the little starflowers. Hearing the old man's voice, seeing the flowers, hearing his own laugh at the sentimental old fool's words, Crel's grief for his loss of Wiss struck him in a way he had not allowed it to yet. No blame, no anger at himself, no pain, just the loss; and Crel's eyes began silently to fill with tears.

He looked away stiffly, stared up at the rafters, heard a soft footfall, looked in time to see the witchwoman leaving his room.

"Do you have a name?" he said.

She paused, her hand on the curtain. Then she turned around, met his eyes. He saw a flicker of movement across the veil over her lips.

"Yes," she said and left the room.

~

If anything, *that* smile made him mad.

As he lay there thinking about it, seeing the flicker of her veil move again in his mind taunting him, he swore at her, using every epithet he had ever heard against the Capsen tellerwomen, against their evil eye.

Against the grey flecks in her eyes that reminded him, cruelly, of Wiss.

And *what* was she doing to him? She and her evil eye, if the stories were true. As he lay here helpless in her power. He had come from a fishing village, full of quaint superstitions and beliefs. He had grown beyond them, traveling the road with Wiss. But he'd never forgotten, he knew such powers could be real. It was the men there, one family of them, who played the mind tricks on them. The

40

Village Father who controlled everything and everyone. From the day of first planting to the time for fishing and laying the nets to the time of choosing the destiny of every man when he was seven. Even his own son... Crel stared up at the lines in the rafters. Ver had been his name. His best friend when he was very young. Crel had never forgotten him either. Ver used to play the mind tricks on him, teasing him. He'd vanish standing in front of him, then laugh at him from the trees, and Crel never could find him. On long dark nights in the woods since, listening to the unseen sounds of night, Crel would often remember Ver's hidden laughter.

Now, here he'd lain vulnerable for days under the grey-flecked evil eye of a Capsen tellerwoman. The stories about them, that called them witchwomen, could be true, despite whatever the Badurian priests were claiming true instead.

Crel flung the blanket off him, rolled to his side, sat up. Then he gasped in a breath. His sides screamed at him; the numbness was wearing off.

Good thing, Crel thought. He could use the pain to sharpen his anger. She had smiled at him. Or had she, under that veil?

He found his clothes on a bench a few feet away. The only other things in his small attic room, the extent of his world the last few days, more confined than ever, was the bed. And the flowers she'd left for him on the window sill.

He clutched the walls, supporting himself, as he went down the circular stairs.

He heard voices finally, and he paused before entering the hall on the ground floor.

"The army will be here in less than a day, the hornblower said." It was a young voice, male.

"Then anyone else who wants to go, must leave now." The constable's voice, Crel recognized.

"For the rest of us, the day must go on as normal. Spring Tree at four bells--" *That* was the witchwoman. Though Crel had only heard her speak three times, he was certain.

41

Crel rounded the staircase into the hall. He recognized where he was now, he'd been here before. The ale room of the bear clan's grand hostel. The one with Alred glowering down from the mural onto the street outside. Wiss had brought him here for festival week every year. The witchwoman had called Wiss her uncle, she was bear clan too.

A gathering of men and women, young and old, stood in front of the open stone hearth. The constable and the witchwoman were among them.

Crel strode over to her, as forcefully as he could. Every step wrenched at his sides and made him grin.

"So that is your name, '*Yes*' is it?"

A flicker of her veil moved above her lips. She shook her head slightly. "No, '*that*' is not my name."

He heard her emphasis on the word 'that,' but before he could say more in front of the others, she had turned away from him and touched the constable's sleeve. "Orist," she said.

Orist's old rough hands went to Crel's shoulder gently and he turned him away from her.

"Lad," he greeted Crel heartily, "it's good to see you up again! We need to get you going--"

Crel glanced back at the witchwoman, saw her already slipping away.

He turned around, faced the constable. He did need to settle matters with him too. "Wiss came here to pay his taxes," he said. "I need to talk to you."

The old man lost his smile. His grey eyes narrowed at him.

"All Wiss had, his wagons and his goods, belong to his clan now, I know," Crel said quickly, to be certain they understood that he had no misconceptions about inheriting any of it. Wiss had told him years ago how it would be. "But there is one thing in the wagon that was not his, one lantern I made myself for my masterpiece. It is all I own, all I can offer you to pay the last of our taxes."

Orist stared at him, his grey eyes duller than they had been.

42

"And then I can be on my way," Crel added, when Orist had not spoken. "You seem...to be entering a situation here that you want to keep me out of, that is none of my concern. And if it has anything to do with that king's hand outside your gates, I agree with you. If there's one thing Wiss taught me about plying a trade on the road, a tinker, when I have a chance to become one, must be loyal to whatever new king rules the realm."

The constable was still staring at him, saying nothing, making Crel feel more uncomfortable.

He clenched his hands into fists at his sides. "All other matters," he said simply, "are beyond me." As if that somehow excused him. "I appreciate what you've done for me. But I have no way to pay for it yet. I will have to bring some money back to you someday."

The constable's hand dropped from Crel's shoulder. He turned on his heel, motioned some men to him. "Then, tinker, let's go see what you say is yours. The wagon's out back." There was no friendliness left in his voice.

~

They followed Crel out to the wagon in the stables behind the hostel. The animals were in separate stalls, the ox, the little mare and her mule colt, and on the end, taking up two stalls, sitting in a bundle wedged into a corner, her back to the world, swaying back and forth, Jesser. Crel clenched his hand around the top bar of her stall, then walked over to the hutwagon.

He crawled into the wagon, started handing out can after can, pot after pot, weather vane after finely wrought weather vane of Wiss's work. He described the value of each as he passed them out to members of Wiss's clan, saw that one clerk was noting down what he said. He started describing each piece in greater detail, including finally the tools and how to use them, the stakes, hammers, rivets, eight sheets of tin, the trunk of oddities that Wiss used in towns at night with his trained bear.

Then last Crel unwrapped his own masterpiece, a copper lantern with an inner cylinder of tin and glass. Holes were punched through the sides of the copper cylinder in shapes that would cast shining moving images onto walls, magic-like images of seals and dolphins jumping through waves as the owner twisted the inner tin around and around. The soft squirrelskins he had wrapped the lantern in had kept it highly polished. Strange, holding it, this one piece did not mean as much to him now as it once did. He handed it down to the constable.

The constable took the lantern to the doorway to inspect it in better light. Crel saw that the witchwoman had come outside and was standing near the stable door. The constable handed her the lantern for her to try moving the images cast by the sunlight.

Crel climbed out of the front of the wagon's painted hut onto the seat as he waited for the constable to come back. His hand, as he sat down, settled onto something soft on the planks beside him. He picked it up.

Wiss's tinker hat, folded flat and waiting for him.

Crel's fingers closed around the soft tiny curls of lambswool on the outside of the hat. His throat constricted and the tears he had tried to keep inside earlier threatened again. This task, emptying Wiss's wagon for him, had been harder than he thought. He swiped his hand across his eyes, as if swatting a fly, and waited for the constable.

Orist returned, nodding. "We'll accept this in payment of the tinker's taxes."

Crel nodded grimly and climbed down from the wagon. He held out the lambswool hat. "This was his hat," he said.

Orist did not take it. "What use do we have of that? We have no tinker in our clan now."

Crel lowered the hat slowly, his hand closing, reclosing silently on it.

"You can keep it, if you want," Orist said, watching him.

Crel nodded numbly.

"And the animals?" asked one of the men.

Crel glanced at the stalls, let his eyes stray back to the constable's. "They were all Wiss's," he said.

The constable shook his head. "They were his personal friends. They do not belong to the clan. They'd go to you now, as his partner."

Crel had not been Wiss's partner; he could not become more than his journeyman until he'd sold his masterpiece and become a tinker himself. But the animals did not belong to the clan! This was a windfall he hadn't expected. He could at least ride out on the mare...

Then he glanced towards the doorway and the witchwoman standing there. He still had a debt to pay.

"Will you buy them then?" He nodded towards the woman. "To pay for my care here?... The ox. The colt. I can use the mare."

"And the bear?" asked a red-headed young cobbler.

Crel's hand gripped around the lambswool hat. It took a moment before he could answer. All the men were watching him. "I'd like to talk to her first," he said. "She probably doesn't understand any of this."

He went into her stall and stopped beside her.

"Jesser," he said.

The bear turned around to his voice, looked up at him sadly.

Crel held out Wiss's hat to her. She sniffed down at it, looked back up. Her little bear eyes in so large a head seemed to ask more questions than he could answer.

He finally broke apart, standing there in front of her. He sank down closer beside her, hugged her shoulders, buried his face into the thick ruff around her neck, and cried silently. Jesserlinellian blew out softly across the top of his hair. "You don't understand any of this, do you, Jesser? He's dead. Poor beast--" he gripped her fur "--I guess I don't understand his death any better than you."

He lifted himself back up. He laid his hand on top of the bear's head. She leaned her head sideways into his hand so he could scratch the soft spot behind her ear. "I have to go, Jesser," he said. "It's not all those times I swore I'd leave you first chance I'd get. It's just...I have no way to take you with me now. And you'll be...comfortable here. They'll feed you well."

45

The bear looked up at him. He smiled thinly, opened up Wiss's lambswool hat, and left it for her on her head.

Then he turned around and left her stall.

All the men in the stable, twenty or more by now, had gathered around her stall, watching him. They moved back into a circle.

He met the constable's eyes. "You'll feed her well? She likes carrots and apples best."

Orist's steel eyes narrowed at him. "You're selling her then?"

"No," Crel shook his head. "No. I'm giving her to you if you'll take her, if you'll take good care of her. I....I could never sell her."

Twenty faces around him all broke into wide, toothy grins. The constable slapped him on the shoulder.

"Lad! Son! Wiss's son! That's all we've been waiting to hear! Of course you can't sell her. You're Wiss's heir. She's yours now."

Crel shook his head, gestured helplessly. "You don't understand. I have no way to take her--"

"The ox cart and the ox! It's been good enough for her before."

"But--"

"And the tinker's your trade too, son! We saw your work on that magic lantern. Wiss taught you well. But those animals on the rocks by the sea on it are not bears."

"Sea lions," Crel answered. "But the bear--"

"Is yours now. To protect her as she will protect you. It is the way of our clan. And she must have a new name now. You must add Wiss's name to it. She carries his soul here on earth for you, to remind you of him as long as you are with her."

Oh Goron, Crel thought numbly. Jesserlinellianwiss. He'd never be able to say it before she'd be bounding off in the other direction. But then, ...what was he saying?

"No, I can't--"

"Crel, lad. Wiss chose you. We've known for years. The tinker wagon's yours, the mare, the cart, the ox,

46

the bear, all the tools. We'll take the colt in payment for your care here. The lantern for this year's taxes. And whatever pot, sign, spoon anyone in the clan needs, to replace one that's worn out. Everything else is yours to sell wherever you can--to buy the bear her apples, if nothing else." The old constable was grinning at him broadly.

"But Wiss wanted everything to belong to the clan."

"And you too, Crel! You too. That is, if you'll accept the bear, and keep her safe for us. She should make some of her apple money for you on the side, dancing at night for you, right?"

Crel had doubts about that, she'd danced only for Wiss before, never for him.

"What do you mean, me too, belong to the clan?"

The constable's grey eyes peered at him. "Do you want to, lad? We'll accept you as a member and a leader-- Alred's heir if you remember, what with your two bear wounds on your sides, just as Alred had-- if first you'll agree to accept the bear and protect her. Wiss accepted you already."

Crel looked at him, saying nothing. He glanced at the tinker's wagon.

Orist followed his glance. "The clan needs a new tinker," he said, tempting him. "To make our pots. And to wander the towns and countryside to gather our news."

By the Goron, he was tempted. Even if it meant keeping a pest of a bear with him he'd never wanted.

He looked up into the old man's eyes. "I don't share your beliefs," he warned him.

"Ah lad! We watched you with the bear. You share enough to become part of the clan."

The constable held out an old rough gentle hand, waiting, until finally Crel broke into a smile and took it. And in the handshake he wondered only fleetingly what else in the Goron he was agreeing to.

The constable laughed and slapped his shoulders. The others in the circle pressed around him and congratulated him.

"You'll need papers," the constable said. "A tinker's passport before we can send you on your way."

47

"But that'll take weeks, months, to go through the king's court."

"Or hours here." The constable grinned widely, and if he hadn't looked so much like a sea lion with his long pointed mustache, Crel might have thought of him more like a highwayman who had just stolen the king's diamond and was laughing for the thrill of it as he escaped. "We have our ways, lad, if we are wise enough, to have papers prepared very quickly, with the signature of the king himself on it, if we need it." He winked.

Forgery? "But what you're talking about is–"

"Not something we speak of aloud. Your papers can be made ready by three bells. Come to the Count's palace by then, and be ready to leave quickly. Wiss's niece can show you where to come."

Wiss's niece? The witchwoman. He glanced back for her near the doorway quickly, but she was gone.

~

That same morning, four hundred leagues to the west, Verl sat on a rocky hillside and watched the sun come up. Grander music than he'd ever played. He'd grown content in the last six months; for the first time in his life since he was seven, free. The colors of the sun stretched upwards through the sky and coursed through his veins, filling him, day after day, not with music, but with warmth. And, finally, forgetfulness. It made him smile.

The call of a sea gull scratched through the sky. The bird he'd once blamed for eating his dreams. Verl watched it circle, graceful in the sky, its pure white back, black wing tips catching a hint of colors from the rising sun. Verl stretched back on his elbows lazily, and watched the bird fly down toward the city below, past Singerhalle, past the grand palace of the king, out to the whitecaps of the sea beyond. First bell had barely rung to wake anyone in Norgarth. Nothing was expected of Verl yet, nothing was demanded from him. He basked in the spreading silent warmth of the sunlight.

He closed his eyes, fell half-asleep, woke to the sound of stones clattering behind him. The king's courier had come.

Verl lifted himself off the ground, went to meet him. Lollander, his master, strode out of the hornblower's hut and reached the courier's side first.

"Gooden news to you, day," greeted Lollander.

The courier pulled from his pack the sealed scroll of the day's official news, or at least as much of the news as the king and his counselors wanted spread across the realm. As he handed the scroll down to Lollander, the courier caught Verl's eyes and grinned. Everyone took the old hornblower Lollander to be sun-struck, his words never quite making sense.

The courier doffed his cap and spun his horse around. In his bag, he carried the more secret scrolls of maps and orders to deliver in hand to the king's troops and liege lords. It would take him a day's ride to reach the next hornblower's hill where the 'court news' Lollander held in his hand would be received in less than an hour.

Lollander and Verl took the scroll to the stone table on top of the hill where the long mountain horns stood ready. Together, silently, they opened the scroll and started to transcribe the words into musical notes.

Verl worked almost as quickly as Lollander now. As the old hornblower checked over Verl's transcription, he chuckled, swaying back and forth. "The day's a gooden come."

After half a year, it sometimes seemed to Verl that Lollander's words made their own kind of sense. "The music's in the eye of the listener," the hornblower most often had told him, chuckling at him, each time Verl soured a note during those first few months he had struggled to learn the horn from him. Other apprentices from Singerhalle who had never earned their chain of mastery but who still had a good ear for music had tried learning from Lollander in years past, Verl had been told, but none had stayed past those first few months before moving on as quickly as they could to other hills around the realm.

49

Yet, as Verl had discovered, Lollander, for all his oddities, never missed a note, and never confused his words when transcribing the king's news, nor when translating the evening's reply from the distant horns. If anything, Lollander's translations to and from the high language of the court was more clear, more precisely worded than what he had received.

Verl respected the old--no, not old, he corrected himself, looking at the hornblower's weatherworn face as he chuckled over Verl's transcription--old before his time, perhaps that was it. The grand masters in Singerhalle had been much older in years, but they lived inside, sheltered, with someone else to talk to besides a horn and a half-crazed youth who had arrived six months ago, half-crazed with bitterness, delusions, expectations-- Failures.

The crazed old hornblower had taught the half-crazed youth his silence. And his music. A music that spoke words, not light. Clear, precise clarion calls into the morning sun. A music that had a use. No demands came with it. No broken dreams.

And gradually, Verl had started appreciating his new life; and when he let that happen, his insatiable curiosity, always a curse of his, bound him to it. Every morning now he waited to hear what secret news had happened in the realm overnight. Each time he sent back the king's reply, he obsessed throughout the day wondering what might happen next. Even in just relaying orders for new troop movements, he could envision the encampments, the far-away town gates, the horses and wagons and flags as far as the eye could see. Verl had once spent long nights at Singerhalle studying the old histories and legends of the land. Now he had become a link in the writing and reporting of new ones. His life, like his music, had a use now.

Verl looked into Lollander's weatherworn face and saw himself in twenty years. He felt a satisfaction he had never expected to find here.

Under his straw bed in the stone hut lay his lute in its pouch, untouched for half a year, denied, and, more nights now, forgotten. Verl picked up his copy of his share

50

of the words translated into notes and climbed the ladder to the mouthpiece of the long mountain horn on the right, the horn that would be his voice from now on, for the rest of his life.

Chapter 5
Veil Dance

By the time two bells rang in the Capsen city of Drespin, Crel was reloading the tinker's wagon. He would be riding out of Wiss's town like a highwayman, with almost half the tinker's wares returned to him. The clerk who had recorded each piece of Wiss's work had gone around town shouting the list, then every townswoman who had needed a pot, ladle, or watering can replaced had come to the stable and taken her ample share; but most had traded in an old broken pot for Crel to rework into a new one someday. Now what he had left to take with him of the old tinker's wares plus his new stock of broken pots was worth a small fortune to a young tinker starting out on his own.

He was not sure, having had several hours to think about it, what exactly he had agreed to this morning with his handshake; but so far, accepting inheritance of Wiss's clan membership had been to his advantage. He hoped he could keep it that way. He had heard a commotion in the streets earlier, had peeked around the alleyway, and had found townsmen up and down the broad avenues bolting front doors, loading wagons, and leaving town in a hurry. Crel was more than ready to leave too. One of the joys of traveling, Wiss had always said, was that promises and problems could be left behind at the last towngate and be forgotten.

With that warning on this town's gate, and with many of its townsmen suddenly on the move, it was time to leave trouble and handshakes behind him again. As soon as he got his traveling papers, he'd be gone.

He stepped out the back of the wagon's hut after hanging up the last tin cup and found the witchwoman waiting for him. He stood in the dusty shadows of the stable with her, seeing the nonsmiling grey flecks in her eyes and the thin yellow silk veils that hid her expressions.

Without saying a word, she held out a sheepskin pouch. He took it and found in it a fresh supply of linen

52

bandages and a small bundle of dried herbs for the road. He nodded, stowed the pouch in the wagon and latched the two wooden doors. The lone scraping of metal against wood as he fitted the bolt was the only sound between them in the vast barn.

He held his hand out to the witchwoman and helped her up to the seat of the wagon. He grabbed the mare's reins, and led her from the stables, away from her mule colt. The tarney ox, as dim-witted and placid as ever, followed behind, pulling Jesser's cart.

Before they entered the alleyway, Esra's colt began braying frantically. Crel felt the twang of guilt he always did each year they sold a colt. He'd left an extra handful of oats in the colt's stall when he led Esra out. The colt had blown at the oats, making them fly up in a cloud, wasting them; then it skitted around the stall trying to make its way out to come after its mother. Crel pulled on Esra's reins until she trotted away faster. Weaned for over a month now, the little fellow would forget about her soon. And Esra, about him, sooner.

When they reached the street, Crel climbed up into the wagon beside the witchwoman. He snapped the reins, then felt her watching him. He glanced over, she looked away quickly. He studied her veiled profile in the sunshine, but he could only see her one eye. A breeze flapped her veil against the rest of her face. He would never be able to tell if she smiled behind it.

But this silence, dammit, was not in his nature.

Babbling to her, telling her his life stories, had not worked. But in this sunshine, with a beautiful young woman beside him ignoring him, made him feel more awkward with her than ever.

There was one thing she had responded to. "So it's not 'That' either?"

She turned her head slowly to him. He could swear the sun glinted a second in the grey flecks of her eyes. If that wasn't a smile, he sure as the Goron didn't want to know it.

She shook her head, turned away. "No, it's not 'Thateither.'"

53

"Ellen?" he asked her.

She glanced back to him, cocked her brow at him--ah! a much more definite reaction.

He turned from her quickly, stared straight down the road, and grinned.

"Arin?... Jerryl? Aly?" One after another. Without looking at her, he heard her starting to chuckle.

He glanced back at her, winked. "Someday I'll get it right."

He faced the road again. He shoved his hat slightly askew on top of his head, eased the mare onto the broad avenue towards the Count's palace, and started to whistle.

~

For the size of the 'palace' outside, Crel was surprised by the sense of splendor he found on the inside. Perhaps...sense of treasure was more what he felt. Foreign treasure. Filigree carvings on wooden lace screens divided the room. Porcelain herons stood nearby, some as tall as his knee, some as tall as his waist, all delicate and fluid, as if waiting for a word to take flight. Bright murals were painted on the wall of clan animals and of...he was not quite sure...eyes in the forest, or in the hills and in the sky. Light falling on the leaves and clouds from different angles changed his idea of what he saw. The floor was tiled in an odd pattern of reds, browns, and yellows, reminding him vaguely from one side of the room of the back of a tortoise shell.

Nothing in the room quite seemed to belong to the world as he knew it. Not that he had been in a palace before, count or otherwise. But somehow, the ostentatiousness, the belittling enormity of the audience hall downstairs seemed *right*, seemed what he expected. But not here. Here in the private waiting room of the count, the witchwoman had called it, with the light playing tricks on him, Crel felt he had stepped into another world. Or a lost world. Treasured relics surrounding him from a lost world.

His own copper lantern, sea lions and sea cliffs and dolphins from his past stamped into it, stood on a small

54

carved table by the balcony, sunlight streaming on it. Beside it was a silver wine flask and two goblets. Crel tried to avoid looking at his lantern, tried to avoid thinking it had been placed here in the count's room deliberately. To be a promise or expectation binding him to his handshake this morning.

The sooner he got his papers and got away from this town, the better.

He started pacing the room. He had heard the horns a few minutes ago. He didn't understand the language of the horns that spread the news from town to town, hilltop to hilltop---news that never affected him, news from a far-off capital where people lived by different rules, not as tinkers, and smiths, and buyers and sellers. Anything he ever needed to learn from the horns, new kings, new religions, new taxes, would filter down to him at a toll bridge or at the next town gate. Or, if he were luckier, in the alehouse on the road ahead of a toll gate, warning him to avoid it. Otherwise, it was said, only hornblowers needed to hear anything but music in the song of the horns, and it was their loss they did.

But the horns that sounded a few minutes ago had been enough to bring expression to the witchwoman's eyes. She listened, then virtually ran from the room, leaving Crel to wait alone for the count.

He heard the door open behind him. He turned and dropped to a knee. "My lord."

If that was what was expected of him to do or say in the presence of a count, he didn't know; but he hoped it was safer to do so than not.

Eyes downcast, he heard the constable's voice. "Crel, lad, we need to hurry."

Crel looked up, saw the constable before him, dressed like a lord, in an emerald green tunic and yellow hose of the finest Solenzian silk. A short mantle hung from his shoulders, intricately woven in a wild pattern of blues, greens and yellows that imitated the paintings on the wall. The constable's sea lion mustache had been combed, and his old man's beard clipped shorter.

If it was the constable... For all his finery, he no longer wore a constable's sash of office.

"Orist?" Crel asked.

Orist brought his rough, gentle hand to Crel's shoulder. "I have not thanked you properly, lad, for bringing my brother home."

"Your brother--?" Crel caught himself, did a quick calculation. "You're the count's brother too, my lord, in disguise?"

The old man laughed heartily. "No, Crel, the tinker was my only brother. Come, we must get you out of here." He handed Crel three papers, a letter of passport, a license to trade, and a note of safe-conduct, all claiming Crel was a right and true member of the Capsen tribes and a freeman. The papers were stamped and dated a year ago, and signed by the old king's name, in the royal script all tradesmen had seen before, and countersigned by Orist, Count of Drespin.

Crel stood reading the papers silently. He wet his lips, not sure how to react. Orist was waiting for him, his grey eyes peering through him. "How far can these get me?" he finally asked.

Orist nodded, dropped his hand from Crel's shoulder. "Wherever. But not for long. We have no copies of the new king's signature yet. You have three months left before all craftsmen must have new papers. By then, I suggest you get true papers from the liege lord of your own home town. The less mention you make until then that you have any connection with my people, the safer, I'd wager, you'll be."

Crel had questions, but questions whose answers, he suspected, would only entangle him here longer. There was one answer though, he did want to know. "Is there anything in these papers that is true?"

Orist grinned. "You mean my signature? That, lad, is still good, through today at least. And with the date on it a year ago, when it carried more weight, we can hope you will be challenged less than you might have been if it had a...more accurate date. Now, lad, we need to get you, and that bear, out of town."

Crel folded the papers away into Wiss's old felt pouch he wore under his tinker coat. He felt Orist watching him, expecting him to say something more. Crel met his look.

"I thought you were a constable," he said.

The old man rocked back on forth on his silk-stockinged boots and chuckled. "I am, lad! Or more a constable than a lord. Our people have no lords, only leaders. But we've lived here in Norgondy for two hundred years. To keep our valley our own, we've needed someone to wear these fancy clothes," he gestured expansively at himself, "whenever the king's men come calling. To all appearances, we must live like everyone else in this fine land." He paused, and his expression grew slightly more serious. "You see, lad, we're expecting visitors later today."

He waited again for Crel to comment. When Crel did not, when he lowered his eyes instead, fumbled with the tie on the pouch, and took his time buttoning his coat over it, Orist tightened his lips, making his sea-lion mustache droop just as Wiss's mustache used to whenever he was disappointed with Crel's work. Wiss had been the kindest of masters, rarely reprimanding Crel even in the early years. But his silent disappointment that Crel learned quickly to recognize always made Crel strive harder to never sadden the old man again.

Crel swallowed. "You were Wiss's brother," he heard himself say. "I owed him everything. If you need me to stay and do whatever I can when the king's men come--"

Orist's laugh was bombastic and good-natured. "Crel, lad! You've spent the last few days telling Merind and me in every way you knew how that the last thing you wanted to do was get involved in our troubles."

Merind? So that was her name! But his quick stray thought was not enough to forestall the embarrassment he felt at hearing the truth flung back at him. Never get involved had always been his motto. Keep his world small, pass in and out of the backdrop of town after town, then move back home to the freedom of the road. Be loyal to

57

whatever new king ruled the realm, Wiss had droned into him. Loyal to whatever oath he needed to make here, or there, until he could move safely on.

Move safely on---with Wiss. And because of Wiss, he had shaken Orist's hand this morning, had accepted Wiss's membership into the clan. In exchange for Wiss's hutwagon, he had, this time, accepted Wiss's entanglements. "I--" he started to protest.

"No, lad." Orist had stopped laughing but his grey eyes were still moist and bright. "You were right all along. You saw that warning outside our gate. You need to get away from here. When the king's men come, those of us who have chosen to stay in Drespin will most likely be dead by tomorrow morning, if we're lucky, or the more able-bodied, taken for slaves. The new queen regent has always wanted our valley back in her family's holdings, and what little power we once held in her former husband's court back in her own greedy hands. And, worse now, her priests want our souls. Drespin is the perfect town for them to set an example of what her tyranny will be like in the coming years. At least, until her child king comes of age."

Crel was horrified. Not by what Orist said, but by his calmness saying it, his good-humor still---and by Crel's admission that he himself had expected what kind of fate the town faced from the first moment he had seen the dead king's hand nailed on the post. He hadn't wanted to know for sure, never wanted to ask about it, never wanted to get involved.

"Then why are you still here?" he asked. "Why haven't you taken that warning and run, before the king's men come?"

Orist raised his shaggy brows, and it felt to Crel for a moment as if he were looking straight through him. "Most of us have, lad. Women, children, young men mostly. But enough of us have chosen to stay so that the others could escape to the hills without their numbers being missed whenever the guardsmen came to check on us." Orist brought both his hands firmly to Crel's shoulders. "Wiss chose you and trusted you, Crel. Because of that, I feel I can trust you will never tell anyone what I just told you. Many of us will die today, but if you keep our camps in the hills a secret, our clans may have a chance to live on."

Crel wet his lips. *Many of us will die today...* "Merind?" he asked dryly.

Orist dropped both his hands, walked over to the table near the window where Crel's lantern sat with the sunlight streaming on it. He rested his knuckles on the table, turned back around. "She is needed here until the end, she decided. But her mother, Ailil, and her baby brother are safe in the hills, and that's what's important. You perhaps, lad, may come back here someday and find out what happened to my niece...for them."

Crel gripped his hands at his sides, stepped forward with a promise. "I'll take her away now--for you. Keep her from being slain tonight. Or worse."

Orist's fingers closed around the table's edge behind him. His grey eyes were as steel, his voice firm. "Merind has made her decision, lad. It was her choice."

"And I?" asked Crel, meeting his stony stare, saying more than he'd intended. "You're giving me a choice too, aren't you? You're telling me to go. But if I choose to stay?"

Orist shook his head. "That's not what we need of you." His voice was still firm, but he was smiling thinly again. "Come, lad, pour us a drink, and I'll tell you what we do ask of you." He gestured at the table with Crel's lantern, the silver wine flask, and the two goblets on it.

Crel went forward, picked up the flask. It felt too light. He took a goblet, tipped the flask into it. Nothing came out.

He looked at Orist confusedly.

"We all have expectations, lad." He took the goblet from Crel's hand, picked up the lantern instead, poured wine from out of the lantern. "And knowing this, appearances can be used to control someone else's expectations fairly easily. Your papers have the appearance of a king's signature on it dated a year ago, just where a guardsman who asks to see them will expect to find it. You felt the wine flask to be empty, but you saw it for what it was and tried pouring from it anyway. You expected your lantern to be empty--you believed you knew everything about it, you made it after all--so you never considered that, with its intricate engravings, and inner glass lining, it might make a more beautiful decanter at a lord's feast table than a simple silver flask." Orist reached for the second goblet, poured himself some wine, and toasted Crel with a crafty grin. "Appearances can control expectations; expectations control beliefs; and truth..." he took a sip of wine, winked, "sometimes knowing the truth destroys everything."

Crel was not sure what Orist was saying. He'd learned years ago from Wiss that appearances matching common expectations were the basis of many tricks for an illusionist and a part-time bear handler; but Orist seemed to be implying something more.

"Crel, lad, my people have beliefs. I don't want you destroying them. It's that simple."

Crel said nothing, still not following him.

Orist went to the balcony and stood a moment looking out at his doomed city until Crel joined him.

Orist said slowly, "You shook my hand this morning, joining my people. Before you did, you warned us you don't share our beliefs. I didn't tell my people how much that is so. They expect so much more from you than I do. They've heard of your two bear wounds, and so you've become their hope of a future beyond tonight. You are their reincarnation of our hero Alred who led us here to freedom.

"But as for me, lad, I've heard you all week. You have no intention of becoming Alred. You shook my hand, accepting my brother's wagon and his trade from us this morning, since we were so willing to share it. I would too, if I had been you." He toasted Crel with his wine, drank it, then returned to the table, and poured himself some more. "In exchange, you promised to take care of our bear. That is enough for me. She is the soul of our people. Or so we like to believe. As long as she lives, or her daughters, or her daughters' daughters, so will we. You take her away from here, keep her safe, that's all I'll ask of you. That, and take a few things from this room, those porcelain herons, the flask, your lantern. If ever you meet more of my people in the hills, you can return them to us.

"The last thing I ask of you, the most important, don't disillusion my people. Don't tell them the truth that you have no wish to be involved with us. Their belief in you is their only hope. Let them believe in their legend for as long as possible. It may be the only thing that'll give them the strength to survive the next few days, and maybe even, if they can hold onto their beliefs, the strength to change our world again someday. If we can be allowed to lie to ourselves long enough in the face of our worst disasters, belief can sometimes be the greatest power of all."

~

Three polder windmills along the River Oakes mushroomed ahead of Crel, black against the sunset. Their sails furled for the night, the skeleton framework of their blades flailed at him, looking like crossbones under the skull cap of their thatched roofs. He patted his coat pocket to make sure he had his papers with him.

He'd become too involved this time, made too many promises, his tinker wagon was loaded with treasures that would be hard to explain. It'd taken him too long to pack them up, and so he'd barely left Drespin out the rear Millgate just minutes before, it sounded like, the king's troops were demanding entrance to the city through its eastern Bridgegate.

He whistled courage to Esra, his pony now, and drove on. He was still too close to Drespin. He could hear the screams, loud crashing behind him. He glanced back, saw a tall fire already rising above the rooftops. He clicked Esra into a trot.

~

Bright wild melody banged out on three accordions. A ripple of bells jangled from every dancer's waist, shoulders, and hair ribbons. The flurry of men's faces beyond their dance blurred, all laughing, drinking, chanting lewd encouragements as the maidens from the five clans

61

twisted their long silk streamers around the Spring Tree. The images of the veil dance swirled through Merind's mind, and the music and the stomping feet beat loud breathless rhythm through her.

She held on to the long green silk streamer of the bear clan and, singing, wove into the pole and out. The tangle of maidens from every town in the valley pressed in ever closer as their lengths of ribbons that were left untwisted around the pole shortened. More scantily dressed than usual, already stripped of three layers of the dancers' silks, the bare shoulders and bellies on the women glistened in the heat of the fire and the heat of the dance. Merind tasted the salt and excitement on her lips from the sweat running down her cheeks under her veil.

With each pass, the men stepped in closer, and the music came faster, until the mass of women at the base of the pole had trapped themselves, breathless, their hands held high above their heads to the last short stretch of twisted ribbon. The young men stopped, an arm's length away, waiting, their eyes flooded with lust. The sun had set, the new moon of the Springing had crested above the horizon; the night was perfect.

It was up to Merind to control it.

She started singing in a clear ringing voice, the power of her song loosening the maidens' frozen grips on the ribbons, slowing their breath, dulling the gleam in the men's eyes, bringing back memory of who they were and why they were here.

Merind let go of her streamer, started dancing away from the press of maidens around her. The men's circle widened, parted, leaving a path to the fire. In a long sinuous line, the maidens, singing, danced behind her, all but one. Merind and her line of dancers wove towards the men. The men fell back farther, leaving only one young carpenter standing alone, his gaze fixed on the maiden by the pole. Merind circled around him and the long line of dancers brushed past him before following her to the fire.

The women drifted away when the song ended to join the men encircling the Spring Tree, leaving the two young lovers alone in the center.

By herself, Merind took a brand to the bonfire and set it ablaze, then brought the brand closer to the wedding tent on the far side of the fire. Reflecting the fire's glow, the tent's quickly erected silks shone white in the night.

Merind stopped at a cauldron of water, lowered her fire brand to the kindling under it. She sang while the water began to boil. She immersed her hands, her arms into the rising steam. Her delicate, quick fingers shaped the steam into small clouds of flowers as she sang. The smoke from the bonfire beside her rose in clouds of circles, each higher and thicker, into the night sky.

The mother of the young carpenter placed a broom on the ground near the threshold of the tent for the young couple to jump over on their way inside. It was never a surprise each year who the Spring Maid would be---a maiden already promised to a young craftsman or farmer from whichever town won the right to hold the Veil Dance under the only Spring Tree left standing at the end of Festival Week.

Usually the ceremony was held in Drespin. The capital city, walled and more populated, had less trouble defending their Spring Tree from the midnight attacks by the guildsmen of the neighboring villages. Drespin's own guildsmen had become efficient in recent years in pulling down the rivaling Spring Trees in the smaller town squares. It was a matter of insensate pride among the guilds of Drespin that their teams had become the best.

Still it was not that unheard of when a neighboring village won the week instead. Every six to seven years maybe. Of all that had happened since Henrik's beheading, Merind could feel it fortunate that the army of the new king would finally be descending upon her people during Festival Week. It was their one stroke of luck, giving the few young men and women who were left in Drespin an excuse to vacate the city without arousing suspicion that most of the other Capsens had escaped to the hills. Celebrating the yearly dance in the village Alin, one league downriver from Drespin, would keep her brave followers out of the thrust of the main attack in Drespin tonight. And so, perhaps, keep them alive.

That was Merind's one hope that sustained her tonight. Sustained her friends too, she knew, until one by one through the dancing and the forgetting, they'd allowed themselves to believe it.

A hush fell around Merind. She looked up from her flowers of steam to the northern horizon, saw a tower of smoke rising from the direction of Drespin. Her throat constricted, her fingers faltered. Her home, Orist...who else was still there?

She had no time now to wonder, no time for grief. She had to stay in control, had to keep her people strong. She sang louder, worked faster. She shaped the steam flowers and blew them towards the couple coming towards the tent. The smoke from the bonfire bent down, began to encircle the couple. She had to work faster. If the clansmen here could see the smoke over Drespin, the king's men could be spotting their bonfire in the night sky too. It'd be a beacon to them; they might come here after all.

~

A league beyond the fires of Drespin, another fire was rising above a village to the south of a crossroads when Crel was halted by two Norgon guardsmen. He dismounted the wagon and handed over his papers.

He explained, with an appropriately nervous laugh, that he'd planned on spending the night in Drespin and do some trading there tomorrow. But when he came to the warning of the dead king's hand posted on the bridgegate, he passed by the city, took the warning, didn't go in. Good thing too, he nodded back at the burning city, but that's why he was still traveling the road so late at night, so he could get far enough away, set up his own camp, move on in the morning.

He unlatched the back door to his hutwagon and handed one of the guardsmen a coach lantern to inspect his goods.

"You don't have the accent of a Capsen," said the other guardsmen, standing in the light of the other lantern, rifling through Crel's papers.

"No... Not much, I've been told." Crel walked over to the guardsman, thinking fast. His passport and license were signed by Orist, forged with the old king's signature, dated a year ago, giving him authority--from the Capsens--to trade and travel. Tonight was no night to claim he was Capsen. "My master was Capsen. He died last year on our way to Drespin. His count transferred his license for me. I spent this last year finishing out his old circuit, and am now on my way home to the Eller Islands to get my own papers before my year is up."

"Most papers are signed by the new king now. Most merchants have not stalled even a month getting their papers changed. Unless-- Whose man are you, tinker?"

Wiss had taught him that answer years ago. "I'm loyal to the king who sits the throne."

"Of course. ...Whichever one that is," finished the guardsman for him in a low conspiratorial mutter, then he chuckled and handed Crel back his papers. "You and me both, tinker. To whichever one signs your license, to whichever one pays my board."

Singing rose in the night sky from the village to the south. The bonfire Crel had spotted from the road climbed higher, and in its glow he could see dabs of color wrapped around the top of a Spring Tree pole that towered above the village's thatched roofs.

"Sounds like a festival, tonight of all nights," the guardsman noted.

Crel nodded. Merind would be there. As witchwoman, she'd be there, he hoped. Not in the burning, screaming city of Drespin behind him. "Their springing dance. I've seen it in other years. Quite a sight, some of those dancing girls in their ribbons, and a coupling right there in the open, blessing the ground, as they call it. Makes others before the night's out," he winked at the guardsman, "more than they're usually willing to take a stranger home. In other years, they've held the dance in Drespin. Good thing it's not there tonight."

"Tonight's not a good night to be a Capsen anywhere."

Crel met the dark in the guardsman's eyes, then glanced away quickly.

The second guardsman climbed out of the hutwagon.

"You have some unusual cargo in there. If, as you say, you are a tinker."

His voice had more threat of authority and danger in it than his companion's.

"Does he have a license for it?"

"His papers were in order," the first responded. "But--"

"But not for that," Crel admitted quickly, while he still might have a chance to explain. "They're trade goods; but not anything I can sell. Unless you'd like to buy them...?" He shrugged at their looks. "Two counties ago, I did some work for a Countess. She kept me on for almost a month, making a hundred matching goblets. Did she pay me? Not a cent to eat. And when I left," he scoffed, "*that* was her pay. Said it was worth gold. Gold, ha!, gold I could use. Or even copper. If I can't sell it--or give it away in the next town--into the river it goes."

A troop of maybe forty, fifty guardsmen came riding towards them from the direction of Drespin. Crel saw them behind the tall sterner guardsman. The guardsman heard them too and glanced behind him, his attention diverted.

"Am I free to go, sir?" Crel asked.

The guardsman grunted, handed Crel his coach lantern, and hurried to his horse.

Before following him, the more friendly one muttered to Crel. "Aye, get yourself gone. As far away from here as you can. And no stopping, no looking back tonight, if I were you. You've been lucky. So far."

~

In the village, the young carpenter took the Spring Maiden's hand, gave her a brave nod, and jumped with her over his mother's broom. They would perform the Springing ritual openly in front of the cheering crowd as they physically blessed the year's fertility; but they would

66

be married and tented first, his mother had insured. Such was not always the case in Drespin where morals were often looser. Merind sang louder, happier. She loved her people, their customs and beliefs, in all their different forms, loose and citified or stricter and more parochial. The couple ducked into the tent, and the smoke Merind sang from the fire billowed into a thick cloud around the tent, hiding it, as her fingers worked swifter circles of steam into tighter flowers.

Soon, where the tent stood, where the young couple lay blessing the ground, it looked as if it were only a mushroom cloud of smoke rising from a large smoldering bed of coals. No one who had not seen the tent before would guess it was there. Nor would the Norgons if they came.

A surprised giggling came from within the smoke. Listening, some of the young craftsmen cheered their friends on. Others guffawed and drank more swigs of the numbing wine. Merind sang on, kept the smoke thick and circling. She spotted the young carpenter's hag-faced mother, grinning toothily, laughing to her neighbor, enjoying the night's desperate ribaldry after all.

Then, from somewhere else in the crowd, a murmur arose, grew stronger, urgently warning everyone, the young couple especially, to keep quiet. In the next instant, the only sounds left were the crackling of the bonfire, Merind's clear, ringing song, and the pounding, clanging beats of horsemen coming up Alin's one lane of cobblestones.

~

The Norgons mowed down many of the Capsens in their first pass. The clansmen had planned to surrender, but the Norgons never gave them the chance. They pulled their horses around at the end of the square and returned, swords swinging.

Some of the Capsens tried fighting back, some of the young men, the older villagers, some of the women. Others ran or tried to hide. Many of the women in the confusion came back and cradled butchered friends and husbands, wailing their stunned grief. They were left for the moment alone. Merind could do nothing to help them. She could only keep singing to keep the smoke hiding the only two she knew how to save.

Six guardsmen dismounted and surrounded her at the cauldron and bound her hands. They kept their swords pointed at her as she kept singing. They made signs of protection against her, crossing their left thumbs over their third fingers. They called her witchwoman and cast fearful glances at her bound fingers still constantly moving, still shaping flowers in thin air over a cauldron of water that had long ago stopped steaming. Merind sang on.

In the hell beyond her tormentors, Norgons rode down escaping Capsens, captured them, slay them. Other guardsmen ripped clansmen from their hiding places, kicked in doors, started fires. One young maiden dressed in heron-clan orange was drug by her golden hair out of a gap under the stone steps of the town hall and was raped by three men directly in front of Merind. She sang on. She watched, full of hate, and sang on.

The guardsmen came back for the women in the square who were cradling their fallen loved ones. Most they took prisoner, the younger ones, the prettier ones, the stronger ones to be sold later in the slave markets of Elkhorn, along with the few young men still alive, already bound in chains. Older women left in the street were butchered to stop their wailing, or were stripped first before their throats were cut.

Merind sang on, keeping the smoke billowing, still hiding the two young lovers who were doing their duty blessing the year ahead for the Capsen people. Merind made sure with her song, her weaving fingers, that they would never know what had happened around them until morning.

A Norgon captain in his red cloak and shiny black boots dismounted in front of Merind.

He came closer, stared at her singing. Undaunted, she stared back. He had a fresh gash in his left cheek where a well-aimed stone, she hoped, from a dying clansman had left its mark. If she were not singing so sweetly to keep the smoke swirling thickly, she would change her song to make her image of the stone cut deeper, to make the gash appear to bleed and bleed and never stop. The captain had deep-set eyes, yellow teeth, hot foul breath as he raised his hand to her veil. His other hand, she noted, twisted a quick sign of protection against her. She kept singing.

The captain ripped her veil off, then gave a howl of triumphant laughter.

"Keep her!" he snapped to his men. "She's not the witch we're looking for. But she is her daughter! She'll bring a ripe price from the queen when we're finished with her."

Chapter 6
Weep my Fortunes, Take my Eyes

Crel took the guardsman's advice. He did not stop when he heard screaming in the village behind him. Nor when he heard galloping hooves and people running. Nor later when he saw colored movement in the woods beside him. He clenched the reins. He had made the promise to take the treasures away, he told himself. That was all he could do.

But when he rounded the next bend, a young man stood in the middle of the road, covered in blood, halting him.

"Please, sir, you're the one... Aren't you? With the bear wounds? Like Alred. Save us!"

Crel stared at the apparition, the sudden ghost of a bloody man, or of his own guilty conscience perhaps. Maybe not real, he barely heard him.

"Please, sir!" The apparition limped closer, grabbed Esra's bridle, gasping in short words, "Save us." He lift a tattered arm towards the dark of the woods. Two women, one old and crying, one young, stripped half-naked, bleeding, tottered into the light cast by the coach lanterns.

"*Please.* There's more guardsmen following!"

Crel heard his words then, understood them enough to snap into action. No vision, no apparition of his conscience, guardsmen were real, gave him no time to think. Guardsmen if they came would question him stopping here. Seeing apparitions or not.

"In the back!" he said, swinging down from the wagon, unhooking a lantern as he jumped.

He helped the old woman hobble towards the back of his wagon, swirled around. She almost fell against him. "No, wait. They'd find you in there. The bear cage! Under the hay. Jesser, these are friends. Protect them. –Go in.

70

Don't make a sound. No one will think to look for you here."

Before he heard hoof beats beating behind him, Crel was back in his seat, geeing Esra forward, whistling to her in the night as calmly as he could. His world was not small enough any more.

~

Merind cupped her hand into a quivering shaft of golden light. She stared mutely at the intricate designs on the stained glass windows. Panels depicting herons in flight over sparkling cobalt lakes and herds of bison and wild horses racing over the wind-swept prairies of the Midlands alternated with the panels of foxes, wolves, rabbits, deer, and bears roaming the woodlands, canals, and fields of this valley in Norgondy that her people had settled two hundred years ago. In celebration of finally having a land of their own, Capsen artisans, famed for their work in wood and stained glass, created this grand corridor to lead into the audience hall of their "count."

The corridor tonight was their prison. A long wall of mirrors to the backs of the dozen young women enslaved at the Veil Dance faced the wall of the stained glass windows. Fires still raged outside in the city. Reflections from the mirrors danced a mockery of tiny blazes throughout the long hall, flickering over herself and her friends.

She tried not to look at her friends. Disheveled, their dancing silks torn, sitting straight with vacant staring eyes, or huddled two or three together in the slow rock side to side of shared grief. No one wept. Husbands lost, or brothers, or lovers, each of them raped of their self-worth, some of them many times tonight. Three women had been dragged away several hours ago and had not been returned, maybe dead now, if they were lucky.

Merind herself had not been touched. Except by the captain last night who had yanked the veil from her face. The rest of the guardsmen were afraid of her, kept their eyes averted, their third and end fingers crossed when they passed by her to take another girl away.

71

They were afraid of her power, of what she might do to them. The irony screamed inside her. She had no power. Illusions only. Mind tricks only. And not enough to protect so many. She could protect one, maybe two, but not all her people. She had no power to. Not yet--

Not yet. The words scraped inside her like a promise. She clenched her hand shut on the shaft of golden light, felt its shard cut into her hand like the words cut into her soul. *Not yet.*

Someday her people would have their vengeance for tonight. Someday she would have the power to avenge them all.

When two guardsmen stood before her to take her away to the captain's room just before dawn, she squeezed her hand tight around the captured shard of light and, keeping it with her as her one weapon, she followed them.

~

Merind was taken to the count's bedchamber. She hadn't seen Orist nor had heard yet what had happened to him. She realized that most poignantly here in his room surrounded by his possessions, the carved pendulum clock on the wall he'd had Wiss fix last year, the quill on his writing desk, its long feather from the black swan in the aviary down by the river, the painting on the wall he'd done as a young man---of her mother, scarcely grown into maidenhood, standing on a hill with her hunting dogs, surveying the vast domain of their river valley. Merind didn't even know now if her uncle was alive or dead.

But she couldn't think of him now. She had stopped struggling to escape half an hour ago. Her wrists were raw, rope burned, tied tighter to the bedposts than they had been when they were chained on the long walk back to the city. The men's laughter had been lewd as they'd cinched her arms to each side of the rumpled bed, leaving her there.

"The captain said he don't want to take no chances with you, witch. Tie you up good till it hurts." The one with the acid breath had laughed as he leaned over her, undid her veil from one side, bit her hard on her lips. "You can't do nothing with yer hands tied, he said. But he wants you to hisself."

It wasn't her hands she needed. She waited. Tried not to think. Tried not to see the captain's gear thrown across Orist's chair. Tried not to worry about anyone else. Tried only to lay calm, reliving over and over in her mind the screams, the slaughter, the rapes in the village square last night. Reliving more memories too, the parade past the piles of burnt bodies here in Drespin. She whetted her courage with the memory of each face, she sharpened the shard of colored light still imagined in her hand with each relived scream. Her people would have her vengeance for last night.

The heavy iron-bound door scraped open. Merind held the shard of light in her tied-up hand, heard footsteps padding closer across the carpet.

"Witch," the captain said above her.

He leered down at her. Dawn light coming through the window reddened the jagged scar across his left cheek. She closed her fingers tighter around the shard of light. She could cut the scar open in her mind as she had thought to do last night, make him believe it would never stop bleeding. But that wouldn't be good enough. She stared at him. He had no beard, no mustache, but he had nose hairs.

"Do you have a name, witch?"

His voice was not unkind. She flicked her eyes up to his, saw duplicity, saw the side of his lips twitch.

"It doesn't have to be this way, you know. You could stop the horrors of this night any time. I told you that last night."

He touched her cheek with the back of his hand, lifted her veil and hair aside gently, trailed the back of his cold fingers down her neck, stopped at her throat, lifted her chin up hard.

"Or you can have it like this." He bent down, crushed his face into hers. She could feel the rough wedge of his scar against her cheek, his hot breath as his lips jarred hers open, his hands cupping her breasts, squeezing hard.

She lay mute, did not resist.

73

He lifted away, stood back, leered down. "It's all up to you."

He started untying his tunic, pulling it off. "The queen wants you. You'll be carted to her alive, paraded in a cage down the streets of Norgarth, your hands tied to the bars above you. You'll be able to eat the tomatoes as they're tossed at you if you can catch them in your teeth." He sat down on the edge of the bed, pulled off his boots, one by one. He patted her hip. "Or you can escape it all. Decide to right here. It's your mother the queen wants to find, not you. Your mother and baby brother."

He shook his head when she did not answer, started pulling off his leggings. She clenched the shard of light in her hand. She could not panic now. She would have time for one attack only.

His throat was no good, she rejected it as no better than reopening his scar. She could slice open his throat, make him see the illusion, believe it in his mind until he bled to death.

But death that way would come too quickly. She wanted something slow, painful, ever-lasting. It was the captain who gave the orders for last night, not just the queen.

"Tell me where your mother is," he said one last time, as he stood beside the bed. "And I'll let you go. Let all your people go. All that's left of them." He smiled his leer of a smile. "Her one life for everyone. I've heard she once would have wanted it that way." He reached down to take off her silk top--

She gripped the shard of light in her hand, sharpened its ragged edge in her mind, swept her eyes down his black-haired chest to the curls of hair at his loins. Then she began humming a wordless tune.

He pulled back, grinned quizzically at her, then he laughed darkly. "Have you gone mad, witch? Or is this your--"

"Answer," she finished for him. She thrust the shard of light into his mind, thrust her visions, her memories she'd sharpened for him into him, until he relived them with her. Until he heard the screams over and over.

Until he felt the shard of light cutting through him, and down, like a knife, castrating him, with slice after slice of the slaughtering swords against his own loin, making him feel the pain of each sword thrust, each rape, each death.

The captain backed away, caught at himself, screamed agony. He doubled over in the center of the room, in the center of the carpet. She forced him to look down, see himself bleeding, severed, what lay in his cupped hands, shriveled and bloody. She forced him to see the vision in his mind, believe it real, feel the pain, and cursed him never to forget. "Each time," she promised him, hypnotizing him with the thought, "each time you try to take a girl or a man, in love or by force, so shall it be. Useless. Shriveled. Feeling my people's pain for the rest of your life."

She withdrew from his mind, leaving only the shard of light within it to cut the vision into him each time. He was bowled over himself on the carpet. She lay on the bed staring up at the ceiling.

"What have you done, witch?" she heard him moan a few minutes later, that must have been when he first realized he was free of her. "*What have you done–?*" She heard him rise, rush to the wash stand, pour water over himself, washing the imagined flow of blood away from his loins, until, moments later, he'd had time for the visions to finally leave him. She heard him come closer, grab his clothes, pull the bell pull, still dressing quickly as the guardsmen came in.

"Take her away," he ordered. "Take that damned witch away. Bring her to court, bound and gagged, when I call for her."

As the guardsmen untied her, led her away, she glanced back at him. *For the rest of your life*, she promised him. Revenge. She could not do much. Not yet. Not against them all. But one day, no matter how many years it took, her people would have her revenge.

~

Crel was up before dawn stowing the treasures from Orist's palace under the hay mound in the bear cart. If the hay was a good enough hiding place for the three Capsen refugees last night, it would be a good enough hiding place to keep the treasures safe from being stolen by the refugees in his camp today. Jesser, he trusted, would make sure of that.

The porcelain birds and the carved screens were too tall to be hidden under the hay, and Crel did not want Jesser's crushing weight anywhere near them. These he carried into the woods and hid them behind a stumble of three large boulders he'd found when he led Jesser, Esra and the ox down to the river. Strictly speaking, the treasures belonged to these Capsens in his camp, but Crel didn't know a one of them, and he had promised to deliver them to Merind's mother's people hidden in the hills. That was what he intended to do, just as soon as he got back. A life spent traveling on the roads taught a tradesman to never trust nor depend on anyone but himself.

By the time Crel led the animals back into camp and gave Jesser her morning apples, three of the Capsen women and two of the men were up, fixing gruel and one of them, by the oily smell of it, boiling castor beans and numbstools for medicines. The other four Capsens still slept fitfully. Crel had not driven much farther last night after picking up the first three Capsen refugees before he came to the trail off the road leading to the campsite he and Wiss had used every year. Once they had made camp, the young Capsen carpenter had set off back into the woods to find as many escaped friends from his village as he could. Now, with nine people in his camp this morning, it felt more overcrowded and loud to Crel than staying in a city tavern ever felt. He cast a baleful eye at them as he brewed himself some jasmine tea over his own separate fire.

After drinking the tea, he hitched Esra back up to his tinker wagon. The one news he had not wanted to hear came from a young woman who had waited long after the soldiers had gone last night to crawl away from her hiding place in a root cellar near the village square. She was the only survivor who had seen what had happened to Merind, marched away in slave chains with maybe twenty others back to Drespin.

If Merind were still alive--

The temptation to go back, find out, get involved went against every principle Crel had set for himself in his life.

But then, maybe he could confirm for himself what had happened to Orist. Wiss's brother. He might need to report that news to Merind's mother someday.

The sun was still rising, the morning fog still greying the trees when Crel's tinker wagon was back on the road towards Drespin. He whistled to Esra, snapped the reins. He'd left the nine refugees safe in the camp behind him, and it felt good to be alone again.

~

"Tell me where your mother is. That's all you need to do to stop this."

From her earliest memories, down by the river one sunset, Orist had taught her about colors. How to paint with them, how to change perspectives with light and shadow.

"Tell me," the captain said. "We'll find her anyway. With or without your help. But with your help, we can stop this right now."

Merind was not listening to the captain. Trying not to. She stood staring at her uncle. He sat bound to a chair, beaten, cut, bruised, bleeding. His eyes were blue, steel blue. Meeting hers, saying goodbye. Blue is for the river, Orist had taught her. The water of life that fell from the sky to the fields and the river.

"How can you people be so stubborn?" The captain cupped her chin up with his hand until she was forced to look at him. "How?"

When she said nothing, he swirled around, nodded to a guardsman. "Do it."

The guardsman held the count's head steady, dug a thumb under Orist's right eye lid, pushed past the tear ducts, and raked the eyeball out.

Orist's agony screamed through Merind, screamed louder than the screams of the rapes last night. She dropped her head, squeezing her eyes shut, squeezing the sight out.

"No!" The captain yanked her head up, forcing her to see. "Watch! Watch what you have done to him. To all your people."

Where Orist's eye had been, the lid half closed over a sunken hole. Blood welled out, streamed down his cheek. Red is for. Orist had taught her. Red is for--

A scream ripped out of her, subsided to sobs. The captain said gently:

"Tell us. That's all you need to do. He has one eye left." He put a hand to her shoulder. "Save him. Save it."

Merind looked up at the captain blankly, not seeing him. If you could walk inside the painting, Orist had taught her, she would see the tree from the other side or could look back at herself holding a brush. Walk inside an eye. Look back at yourself. Perspectives changed. Red is...

Fire.

And gold? A shard of light emblazoned last night by the fires outside. Merind shook her head, numbed to what she had to do.

As Orist yelled the torture of his last eye being ripped out, her mind exploded until she was seeing only shafts of golden light--

"Break his legs, throw him out among the others," the captain said. "He's as good as dead already. No need now to let him die sooner. Neither one of them will ever talk. Take that witch away. If I never see her again, it'll be too soon."

--And gold is. Gold is only a shard of imagined light. She had no real power to save.

Chapter 7
Prisoners

Two of the three young women who had been gone for hours last night sat huddled with several of the other prisoners. Merind saw them as soon as she was pushed through the double doors back into the hall of mirrors. The third young woman, Caris of Alin, a friend Merind had grown up with, learning to ride and to train their herding dogs, sat alone on the other side of the hall, her back against a window.

Caris's eyes were vacant, staring ahead at the reflection of herself in the mirror across from her. What she saw in it, Merind did not want to guess. She had sung at her friend's wedding a year ago. Last night, Caris's husband had been cut in half as he stood protecting her in the Norgon's first sweep through their village.

Caris had been beaten and bruised cruelly since Merind last saw her. Her right cheek was swollen under a fallen tangle of auburn hair, the same dark rusty shade as Merind's own. The rest of her arms and face were starting to blister, with patches of skin a brighter red than where she had been beaten.

The blistering was a torture self-inflicted, Merind saw with horror. Caris had always been allergic to skin contact with many plants; yet in her hands as she stared at the mirror, she twisted a small yew branch around and around. She must have been brought back into the hall through the courtyard, past the yew hedge maze, she must have broken off a branch as she brushed by. Perhaps in her own way, staring into the mirror, wringing a yew branch in her hands, as allergic as she was to it, Caris grieved for her husband. In the villages, yew hedges, bright green with berries through winter's long death, were planted around family graveyards as a promise of being remembered, and as a promise of the day of return.

Merind walked over to the windows, careful not to disturb Caris's silence. Afternoon sunlight streamed through the colored glass--colors Orist would never see again-- She could not think of that. Refused to. The city outside was no longer burning. She noted that, saw nothing else.

She sank to the floor, let her eyes stray again to her friends. Seeing a reflection of herself in their faces took less courage than looking across into a mirror to see her own reflection, as Caris sat doing. The last time Merind had seen a reflection of herself had been in the captain's eyes-- Orist's agony had not stopped screaming through her.

These women, her friends, in torn dancing silks, bright ribbons, young wives, sisters, had all lost more than she.

Caris, sitting a few feet from her, stifled a moan, catching Merind's attention. Merind glanced over, then, pull of grim fascination, turned to watch her. Caris had started rubbing the twisted broken needles of the yew branch across her blistered arms and cheeks, and pressing them into her open sores. She brushed the branch gently across each tearing eye, caressed it down the line of her nose like a lover's touch, opened her mouth, stuffed it in-- *No!* By all the Goron, no!

Merind scrambled over to her on her hands and knees, and lunged at her as fast she could to grab her hand from her mouth.

"Spit it out, Caris! Spit!"

Caris focused wildly bleared eyes on her, shook her head. "Too late." She managed a thin smile of recognition--or triumph, then swallowed the poisonous wad of berries and needles.

"Too late," she repeated. "I have chosen, Merind. You asked us to, a month ago. We chose to stay, that others might live, Ari and I. We chose to stay." She bit off more needles, chewed them. "As I choose now to join him."

"Caris." Her name was a sob in Merind's throat that never came out.

"You'll have no pain," she promised her finally with a kiss. There were few poisons that could kill as quickly as valley yew when swallowed.

She cradled Caris's head against her, hugged her arm tightly around her shoulder against the first hard quaking that wracked through her friend's body, then helped her gently as she began to vomit. And as calmly as she could, she slipped inside Caris's mind, gave her visions and memories of the times they had shared. The fresh spring dawns racing their growing shadows over hills with their dogs barking. Lazy golden sunsets they had learned to paint; and that one evening they had painted the pastel sunset clouds on each other's faces. Brisk fall mornings binding armloads of sheaves at harvest times, whispering back and forth in excited secrets as they worked next to each other. Childhood days spent herding goats down from the hill pastures. Summer afternoons spent wading through the shoals of the river above the village Alin, laughing at the splashing cold water as they tried to catch fish with their bare hands. Caris's wedding. The brightness of the fire reflected in Ari's eyes as he jumped over the broom with her, danced with her, laughed at her. Merind felt every constriction, every convulsion of the poison coursing rapidly through Caris's veins; but she made sure Caris saw only memories and felt only the slowly spreading warmth.

Weakly Caris's eyes fluttered open, tried focusing over wet swollen cheeks. She raised an arm. Merind caught her hand, held it. Caris squeezed back for concentration. She opened cracked blistered lips, mouthed words. Merind slipped out of her mind and leaned close to hear her.

"Promise. You must. Change with me. Change clothes. Let them. Think I am you." Her hand squeezed tighter with her meaning. "Live, Merind. Promise. Live. For all of us."

Her body jolted up and down in a violent contraction; and when it passed, Caris lay dead in Merind's arms.

All Merind could think was left to do was to stroke Caris's hair away from her face. Again, and again. And again.

There were the other women crowding around them, pulling Merind's hands away, crooning soft words Merind could not hear, pulling her away, rolling Caris's body away from her, separating them. "She was right," they said, she heard those words among them. "She was right." They began undressing her, undressing Caris, exchanging their clothes. There was vomit on both of them. Merind felt numb, shaken, barely aware of their hurried fingers, low murmuring. She was right, she was right, the words repeated inside her. Live, for all of us; live--

Her mind snapped clear. She felt more certain of herself than she ever had. She felt purpose. And power. She would have power someday. She'd be a shard of light cut sharp for all of them.

Gently, purposefully, she unwrapped her headpiece, undid the veil, fastened it around Caris's head, smoothed the hair inside, fastened the veil. Under the veil, blistered swollen cheeks made the face unrecognizable; Caris's hair was shorter, but not by much, and it was the same color. *The witchwoman was dead, daughter of the royal witch had poisoned herself.* This witch had more courage than Merind had ever had.

She slipped off her soft boots, started to trade them with Caris's clogs, paused a moment, one clog in her hand, and looked at the window. Purpose. More certainty than she ever had. There may still be a way out.

She tapped the heel of the wooden shoe softly against the window. A woodland scene. A stag, the stealth of a hiding fox; colored glass, yellows, gold, greens, trapped prismed sunlight streamed onto her arms. She tapped, and a small pane of glass gave way and broke silently outward. More; softly, quickly; then a large hole opened, shattered and crashed in loud thick pieces all around her.

No time to think now. If the guards heard that crash, they would unbolt the doors quickly.

She ordered the women through the jagged hole one by one. "Hide among the bodies in the streets," she whispered. "Meet in the hills when we can."

Six through, starting to help the seventh when the doors shoved open. Certainty, the straight path of colored sunlight ahead of her darkened, waited for a later time. Merind became as meek as the other caught slaves. They were surrounded, sent into a corner, Merind hiding among them. The witchwoman lay on the floor in her own poisoned vomit under the broken window. One guardsmen was sent to tell the captain, two others ran out to capture the six women who had escaped.

By the time the captain was yanking aside the veil, confirming that the swollen mass of a face must be Merind's, kicking the body with good riddance, three of the women who had escaped were being hauled back among them.

--*Only three.* Meaning three were still free!

Merind's eyes flashed with determination. And her people's first sign of hope.

Chapter 8
Court News

Verl savored his peach, from the soft fuzz that pricked his lips as he first bit into it through the sweet orangey flavor of spring that melted in his mouth, its juices dripping on his fingers. This one peach had cost him most of two week's wages, but he'd had one once before in his life at a celebration at Singerhalle and he'd never forgotten it.

He wandered through the crowded market. Past the blue awninged stall of the fishmonger with long eels hanging up from wide sucker mouths and with piles of red-eye salmon on display, flies buzzing around and resettling each time the fishmonger fanned them away. Past the multicolored tent of the seller of fine Solenzian silks where Verl kept shaking his head sadly and finally had to show his empty purse, empty except for one half copper---good for nothing but good luck, as the gamblers would say. It might as well be for luck, the coin he'd gotten back in change for the peach would not so much as buy him a fly from the fishmonger. It was proof enough to the silkseller though, who, nose raised, shoved past him to hail a passing lord. Verl might look the part of courtier--wearing his one set of silk tunic, leggings, and matching blue velvet high boots given to him when he left Singerhalle half a year ago --but today especially, he had no funds to match.

He ambled on, sucking the last of the peach juice from his fingers and throwing the pit into the mud beyond the narrow boardwalk. Peasants bowed their heads respectfully and stepped off the walk to let him pass, lest his velvet boots got soiled. He paused once as a belled handcart of a sausage and nut vender shoved past. The aroma of fresh chestnuts roasting in its pot-bellied stove covered for an instant the market day stench of dung, fish, and the close hot sweat of too many people.

Bells in the clock tower struck five. Verl watched the mechanical dancers spin from one partner to their next.

He was in no rush, there was an hour before the king would hold audience. Past experience had taught him the scroll of news under his cloak was not emergency enough to warrant disturbing the king--or rather, the queen regent--before then.

He mingled with the crowd in Council Square to watch a midget do high flips between the stomping 'legs' of a delta stiltwalker. Closer to the clock tower adjacent to the palace, seven Badurian priests shook their belled staffs over newly professed converts, anointing their foreheads with the black feathers of the Winged One dipped in myrrh.

Only a few feet beyond the priests, on the low steps of the Victory Fountain, was a makeshift stall. A painted sign hanging from it proclaimed its owner knew the dark secrets of the Eller Islands. In Norgarth society that meant he was a dream interpreter. Verl drifted over to it curiously.

Last year, market day would have been more crowded, jammed with the bright green and yellow hutwagons of Capsen tellerwomen and the dark threatening tents of Morris stargazers as well as the little slapboard stalls, such as this one, run by those who claimed to be dream interpreters from Verl's native islands. Now for the last few months, the Capsen tellerwomen--witchwomen, as most people called them behind their backs--were gone, their powers outlawed by the new king and his priests, and all belief in Capsen magic publicly and vehemently denied, if you wanted to keep your tongue here in the capital city. But, so far, fortune telling by stargazers and dream interpreters had escaped the royal order. Official policy said there was no true magic in their predictions, no threat at all to the realm, guesswork only. And as every townsman had a dream, he had as well a king-given right to guess what his dream meant, or to pay someone else, if he wanted, tax included, to guess for him.

Yet it was rare these days to see a stargazer or dream interpreter still practicing inside the city gates. Most had been wise enough to leave their profession early while they still could, becoming card shifters, or shell game dealers, or some other form of out and out thief, their taste

85

for larceny already well trained. Verl had never found an 'Eller Island' interpreter who knew anything about what he was saying.

This one had suckered in a rich merchant for a customer. The merchant, his hair thinning and streaked with grey, wore a long packerwool traveling cloak trimmed in sable fur. His back turned to Verl, his shoulders hunched, he was looking down at the counter where the interpreter was drawing a design in a tray of sand. A shell full of saw reed and numbstool was smoking on the left side. The thick, intoxicating smell brought memories to Verl and he stepped closer behind the merchant's back to listen. The interpreter wore a turban, he noted with disdain, not even knowing that a Village Father would never walk into a dream still turbaned. Verl's gaze dropped to the sand drawing, and his breath caught.

Precisely drawn with a stick in the sand was a power sign of one of the five that guided men's destinies: the web of guilt.

Verl restudied the interpreter's face sharply. He had an old man's curled mustache, a scar below his left lip, his accent was not at all of the Eller Islands. How had he seen a secret sign of one of the five?

'You tell me your dream,' the interpreter was intoning. 'Now see its name. This is the knot of love.'

Verl's chin tightened over his effort to keep from shouting out his reaction to this imposter, more severe than he'd expected. He'd left the Islands years ago, had outgrown most of its beliefs, and had years ago stopped feeling insulted on its behalf. Or so he had hoped.

Still, this interpreter had precisely drawn the web of guilt; misnamed it, yes, but the design itself was considered dangerous for anyone to see. Verl himself might no longer believe that it was dangerous, but he still respected his homeland's belief that it was.

"You will meet a black-haired lady tonight," the interpreter was telling the merchant, "beware the entanglement--"

Before he dishonored the symbol more, Verl bumped against the merchant, then grabbed his arms enthusiastically and swung him around. "My friend! There you are! We've been searching the market for you. We're due at court in an hour."

The merchant in his greying beard raised a brow at Verl in surprise and wariness, but he said nothing.

"Burn's been to the taverns!" Verl went on. "And there..." He laughed a jeer and leaned close to the merchant's ear as if to whisper of a lewd encounter. He whispered instead, "My friend, be quick. He lies to you. Hold your purse and come away."

"Come, my friend, come!" he said aloud. "The night awaits." Verl took the half copper from his purse and set it down on the interpreter's tray of sand, carelessly destroying the intricate design. "For your troubles, my good man. For your trouble!"

Verl slung his arm around the merchant who, thankfully, was eyeing him only still, yet was allowing himself, quite willingly, to be led away.

From among the few passersby who had paused to watch the commotion he had made, Verl spotted a youth in a blue cap and a woman in a grey shawl. As he hurried the merchant between them, Verl cast his voice, something he had not tried doing in years.

From the direction of the woman came a panicked scream. "I've been cheated! He stole my money! He told me lies! Lies! Arrest him!" The woman looked around her in surprise.

From the youth, "Liar, fake, thief! Guards, help! Thief!"

As Verl shoved the merchant quickly before him into the gathering crowd, he glanced back. The interpreter was grabbing his shell, pouring out his sands in a hurry, packing his bags, while two constables were pushing their way through the crowd to arrest him.

~

"Well!" said the merchant when they gotten safely away. His dark eyes glinted. He planted his feet, refusing to be shoved a step further, and faced Verl squarely. Verl dropped his arm from the merchant's shoulder.

The merchant raised his arm to Verl's shoulder and tightened his grip. "Come, my friend, come! Shall we go to that dark tavern you promised?" He began pushing Verl in front of him through the streets much harder than Verl had pushed him. To all appearances, they would look the best of friends. Verl was not sure now how he could get away.

Two tall men, dressed as merchants, drifted away from the crowds and started following.

~

"It seems I owe you a favor," the merchant said, his black eyes glinting. "What is it, lad, *you* want?"

They sat in the darkest corner of the darkest tavern in the first dark street the merchant could find.

Verl swallowed. He had acted rashly, interfering in someone else's business. "Nothing, sir, I swear to you. I only wanted a stranger to be treated fairly. That interpreter was no more than a thief." For all he knew, so was the man in front of him.

The merchant sat back against the wall and laced his fingers under his chin, his elbows propped on the table. He studied Verl for a long silence. The room was full of smoke; the straw on the floor stank of old beer and vomit. The two merchants Verl had spotted following them were blocking the door, talking to the keeper.

"So you're taking me to court?" the merchant said.

Verl spread open his hands in a helpless gesture. Singerhalle training kept his voice more calm than he felt. "I meant nothing by that either, sir."

"Come, lad! You listened over my shoulder. You heard that interpreter say I'd be entangled in a knot of love, that I'd meet a black-haired lady. Is not the queen *raven-haired?*"

How could Verl answer without admitting he'd been to court? And right now, he felt certain, was no time to admit anything.

The merchant leaned close to Verl. "Well, is she?"

"I've heard it said so, sir."

"Ah, but we're forgetting; you're the one who said that interpreter lied to me. Perhaps, when you take me to the queen, she'll be golden haired."

Verl felt his pulse pounding hard enough to hear. If he said anything, yes or no, would he be agreeing to escort the merchant into court?

The merchant smiled after a moment, showing his teeth in the grim light. "You are young. You do not trap yourself so easily a second time though, do you? Not as you did outside."

"I never meant to interfere with your business, sir. I only meant to warn you--"

"To be more careful?" the merchant finished, with his spectral smile. "I would hope that was your only intent. For your sake. I am not one who takes kindly to being a pawn of a more dangerous thief than a simple market interpreter. Now tell me. How did you know that scoundrel had cast a web of guilt around him?"

Despite his Singer-trained control, Verl gave an audible start, his lips parting before he could force his expression blank again. The merchant had recognized the sacred symbol.

The merchant leaned closer. Verl could feel his hot breath in his face. *"Where are you from, singer?"*

"I am no singer." Verl could deny that truthfully.

"No?" The merchant looked up and down Verl's silk tunic dyed the purple blue of Singerhalle. "You wear no chain of mastery, I noted. Although that is hardly something to sport around in the open market--or...in a darkened tavern?"

Verl kept his face blank, his breathing as calm as he could.

The merchant reached into his black cloak, pulled out a jeweled knife, began trimming his fingernails with it. "So you say you are no singer. Perhaps so. But you have had years of Singerhalle training, I'd warrant. Perhaps even"--the knife paused, he stared straight through Verl-- "you've become a hornblower by now? How convenient. I've found someone who knows all the secret news of the realm."

89

Verl's pulse stopped; then sharply, he rose, tried walking away. The merchant grabbed him by the wrist, his grip surprisingly powerful and certain.

"You have not finished your drink, my lad!" The merchant reached for Verl's half-empty mug, refilled it from the jug of room-temperature thick brown ale the keeper had served.

Forced by the merchant's strong grip, Verl sat back down. He crossed his arms in front of him, refused to take the drink. Out of the corner of his eye, he saw the two merchants who had followed them come sit at the table behind him. One carried a jeweled casket the size of a melon.

"Drink, my friend," encouraged the merchant with a sly, toothy grin. "I mean you no harm. If you are what you seem to be, that is. But as you tried to warn me outside, one can never be too careful these days. I'm a jewel merchant, come from afar. With my two friends here. We bring the queen a rare jewel in that casket. Tell me, lad, do you think she'll like it? It is almost time for our court date."

Verl kept his arms folded. Why would a jewel merchant reveal the contents of casket to a stranger, especially if it contained a rare jewel? It sounded like information revealed only to someone who would not live beyond the telling. Three to one. Verl had never learned how to fight.

He wet his lips. "How did you know that symbol was not the knot of love?"

"Ah, lad!" The merchant nodded his head as if in approval. "I am a merchant. I've been to the Eller Islands. *And you?*"

Verl thought fast. He kept his arms folded, his face calm. But inside, he panicked. He had never been in a situation so desperate. He only came to Norgarth once a month on market day when the King's usual courier paid him a silver talent to take his place, having other business of his own that night, he always claimed. Never before when Verl had come inside the crowded city had he spoken to anyone, at least not while he still carried the king's news.

And he found right now, it was the king's news, the scroll inside his tunic, that worried him. Three to one. If they killed him, they would find it. His life without a dream had become free and peaceful, but no longer worth, he knew, so much as the half copper he had thrown down into the interpreter's sand for this merchant. His duty though was worth much more; the scroll inside his tunic was what he had to save.

While he waited for an answer, the merchant took his knife to the round of cheese on the table, cut off a chunk, and began to eat. The other merchants were still behind Verl; he could not escape them. Yet perhaps--

The memory struck. Something else he had not tried in years, like casting his voice to escape the crowd, something he had not done since he was seven. His arms folded, his fingers dug into his sleeves. He closed his eyes, saw a beach, his boyhood friends searching for him as he stood in front of them, suddenly invisible to their sight. He remembered the blackness, the queasiness, the world wavering, becoming unreal, as if seen through water, between his friends and himself.

He sought that place in his mind again, opened his eyes, and stared straight into the black, stern eyes of the merchant, and disappeared.

He heard a scuffle behind him as the two merchants rose in astonishment; but the merchant in front of him calmly raised his brow, then made a gesture to his men, pointing to either side of Verl's bench. Then he cut himself another chunk of cheese.

Before Verl could get away, the two merchants were pressing in on either side of him. They could not see him, but, shoulder to shoulder, they could feel him. Verl sank back down on the bench between them.

The merchant ate his cheese. "A mistake, my friend. Your third in one day. You react to a magic symbol. Excusable, if you are in the habit of warning every fool not to deal with false seers. You cast your voice to put words into a woman's mouth and a young boy's. Again, a trick many people can learn. A ventriloquist with his woodenhead can be found on half the street corners of this realm. Amusing, but not necessarily magical, a trick not yet against the king's law.

"However..." the merchant paused to bite into his cheese, then he reached across the table to offer the next bite to the invisible air in front of him; he shrugged when Verl did not take it, and ate it himself, "however, what you are doing now is most unwise. An act only one with the blood of a lakeman can attempt. And, as we all know, having read the king's decree, lakemen and their magic don't exist. To be caught attempting such a trick could cost you your head. Especially here in his fine city."

Verl felt the queasiness, more sickening than he remembered, saw the waviness, the uncertainty of the world around him. It was totally unlike the visions, the sharp detail his music and dreams created. He swayed against the solid, muscular shoulders of the two men beside him. He said nothing to the merchant; he knew nothing of lakemen. He had come from the Eller Islands.

"Now, lad, I'd like--" The merchant looked up past Verl and his men suddenly. His thin mouth tightened. He leaned forward, whispered a quick warning. "Whatever you do, stay as you are and don't make a sound."

Then he calmly cut each of his men a piece of cheese, looked up as the keeper of the tavern approached followed by three Badurian priests. Verl froze. His fate was certain now, no escape was left him. All the merchant needed to do was reveal his presence to the priests, and he would be strung up on the tower gate and left for the crows to eat by this time tomorrow.

The keeper led the priests to a nearby table, then came over to their table. The merchant calmly waved his knife in greeting to him.

"Where be your young friend?" the keeper asked, as he offered to refill the jug of ale.

The merchant gestured no to the ale. "We've had enough; we have an appointment to keep. Unfortunately our enterprise with the young man came to no sale. He wanted a ring for his mistress; I wanted more gold than he had."

The keeper guffawed. "Then I leave you to your ways." But instead of leaving, he stood waiting, dirty beefy hand outstretched.

The merchant nodded to his man closest to the keeper. So pressed up against the man as he was, Verl felt every movement the merchant beside him made as he reached for his purse, withdrew a silver talent, and placed it in the keeper's hand.

The keeper took the coin, bit into it, and wheezed another laugh.

"Gooden days to you then, me sirs."

The merchant in front of Verl sat watching the keeper leave. Then he reached for the purse sack from his friend. He opened it, took out a large coin, and set it on the table in front of Verl.

"Now," he said, with his sly grin, "shall we say, I'm always in the market for information?"

Verl stared down at the coin. Through the sea-water waves between him and the world, it shone in the darkened tavern. A full gold talent. More than half a year's wages. He left the coin where it was and did not touch it.

The merchant grinned again, less toothily this time, and took out a jeweled ring instead from his own purse. He set the ring on the table beside the coin.

"An honest man!" he said in a lower voice. "There are a few like you these days. You do not intimidate, you can not be bought. Even when, shall we say, there are those in this room--" he nodded at the priests "--who would be very interested in you if you could be bought. Take the ring; it is yours. Nothing asked in return. Except that you take the coin too. I would not care to leave so fat a tip to so greedy a keeper." He nodded to his men and stood to leave. He leaned back over the table to grab his knife and whispered to Verl as he pocketed it. "One last word of advice, wait till you're long gone from this tavern and those priests before you come back to this world. I would not like to hear that so young and honest a man had lost his head tonight."

Verl sat frozen, his heart still pounding in his throat, long after the merchant left him.

Then in the last seconds before the keeper came to clear the table, he grabbed the ring and coin and ran for the door.

Still panicked, leaning hard against a wall two streets away, he finally slowed his breath and reappeared to the world.

~

After the six times Verl had come to court in the last half year bearing the king's news, he still felt ill at ease when he entered the throne room. He tried not to show it; a good mimic, quickly observant, he imitated the erect bearing of the most dignified courtiers, keeping his back straight, his step assured, his eyes focused unswervingly forward on the boy-king Laird seated upon the throne and on the regent, his queen mother, beside him.

It was the sea of dancing lights from the high rows of stained glass windows that Verl did not want to see. This hall, built by Alred and his Capsen artisans almost two hundred years ago in gratitude to King Edoff for granting them land of their own, was famed throughout the realm as the Jewel of Norgondy. Its dazzling brilliance by daylight, even its subdued shift of colors by full moonlight outshone the splendor of the crown jewels. Or so the songs said.

It was that splendor of colored lights that crazed Verl every time he came to court. That made it too constantly hard in here to forget that he'd failed to become a Singer in that one other famous Capsen-built hall of stained glass windows. Try as he might, that memory from half a year ago was as alive in here as if it had all happened yesterday; and it confused and haunted him. He stiffened his back and waited for the Way Lord to signal him forward.

The merchant who'd detained him and his two henchmen were kneeling before the king. Verl felt the pouch at his side, the gold coin and the ring inside it, wondering if he had sold himself to the merchant in taking them. He denied that train of thought. He'd grabbed them at the last minute rather than leave them for the keeper, that

94

was all. He hoped he could find a way to return them to the merchant, to make sure he knew he had refused them.

Queen Felain spotted Verl. She signaled her son; he nodded regally, dutiful puppet; and the Way Lord called for the courier's news.

Shards of the colored lights went forward through the hall with him. As Verl passed the trio of court singers, a harpist, a flutist, a singer, playing softly to one side of the courtiers, he dared not look at them, no doubt he'd recognize them. *Music is in the eye of the listener*, Lollander would say with a wink and a half-sane laugh.

He knelt in the center of the "bear claw," and handed over the scroll to the Way Lord. Then he retired among the crowd of courtiers. He would not be needed until the king and his mother gave their answer.

He noted the merchant had stepped aside for him. His rich hood pulled forward, his face hidden, the greying beard stiff, the merchant nodded slightly to Verl. Verl looked away, clenched his fist. Perhaps he should have left the coin and the ring on the table, as he had first been tempted to. This merchant, nodding at him, as if expecting a bond between them now, was wrong if he thought that. Verl owed his loyalty to the king. The boy was only seven, a hard age to be alone.

King Laird untied the scroll and "read" it to himself, but the scroll was turned upside down. The boy-king handed it to his mother to read. The singers kept playing softly, their fractured notes streaked across Verl's thoughts like fractured lights. Music was in the lights on his fingers, he had once tried arguing to Lollander, and the old man had laughed.

How he hated the disorientation he always felt here.

He felt it worse today with that merchant watching him.

The colored lights sparked most vividly on the white marble inlay of the giant bear claw design in the floor before the king's throne. Verl could never avoid looking at the design. The oval pad of the bear's paw was in front of the king, the five circles and scratch marks of the claw tips pointed outward, warning the world away. Verl controlled his breath and listened to the queen announcing the message from the scroll.

"Drespin has been taken, and the daughter of the Capsen Witch captured. The Witchwoman herself shall soon be ours."

Fractured words, broken lights colored the queen's face. Raven-haired, the merchant had called her. The queen was beautiful in an unsoft way. Her rival, her husband's mistress long before their marriage, and long after, the rumors held, must certainly have been more bewitching behind her tellerwoman's veil. The Capsen Witch, the queen now dared call her. Singerhalle training had taught Verl all the scandals of the realm.

But it was what the queen had not read aloud, any mention of the Capsen massacre, that struck Verl with irony. Broken colors fell across the white inlaid marble bear claw on the floor in front of her and her son. It was a wonder she had not ordered the bear claw torn from the floor as she had ordered the Capsen people torn from the land and their Capsen magic torn from the people's memory. Verl looked at the sickly boy-king. He had made the oath half a year ago to join the boy-king's service. It had been easy for him then to disavow any belief in magic. Its visions had given him nothing; its promises were as false as dreams. The music of the court singers scratched through him like broken shards of light.

He watched the merchant stride forward to the center of the bear claw and kneel before the king.

Perhaps the queen did not know the origin of the bear claw design, perhaps that was why she had left it alone. Common knowledge held that the marble design was the rising sun, spreading out its rays from the king to his people. That it represented a bear claw instead left as a signature of the Capsen artisans after building this hall with its intricate lattice work and marvelous array of stained glass windows was little more than a side note in the histories of the realm taught in Singerhalle. Verl would have forgotten it himself, had it not been for an older memory of a Capsen child's counting song he had learned in his first years at Singerhalle. Child games, used to teach

96

the young students the different languages of the land, would often have words that made no sense. But the words of the Capsen counting song, as obscure as any, had always made Verl curious. Allowing for the differences in its language and that of his own native tongue, the Capsen song named the five power designs his father would have drawn in the sand to seek men's dreams. That it was Capsen artisans who had built this king's hall still intrigued him.

Verl listened as the merchant swore fealty to the boy-king and asked for his protection. Laird sat through it looking attentive, glancing up once for his mother's approval, only one stray finger drawing little circles on the arm of his throne. If the king had ever had a chance to learn a child's game, Verl doubted it. Shards of the colored lights from the windows above broke in half-moon circles across Laird's face, broke across the back of the merchant standing before him. In his black fur-trimmed hood, oversized cloak, the hulk of the merchant could have been a bear standing in the center of the claw—

> Dancing Bear, dancing bear spin around
> Moonstar lights touch the ground
>> Counting one, two
>> Guilt spun right

The words came crazedly, the child's song breaking the rhythm of the court singers, crowding his mind in counterpoint to the fallen lights across the bear's back. Verl did not want the merchant to spin around, did not want to face him, did not trust him. He felt the hardness of the gold coin in his pouch, swore again he had sold the merchant nothing of himself in taking it—

> Dancing year, dancing year spin around
> Bear claw clan comes to town
>> Counting three, four
>> Song spun woe

Verl had seen the merchant's face up close in the tavern, the high brow, black eyes, sharp nose, greying beard, and he'd heard his accent. The merchant was not of the bear clan, he was not Capsen. Verl tried to erase the refrain running through him, tried hearing instead the soft melody of the court singers. The colored lights broke lengthwise on the merchant's long black cloak, broke in more sharp, vivid designs on the white marble claw at his feet. *Music is in the eye of the listener*, Lollander would laugh.

One of the merchant's two companions passed the large melon-shaped jeweled box to the merchant to present to the queen regent. In the cavernous hall, the merchant spoke, his voice deep, ingratiating.

"...a jewel beyond compare, my lady, I found it for you in a town along the way...a jewel most fit for any crown..."

Dancing stars, dancing stars spin around
Bear claw man wears a crown

The queen nodded graciously, the merchant opened the lid. Verl could hear murmurs among the courtiers nearby; the jeweled box itself was a treasure beyond compare.

Spinning count five
Forget star light

Five... The five toes of the bear claw, the five corners of his father's pentagon for walking into dreams. The five white circles on the floor behind the merchant's feet, fractured lights from the five windows above breaking into sharp, defined patterns on the white circles, the long lines of red in the first circle looking like--the web of guilt.

Verl looked up quickly to the rose windows in the ceiling--a trick of light, no doubt, a trick of his own confused memories in this hall of broken lights.

But the merchant had recognized the secret dreamer design drawn in the sand and had named it correctly. *The*

98

web of guilt. Verl stared back hard at the merchant; his head clearing of all music, all confusion. He watched intently as the merchant put his hand inside the box.

The courtroom gasped, the boy-king squirmed, and hid his face in his hands. His mother the queen regent grasped his arm to control him.

"Do you not recognize him, your late husband, my lady?" asked the merchant calmly. He raised up higher for all to see the decapitated head of the dead king she'd had defeated, drawn and quartered, his body parts sent in warning to his followers across the land. Long strands of blond hair still hung from the yellowed skull and what skin was left stretched across it in dried patches of boiled leather.

"Guards!" The queen's word, sharp and cold, drove like ice, like a stained glass window shard through the room.

Guardsmen appeared at every corner, every door, every window, perhaps twenty of them, and two to either side of the king's dais, swords drawn. The queen regent and her priests and counselors edged closer to the throne.

Amid the confusion, the positioning of the guards, the quick stirring throughout the Hall as the courtiers near Verl eyed escape routes, if there were any, or set hands to their rapiers, if they had one, the merchant quietly replaced the old king's head back into the jeweled box and closed the lid.

"Sire," he approached the throne and presented the box, "your father."

"Seize him!" the queen commanded.

Three guardsmen shoved through the courtiers and stood, swords drawn, between the courtiers and the merchant. The two other merchants positioned themselves behind their leader.

The merchant held up a hand to the queen, the courtroom went silent, no guardsman had seized him yet.

"Sire," he said, his voice as certain and slow as it had been in the tavern when he cut his knife through the cheese, "may I advise caution? You are not long upon this throne."

As if to add threat to his words, the merchant bent down and left the jeweled box on the lower step of the gilded dais, then turned his back on the king and returned to the red-stained circle on the bear's claw.

The queen was in fury. The priests and counselors bunching closer to her looked around at the inaction of the guards. One of the four guardsmen protecting the dais shifted his head, and Verl caught sight of his face, his curled mustache, his harelip-- Verl froze; his breath trapped in his throat, the gold coin in his pouch felt heavier. The guardsman standing closest to the queen was one and the same man as the fake Island dream interpreter the merchant had visited.

He needed to warn the queen about the spy. But could he? With the gold coin and the merchant's ring in his pouch? He tried to push through the courtiers to get to her, but the guards stopped him.

"Guards, seize him!" the queen ordered again, pointing at the merchant, her voice raised barely a key from what it had been.

The merchant bowed extravagantly. "Consider what you ask, my lady." Verl still fought to push through. The guardsman in front of him shoved him back among the courtiers, allowing no one through.

The merchant continued, "I pledged a few minutes ago my fealty to the crown. The young king in accepting it has honor-bound himself to protect my life as I am now bound to protect his--at least as long as I raise no sword against him and break my word. Is his father's crown so secure upon his head that my young liege can afford openly to break his word and, in front of all the court, arrest me, perhaps behead me, even as you have done--" with a swift hand, he flung back his merchant's cloak off his broad shoulders and lowered his hood "--*to my brother?*"

The courtroom reacted in one audible gasp. Verl heard snatches of a name whispered and confirmed back and forth around him. Prince Rayid, Duke of Navarn, from the duchy to the east created by the old king's father when he split the kingdom for his two sons. The other half of the news Verl had delivered to the queen tonight concerned the

100

rapid movement of the duke's army, camped now five days away, the last horn had reported, while the queen's forces were still mustering beyond the gates of Norgarth to meet them.

"Guards!" the queen repeated, as if her safety were trapped in that one word.

"Sister," the duke said with a note of condescension. His hair from behind was a bear's head of black turning white on the sides. "No use in calling. Those who would respond to you most willingly you'll find later, locked up in the guardhouse below. Shall we talk?"

She did not answer. Her fingers fluttered a second at her sides. She inched a step closer in front of her son. The colored lights streaming down on the throne sparked from her eyes.

"Call this a friendly visit, shall we, my lady? Between two neighbors. It won't last long." The duke turned to one of his two men dressed as merchants and accepted a scroll. "Here are the maps of our two kingdoms, the boundary between them marked in red, as charted by my father. By your grandfather, sire. It is my wish, my one desire in entering your realm that that boundary line never be marked in blood. That I assure you."

He handed the scroll back to his companion who took it up to one of the priests near the throne.

"And what do you call this? Your invasion. Not being marked in blood?" the queen asked.

The duke bowed his head to her. "I came to do as I have done. To offer my fealty to my young nephew. To guarantee that our borders be not crossed, despite recent..." he gestured at the jeweled box with his dead brother's head in it, "events within your realm. To insure the alliance still between our two countries, and to insure the independence still of my own. To give warning, my sister, I will not have my border crossed." He paused, emphasizing the threat behind his words. "I have come in person to do as I have done. Considering recent events here, I thought it most wise to come with friends. More friends, as I know you know, are camped five days away. They could be a troublesome lot for you, if I do not come back to them in

101

three days. Most bloody then, the border line drawn between us. But if I do get back in time, we turn around, go back home peacefully. My friends again insuring that I can return home--shall I say?--as I came, in person."

"Now. Shall we make a deal?" He held the court in abeyance, the scene more like a history drama played out in song each winter festival at Singerhalle, a hint of the unreal in the air around Verl, in the streams of colored lights highlighting the players, in the silence of the room straining to hear the duke's next word. The fury of the queen's breathing was palpable every time Verl glanced at her. He'd been too late to warn her. But if he had, what difference could it have made?

"What are you offering?" the queen finally said. She held her head high. The lights hitting her raven eyes glinted.

~

Queen Felain was in a rage. She paced the small council room demanding answers. Who let the duke and his men into the city--had no one checked his papers? How could--she swirled to the captain of the palace guards--how could all her own guards be so easily trapped inside their guardhouse? Their uniforms and swords so graciously donated to the duke's men?

The captain of the guard stood tall. A solidly built man, he looked too tall, too muscular for the stretched, short fit of what must have been the only uniform he could commandeer quickly enough to answer the queen's summon. He did not speak in any but tight, one word excuses; but his lips were pressed thin, and his nut brown cheeks flushed a shade darker with each question she asked. The fierce silence in his black eyes spoke more and more of the vengeance he would extract the next time he faced the duke.

In the alcove by the door, pressed against wall, wishing he could disappear altogether, and fighting the urge to do so as he had done in the tavern, Verl watched the captain. He felt embarrassed for him, for the comic fit of his uniform, for all the questions he could not answer. But he feared him too. It was Verl's hope that the queen would never see him now, would never think to ask a faceless hornblower if he had met the duke before, as she had asked everyone else in the room. The duke's gold was in his pouch, and more identifiable no doubt, the duke's ring that would condemn him. No one would listen to an explanation, no one would believe him. They would have found the duke's spy. All blame would be his. Verl could see what would happen to him in the captain's eyes.

He stood pressed against the wall, awaiting the message the queen had said she wanted to send back with him. And then--he would fly away from here, just as fast as he could run, back to Lollander's hill. And on his way Verl would pitch the coin and condemning ring, any connection at all to this night, as far away from him as he could.

He watched the boy-king fiddle with the markers on the maps spread out on a large table by the window, moving some of the markers, replacing some of them, being ignored by the queen. Laird reached far across the large unscrolled map the duke had brought of their two kingdoms, traced a short finger along the border edged in red. He went back to his own kingdom's more detailed permanent map with the tin chess-piece-like soldiers showing the most recent movements of his forces, one small troop centered in Drespin triumphant over the green and yellow Capsen peasants, more of his guard in red and gold outside the gates of Norgarth readying to face the duke's army in blue that was camped in Halett's Valley. Laird picked up the crowned blue marker that was the duke and his own crowned red marker from inside his palace in the center of Norgarth, one marker in each small hand, looked at the them, cocking his head at them a moment, then banged them against each other, twice as children would. So the boy-king, Verl mused, was allowed to play after all. The queen was still talking to her priests, counselors, and guardsmen.

"As much as I want to stop him now," the captain told her. "I have to advise against it. His army will march against us if he doesn't return to them in three days. We

103

don't have enough men here yet to stop them. The city will fall."

The high priest shook his belled staff. "Have no fear of that, my lady. I tell you, the Winged One shall lead our men to victory. Her city shall never fall!"

The captain pressed his lips thinner, said no more. Was it so unwise for even him to counter the high priest?

Laird scrambled back to the duke's map, stood his own crowned marker firmly in the center of the duke's hills of Navarn. Then he untwisted the duke's crowned head off its narrow peg from its body and grinned up at his mother.

"And now, my lady," he interrupted her, "do we behead my uncle too?"

Chapter 9
Whale Dreams

In the red pulsing heat of the forge fire, Yarisol
tempered the scythe blade down to just the right bee's wing
color and quenched it immediately. He struck it on the anvil
till it sang to the darkest corners of the shop with the bark of
a seal and, as he sharpened its hard whining edge on the
wheelstone, he knew that this was the blade from his naming
dream. He wished his father could have lived one more
week to see it. A selfish wish perhaps, aye, but there it was.
It was the sixth weakness of man to be selfish.

The scythe blade was shorter, wider than one he
could sell to the mainland. But this was a reed cutter's
blade, an islander's blade, true, strong, mated fair well to its
soul. It would one day cut the flax fields of Clayl's bride, as
well as, in the fullness of deed, cut a path for Clayl down
through the reeds to his boats on the river. For in islander
tradition, the best wisest work of Yarisol's hand was not for
him to sell, it need be given away to a brother. In the time
beyond tall tale when the first isle was the hump of the
whale and first man its second dream, the wisdoms and
mysteries of all trades were given freely to brother man
from father whale.

Clayl was not one of his mother's four sons, this was
true, not a brother by shared blood. But he was Yarisol's
yearmate, born in the same dreamyear of the whale, and
Clayl had shared his mother's milk---Clayl's own mother,
and that of his twin Crel, having died in their birth. To
Yarisol's way of thought, Clayl was as close as any of his
three brothers. And tomorrow, when Clayl would take his
bride and her Village Father's son into his wedding boat
over their first waves together, Yarisol would present them
with a scythe to take with them for all their years of
prosperity and whims of good fortune.

Yarisol stopped pumping the footpedals of the
wheelstone and he held up the shining blade, sighting down
its edge, no nicks, smooth. He needed only to weld the

small loop of steel at its base for the sliding hook to go through---unlike a mainlander's long cumbersome mower's scythe, the blade on a reed cutter's scythe was collapsible against its handle when not in use.

Yarisol chuckled a wordless tune as he worked, picturing Clayl as a farmer. Aye, but Clayl said his bride would be sitting at his side learning to make fishing nets and baskettraps with him come the winter. Yarisol shook his head. Thanks be to the whale that his own wife was a villager like he was, that she was content to spend her mornings parading her two-year old son back and forth to market, content to spend her afternoons gossiping in the women's long house where she sat hours spinning her colorfully designed tunics of fine linen for her son to model when the merchant ships came in, hoping she could win their fattest orders. Thanks be to the whale too, his life with her seemed good enough mating. He never expected her to turn three times to divorce him, for in full deed, she and her son did come willingly each night to his hearth; aye, and willingly each cap of midday to his forge with a welcome basket of fish, apples, cheese, and a brew of frothing ale.

Still, islander women were seals and sirens of seals in their other lives, and no man should ever feel secure about them. And yet, when his wife's son would turn seven and go alone to the stone cliffhouse to become a man, Yarisol did hope he would dream the whale dream to walk the path of the blacksmith, as he and his own father had done before him. For then, Yarisol would know he had made a true son.

The blade, he judged well, was ready for its handle. No thick ordinary oak handle from the mainland would do. Nor a handle of the lighter but too soft island cypress. Neither one for the blade of his dream. Instead rolled in soft sealskin, waiting since midwinter when he'd finished carving it, was the soul to match the lifework of the blade. Ivory, gleaming ivory, whalebone, to last a lifetime and beyond. Carved intricately into fields of flax, wave upon wave of the grain, until their waves rolled into a sea of watery waves, and when those crested, dolphinmen and sealwomen jumped over them, diving through them; and as

106

the spume of the waves curled down, he had carved the crash of their breaking into spiral after mystical spiral of the path to the whale's dream. He unrolled the handle carefully. Two areas along its length he had left smooth and polished for hand grips. And the tip of the handle was shaped and smoothed too, ready for the tight fit of the base piece of the blade. It would not take long now to finish the scythe.

He hummed as he fitted and riveted it, advising the spirit within what he was doing and giving it the fairest of warning. And thanking it again for having beached itself upon the sand bar beyond the bay last fall. The village had prospered in full deed with the whale's gifts, its smooth slick skin making new boots and capes for the fishermen, its flesh feeding them grandly through all the long winter, its oil lighting their lamps and bringing them the highest of prices in trade with the merchants. And this rib bone now to become a scythe. Father whale had taught them humility and gratitude once again with his example. And when his own father had walked back out of his dream of life last week, it was with full gratitude and faith that Yarisol could set his body free beyond the last wave for he knew the whale was content now with their village and would open wide his mouth for his father's raft and welcome him home.

He hefted high the scythe when he finished it, swung it wide with ease, noting with satisfaction the weight of it felt full more natural than any long oak-handled scythe he would have made for the mainland. He released the hook, dropped the blade, wrapped the scythe again in its soft sealskin. Merchants were by far a queer lot, never understanding the right value of things, disdaining what islanders prized, wanting only those soulless tools that Mainlanders wanted. Aye, soulless, that was the right word for them.

And small be it wonder. He had heard the merchants say yesterday that the new king of the realm was destroying people who believed in powers and souls beyond themselves, the caravans and wagons of the brothers of the bear disappearing from the cities and main roads already.

But Yarisol knew his own people had nothing to fear, their village had little to do with the mainland. And

107

naught but merchant ships sailed to the Eller Islands. Who was the islander fool enough to trust a merchant with his truth?

There was truth and there was truth. Merchants were cousins of sharks. Or the best of them, perhaps, the clattering sea gulls that followed them here, that fought day and night over the racks of drying fish down by the docks. Islanders were *men*, the second dreamed, their brother the stealth of the island fox, their sister, the eye of the pelican. The moon was a pelican too, watching over them at night, teaching them to keep their secrets, and spying on the mainlanders in her silent glide past them. Islanders would have nothing to fear from the mainlanders, if they kept their dreams to themselves.

Aye, but there was truth and there was truth. And merchants knew much that an islander had never told them. Many a grim time, a merchant would share an ale and begin a sea gull laugh, speaking loud of a funerary raft they had passed, crashed upon the outer rocks, the body fallen off it, rolling back and forth with the tide, feed for the sea gulls, they'd say, not a whale. But there was truth and there was truth. And any islander knew the facts in the matter, from day one on. For as many rafts came back to their shores from the bay as ever had crashed against the rocks beyond. The shell of the body they sometimes still found within it was not the true body they had sent out to the whale, nay, its discarded shell only. The facts were not the same as the truth. The dream of the islander and the spirit of his raft were back home in the mouth of the whale.

Aye, there was truth and there was truth, surely. As here in this scythe wrapped in its sealskin, the blade sharp, forged of iron, a thing to kill the reeds and tall grasses, a knowledge to use and be useful, as well an islander knew the facts as a mainlander. But like an islander taught to keep his secrets, this blade was mated in silence to a handle carved in magic spirals to the dream. The scythe had a life and soul no mainlander merchant seemed to see.

The merchants would have nothing of their beliefs to report back to the mainlander king. The islanders would stay silent and safe for time on end.

108

Yarisol cradled the scythe in its sealskin and took it to the Village Father to be blessed. Tomorrow, its spirit awakened, he would give it to his brother Clayl and his new bride.

~

It was late afternoon by the time Crel was sifting through the ashes of the bear hostel. Ever so often, he found a chunk of charred wood that still showed a trace of paint from the glowering mural of Alred. The long history and dream of the Capsen people crumbled in his hands as he tried setting those pieces aside. A guardsman was watching him, growing impatient.

The only thing of value left in the hostel's rubble was its collection of tin cups and spoons, copper doorknobs and keys, and a few silver platters and mugs he could clean up and salvage. He was lucky, he had told the guardsmen at the gate, that he had come upon the burnt city so soon after its destruction, while a fortune in wares would still be there, before other merchants or peasantfolk discovered them first. He'd already been to the troop's quartermaster, traded him a good share of newly worked plates and mugs in exchange for dented ones and for a licensed right to salvage through the city's rubble for whatever metals he could find.

He hefted his last burlap sack full of clattering wares onto his shoulder and nodded thanks to the guardsman as he went back to the cobbled street where his wagon was waiting. The city smoldered around him. Only a few buildings remained standing. The palace and the grounds across the square were untouched, that's where the captain and his officers had bivouacked and had held a few prisoners. And, by some miracle, half the stable behind the bear hostel still stood. Stepping over rubble, bricks, burnt timber blocking the stable door to go inside it earlier, he'd found the frightened colt. The guardsman had shrugged when Crel asked if he could take it.

The colt and the collection of wares were Crel's only reward for coming back. That, and news. The quartermaster had been friendly, had told him everything, with little questioning on Crel's part. They'd caught a witchwoman at some ceremony in another village last night, not the one they had come for, not the former king's "bitchwoman"--the quartermaster had laughed that word with his garlic-blasting chuckle--but the bitchwoman's daughter. She'd killed herself, the quartermaster said in a lower conspiratorial voice, glancing around, making sure no one else would hear, the daughter had poisoned and disfigured herself rather than tell the captain where her mother was. The count hadn't talked either before he'd died, and the captain was furious, had already given orders to get the hell out of here. Only a handful of Capsens remained alive, except for those in the outlying villages. Men had been searching through them all day for the witch the queen wanted, and were returning empty-handed. Here in the city, the few slaves that had been taken had already been marched off to the slave markets in Elkhorn. Hearing the quartermaster say that, Crel held his breath. He'd had to wait while a parade of a dozen young women and five men were marched in chains through Bridgegate before he could cross into the city. One peasant woman had reminded him of Merind, she had glanced at him, and he could have then almost believed it was she--but no, he knew better now. Merind had poisoned herself, the quartermaster had said, and she and her uncle lay among the piles of burnt and slain bodies that ringed the courtyard near the palace.

Crel stowed the burlap sack full of salvaged wares into his hutwagon with the six other sacks he had collected and climbed up onto the seat. He drove past the piles of bodies one last time around the square on his way out of town. The guardsman had gone on to his own business now, and Crel was alone, a tinker leaving town was no longer suspicious. Still, Crel glanced up and down the streets before he turned into a shaded corner under the south portico of the palace. Earlier he thought he had heard some moaning, seen some movement near one of the piles when he and the guardsman drove by.

He walked slowly from one pile of the bodies to the next under the late afternoon shadows. Air gagged him, continually catching at a sick lump in his throat, but it was not just from the smell of burnt flesh. No world could be this foreign to his own small view of what was right. No people could be so dangerous to a far-away king to deserve this. Rats tore unafraid at the bodies, and already vultures lorded over the feast.

All the Capsens the Norgons could find in the city, the quartermaster had told him, had been drug out into the streets to count their numbers, and when the final tally was in, the captain had been more furious than ever by the outcome of his mission–less than a quarter of the populace of Drespin could be accounted for. The royal witchwoman was not the only one missing, despite all the assurances from their spies and messengers that life in Drespin had continued undisturbed since the warning bans had been posted on the city's gate. The Capsens had not just been waiting docilely for the guardsmen to come.

Too many had waited, Crel thought as he hurried past the last pile of bodies. Too many, just to keep up appearances of a full city, giving too few the chance to escape. He had understood their sacrifice in principle when he had first heard about it; he didn't understand it all now seeing and smelling the bodies of the slaughtered and burned.

He started back for his wagon when he heard another moan. He paused, looked again at the nearest pile, saw eyes staring at him from inside the center of it, then heard a whisper.

"You're alone?"

If dead women talked, if they watched you from beyond the next world, Crel couldn't have felt less jumpy. For a second, he just stared, then, gathering in his breath, he hurried closer, knelt down.

"Are you alive?"

"Three of us. And Orist is too. But he needs help quickly."

Crel knew he had never sweated fear so much as he did at the gate waiting for the guardsman to inspect his load and papers. Seven burlap sacks filled with clattering cups and spoons covered four that burgeoned with softer lumps in the back of his wagon. But the guardsman at the gate only opened the top two sacks and poked at the rest. Then,

111

grunting dismissively, he handed Crel back his signed license to salvage and let him pass.

~

Finally out of sight of the guards, Verl ran towards the hornblower's hill. Halfway back, he paused, panting, and stared up at the stars.

His father would have called them pelican eggs, and the moon a pelican. In Singerhalle, he had learned they were balls of skyfire, and there were far many more of them than he could see through the masters' telescope.

Either way, the stars were silent tonight, giving him no answer. Hidden in his tunic were the queen's orders she had commanded him to send to the next two hills and the town beyond, orders to arrest the merchant, the Duke of Navarn, and have him killed. He could hear the child king's voice, *when do we behead my uncle too, my lady?* The boy was only seven.

Then louder in his mind again, he heard the captain's warning: *If the duke doesn't return to his army in three days, the city will fall.* Verl had translated all the troop movements around the realm himself, and he could easily envision the overwhelming number of men in the duke's army crushing the queen's forces in front of walls of Norgarth and overrunning the city.

Inside his pouch were a coin and the duke's ring. He had planned to toss them far from him. He could now.

He didn't. The duke had saved Verl's life, had not turned him in to the priests. And if the captain were right? If he were? Verl clenched his fist, ran on. The stars had given him no answer.

In the morning, long before dawn, Verl took the lamp, climbed to the stone table above the horns, and unscrolled the court news. He translated it into the hornnotes himself, before Lollander woke up. He translated half the news, half the queen's orders, leaving her first order for the village beyond undone. He rolled the scroll back up, burned it.

He'd hid the coin and gold ring inside his forgotten lute under his bed, never to use them. The merchant had not bought him, he was still loyal to the king. But no, he would take no part in killing the duke for him. His fingers still shook with his decision.

He'd sent orders to armies to march before, he'd received reports back of success and death toll. But this, this was different. This was a man he had met face to face. A man who had saved his life from the priests. To send orders to kill him...

Verl was no Singer, he had never taken the Singer's oath to kill no man, to do no harm to another. But this time, this morning, he had found...he just couldn't send it...

Call himself a failure again. He was no true son and heir to his father. He was no Singer. And now, he was no killer either. Not even for his king.

Chapter 10
Nightmares

The king's screams shrilled through the palace. The captain of the guard hesitated mid-sentence and waited for the queen regent's reaction.

Queen Felain kept her composure. She took the duke's marker off the war map in the council room and handed it to the captain. "Continue," she said. "Show me where."

The captain nodded. "At his army's slow pace, the duke is still two weeks from the border. He'll keep to the river road, and that will take him over Moxie Pass--here." He set the marker down in the midst of the hills bordering Norgondy and the duchy of Navarn. "With half your army carrying out the priests' orders around the realm, and other units still chasing down remnants of the old king's followers, you would be ill-advised to try fighting the duke before the Pass. He outnumbers what troops we have following him–"

"No more units can be taken away from the holy task of purifying the realm of false beliefs," the Badurian High Priest interrupted. Again, Felain needed to compose herself; she had not asked the priest to speak. It had been necessary to align with the Badurian Order in the early days of her son's rebellion against Henrik and his Capsen whore. It had been convenient too, afterwards, to allow the Badurian priests to "purify" the realm against her enemies. Plus, in stripping her people of their false beliefs in magic spells, love trinkets, and other scams her husband and the Capsen witch had allowed to infest the land, Felain knew she had needed to give her people a new belief to replace their old. A winged god that dwelt in the Black Hills of the east seemed far enough away to be innocuous. But now, the Badurian priests were "converting" so many by force or fire, they were becoming too powerful, and Felain herself had to be careful. That she had to endure the high priest as a member of her council had become a necessary evil. But to endure him when he did not wait upon her word to speak, when he considered himself, in fact, her equal in policy making was becoming unbearable.

She watched the priest pull out his silver snuff box from the folds of his voluminous scarlet robes and lift it to the shaded darkness of his hooded face. The air pungent and dusty as soon as he opened the lid, he sneezed in the visionary powder noisily. Felain turned from him pointedly.

"But in the Pass?" she prompted the Captain.

The Captain's expression was grim and she saw him take in a breath as if reluctant to answer her. "Yes. Your forces would have more chances against the duke there." He lifted up the duke's marker, revealing a small valley in the hills that had been hidden beneath it. "Here in the flats of this valley is where his wagons must ford the river before the road narrows again. It would be easy for one unit each to close off the defile on either side. Three, four more units can hide in the hills above the ford and wait for him. If it is still your intention to attack the Duke before he crosses the border, this would be my only recommendation."

His answer had been stiff, forced. "But you still don't agree?" the queen asked, watching him.

The Captain opened and closed his hand against the map before he spoke. "Suicide still, my lady. Or near. We'd have the advantage, but he'll be expecting us there, if anywhere. We can kill many of them, but I cannot guarantee we can get close to the Duke himself. He'll have too many men around him. And if we don't get the Duke, no matter how many others we kill, we will have started a war your forces are in no position yet to fight. And..." he glanced at the priest, "never will be until more of your men can be released from duties elsewhere."

The Captain was a tall man with a noble profile, high stiff cheeks the black brown of a walnut tree and as strong. His cheeks flushed darker each time he mentioned the duke. He hated the duke as much as she did--what the duke had done to embarrass her palace guard, none of her officers would forget. Too many had lost name and rank over the incident. If there was any way possible to get to the duke and kill him, her Captain of the Guard had sworn to find it. She had to take his advice that now was not the time.

She walked to the corner of the room where the melon-shaped jeweled casket with her dead husband's head inside sat on a pedestal. She rested a hand on top of the casket, met the captain's black eyes. "We wait then--again."

~

Queen Felain swept through the halls towards the king's chambers. Her page, not much younger than her son, ran to keep up with her, his lantern jerking long shadows that passed like dark clouds over the murals of the masters as they climbed the grand staircase. Ahead light flooded the gilt corridor leading to the king's apartment.

The hall was crowded. Servants, guards, doctors, and a cabal of priests parted to let the queen through. A priest waved his belled incense burner over her path behind her. The smoke hung heavy and hot in the king's bedroom from the legion of holy burners infesting his room. No wonder her son had nightmares.

Laird sat propped against his pillows, his nurse standing waiting on his left side, and his tutor, a Badurian priest, hovering on his right, reciting a prayer with him. Felain held her breath. Her son needed his tutoring. The library in Sorenzia, the greatest treasury of the realm's histories and literature, was now under Badurian control. And, perhaps more importantly, full knowledge and understanding of Badurian beliefs would one day give her son the power he needed to stand above them.

Felain would just have to make sure herself that Laird would learn the difference between peasant-dreamed beliefs and reality. Her son, the king, would need no god beyond himself.

For now, she waited at the foot of his bed.

When the priest finished his chant, he turned to her and bowed. She inclined her head in acknowledgment as she would to thank a servant. "Leave us," she said.

With the priest and the nurse gone, the first thing Felain did was open the windows and balcony doors, letting the sea air cleanse the room. Then she sat down next to her son.

"Did your screams chase away your monsters yet? Or perhaps it was their screams I heard tonight as you took your sword against them and slew them."

He grinned bravely at her suggestion. "One day I'll make it happen that way, Mother."

She combed her fingers through his golden hair and nodded her approval. "That's my hero king." He looked back at her through her own raven eyes. His high brow, high cheeks were also hers. But his golden hair, weak rounded nose, pale thin scholar lips came from his father. His pale skin that blistered in the sun was something else he would have to overcome. She would tell his weapons master tomorrow to start increasing his training outside. One day he might have to ride and fight all day in the sun.

"Tell me what you saw this time," she said.

His eyes widened, he clenched his pudgy hands around his sheet, but he answered her. "The same as last night. The same as the night before. A giant head, made of glass or water or something. Coming up out of the sea. White as the sea foam. But I could see a blue light shining through it. It was...it was my father's head."

She cursed his father under her breath. And the Duke his brother. For years, Laird had had nightmares of his father bullying him, killing him, or laughing at him. His father--her husband--the monster. But even during the rebellion, even after they'd won and the father had been quartered and beheaded, the nightmares had only come infrequently, once or twice a month. But since the Duke had come--Felain's blood started to boil remembering him, hating him--since the Duke had come delivering Henrik's head, Laird had wakened every night screaming as his father's head chased after him in more and more terrifying dreams.

"Did the face say anything?"

He shook his head, his eyes starting to fill with tears, but a king does not cry in his waking hours she had drilled into him. "I stepped up onto his glass lip. I was cold. His mouth was open, as big, as big as this room. I kept hitting at his teeth with my sword. I heard him laugh above the clatter

117

the sword made. Then he ate me. And swallowed the city whole in a giant wave. I couldn't save it."

"Perhaps you woke too soon," was all she could think to say.

Suddenly, he reached for her wrist. He dug in his nails, as earnest as he was with his question. "Did my captain of the guard kill my uncle yet?"

She shook her head. "We can't yet."

He released her arm, stared up at the ceiling. "I don't like that Duke. He's a bad man. I have a place on the shelf over there where I can put his head and spit at him every morning. And I will stuff the duke's skin with straw, my swordmaster said, and use him for practice."

Felain searched her son's expression, his hardness. She felt more cold than heat run through her veins when he said things like that in his young child's voice. And she hated her husband more than ever for what he had done to her son.

She hugged her arms around him, held him to her hard, then laid him back down, kissed his forehead. He would be stronger for all this someday. He would have to be. His hate would teach him to be. As it had her. "You do that, my hero king. But sometimes we have to wait until we have the power."

She started straightening his sheet when her fingers scratched across a roughness. She lifted up his bed robes and looked. The sheet was embroidered with white thread on white in a large intricate pattern.

"Where did this sheet come from?" she asked her son, keeping her voice calm, despite her instant fury.

"The nurse gave it to me, said it might help my dreams."

"Did she?" Felain said, as she blew out his candles, masking her reaction. "I'll talk to her then." She sat by his side, singing to him softly as she used to do when it was just the two of them in all the world, and watched him nestle down and fall asleep.

Then she yanked the sheet off him and twisted it into a small hated ball. Capsen symbols had been outlawed, their magic patterns and prophecies of good fortune were nothing but lies that gave you hope when there was none.

The Capsen witch Ailil had returned to court in the early years of Felain's marriage to Henrik. Felain wrung the sheet, remembering. Ailil had blessed their wedding chambers and their bed with patterns such as this dream web on Laird's sheet. She had trusted Ailil as a friend then, and thanked her heartedly. And her husband, apparently, started trusting the witch and thanking her even more. Then came stillbirth after stillbirth of Felain's and Henrik's children--all conceived under the blessed protection of the witch's patterns. False hopes, lies. Felain clenched the hated sheet.

Ten years later when her husband came back to her, roughly, only to make an heir, Felain had finally understood the witch's "magic" and had rid her chambers of all Capsen designs. Laird survived his birth, but barely.

Henrik had been interested in Laird at first. For a year or two. But Felain would not allow the whore Ailil anywhere near her son when she came with him. Finally Henrik stopped coming. He saw his son only in public then, at feasts or parades, where he would laugh out loud at Laird when he toddled and stumbled, and, after his laughter subsided, he'd order Felain to stop Laird's crying.

The next few years of exile on the coast followed. Only the three of them, she and Laird, and Laird's nurse. Planning the day of vengeance and restoration, they waited. Laird was safe and still growing—Felain's only road, she knew, back to power.

Then came the news that the whore carried the king's new son and heir.

The itinerant Badurian priest who brought the news was not the only one, he told her, who feared for Laird's life, true heir that he was and great king that he would be, ridding the realm of the unholy scourge of the witch's magic. Laird had supporters everywhere. And from that day a year ago, Felain had truly learned what hate can give you the power to do. There was no turning back now.

Clutching the sheet embroidered with the Capsen curse that had given her son nightmares, Felain strode softly from his room and closed the door behind her. Then she turned to the nearest guardsman and gave him the order to arrest the nurse for treason.

~

A week of wondering was over. The clattering coming up the road to the hornblower's cabin was too loud to be made by a single courier rider.

Perhaps Verl should have run before now. But if he had, he would have been admitting guilt. And worse, he would have left Lollander alone to face the queen's justice.

Verl kneaded flour into hardtack dough and punched a clenched fist into it as he tried to calm his nerves. He'd heard three days ago that a hornblower over on the next hill had been arrested for not delivering the queen's order to kill the duke. The hornblower had come from Navarn and so surely, he must have been the duke's spy. For all Verl knew, remembering the gold the duke had offered him, the Navarn hornblower could very well have been one of his spies. Most likely the arrest was justified on that count, the Norgon guardsmen must have surely found out more proof against the Navarn hornblower, and Verl had decided he could keep quiet about his involvement, and thereby keep himself—and Lollander—from being arrested too. Verl had even convinced himself by then that what little he had done was for the best. The duke and his army had turned peacefully around back to Navarn, as he had promised, and the king and the citizens of Norgarth were once again invincible, safe from attack, thanks be to the holy wisdom and loving protection of the Winged One, the king's scrolls had announced.

Indeed, Verl had heard nothing more since the arrest, and since yesterday, he had started to relax. But not now... He cut a biscuit. It was misshapen, his fingers were visibly shaking. Above the clattering of the horses, Lollander started to chuckle.

"Hills ride the horses night!" The old hornblower tapped a rapid cadence imitating many hoof beats with his ladle against the side of the bean pot he'd been stirring. "Snow flurries come early, spring flowers too late."

Lollander neighed like a horse then chuckled over at Verl.
"More than flowers know you why?"

Verl shook his head no, started cutting out biscuits,
and tried to guess Lollander's meaning. Foxfire Night came
early in the winter, bonfires built high upon all the hills as
townsmen and county peasants festooned their cows, dogs,
and horses with bells and holly and tied cups and spoons to
clatter behind their tails, driving away the spirits of the
howling wind beasts. Any thief caught that night would be
hung as a scapegoat.

But those were no spirits halting outside. And it was
spring, not winter. Lollander was watching Verl's hands.

"Ho, inside! Come out, in the name of the king!"

Lollander laughed, tapped another quick sound of
hoof beats against the iron pot and yelled back. "In the
name the king come I! What name call we the king and I
now?" As the hornblower stood, he shot a clear, uncrazed
eye at Verl and nodded his head. "More than flowers know
you." He spilled a spoonful of beans into the fire below his
pot, then hung up the ladle. "Feeding our fire, friends come
here night!" he called back out, and then to Verl, as if it
were a warning, "Feed your fire high."

"In the name of--"

"Of Lollander come I!" He swaggered outside
chuckling aloud and closed the door behind him.

Alone, Verl shot a glance at his cot. Every chance
he'd had during the past week when Lollander was out of the
cabin, Verl had worked on opening up the planks under his
bed, chipping out a hole in the rock, hiding his wrapped-up
lute with the Duke's ring and gold stuffed inside it, and then
finally yesterday carefully recovering the planks with straw.
He had nothing to do now but wait. He considered once
disappearing into illusion as he had that day in front of the
duke. But then, Lollander would hang alone.

He heard nothing outside for long minutes other than
an occasional horse nicker. As he waited, as calmly as he
could, he scratched the four protection signs he knew from
the pentagon onto each flattened mound of biscuit dough.

He'd begun setting the biscuits into the oven when
the door burst open behind him, and three of the queen's

guards came in to arrest him.

Chapter 11
Stone Tracks

Late spring hail pelted Crel and bounced in sharp pings off the slick rock around him. Determined not to retreat from its battering, he bunched himself inside his whaleskin wrap, a treasure from Wiss's and his last trading trip to the Eller Islands, and waited. The tough slick skin kept him dry, but did nothing to keep out the cold of the mountain storm.

It was the strong smell of wet stone that Crel noticed most. He was more familiar with rain storms in the forests or open prairies--rarely had Wiss and he ever crossed mountain passes, keeping to the low roads of the main trade routes. Wet stone, he noted here, did not smell like rain-soaked earth nor the soggy decay of forest humus. Instead, more like the hot tin he hammered into the inside of his copper vessels around the campfire at night. The same dust-like sting to the odor, stronger here because there was nothing but the wet stone to smell.

The hail pellets stopped as suddenly as they'd started. But rain now came from the west and drove slanted into his face, blinding his squinting eyes and hitting as hard and cold as the hail had against his cheeks. His troupe of Capsen refugees, numbering almost twenty, huddled with his wagon and bear cart under the overhang of the mountain wall, well protected. But Crel hunched out here in the punishing storm by the creek bed, refusing to move, waiting for the idiot carpenter Harris to finish scooping water out of one of many oblong puddles on the exposed rock shelf.

Perhaps if Harris had the sense to wait out the storm, he'd have more luck seeing the shape of the dent in the stone from which he kept trying to scoop the rainwater. But if there was one thing Crel had learned in the last two weeks, Harris was not one to listen to his advice. Crel had lived his life on the road, but villager Harris had appointed himself leader of their troupe, giving the orders, nosing into everyone else's talks at night, overseeing the healers, and only once a day giving a perfunctory report to blind, lame Orist. Just that once a day was fine with Crel. With both knees broken, with eye sockets still bandaged by a silken scarf, Orist had the unchallenged privilege of all the wounded to ride in the tinker's wagon and be Crel's responsibility. The less Crel had to deal with Harris coming to discuss the route to the Capsen hideaway with Orist each day, the more he could ignore his blustering.

As the rain softened, Crel glanced up at the billows of the dark grey storm cloud shouldering the peaks. At least the rain did not smell like lightning, exposed to the elements as the rock shelf was.

Harris was finally cupping water from the stone faster than the rain filled it up, and Crel, standing close, could study the odd shape of the hole. If the stone had been mud, if the hole were only a quarter of its size, he could have sworn it was an animal track. A bird's maybe, a heron, or something heavier, a lizard? given the width of the "toes." Three toes forward, one clawed toe back. As if someone had carved a giant track in the stone. The length of the hole from toe to toe was longer than Crel's two feet, one in front of the other.

Harris lifted his finger from the middle front toe and pointed to one of the two crevasses between the cliffs in the pass ahead. "That one," he said. "That's the way."

~

By midday, the rain had stopped and the sun shone full on a meadow atop a rise. A few young pines and scrub bushes were scattered nearby seeking to reclaim the meadow from the flowers and stony ground, but the hilltop looked more like a fire had burned through it and laid it bare. Fallen logs, a forest of whitened tree stumps had been left--or so Crel had thought when they first came upon the clearing. He sat on one of the stumps now, eating a sausage. Orist sat on a litter beside him. The stump was mostly white with some orange brown coloring streaking through it, adding to the effect that it had once been bark. And he saw a faint tracing of tree rings before he sat. But he had kicked at it, scratched at it. It was stone not wood.

Years ago when he was very young, Wiss and he were traveling down the Purlish Coast when a quake shook them off their feet and felled their wagon. In the distance, fire and smoke plumed into the sky, from a volcano, Wiss had said. In another week traveling south, they would have been caught in the sea of its lava flow. As it was, they turned inland instead, and listened to tales ten years later of villages still being found in its ashes, the people, dogs, horses, the tree stumps, everything, the frightened contortions on the people's faces all turned to stone.

Perhaps that was what had happened here. The hill they were climbing had the conical shape of an old volcano.

But that didn't account for the intricate carving on a flat rock near his foot. A dragonfly imprinted into it, twice the size of any dragonfly he'd ever seen, but definitely identifiable. The wings so delicately laced into the rock, it had to have been a masterpiece. Yet it was thrown aside here on top of a mountain.

Crel chewed off another hunk of sausage and didn't mention the dragonfly to Orist. He'd asked about the odd carving by the creek bed that looked like a giant bird print, and Orist had chuckled.

"Carved, you say?" Orist's walrus mustache twitched with each chuckle below his red scarf bandage covering his empty eye sockets. "Not by the hand of man, lad. Our people are artists, yes. But we can only copy nature's carvings. We don't work in stone any more than you do."

A Capsen woman brought Orist a tambour. From his litter, he banged it and shook its bells after every meal while others played flutes, drums, lutes, and a prized accordion salvaged from their village after the guardsmen left and before Crel had returned to them. Some of the women sang and a few of the men danced. After evening meals, Jesser danced with them, the bear twirling her pirouettes in the center of their circles, grinning with her long bear teeth, enjoying herself more than she did performing in the towns around the realm where she danced for a hatful of copper talents and an overripe apple.

Crel rose from the stone stump, careful not to step on the dragonfly rock, and went to water the animals and to give Jesser an apple when the singing started. Listening grated him. It sounded as if all memory of grief and devastation of two weeks ago had been forgotten. Until, that is, he looked into their eyes at night, dark and haunted, or into the long somber draw of their faces in the early morning. These singing, merry-making refugees had a courage he could scarce understand, he could grant them that. The memory of finding Wiss's body, half-eaten by the crested bear, still pulled at him and he had never felt like singing.

~

Crel felt eyes watching him. Not the Capsen refugees watching him, he'd grown used to their intrusion into his world. But the eyes of something else hidden in the rocks, behind the red manzanna bushes, or darting behind the wind-sheared pines along the trail each time he glanced over to see. Nothing was there, except at every turn he noted another rock carving set into the face of the cliffs. Plaques of animals, insects, fish, birds, or skeletons of something larger engraved into slabs of red sandstone and mounted like altars in the grey granite cliffs. From the fossil beds, Harris had said, laughing at him when he caught Crel looking at them. Crel was beginning to detest Harris intensely.

As Crel studied one of the carvings that seemed to move whenever he wasn't looking, he remembered the tapestry on the wall in the treasure room of Orist's palace, eyes staring at him from animals hidden in every color and swirl of green leaves. Crel rested his hand on Jesser's neck as she lumbered beside him, the rest of the caravan taking a welcome break as he walked her and rested the mare and the ox from their long climb. Jesser was neither bristling nor growling; she paid no attention to the animal carvings along the trail. The sensation of something watching them must only be in Crel's imagination.

126

Jesser paused to whuff at a clump of mountain dewberries that were just turning black. She grunted happily and sat down on her haunches to eat.

~

Sunset came early to the mountains, firing the rocks ahead and casting long shadows that loomed over Crel and darkened his imaginings. From the corner of his eye, the carved animal skeletons along the cliff walls hunched on their bare kneebones and shifted the twist of their broken necks to watch as he passed by. The play of the slanted light on the carvings etched them sharper, deeper into his thoughts, he couldn't tear his mind away from seeing them move, or from listening to the sounds he thought they made. But the clicking of horse shoes on the rocks, the rattle of the wooden wheels and the groan of the wagons, the snippets of conversations among the refugees walking in twos and threes ahead of him, the howling whine of the wind through the pines was what he heard, nothing else. He had never been one to give way to imagined fears.

He looped Esra's reins over the front board and crawled into the back of the hutwagon, opened the half-lid of the water barrel and dipped his cup in. He shut his eyes as he drank, safe for the moment from the shadows and carvings that watched him and crowded in behind him when he wasn't looking. He took off his wool tinker's cap and scrunched it in his fist as he swiped his brow. Beads of sweat had formed along his hairline. He took another gulp of cool water and splashed the last few drops across his face. Then he closed the lid and crawled back onto the seat beside Orist and picked up the reins.

He counted three horse shadows ahead of him. One was Esra hitched to his wagon. One was her mule colt following by her side. And the third... The third was for whatever horse that wasn't there. A carving on the cliff wall twisted its broken neck as they passed by.

Crel settled his cap jauntily to one side of his head, started whistling between his teeth, and drove on. Perhaps Orist beside him didn't know how lucky he was being blind.

Twilight lingered, and the shadows lengthened. The caravan of refugees marched on ahead, oblivious to the moving carvings, oblivious to the nightfall. Crel halted to light his lanterns then hurried to catch up. He would follow as long as it was safe for Esra to find her way on the stones.

But when he rounded a cliff, he pulled to a halt.

Ahead the road narrowed and passed under two giant slabs of granite arching into each other. Where the slabs touched, a rock carving, a monster skull, had been mounted. Its eye sockets were caverns that swallowed the light, its snout was long and broad-tipped, its jawbone opened around fangs half the size of a man. Swirls of smoke or evening fog curled out through the pass under it, and out through a cave in its mouth. In stone silence, in the hunger of a predator waiting, the stone skull leered down on the refugees marching towards it.

Sweat beaded on Crel's brow again. He swiped it. He wanted to shout out, warn of shadows of horses that weren't there, of stone necks twisting as he passed by, of eyes he never saw, stalking him, crowding him, of monster eye caverns that leered down with an emptiness that swallowed the sun's setting light. To warn of fangs that gleamed faint sunset orange dripping sharply through the smoky fog curling through them. Crel's grip turned to stone around the reins. The refugees kept walking. One by one, two by two, laughing. Not seeing the gleam on the teeth reddening brighter, the black lips curling back, the grey leathery skin stretching, filling out into a long body, wrinkling across the broad snout, empty eyes gleaming--

"What is it, lad?"

Orist's voice beside him startled him, brought him back to himself, back to reality. Crel looked at the old man, his shaggy white brows lifting above his bandaged eyes, waiting for him to answer. In the calming aura of the old man's silence, the shadows receded from Crel's mind, and he could breathe again, certain of himself, certain of the old man. "Been seeing things that aren't there," he admitted. He laughed. But his fists were still clenched around the reins.

"Describe what you see," Orist said. His voice was serious.

Crel told him hesitantly. And the more he told him, the more a fool he felt. And the more relieved to have someone to laugh it over with, to dispel his imaginings.

But Orist was not laughing. "Is your mare worried?"

Crel looked at Esra. She was standing waiting, her left rear hoof tilted forward, calmly resting a leg. Her tail switched lazily against her harness. Her colt was cropping a stand of grass.

Orist took the reins from Crel. "Among my people, lad, let your animals guide you. Learn to see as they do. Learn to see what is there, not what you believe you see."

Blind Orist snapped the reins and geed the mare forward.   "Dragon's Gate," he said. "Few outsiders ever pass through it. Especially with Merind's mother on the other side. Hold on to your seat, lad. Shut your eyes if you have to. There's rope in the back, tie yourself in before you start thinking about running. We're going through. -- Damn," he muttered softly a moment later, "Harris should have warned you."

Chapter 12
Treasure Cave

Thick steam swirled in front of Merind's mother as she sang and stirred her cauldron.

Sitting with the Capsens who encircled her, Crel studied her. Ailil was beautiful, even behind her tellerwoman's veil. Beautiful eyes, grey like her daughter's. Or maybe silver, if he could call them that. That hint of silver shine on polished pewter when he embossed a mug and it caught the firelight.

There was a beautiful calmness in her too, a gentleness--this peace he felt inside him to be sitting near her. The same quiet assurance that had wrapped his world inside the safe circle of a fire's glow during the long nights traveling down the road with Wiss. Rarely had he felt that secure, that accepted among strangers. More rarely had he felt a stranger was someone he would accept into his own small circle of the world.

More than accept, and his gaze was lured down again by the soft contours and breezy wisp of her dancer's silks. He had to remind himself how old Ailil must be. Merind's mother. A witchwoman, like her daughter. The dead king's consort. And the queen regent's oldest, most hunted enemy. Stories of the politics of the realm had always been distant, inconsequential in Crel's life. Never before had one stood in the flesh in front of him, singing, scantily clad in her last stripped-down layers of ceremonial silks, sweat gleaming on her brow in the heat of the fire and steam rising between them, her bright silver eyes piercing through him--

Crel shifted away, broke contact. He had to remind himself of Orist's warning. "Trust nothing in this land you see with your own eyes. Trust nothing, until you know for sure the difference between seeing and believing."

Ailil's infant son by the dead king was wrapped inside his cradle board and mounted on a tripod near the tents. He turned his small head away from watching his mother and laughed straight at Crel, gurgling at him. Trust nothing, Crel repeated, as in liturgy.

The witchwoman's song reached inside him and pulled him back to her. He watched her quick fingers curl steam above her cauldron, shaping flowers, birds, and as she sang on, a bright waterfall cascaded down from one hand to the other. She took her lower hand away, and Crel saw the waters splash upon steam turtles on steamy rocks of a woodland stream. There, where the shining waters splashed, the steam rose again, grew wings, opalescent butterfly wings, that crowded open in the spiraling steam into a rainbow's suggestion of colors. The butterflies flew up, circled, scattered, and faded away among the stars.

Crel heard the baby laugh. *Trust nothing.* Not the beauty, not the peace, not the exaltation in him that sang in butterflies among the stars. Crel shook his head, hearing his own words. He banished the song's effect on him, banished his words, his interpretation of it, must be--

The baby gurgled and laughed. Merind's baby brother, strapped inside his cradle board. His head was the skull of a dragon, fleshing out: his crinkling leather snout snarled above giant crested bear teeth that salivated steam and spouted fire. Its jaws reached down, closed upon Crel in his wagon, as fire leapt around him.

Then the baby laughed.

And the skull was stone again left behind him at the entrance to the dragon's gate, at the entrance to this valley, and there was no such things as dragons, Orist had said, stories, and the fear of stone skulls only. And the baby was just a baby, he had a child's face, grey cave eyes laughing. Crel shivered in the fire's close heat. He wet his lips, and braved the flames he imagined still around him, and the song scorching through him.

The song changed note. Ailil reached up, caught one of the spiraling butterflies.

She spread its rainbow wings apart between her hands. Wider, larger. Holes in the steam rented open between the wings, two for eye caverns, one for a mouth. She spoke a name, the swirl of steam between the wings became a face, a figure of a man, of one of the dead they had left behind at the massacre in Drespin.

She sang his name, and the Capsens in the circle around the fire with Crel sang his name, and the figure of steam with butterfly wings on his back took flight, rising, fading out, vanishing among the stars.

There were tears at the corners of Crel's eyes, shivers along his spine, beads of sweat from the fire. The baby laughed. The song exalted through him and resounded among the stars.

From the other side of the fire, Orist nodded, and Crel heard himself singing then too, through his tears, singing the names of the dead arising. The refugees in the circle beside him, wives, daughters, friends of the slain, were laughing, singing too. Ailil's nimble fingers, fine voice pulled open butterfly wings of steam, and the names they sang one by one, hundreds of them, all night long, shaped their memories into spirits and released them. Crel sang and cried in joy with them.

The last song of the night, the last steam butterfly Ailil caught became Wiss.

Crel froze when he heard his name, couldn't repeat it. He watched Wiss's face, wizened body form in the steam between the wings of the butterfly. The baby had fallen asleep, couldn't laugh. As Crel watched, Wiss fleshed out, became more than steam, unlike any of the others who had only been names to him. His cheeks creased with remembered wrinkles, his long walrus mustache chuckled above his thin cracked lips, his fly-away hair steamed freely above him. Jesser had his hat now, Crel remembered, no way to keep his hair from escaping. Through tears, through a rush of memories, Crel mouthed the old man's name, and Wiss, released, opened his eyes and winked at him, then took wing and flew away, fading out among the dwindling stars.

Crel stared up at the hole left between the stars, long after the others around the fire started drifting away, long after the sky started brightening in the false dawn and the stars disappeared. Then, he smiled. There was no guilt left in Wiss's passing, no blame left. Peace only. Seeing is believing, Crel muttered to himself. It had to be. He had to trust it so. And he hoped Jesser had seen Wiss too.

"Crel, lad."

Orist's voice broke through Crel's thoughts. Crel looked up at Wiss's brother standing beside him, the bright scarf tied over his empty eye sockets. Crel rose, his legs, back, neck stiff from sitting all night.

"You sang too, lad," Orist said, chuckling below his mustache.

Crel nodded before remembering Orist couldn't hear a nod. "Yes," he said aloud. "I did. But," he wet dry lips, "We never sang Merind's name--"

Orist turned his head sharply to the sound of Merind's mother approaching. She had finished raking the last embers under her cauldron into the sand.

"Merind?" she asked.

Crel paused, confused; apparently she hadn't heard of her daughter's death. "I'm sorry," he said.

Ailil stared back a moment, then she nodded. Her eyes above her green silk veil were grey in the rising sun, not silver as they had looked by firelight.

"No one told you," she said.

Crel was more confused. She looked to blind Orist, her brother, as Crel answered softly, "One of the Norgon guardsmen did, a cook actually. Told how she poisoned herself, scratched yew across her face, ate it--" Crel swallowed; Merind' mother was staring back at him again. He shouldn't be the one to be telling her this. "I'm sorry."

Ailil put a hand on Crel's arm, stopping him. "That was my daughter's friend. They grew up together, looked quite alike, until Caris had the courage to do that to herself. She always was allergic to yew. Caris is the second soul we freed last night. When my daughter changed clothes with her, the Norgons never knew the difference."

Crel's breath stopped, then rushed out suddenly. "Then she lives--" His eyes searched across the vast expanse of the lake in the crater of the old volcano that hid the Capsens' last refuge. Fog rose up in the early dawn light and curled above the lake, like the steam had above the cauldron last night. He half-expected to see Merind come

133

walking towards them out of the fog. Or else, he could go find her--

"Lad, no." Orist grappled at him blindly on his shoulder and arm, stopping him, then he turned to his sister.

"This is why we never told him."

"I see," Ailil said.

Crel tried shaking his arm free, then paused, finally hearing what Orist said. "What--?"

"We needed you to come here first, Crel, drive your wagon here, bring our treasures, like you promised. It's what we asked of you to do, that and save Jesser. And now, your second promise. Become our tinker, become our eyes and ears across the land. You have less than two months left before you must reach the islands of your homeland and have the leader of your people sign your license with the new king's signature on it, keeping your right to trade and travel. That first, lad, as you promised me, before all is lost. And then, perhaps, in your later traveling, may you find word of Merind again."

Crel stared at the blinded Orist, his fists tightening rebelliously at his sides. Orist's walrus mustache, so like Old Wiss's, held him trapped.

"Right," he said stiffly. "I promised."

Ailil closed her fingers around his arm, fingers that had shaped visions out of steam. She met Crel's look unflinchingly. "In the meantime, Crel, my daughter can take care of herself." But in silence, Crel nodded another promise to her, one Orist never heard, and Ailil nodded back. He *would* look for Merind.

"Come," she said, "we'll unload your wagon. I'll show you where."

~

It was late afternoon, after eating and resting, before Crel drove Ailil to the caves on the other side of the crater to stow the Capsen treasures. Crel set his hat jauntily on his head and whistled to Esra as she trotted along. Her ears flicked constantly back to listen to him then forward to study the road. Her mule colt sported along the rushes and flirting dragonflies beside the lake, until he startled a nesting

134

swan. The swan rose up, stretched her mighty wings, arched her neck down, and charged after him, honking, her string of cygnets yapping after her. The colt bounded back to Esra for protection. He huddled so close behind her that Esra's cropped tail slapped his face for his cowardice and he brayed piteously. Crel chuckled and drove on, Ailil beside him.

They passed seven, maybe eight separate villages of her people. More had been set up along the north rim of the cauldron. Most of the refugees were living in tents, with clothes drying on ropes strung between them, and barking dogs chasing children everywhere. But some of the villages already had stone houses, gleaming granite fronts crisscrossed by bricks of lava for color, stubbornly reminiscent of their half-timbered villages they had abandoned to the Norgons in the valley below. These new houses, hidden from the world and built of stone, would never burn like Drespin had. Or so Crel hoped for them. Across the faces of two of the buildings Crel had seen young owners and their wives on scaffolds painting murals of the Capsen histories and legends, miniatures of the great murals that had once adorned the hostels in Drespin. The Capsens were rebuilding their lives to stay here forever.

"No," Ailil said. "not forever." Crel turned to her and blinked, her sudden words seeming to answer his thoughts. Her grey eyes sparked with a silver gleam in them again, this time, perhaps, reflected off the lake. "We are a wandering people always," she said softly, speaking to herself maybe, instead of to him. "We've rested in our valley for two centuries too long. That was never Alred's promise to us. This is our sacred land, as he promised...a place well hidden, safe for dreams and training; but no, this is never our home. We will not rest here forever."

Crel turned his attention away, giving her musings privacy. He listened to Esra's hooves thudding on the lava stones and to the heavy rattle of the wagon wheels. He would have to oil the axles soon, that was sure. Whale oil would be good for that, as soon as he got home to the islands.

135

Ailil turned to him. "That we promise *you*, Crel. We will not stay here forever. They said you have Alred's scars."

Crel took in his breath, held it. Then he turned from her, never answered. He was committed to too many promises already. He had sworn to Orist he would not tell his people he had no intention of becoming their legend. And certainly for himself, he had no desire ever to talk about it.

Past the next bare stone beach, around the next turn, they arrived at the caves. Crel pulled to a stop.

For the first time since the pass leading up the mountain, Crel was facing sandstone plaques of animals inset into the cliff walls. Fossils, Harris had called the carvings, Crel remembered with distaste for the carpenter still. Four giant animals, life-size full skeletons almost, if unflattened, if their bones were untwisted, guarded each side of the mouths of the two caves. Two were bears, one a giant lion of some sort, the fourth as large a seal with a long neck and a pointed mouth with vicious teeth. Crel did not see any of them move.

"You are in their memory now," Ailil said, nodding at them.

Crel looped the reins around the whipstand and swung down from the wagon. He went around Esra to help Ailil down, but she was already swinging down, landing lightly. She looked up at him, the silver in her eyes laughing. Unlike their situation last night, he realized suddenly, he was alone with her. She wore a simple yellow tunic, belted at her slender waist, light green kirtle to her knees, her blond hair was pulled back on top and cascaded down to either side of her veil. Merind's mother, Crel reminded himself. Old enough to be his own. A king's consort-- The dead king's consort. Crel made a fist. He had seen the decayed quartered arm of the king posted on the gate in front of Drespin, its curled fingers pointing at him, warning him away.

Ailil laughed, and her grey eyes sparked silver. Crel had no idea what they could be reflecting this time. She was not facing the sun or the lake.

136

She went around to the back of the hutwagon and opened the doors. Crel joined her.

He showed her the treasures from Orist's palace, unwrapping each one carefully, the porcelain herons ready to unfold butterfly-colored wings and take flight, the delicate lattice screens carved in turtles and rabbits and hutwagon caravans, the stained glass bowls, the silver flasks, the gold sheep, lizards, deer figures, and the tapestry from the wall, animals hiding in its green and yellow leaves. And last, he unpacked his own masterpiece, the copper lantern he'd spent every night for a year engraving with seals perched on rocks, waves splashing over them, from childhood memories of his island homeland.

Ailil took the copper lantern outside the wagon, studied its intricate designs in the sunlight. She pointed to the cave on the right, and waited while Crel unloaded the other treasures into it. "They're safe in there," she told him. "The guardians will let no one else pass." Crel glanced up uneasily at the stone lion and toothed seal each time he passed under them. Even from the corner of his eyes, they never once looked at him.

When he had finished unloading the rest, Ailil handed him back his lantern and pointed to the bear-guarded cave on the left. "Take this one in there," she said. "All the way in and wait for me. If you want to see my daughter again someday, you might be very interested in what you see in there." The tellerwoman's eyes sparked silver again.

Crel entered the cave. Unlike the other cave, its mouth was only large enough for the boulder sitting on rails beside it to fit it, a door Crel assumed. The mouth opened into a long low tunnel. Ailil had said all the way in, and Crel bent to follow the tunnel. White cave spiders crawled everywhere just above his sloped back and lowered head. It smelled dank; it was getting colder, the light dimmer, the only light was coming from behind him through the tunnel. He came finally to a wide dark cavern.

He stood in the center of the cavern looking into the dark recesses for some table or shelves to set the lantern on. The other cavern had been filled with many treasures. Here there was nothing, the inside bowel of a mountain.

137

He heard a heavy scrape, rock against rock. It took him a puzzled moment to realize what he heard. Then he started to spin back towards the tunnel--but not soon enough before the grey light blinked out.

He spun wildly, disoriented in the sudden complete blackness, not sure now how far he had spun nor in which direction the tunnel was. The lantern slipped from his fingers, he ran forward, seeking the tunnel. He crashed into the smooth wall of the cavern. He clawed his way along the wall until he stumbled into the tunnel, hitting his forehead against the roof of it.

He ducked his head, screamed Ailil's name through the tunnel. He rushed forward, his arms frantically guiding him between the walls of the tunnel. His fingers cracked spiders as he pushed past them. He reached the closed, sealed boulder at the end of the tunnel, his cheeks smashed hard into the rough edges of it.

Trapped. Buried. Betrayed.

"Ailil!" he shouted.

He pounded his fists blindly against the rough stone until they bled, then he sank down to his knees, exhausted. "Trust nothing in here you believe you see," Orist had warned him. "Trust nothing you believe."

"Ailil!" Crel whimpered, not understanding. *"Ailil!"*

Chapter 13
Norgarth Dungeon

Days or nights were defined by blacks or greys, and mornings by three narrow strips of light when the sun hit the only windows in the high tower above the pauper's pit.

One of those shafts of light streaked across Verl's lap. He cupped his hand into the dusty glow and followed its beam upwards to the windows above.

As a free man, he had never paid much attention to the stories of why the dungeon windows were being bricked up last year until only slits remained. The three windows were narrower than arrow openings in ramparts, he saw, too narrow, it was claimed, to allow the witches and demons imprisoned in the pit to fly through them when they changed shape at night.

Verl closed his hand on the insubstantial light.

During the war and since, so many covens of witches, societies of sorcerers, and wagonloads of Capsen tellerwomen had been captured that the dungeons overflowed. The latest scare story he'd heard, told in hushed whispers or rips of strained laughter around the taverns when he came down from the hill each month, was that Norgarth Dungeon was beleaguered by the maddened spirits crowding up against its walls and trying to fly through them --so much so that, despite the bricked-in windows, one or two witches starved thin enough did manage to escape on a full moon night. Battered and squeezed by the pushing and shoving until they lost any last body shape they had, they oozed out like thick foul clumps of smoke through the narrow slits and sank in dark ink splotches through the sea fog to the city below. And that would be why Marn or Race or Race's dog--the victim depending on the storyteller--had been found murdered and eaten in a back alley two nights ago.

Verl reopened his hand. The streak of light made a bright line across his palm, but he held nothing. He turned his hand over in the light, strummed his fingers through the chords of the light, but he made no sound. The irony of his life twisted at the corners of his lips.

They had spent five nights in the pit so far, counting the greys of day. He recounted, just to be certain, the four small pebbles he had piled above Lollander's fevered head as he leaned over and added on a fifth pebble for this morning. During the black nights, he heard the fighting, the moans, the piteous long screams that he didn't want to imagine the reason for, but he had heard no such thing as witches or demons flying into the stone walls above him. He sat awake guarding Lollander the first two nights and napped during the days, though, just in case.

During the long grey stretch of day, he felt safer, but this was the only time it was quiet enough in the pit to hear the rats. Twice he had awakened to find a rat biting near the wound on Lollander's side, and once a rat nibbled on Lollander's blistered lips. Verl checked the old hornblower's brow lightly, not to wake him. He still had a fever.

Verl did not know how much longer he could keep Lollander alive. He scrabbled for food scraps for the both of them when they were thrown into the pit. Their supply of water came from buckets lowered six times a day, but he could bring his friend only as much as his cupped hands could hold or that a strip of his shirt wetted in a bucket could dribble across Lollander's hot face. When he could, when the shirt was wet enough, he would wring the first few precious drops of water onto Lollander's cracked lips. They had each been given a tin cup before they were lowered into the pit, but the cups, their shoes, the tunics and surcoats on their backs were the only possessions they had on them when the guards left and the pit door was pulled shut. They were mobbed for those few treasures and left for dead by the immediate black rush of shadows in the grey--by the gang of the twenty to thirty men and women in the pit determined to be survivors.

Verl learned his lesson from the mob that day. When he regained consciousness on the hard stones and caked mud of the floor, he had cuts and bruises, a sore shoulder and half a shirt, but he was still alive, and so was Lollander. The cut in Lollander's side was open and bleeding though, and his master was still unconscious when Verl dragged his body to an empty spot by the rounded stone wall and claimed it as their own. Lollander had awakened from time to time in the days since and greeted Verl with his ludicrous toothy grin that mixed hope, stubborn odd truths, and insanity as much as his words ever had. Feeding him, bandaging his side, passing the wet cloth across his face, smiling back at that grin that twisted inside him between sadness and love, Verl grew more and more determined he had to be a survivor for the both of them.

There were some prisoners, he'd noted, who had come the same day they had or a day or two later, who crawled to a corner of the wall and gave up, never moving since, never eating, maybe dead already. Bodies were only carted out every third day, and the suffocating fumes in the pit spoke of the one or two bodies the guards inevitably missed.

But because of Lollander, because of that ludicrous grin of hope and faith, Verl could not be one of the ones who gave up. And every day Verl got stronger, quicker, fiercer, as he fought for a bigger handful of the food scraps to feed them both. And while he hadn't brought himself yet to attacking a new prisoner for his cup or clothes, he had been studying the five to ten prisoners who were herded into the cage each morning and hauled out of the pit, with only one, maybe two dropped back in wounded and bleeding each evening, a cup again in his hand.

Eight prisoners had been herded out by a Badurian priest and five guardsmen this morning. Verl passed his hand slowly again in and out of the narrow shaft of light and watched his fingers glow red in the light then grey as they passed out of the light. Seeing his fingers glow and disappear gave him an idea that just might...work.

~

"In the name of the prophet
Badur
Who wandered for sixty days
to the black hills of the east
Badur

141

His soul exiled, blackened to humanity
Badur
His only friend the stars at night,
the sun on his back
Badur
The hills were sharp, black rugged glass
In life, there is no Pass through
Badur
His soul cut naked, lay starved by the river
The unredeemed die of thirst
with water in their cup
Badur
The wolves howled, the fire demons circled--
Protect us, Nameless One. Have pity!
Badur
Lion-with-wings, hawk-with-fangs,
Forked tail stroke of death
Take pity!
The Nameless One came.
Badur
Bring mankind back to me,
Hurl the demon down
The only truth is me
Glory be to the Nameless One!
Badur!

As Arnaby intoned the name of the prophet Badur in
choral response to the High Priest of the East, he peered out
from the hidden shadows of his hood at the eight prisoners
from the dungeon. All were condemned as heretics, but
they were heretics, no doubt, through no deed nor thought of
their own, judging by the way they huddled together in the
center of the arena facing the four chanting priests. A true
witch or sorcerer or illusionist descended from the blood of
a lakeman would stand ready and alert, awaiting the chance
to change his or her fate. These eight instead quaked in fear,
their spirits broken, eyes sullen, they were not looking
around. There was not a shred of power or hope in them;
rat-eaten, lamed, starved, wearing no more than strips of
clothing, they were simply this day's quota of live targets for

142

the mêlée. Time was when the guardsmen trained on straw effigies. That was before the overcrowding in the dungeons.

One scrawny lass standing in front had the matted hair of a straw effigy. She looked young enough to have seen no more than sixteen summers. Another, with a hooked nose, cragged crow face, breathing and drooling through missing teeth, looked worn before her time, but maybe as old as thirty. Her head hung forward in idiocy and her eyes were grey. The other six today were men. Arnaby chanted the name of the prophet Badur and shook stinging smoke up in the air before him with his incense burner.

All eight were victims most probably of a neighbor's zealot conversion to the promises of the Badurian priests who passed like plagues through the towns. Priests could always find among their new converts a good wife professing her new religious fervor so loudly she'd name a wisewoman, or a village harlot, or a neighbor's drunken husband she'd seen at a demon's dance in the woods on a full moon night--condemning not only the village outcast but herself as well for having attended a demon's dance. Most likely there had never been such a dance, the good wife, only having heard such stories that preceded the coming of the priests, convinced herself they were true, believing eventually she had seen them too, and her word made another story true.

But not all the prisoners had once been peasants, Arnaby had discovered in his guise as a priest. The holy purge of the army of the Nameless One was becoming a great leveler of society. Neighbor would name neighbor when the priests came, to keep from being named a practitioner of the demon's magics himself. Or worse reason, in recent months, land owners were being named as having struck bargains to fly with the demon at night in exchange for more land and buckets of gold. As soon as a shrewd neighbor learned that a named heretic's confiscated holdings could be redeemed by his accuser, more and more wealthy landowners were identified as the masked leaders at the demon's dances.

Watching the eight before them, Arnaby could not guess which rank or estate in life any of them once held.

Pauper or prince, they were condemned for having held false beliefs in the power of the demon's magic. For having been led astray from the one true Path to the loving wings of the Nameless One.

Arnaby knew how his friend the duke would laugh in despair at the Badurian beliefs.

"Rejoice!" the priest of the east wind told the prisoners before them. "You are the chosen! The Nameless One sees inside your dreams and knows you stand guilty before him. He has watched you leave your bodies and fly with the demon at night, even though in your hearts you deny it by day. See with him, confess to the truth, let him show you the way."

The prisoners huddled in the center of the arena not moving. Some glanced back at the unit of twenty guardsmen who had herded them here and now stood, polishing their swords, waiting.

"Now, in the hour of your death," the high priest of the east raised his voice and pounded his staff into the dirt, its silver bells ringing, "confess, and save your soul! The Nameless One comes!"

Five or six glanced up at the grey clouds, as if expecting to see the black wings descending upon them. One whimpered out in terror. The woman with the limp head and glazed eyes did not move. Duke Rayid's court had laughed uproariously three years ago when news first arrived in Navarn that the obscure order of new priests in his brother's realm took as their god the winged beasts of the Black Hills. Navarn lay to the south of the Black Hills. Once in a lifetime, a Navarn farmer might spot one of the giant beasts flying off with a sheep. The beasts ate. There was nothing godly about them.

But those beasts were unknown here in Norgondy, and the vision of the wanderer Badur who had spotted one a decade ago struck all the fear of the divine the Badurian priests needed to convert a realm. Their rise to dangerous power had been sudden and quick; their righteous purge of all beliefs and magics not their own had aligned them with Henrik's ousted queen and with many of the high families who resented the power the Capsen sorceress had in

Henrik's heart. In the name of the Nameless One and in the name of Henrik's young son, the duke's brother's head lay in a jeweled casket, false magics were heresy, and Duke Rayid's laughter in far-off Navarn had changed note.

Arnaby wished he could have passed more information to the duke that day in the market square in his disguise as an Eller Island dream interpreter. But before he had time to tell him much more than where the palace guard uniforms for his men lay, that singer had caused a commotion and had almost had Arnaby arrested. Dream interpretation was one magic power not yet outlawed-- Badur's vision of the winged beast was called a dream by the Badurian priests, maybe that was why--but Arnaby could not risk getting captured and becoming the first dream interpreter to be condemned. He had had to disappear quickly that day.

"Confess!" The high priest of the east wind pounded his staff into the ground and rattled its bells a fifth time.

Five of the prisoners fell to their knees, sobbing, confessing to anything to save their souls. Seeing the others, the woman with the limp head kneeled with them, blubbering. The young lass, as wide-eyed and frozen as a trapped rabbit, stood still. A large bearded man to the rear also did not drop down and confess. Either way, their lives would not be saved.

"Welcome, my friends, back into the love of the Nameless One. May he take you under his wings and protect you." At a hand signal from the high priest, Arnaby and the two other priests of the winds passed among the kneeling prisoners, anointing their upraised cheeks with wing-shaped stamps dipped in dark oil, blessing them with a pass of incense smoke, and handing them a staff. The most frightening thing about these priests, Arnaby had found, was that they believed what they said without question. The staffs were to protect the six new converts from the two charges of the guards. The two prisoners who had stayed standing were given nothing. Their chances of survival were the same.

~

On the first charge of five horsemen, the tight knot of prisoners scattered. As happened every day, some prisoners stood too long in shock until the soldiers came within yards of them before they ran for the walls of the arena. They were the first to be hacked dead. Three "converts" dropped their staffs as they ran; only two men tried turning at their last chance to defend themselves. Of these two, one survived the first charge, swinging hard enough against the swing of the sword that it only glazed his left hip. His staff ripped from him, he fell as the horse charged past him.

The bearded man was one of the four to survive the first charge. When the five horsemen rode towards them, he grabbed the hand of the girl who hadn't moved and pulled her with him as he ran for the walls. A guardsman singled them out and pursued them. The bearded man pushed the girl down to the ground and ran for the opposite wall. The guardsman's horse cut towards him. He zigzagged twice more as the horse got closer; the sharp turns broke the horse's stride, slowing it down. The guardsman, cursing, his face livid with the chase, yelled taunts at him and held his sword high, ready for the swing.

At the last second, the prisoner dove to the ground and rolled. The guardsman's sword cut against his right shoulder as the horse jerked to a stop and reared above him, trying once more to shift direction. As the horse came down, as the guardsman pulled his sword back to swing again, the prisoner jumped to his feet and sprinted back towards the center of the arena.

One pass was all the mounted guardsmen were given in the first charge. The prisoner grabbed a forsaken staff from the ground and waited for the next five guardsmen running towards the remaining four prisoners on foot.

The bearded man fought valiantly, and Arnaby watched him. It was a shame he could not be saved and drafted into the duke's army. The prisoner swung the staff furiously, parrying the strikes of the two guardsmen fighting him, almost disarming one. Then a third, fourth, fifth guardsman surrounded him as he fought on, the last prisoner left alive. His right arm streaming blood, then his left side gorged, his right leg, he spun in all directions jabbing the staff against the sword strikes, until at last he fell to a knee. He raised his staff in both strong hands still to defend himself, but then he wavered and fell forward upon it.

From the side of the arena, the swordmaster barked an order. The swordsmen stayed their arms, backed away as the swordmaster came closer. The four Badurian priests, Arnaby among them, reentered the arena to pass judgment.

It would be an interesting verdict. The prisoner was not one of the ones who had confessed and been given a staff to defend himself. But he was the last prisoner left alive, and the convention so far had been for the high priest to show the god's mercy by sending the one or two prisoners left alive each day back down to the dungeon to a slower death there.

Two guardsmen rolled the prisoner over and yanked the staff from his grip. He lay a mass of blood, pulp, torn rags and skin, barely conscious but still moaning. If a sword were in Arnaby's hand, he would have released him from his pain, in respect for his desperate valor, if not in pity. Arnaby swung his incense burner and chanted lowly as he waited.

"He shall live," the high priest said, pounding his belled staff into the ground with his pronouncement. "Unredeemed though he is. It is the demon who saved him. But he fought with a staff that has been blessed. Perhaps the Nameless One still sees a chance in him to win his soul." The priest of the east wind shook the bells on his staff again. "Take him back down to the dungeon."

~

Black. Grey. Nausea. Verl no longer existed. His hand in front of his face was not even a shadow against the grey.

His disorientation, the dizziness of not seeing where his own fingers ended and the grey world began, panicked him more here in the dungeon than the confusion he'd felt that day in the tavern when he'd disappeared in front of the merchant.

That day, like today, he saw the world as if through water. But he still at least had something then to focus on, something to see. Here in the darkening grey of the dungeon, invisible, he had no distinct bearings around him to define him.

He clenched his hand shut, dug his fingers into his palm until it hurt. He tried to believe that touch meant he was still here, bounded by skin and bones.

He anchored himself to the pain in his hand. The rest of him ebbed and flowed on the battering waves of nausea that kept rising in him. Dizzy, sick, he swayed.

His skin was the walls of the dungeon, for all his mind told him. He could keep the ground beneath his feet. But his shoulders, back, chest expanded outwards, became the hard sea cliff walls banking him, drowning him--

It was his last grim hold on sanity that he was losing, more likely. He was mixing up images more than Lollander would.

He patted the rags he wore down his side and hip. Wherever his hand touched became a solid moment of himself.

But still he could not pull all of himself back into his hand, and he swallowed bile once more. He couldn't understand why he had ever thought it fun to vanish in front of his friends when he was a child on the beach.

There were sounds in the dungeon. He could cling to them. Hushed coughs, moaning, scuffling, waiting. It struck him with irony to think that once he'd believed his fingers could extend into light to play music, to translate colors into song. Here instead he ebbed into a grey nothingness, and the only sound was the waiting of the dungeon.

Dark shadows in the grey were his fellow prisoners-- he knew that, the smaller ones, dungheaps, and the black scurry of a rat.

He fought the tricks of his mind and he waited. It would all be worth it, he told himself. To be the first one here when the door above him opened. It would have to be worth it. No one else dared to come as close to the cage landing where the guards would come as he could unseen.

He would be the first one here to get at today's returning prisoners, if there were any.

And then, a tin cup—water for Lollander-- would again be his.

Chapter 14
Merind

The second night out of Drespin, three off-duty guardsmen swaggered towards the Capsen prisoners. The burliest, hairiest ape of them chose Merind for the night.

His breath reeked of the heavy brown ale of the Highlands as he unchained her and yanked her up by the wrists. In front of everyone as she struggled, he laughed and pawed open her bodice.

"This one still has fight left in her!" he leered to the other two guardsmen.

She spat a curse at him. With a calloused, sweaty hand behind her neck, he forced her face up to his and thrust his sour tongue into her mouth. She bit. He slapped her cheek hard enough that she crumpled sideways to the ground.

He pulled her up by the shoulder and hair, and dragged her to a tree beyond the fire's glow.

That was the moment Merind was waiting for. Alone in the shadows with him, she had power over him. She hadn't dared try anything in front of all the guardsmen, but with one Norgon at a time, she could take her revenge. He pushed her down to the ground; and she stopped struggling and began to sing.

He chortled. "You like it now, do you?"

He was down on her, pushing her legs apart. Her song reached into his mind, threaded through his thoughts. When she had him contained, she put him to sleep.

He lay there on top of her, sudden dead weight, snoring. Merind caught her breath and for the first time felt the scratch of the pine needles and sharp twigs beneath her bare shoulders. Time slowed, became real again; and she waited for her thoughts to clear. She could smell the moist earth and last winter's decay as well as his filthy ale and sweat. She could kill him with one simple twist inside his mind, and she wanted to, had to fight herself not to. If she did, they'd call her a witch. The other guardsmen had seen him overpower her; they wouldn't believe she could escape him any other way.

Merind rolled the burly ape off. There was one unnoticeable thing she could do--add to the effects of his ale. She started to sing softly, weaving herself into his dream.

~

In the morning, his friends doused him awake. The guardsman's breath and clothes stank of ale and, in his stupor, he had no memory of what had happened the night before, not after he had started drinking.

"You drunken bastard!"

Merind watched from the trees as the sergeant in charge yelled at him.

"You let one of the women escape! Where'd she go?"

Nowhere. Merind's fingers dug into the soft bark of the pine burl beside her. *Nowhere!* There were sixteen captives here, friends she could not leave behind. She had sworn to the memory of all those she'd watched massacred that she'd rescue her people. When all the Capsens were safe, then she could take her vengeance on the Norgons.

On the far side of the camp, the other prisoners were all heavily chained, and the guardsmen watching them had been doubled this morning in the wake of her disappearance. Merind could do nothing yet to save them.

~

The Norgons did not break camp that day. Instead, they hunted for Merind. By mid-morning, they found her tracks leading into the trees. They set a farmer's three dogs after her.

She could hide in the woods all day easily eluding human trackers. But not dogs. She could walk into camp among the Norgons for as long as an hour without anyone seeing her, without her needing to sing to weave the simplest illusion of all that she wasn't there. But there was no way to hide from the sight and smell of an animal.

The dogs picked up her scent quickly. She ran to get ahead of them, but they followed, barking louder when her scent grew stronger. She circled back, stole food from the camp, and threw it to the hounds, hoping to distract them. Two of the hounds took the bait. The third, a yellow hound, stayed on her trail.

Like a fox she had hunted once, she waded down a river, then doubled back, keeping to the rocks as much as she could. But the yellow hound found her tracks again, and sounded his triumph to the others.

Out of breath, she climbed a tree when they got close again. She lay there, hugging the branch, catching her breath as the dogs jumped and bayed just beneath her.

The guardsmen came and circled the tree. But they could see no one. Cursing the useless mutts, spawn of the dingo cat, they leashed them and pulled them away. The dogs barked and strained against their ropes, as they watched their captured prey, invisible to the men, slide down the tree and escape into the woods.

Out of breath, her side hurting hard, having raced up and down the stream again, scrambling, slipping across the rocks, Merind finally hoped she had gotten far enough ahead of the dogs, when and if they were released again, to lose them. She collapsed, hiding in the high fork of a tree, and tried to get some sleep before nightfall. She heard barking nearer and farther away half the afternoon.

~

Frogs croaked, and the crickets sawed a deafening rhythm along the streambed. Crick-crock. Crick-crock. A thousand voices saying, here I am; come mate with me. Life in its simplest form, its only purpose. Each bug that ate of life proudly sawing its boast that it could make more life, never knowing that, in a week, it would die and be eaten by new life. A thousand years times a thousand million voices. Here I am. Crick-crock. All Merind's ideas, all her fears for her people, all her hopes for revenge against the Norgons, were only a part of the intricately constructed lie she lived in—the world as she knew it—that helped her believe life held more purpose than a simple crick-crock. A

152

thousand years from now the Norgons, the Capsens, everything she knew would be dead, but the crickets and frogs would still be croaking.

A single bull-frog voice boasted lower, louder. As she sat on the creek bank listening, Merind's first impulse was to hear its voice as proof that one voice could be different.

But Capsen lore and the long nights training to be a tellerwoman in the Cave of Initiation had taught her better. Human weakness, her own weakness, was a need to believe two things: that the world was ordered and understandable, and that her perception of the world's order, her interpretation of its patterns was true, just as she saw and understood it. Leaders of the world, from king to priest to village father--to Capsen tellerwomen--were those who took the lie one step further, those who believed that if you could make others see your truth, the way you saw it, you could be the one to change the world.

But just as in the Cave, a Capsen tellerwoman had to constantly learn there was no pattern, no one truth.

Merind pulled a cattail up by its root, rubbed a thumb along its prickly soft head. It was that understanding, cruel lesson though it was, that the world she lived in was false, a creation made to match the beliefs of those who had come before her, that gave her the power to create illusions. In knowing her beliefs were lies, she could create lies for others to believe in.

And what they believed in became their reality. For as long as she wanted it to be.

She pitched the cattail into the stream and watched the waters eddy around it as its stem sank. It was not real power, though. In front of a village at most she could change how she looked to others or she could vanish from their sight altogether. With fire and water and steam as aid for concentration, she could also cloud the sight of almost as many people to hide someone else. But to completely create a new vision for someone to believe in, she could only work on the minds of one or two people close enough to her at one time.

She spread her arms open wide to the night and to its thousand voices around her. What she needed instead was the power to destroy the voices of a thousand thousand Norgons at one time until all the world spoke only with her voice and believed only as she wanted it to. And even then, the Norgons and their false priests would not pay dearly enough for what they had done to her people.

She closed her eyes, stretched her fingers outwards, listened to the crick-crock of the crickets, expanded her awareness farther into their rhythm. The Badurian priests claimed witches could leave their body and fly in spirit at night. If so, this was the closest she'd ever come to it. Crick-crock. Crick-crock. ...Crick...crock. She could not change their song.

And she could reach no farther beyond them. If the crickets had been so many men, she would have had no more effect upon them.

Someday, maybe. Someday.

But tonight, one Norgon at a time was all she could attack.

She rose, crept back towards their camp and walked invisibly among them. She'd waited long enough. They'd finished their meal and had long ago started their drinking.

She stopped first at the dogs and tossed each a squirrel she had trapped and skinned. The first two dogs set into their offerings happily, but the yellow hound planted its feet around its squirrel and bayed at her instead.

"Shut up, you!" ordered a Norgon. The guardsman threw a stone that sailed towards Merind. Invisible to him, she stepped back out of its way.

The hound looked from the guard to Merind to the guard again and stopped barking. Walking calmly among them, being accepted by its masters, she apparently was no longer the hunted. The hound began eating its squirrel greedily.

Merind walked on through the camp. She paused at the three Norgons guarding the chained Capsens. Would that she could release all her friends at one time, but she still had to be careful not to betray the presence of her powers by doing anything so dramatic until they all had gotten away safely.

At the far side of the fire, she saw two off-duty Norgons dragging Capsen girls into the shadows. Merind chose one of the guardsmen and, as she ran between them, she was already threading visions into his thoughts.

The Norgon whirled around drunkenly, wildly. He thrust the girl behind him and drew his knife.

"What goes there?" He stumbled forward--in the direction of the other guardsman.

Merind elaborated the illusion, brought it into sharper focus, made him see the other guardsman as a crouching mountain lion, its bright eyes boring into him, snarling at him, attacking him.

True to his training, the drunken guardsman howled a curse, ran forward with his knife, and attacked the lion instead of escaping.

The second guardsman, caught by surprise, drew his knife in time to parry the first thrust. Both men, busy fighting, left the Capsen women freed behind them.

Merind grabbed the women by their wrists and whispered softly who she was. As the two men raged drunkenly against each other, she pulled her friends away into the night.

~

The next morning, Merind walked back into camp to steal food and supplies. The Norgons had discovered two more missing captives, and the two men who had fought each other so savagely were being questioned. Unseen, Merind paused in the crowd to listen.

"Cleff was the one who had the two girls with him, I did not. He was howling drunk. He came at me with a knife. He left them behind him, let them escape when he came at me. I could only defend myself--didn't have a chance to stop them."

The first drunk, his right cheek slashed, his eyes swollen and bruised, could only shake his head, remembering nothing from the night before. Merind's gift to him.

She rushed back to where the two women were hiding and sent them home with their bundle of supplies. The Norgons would begin hunting for them quickly and she would need to cover their trail before they did.

~

Two weeks later, Merind stood looking over the shoulder of the bursar of Elkhorn. Slate in hand to keep it as invisible as she was, she copied the locations of where the Capsen captives were being sold into indentured servitude.

The bursar worked too slowly and Merind was impatient. She could not concentrate much longer than an hour to erase her presence from the minds of those who looked in her direction, and the townhall clock had last tolled almost an hour ago. The bursar had close to two hundred sales from the auction this morning to record in his pinched ornate scrawl. Merind was only interested in thirteen of them. But she had to wait for him to record them all. No two Capsens had been sold to the same owner. One was bought by a lord of Tuscoy for a washerwoman, one by the silver mines of Moari, one by the silk farms of Sorenz Valley, one by a merchant's galley ship off the coast of Prie. It could take months to find and rescue them all.

If only she could have helped more to escape on their way to Elkhorn. But after she and the first two women had escaped, the Norgon sergeant in charge no longer allowed off-duty guardsmen to take captive women away with them at night. The only captives they did unchain and separate from then on were the men to dig slit trenches to build latrines at each new campsite. That was how, one evening, Merind helped Jevers escape. But his escape had been the last, and from the upheaval it caused, the Norgons now suspected a witch was among the Capsens, exactly the attention Merind had tried to avoid.

Her plan for Jevers' escape started out well. She'd stood unseen beside the guardsman who sat on a fallen log jibing at Jevers as he dug the trench.

"Deeper," he called. "Lessen you want to come back here all night long dig it up after each one of us uses it. I'd bet you'd like that, wouldn't you? I hear you animals would eat anything got meat in it."

An ant crawled across the guardsman's hand as he leaned back against the log. He flicked it away, barely noticing it. Another ant scurried up his boot, got in under his pant leg; two, three more followed it. One bit. Cursing, the guardsman stomped his foot, and swung it hard at the shavings under the log, sign of the ant colony he must have missed when he sat down. He stood up, looked down, and tens, hundreds, thousands black ants were flooding up his legs. A thousand ants were biting his legs, his thighs, his belly, a thousand nerve pulses in his mind copying the sting of the first bite. He shouted, did a dance, a devil's whirl. He was covered head to toe in the black swarm he saw and felt in his mind attacking him while Merind whispered quickly to Jevers to follow her.

But before following, Jevers took the spade and clobbered the maddened guardsman on the head.

Merind had no warning. The guardsman fell backwards, his head bleeding, but the sudden pain cleared his mind of illusion. There were no ants, no bites, but as he told his sergeant afterwards, he heard then the soft song of a witch's humming.

Jevers escaped. Merind sent him to home to the Capsen hideaway in the hills west of Drespin to wait for her there.

The rest of the captives were more heavily guarded than before, and each were questioned on their hurried way to Elkhorn to find out which one of them was the witch. The Norgon sergeant settled on Vanis, she who escaped once by driving one of the guardsmen insane and making him attack his friend one night. She who had been recaptured. The Norgons posted four guardsmen around Vanis continuously. They chained her hands behind her back and pulled out her tongue so she could not sing another witch's spell until they turned her over to the Badurian priests in Elkhorn.

Merind copied down the name of Felnrist, sold to the coal pits of East Warren, her fingers held so tight around the stylus, they were red and stiff. If she had tried to help anyone else escape on the way here to Elkhorn, Vanis would only have been blamed and tortured all the more.

Someday, she promised the Norgons. *Someday.*

Chapter 15
Reflection

Verl fought for the tin cup. Invisible, he dove for it as soon as the wounded prisoner was rolled off the lowered cage onto the rocky ground of the dungeon. The prisoner lay in humps where he fell, looking dead already, but he had a powerful grip on the cup's handle. The more Verl tried to pry it loose, the tighter the big man's bloodied fingers held on. That tin cup meant life or death in the dungeon, and they fought for it.

Heavy cranking signaled that the cage protecting the guardsmen was still rising out of the dungeon. The shadows of the other prisoners closed in above Verl and loomed over him. The door far above pulled shut, and the gang of prisoners pounced.

They scrabbled over each other for the wounded man's cup, and for his shred of clothes, crushing Verl underneath. Knees jabbed into his back, winding him. Hands clawed at his face, raked through his hair. The weight of one man elbowed into his jawbone, pushing him into the sharp rocks. He felt one stone jutting into his cheek, another cutting into the corner of his eye. He held onto the cup's handle, squirmed closer to pull harder.

Other hands found the cup, they pulled on the rim, pried at his fingers. Verl squeezed his eyes shut against the pain, held on. He was no longer the dungeon, he no longer felt himself expanded as wide as the spreading darkness to the dank cold stone walls of its tower. His illusion of invisibility, his invulnerability he felt inside the illusion was lost, the nothingness he'd become to anyone looking at him was meaningless, trapped, confined into his physical body pressed under the weight of twenty men and women. He grunted, screamed agony, his head crushed into rocks, he held onto the cup and pulled. He tasted blood, gritted his teeth, pulled.

Then, for an instant, the wounded prisoner's fingers around the handle slackened. Verl yanked, and the cup came loose. It was his. He could save Lollander's life with it now.

Hands still grappled with his for the cup, but he was the only one who clutched the handle. He drew his arm back bit by bit, fighting for every inch of purchase to keep the cup, to pull it back to him, to hide it under his shoulder. Then, to squirm back, an eternity of effort in every slight push, in every lift of a shoulder against the weight of a hand shoving off him, in every scrape of his knees, arms, body backwards--then out, free, from under the pile of bodies all still trying to scrabble forward to get to the prisoner.

Verl raised himself to his hands and knees, sunk his head, breathed heavily. The cup was his prize. He crawled a foot or two away, took a moment to reappear to the world, then stood.

In the dim grey black of the dungeon, his eyes took another moment to adjust. He watched the darkened forms of the other prisoners lift away from the wounded man and drift to the walls of the dungeon, two or three clutching scraps of shirt as their prize. Verl's eyes played tricks on him, the prisoners moved too slowly, surreal shadows drifting up and away from their victim. Years of Singerhalle training, of staging pageantries played out the dirge to their dance, his fingers of their own volition tapped the macabre rhythm against the tin cup under his tunic. He barely was aware of it, barely felt the tears welling in his eyes, stinging the cut in the corner of one. His cheek was bruised, swelling. He listened to the grunts of the mimers, their moans as they limped and drifted past. He had become one of them. No remorse. No other song left in him. He had attacked the prisoner first.

All for a tin cup. All for a drink of water, for one more day of Lollander's survival--

His fingers tapped out their hateful rhythm and corrected him. All for his own survival.

Then, louder, yanking him back to himself, Verl heard a groan, then a choked coughing from the lump of the wounded man.

His eyes riveted on the shadow of him, and saw a cough rack through him, the slight heave of a shoulder to a bunching of a knee. He was still alive.

Verl had not expected it. The attack on him by the gang of prisoners--by Verl--had seemed a lifetime away, but from watching other attacks on new and returned prisoners every day since he'd been here, he knew it had lasted moments only. A quick kill to get whatever the newcomer had. Verl had barely survived his first day, Lollander still lay suffering. Most victims died.

Verl had thought this too had been a kill.

He was still alive! Still moving.

Verl clutched his fingers around the hard dented cup. It was Lollander's life he held in his hand. He could heal him now. Give him a real drink of water.

The prisoner stopped coughing.

Verl's bottom lip started trembling. He wiped blood from his stinging cheek, clutched his other hand around the tin cup.

Music is in the eye of the listener, Lollander had always laughed. Lollander had never tapped out a dance of death on a tin cup after killing a man.

Neither had he. Neither had he! The man was not dead yet.

With certainty, with calm excited fingers, Verl took a precious moment to secure the cup handle onto a thong of his leggings. Then he went over to the wounded prisoner, raised him up by his heavy shoulders, and dragged him gently over to where Lollander lay waiting.

He had two lives to save now.

~

"Ailil!"

Crel woke in the dark, still mouthing her name.

Pitch black. Still trapped in the cave--

No; turning around, it was not all pitch black. His eyes adjusted. There was a dim greyness ahead, greying the end of the tunnel, coming from the cavern he'd raced out of when he'd heard the cave door closing.

He could swear he hadn't seen anything but complete blackness before.

He groped his way back through the tunnel. The closer he got to the cavern, the grey brightened and blued slowly around him. Upon entering the cavern, the glow dimmed into darkness again in a semicircle five, six feet before him.

Crel shivered looking towards the dimming boundary of his sight. He buttoned up the collar buttons of his tinker's wool jacket. Trapped inside a mountain, he felt damp cold air against his cheeks. The blue grey glow ahead looked cold, weak, not at all the friendly warm glow of a campfire.

Crel wrapped his arms around him against the cold and walked into it.

Here at the edge of the fading light, the glow, so blue and weak, confined him into a smallness he had never felt before. He shivered. He felt the heaviness of the darkness pushing into him, the weight of the mountain piling onto him, onto his back, onto his shoulders—

He shook his head. Such thinking would lead to madness. He had never been one to fear the dark. Or to let his thoughts stray until he did. He refused to do so now.

Here in this dark prison that would be his death—

"Ailil!" he shouted. *"Ailil!"*

Her name raged into the darkness, bounced thinly, impotently, off the walls of the cavern. He thought he heard a fluttering.

He sucked in a cold, damp breath. He lifted his wool cap, brushed back his hair, set his cap firmly back down on his head, and turned back around to the source of the glow.

And there, beside the dark mouth of the tunnel, he saw them, two blue handprints shining distinctly against the black wall.

He went to them, left hand, right hand, matched his own, the blue glassy stone shining forth their shape brilliantly. He touched at the outline of a finger, brushed the powdery blackness away from more of the stone. He whistled between his teeth, and he heard the fluttering again. Bats. Guano. Covering the walls, covering a rich vein of

162

fosfar. The rarity of the glowing blue gem made even small stones of it set into a copper chalice worth a king's ransom. Crel had helped Wiss fashion such a chalice once for a duke. Afterwards Wiss saved the tiny crystals and shavings from the cut stones, and ground them into a dust he'd used in his sideshow tricks to accent his stories in the towns around the realm, throwing out the blue powder to create a magical fire-like glow for Jesser to dance around. They'd collected almost as much money that year from their entertainments at nights as they had from selling their tinker wares by day.

Crel laughed aloud at Wiss as if he were there with him. "Ha, old man, is this where your fosfar came from?" He began brushing more guano off the vein, revealing more of the blue glassy stone, and the cave brightened around him.

He worked like a man possessed. When his hands became blackened so he couldn't wipe the guano off, he took off his jacket, tore off his shirt, used it instead. When all he did was smudge more guano onto the widening veins of fosfar streaking along the walls, he discarded the black ball of his shirt, took off a sock, and began uncovering drawn lines of red ochre on the grey stone bordering the left of the vein.

He stood back, looked at the drawing he'd uncovered, puzzled. It depicted a spider's web.

~

Verl leaned back against the bricks of the dungeon wall and watched a spider dangling from a single thread, swaying back and forth through the dusty stream of light coming from one of the slitted windows far above. Some days when he saw the spider he gave way to the temptation of his fingers to strum its thin single chord to hear the sound it made different from the sound he heard in his mind strumming his fingers through the thicker chords of the beam of light. Some days he pinched the spider's chord instead, breaking it, to spite it for being in truth more silent than he longed to believe it.

But today, he let the spider be, and watched it swing, back, forth, and higher until it reached the web it was rebuilding on the wall above Lollander. Tomorrow, or the next day, would be time enough to swipe the web down, watch the spider start over again.

Looking up at web, barely visible in the dim light, Verl remembered the pattern of a web that the fractured lights of the stained glass windows made on the inlaid bear claw on the floor of the throne room in the king's palace. Identical to the web of guilt, one of the five symbols of power tattooed on his father's skull. One of the five labyrinthine entrances into dreams. Someday, perhaps, he would learn to strum his fingers through that spider's web on the wall and learn to play it.

He heard a scritching, looked down, kicked a rat away from Lollander's leg. He stomped his foot, the sound threatening a smaller rat approaching his new charge on his other side.

Name was Arax, he'd told him, from the Orliand Islands, his brawn, his courage built from years of shepherding ice flows, harpooning the diving bullseals and hauling them aboard, and then wrestling snow bears on his days off. He told his stories as well as any teller at Singerhalle, and Verl loved to hear the natural lilt and poetry behind his rough words. He'd been bringing in a load of sealskins up the coast for springing trade few months back, when he got waylaid in a tavern. Not minding surely that he'd already had a few pitchers of that good keeper's fine ale, he still ne'er would've been overcome were it not for that insufferable demon priest in all his black robes of death, afooling him into arguing about his gods against this so-called Nameless One. The priest ordered him one more pitcherful, urging him to tell him more, while behind his back, the lout signaled to his henchmen to come take him away unawares. He was caged, and although he raged against the bars like a bear for all the good it did him, he still ended up here, dropped into this hellhole where he'd been doing nothing but just abreathing ever since.

For all his wounds from his attack two days ago, Arax was healing quickly, and for the first time this morning he was sleeping quietly.

Verl wished he could say the same about Lollander. The hornblower lay beside him, his noisy breathing coming in jerky gasps with long pauses in between. He moaned when touched, and was barely awake long enough now to eat or drink. Verl gripped the tin cup in his hand; he did not know how much longer he could keep his friend alive.

He sighed, then held the cup into the beam of light, started polishing it again with a torn off strip of his leggings. The polishing was more to pass the time than to clean the grime and soot off the cup. It was an endless chore but it kept his hands busy as he awaited the creaking he would hear when the elevator cage was lowered into the pit. It was from that cage that the morning guardsmen would stand throwing out the chunks of meat and bread and lower the buckets of water to prisoners holding up cups, hands, or strips of cloth or whatever they had to catch the life-prolonging droplets.

Verl winced, rubbed harder on the tin cup. Life-prolonging, yes, that was the way to describe it. Misery-prolonging. But who here would not scramble and fight for one more day of life, for one more cup of water? Questions once argued in lighted halls of Singerhalle of purpose, of sanctity, of the meaning of song and service were reduced here to three words as hollow and dry as this cup, down to the bare scrabbling existence of one more day, one more day... One. More. Day. He rubbed the rhythm of those three words harder into the dent on the side of the cup.

It would must be time soon for the cage to come, for the water to come. He could always tell. Whether he heard some far off toll of the morning bells in the city beyond the stone walls of the dungeon that slipped into him below his conscious hearing, or whether like an animal, he had developed his own inner time tolling, he always knew when, morning or night, the food would come. He rubbed on the side of the tin cup, waiting.

He lifted the cloth a moment, held the cup up in the dusty beam of light. He'd gotten it to shine. It reflected a grey image of himself, a concave misshapen image, elongated, thinned by the dent. He smiled morosely at his meaningless accomplishment, clutched the cup tighter.

165

A beard had grown, he saw in his reflection. He raised a questioning hand to the beard, ran his fingers through the curly hairs, a stranger to himself. His face was gaunt, grey, surely more so than could be accounted for by the thinning distortion the curve of the dent made. His fingers on his reflected beard looked like nails across the tin cup.

He lifted his hand up above the cup into the beam of light, studied it for what it had really become. Long fingers, always had been long musician's fingers stroking his lute, but here weaving in the dusty chords of the light, they were longer, thinner, skin-stretched bones. They may never play anything more substantial than light again.

He dropped his hand. No, he would never play his lute again, he knew that. Why did he let its memory torture him so?

In his mind's eye, in the dusty shaft of light, he constructed the image of who he had been, the image of who he still was to himself. The light, the hope, the luteplayer with a dream that he could be a mastersinger as no other who would play a song that would make his listeners see a cascade of flowers falling upon them.

He compared his delusion of himself to his tin reflection of himself and closed his eyes.

Then, angered, determined, one more day of life, he methodically changed the reflection in the light he held in his mind to match the reflection in the cup of who he was now. Bearded, gaunt, stripped half-naked, mud- and feces-caked, desperate, he made the illusion in the light staring back at him laugh at him.

Then, he paused. He held up the dark reflection of himself in the cup beside the reflection he had made of himself in the light. He passed his hand through the reflection in the light, and made it smile back at him, made it raise its thin ragged arm, made it wave back at him.

Delusional. More crazed than Lollander.

...Or maybe not.

He sat forward. His illusion smiled at him. His tin reflection frowned at him. Illusion, reflection, he himself with a curly stiff beard his fingers could touch, which one was really he?

He shifted, closed the mantle of darkness around him, felt the sickening sea-sway of invisibility delude his mind, suggest he wasn't there. He raised his own hand before his face, could not see it. But there the hand was in the reflection in the cup, there he was staring back at him. And there he was in the illusion in the light, laughing at him, turning around, sitting, waving, doing whatever he wanted it to do.

It was the first time he had cast an illusion of himself separate from himself, as easily and naturally as he used to cast voices away from him as a child. This was something he had never known he could do.

~

Crel woke on the stony floor of the cave. Before him was a mound of cherries on a slab of bread, and his own lantern he had dropped onto the floor of the cave when he first heard the great stone door being rolled across the tunnel entrance, trapping him inside. The lantern now stood upright, and filled he knew again with wine. It had been so every time he woke up. How many days, hours, weeks had he been in here...he had no idea. He sat up, ate a cherry.

The blue glow swathed the cave around him in light and stretched half-way up into the dark which stretched farther up to the restless fluttering of the bats above. He heard one closer, saw it emerge from the mouth of the tunnel. The bats, trapped in here like he was, still flew into the tunnel, searching--each night he assumed--for their escape. There inside the tunnel, they could at least feed on the multitude of spiders and survive.

And feed on a cherry too if he bit into it, threw it to them. He called to the bat, threw a cherry. The bat beat a circle overhead, then swooped down, landed on the cherry, its black wings folded out and flattened behind it as it sucked on the cherry. For companionship, Crel talked to the bats in here more than he had ever talked to Jesser.

He ate another cherry.

167

He had finished wiping the guano off the walls of the cave two sleeps ago. Now he studied the puzzle of the ochered drawings lining the walls three-quarters of the way around him.

Five long rows of them, like notes on a musical scale. No other order to the drawings. No pattern, little repetition, no way of counting which, when, or where an image would be repeated.

He refused to believe it. There must be a pattern, must be a reason to it. The arrangement of the images, twenty-three different symbols he had counted, some appearing only once, had to reveal some meaning, had to tell some story, sing some song maybe, if only he could read it, puzzle it out. If only he could discover the key perhaps to his getting out of here. He had little else to hope for.

He smoothed out the sand in front of him, copied with his finger some of the designs. Some were more intricate, or had a more complicated mix of thick and thin lines as well as sharp curls and precise turnings. For those he used a cherry stem. Five designs were repeated more than any other, and most times all five were grouped together, one on each line. The spider's web he'd uncovered first was one of the five; a harp, a curved knife or scythe, a labyrinth and two adjacent spirals were the other four. He could identify their groupings at a glance now, he could draw them in the sand without looking at them. But what he could not do is decide why the groupings of the five came when they came. Sometimes there were twenty, thirty-some odd symbols drawn between them, sometimes there was only one, or none—one section there were three groupings of the five, following one after the other. Sometimes the five were rearranged, the spiral on the top row, the harp on the next, the web, the labyrinth, the knife below. Sometimes the knife was on top, or the web. It made no sense, no pattern he could predict. And the other symbols drawn between, like longer, shorter messages, sometimes he thought, placed at random on one line or the other.

A song, he kept trying to guess, must be a song. He tried singing it, humming it, whistling each symbol as a

168

note. It never sounded good, there was no order to the notes, no music in it, no rhythm.

The symbols had to have some meaning, some message, some pattern; he refused to believe they didn't. They could not be placed there as random as they looked.

He followed the song without music, the message without meaning to its end behind him. And there, just like the last time he woke up, under the grey empty wall at the end of the drawing was a clay pot full of the ochre paint and two paint brushes, one thick, one thin, waiting for him, tempting him to finish the song, to find the key to the message and complete it. If only he could--

"Ailil!" he shouted. It would do no good, it never did. Except to assuage his rage, bounce it off the walls around him, flutter the bats above him, strike uselessly at the stone door rolled in front of the tunnel. "When do you come in here, Ailil? *When?*" he yelled to the unanswering stone, to the darkness above, to the enigma of the drawings. To the witchwoman who had trapped him in here, and never came in when he was awake.

He lifted the refilled lantern in his rage and took a hard swig of the wine she had left him again. He swiped the drops off the stubble on his cheeks.

What he did not admit aloud, in case the stones heard, in case the bats told her, he'd become intrigued by the puzzle of the drawings, spent hours trying to copy it, decipher it. The drawings had to have some meaning, had to not be as random as they looked---

He took another hard swallow, glared back at the pot of ochre and the brushes, at the empty wall waiting.

"Damn," he muttered. Another swallow. "Damn!" He stood, went to the paint, and began to draw.

Five symbols, he knew them by heart, to start his section of the message. He didn't care what order they came in, he drew one on each line. What else was supposed to come next, he didn't know, he would never know. But did it matter?

Did it matter?

169

He took the thick brush, and in broad red strokes, he drew his own message. One letter after the other, one on each line. D. A. M. N. !.

He heard sudden laughter behind him.

Ailil stood there laughing at what he wrote. Or it was someone who had her eyes and who was wearing the same clothes he had last seen her wearing, the silks soiled slightly with guano. But her face was unveiled. And her skin was laced tight with wrinkles around her eyes. Her hair was more white than blond. She was old enough to be Merind's mother. Or her mother's mother.

She met his question.

"You know me."

"Ailil?"

The witchwoman stretched out a thin finger to his message. "You have just passed your first lesson in looking behind my people's illusions. Men will always look for meanings, look for patterns. A fox will too, when there is a pattern; when a rabbit uses the same run every night, a fox knows it. But when there is no pattern, the fox does not wait to see one. Men not finding a pattern, can't believe there isn't one, and so will still keep searching for one until finally they believe they see it. Merind can hide behind such a pattern if you're expecting to see one instead of her. Or she'll make one up in your mind to fit your expectations, and as you play out her story in your mind, she'll walk away. If you are ever to someday find my daughter as you wanted to the other morning, you must learn to see as an animal does. Jesser walked past the stone fossils, seeing them for what they were, not seeing the dread and fear you thought you saw in them. Learn to see as Jesser, look behind the illusion, beyond your expectations. Learn to see what is there, and what–" she passed a hand in front of her face, grew young, beautiful again, "--is not."

She smiled, and her eyes sparked silver through the blue glow.

Crel drew in his breath, then glanced at the drawings along the walls.

"Then it didn't matter what I drew?"

Her smile widened, showing a trace of wrinkles around the eyes again. "Didn't it? I'd say it mattered to you. When you could find no pattern to the drawings, you made up your own answer to their puzzle. Each tellerwoman and lord of my people, for the last two hundred years, has been in this cave and discovered as you have discovered: we can't accept that the world can be without an order, without a meaning, so when we find no pattern, we make one up. Each one of us has added to this wall, guided by our own final answer. Then ever afterwards we're forced to see that our visions, our beliefs, our ways of life might likewise only be creations--whether our own or those others have passed down to us. The patterns, the answers we see in the world around us may be false, they may have very little to do with anything real outside of our mind's perceptions. But it's in knowing how easily we believe that what we see must be real, that we learn to create new patterns---illusions---a new reality for others to believe in. It's part of what will give a tellerwoman like my daughter her power over you."

Chapter16
Dream Singer

Lollander died two days ago.

No... Verl scratched a dream pentagon into the dirt with a stick. No. They carted him away two days ago. He died six days ago. Verl had stones piled up behind him, proof for each day. He could count them again if he wanted.

He etched in four of the corners of the pentagon. The web of guilt, the song of gifts, the edge of sorrow, the path of right. Then, gritting his teeth, giving himself no mercy, he etched in a skull shape that circled and circled and never met--as good a sign as any for the fifth corner symbol he could never remember, if he had ever known it, the spiral of forgetfulness. Lollander's death he would never forget. If Verl had only sent the queen's message to kill that duke, Lollander would have never been down here, would have never died in this hellhole.

Always before when Verl tried making a dream pentagon, he'd drawn a seagull in the center of it, the seagull that had pecked the eyes out of his puppy when, as a young boy, he had found it dead on the beach. The seagull he had drawn eating his dreams ever since. This morning instead, in the shaft of dusty light that came down from the dungeon window, he drew the real dream eater: himself. A stick figure, as crude a symbol as the seagull had ever been. In its right hand, the stick man held the one detail lovingly drawn. Leidel. The lute Verl would never play again. After he traced in the sixth and final string of the lute, he clenched the stick in his fist, raised it over his shoulder, and stabbed it down through the heart of the stick man.

Then, he dropped the stick, sunk his head. His fists fell heavily into the filth, stone, straw of the dungeon floor. If he could, he'd drive his fists further, deeper into the ground, bury himself among the worms, past the worms, into the labyrinth hell of the fire pit that the Badurian priests spoke of. He'd bring the worms with him, to crawl through his bones, to peck out his eyes, his heart. He could feel the worms already burrowing through him, eating holes inside his lungs, twisting his veins, wringing his sinews around them, constricting his breathing...waiting.

Verl raised his head, bit determination into his lower lip, added a stone to the pile of days behind him.

The dusty shaft of light still fell on the wounded stick man. Verl fleshed the image out in his mind. He gave it his face, his hands, clothed its dungeon-thin body in a mocking rich tunic of Singer blue. He made the image of the little man rise to its knees; it grabbed the lute beside it, cradled it in its hands, stood. Dusty light shimmered around it.

Bathed in the light, the six strings of the lute shone like the fragile pearled threads of a spider web in morning dew. Six compelling strings of light. The little dream singer met Verl's eyes in painful recognition, nodded. He positioned the lute, strummed hesitant fingers through the strings and, one silver string after another, played the light. Dust particles sparkled and drifted around him. Floated up from the strings of the lute and fell shining down upon the head of the little singer, as flowers would from above.

False dream. Lost dream. But Verl could not tear his eyes away from the reflection of himself inside the fiery bright pentagon. The little singer raised his head to the glory of light falling upon him, and becoming jubilant, ensorcelled, he opened his mouth to sing.

"What's he singing, mate?"

Startled, Verl glanced up to see Arax watching him. Verl erased the vision of the little dream singer.

Arax looked down at the sketch of the pentagon, empty except for the stick man scratched into the dirt. He waved his hand through the dusty shaft of light above it, squinted back up at Verl.

"Sent 'im away, did you?"

Verl shook his head as if in incomprehension. The bearwrestler's cheeks were ruddy in the dim light above his black beard, even down here after all his months in the dungeon. His eyes had a grey sparkle in them.

173

"Ho, mate, sure now as you know me, I'd not hold the wee one against you. Your friend's as good with me as with you."

Verl held his breath, studied his burly friend. Under his scrutiny, Arax grinned widely, the gap from his missing front tooth showing plainly, adding to the incongruous picture of excitement and mirth on the hardened prisoner's face.

"Ice-cold be truth, I tell you this. My sweet Dell, her mother's brother drew the dream signs for my old island village Walk. Five days north, five days south, and all the land in between came to see him. I was no higher than the muskmite's knee, the one time I sat down before him. Five oil lamps full above me and the circle of signs below, scratched into a clear blue mirror of ice it was. I swear I could see my own face in it before I saw what's to come in my life. ...Truth to tell you, though," Arax paused, glanced around the dark confines of the dungeon, lowered his voice, "for all I did see in it, I never for once saw this damned hell I'd end up in." Arax jerked his attention back to Verl, implored him with his dark riveting gaze. "Bring your wee one back for me. Let me hear him sing. I never see a wee one before. Not even my sweet Dell's mother's brother could have brought one up."

Verl chewed his lip, then stiffly nodded. What Arax had just told him, his belief in wee ones despite all the Badurian priests' warnings, would have been enough to send his friend back up to the arena as proof certain he was a heretic. He would not come back a second time. Verl could do no less than place his life too in his friend's keeping. If Arax had truly seen the image he had made in the shaft of light, then Verl would not deny he had made it.

The irony was, though, that Verl had never known he held the power to make an illusion another could see. Such illusion was far beyond his childhood trick of stripping awareness of his presence from the sight of others. Yet knowledge he could do either illusion--make himself invisible or make moving images that others could see-- would be enough to send him too before the priests. Of all the prisoners down here condemned as witches and

174

practitioners of outlawed magics, Verl was the one never yet condemned of heresy. He had hoped, he realized suddenly, that because of that, he might one day be released. Not now, he knew. Not now.

Verl gazed down into the pentagon at the stick man. "I do not know how to make him sing," he said quietly. He fleshed the stick man out, clothed him, let him stand.

The grey light sparked again in the bearwrestler's eyes. He held his palm out open at the little man's feet, and Verl made the image step up onto his hand. Arax chuckled, his shoulder and hand shaking with his chuckle.

"It's nothing real," Verl said. "A circusman's trick, nothing but air and light." As he spoke, the memory of all the times he'd tried to play the song that would make flowers out of air and light crowded before him. If this illusion had been so simple, so natural for him to make, why had he always failed so before with his music? "I was surprised you could see him," he said.

At that, Arax looked around them furtively, and cupped his other hand around the image, hiding it. "We cannot let anyone else see him, mate."

Verl glanced around too. His corner was growing. New prisoners and those few most recently returned wounded from the arena lay closest by. Many others, those whose cups he'd been first to grab and save from the mob, and whose pummeled bodies Arax had carried over to their circle afterwards, and who had since healed and grown strong in the last two weeks under Verl's care and Arax's protection, had stayed with him too, helping Arax patrol their corner of the dungeon at night, helping Verl feed and minister to the newly wounded by day. Behind Verl to his left was their hoard of cups, some still filled with water from yesterday. There were enough cups now for whenever someone in their group needed a drink. Each morning, afternoon, and evening when the guards brought down the buckets, cups were filled and refilled until everyone in their group, the wounded first, then those able to walk, had drunken all they wanted. Then the cups were refilled again and left inside their circle for whomever needed water later on. Verl even had enough to spare now to clean a bloody wound.

Their hoard of cups was their treasure, the one source of power and life--and war down here, and the other gangs were taking notice. Night raids kept Arax and his unit of guards he'd organized and commanded each night busy. There were six other large prisoner gangs, each centering around its own hoard of water cups, Arax had explained to Verl. If Verl had joined one of them that first week, he would've had the water from the start to keep Lollander alive maybe. But Arax spoke grimly to his friend, clutching Verl's bone-thin arm, describing the horrors he would have submitted to, being one of the scrawniest members of a gang, in exchange for a daily cup of water. The nightmare screams all night long were not just the women getting raped and beaten, the weaker men were kept alive for entertainment too, or bartered to the next gang for a change in flavor. Arax had been a member of such a gang for three months; it was the only way to survive here so long. But as bear of a man as he was, Arax had been left alone, as he had had no taste for joining in on their nightly sports. Not everyone who died down here at night, he said darkly, died of starvation or rat bites.

Verl's gang was new, yet most members stayed gratefully gathered together for more than just the water, and Arax was not the only one who had sworn to fight to the death to keep Verl and their new friends protected. Maybe twenty men and women by now lay huddled beyond the most wounded; all, still asleep. It was early morning, and after a long watchful night and a few skirmishes, no one else had stirred awake yet, as far as Verl could see.

He turned back to Arax. "No one is watching," he said.

Arax held the little man in the open light again. "If he cannot sing, will you let him tell me my dream then?"

Verl shrugged his hand. "He can do nothing. He's not a wee one, Arax. It's just an illusion. No more than a thought. A memory. I'm sorry."

Arax sat staring at him a long moment, then he released the little man back into the center of the pentagon drawn on the floor.

"Then you, mate, you'll tell me my dreams and we'll--"

Verl shook his head. "I've never walked into one of my own dreams successfully, let alone into anyone else's since I too was knee high to one of your muskmites. My father dreamwalked but--"

"Then I'd say, truth most like, you can too." He gestured at the dream pentagon. "But...it is not me I want to see, not my life ahead." He indicated the dark dungeon behind him. "I've seen all of it I want to see. What I'm asking of you, mate, help me see my dreams of home. Let me see my village and its Walk, what all they do there now, in the cove beyond the bay; let me watch the longboats setting sail, casting out the trawling nets between them. Let me see the last ice on hilltops crack and thunder, and the summer flowers popping up all around. Let me see the she bear hunt, and the great white bullseal dive under. Let me see what my sweet Dell dreams tonight."

Verl shrugged open both hands to protest, but he had no words to say. He may fail, surely he would--the worms burrowing through him, twisting through him, knew he would--but day upon day awaiting him down here, what else had he left to do here but try? He could get Arax to tell him more about the Orliand Islands and then maybe he could at least help Arax believe he was seeing what he had described.

Arax was watching him, and nodded when he nodded, their deal made. "And to pay you, mate, we teach your wee one here to be more use to you than air and light." Arax picked up a straw from the ground, broke it in half and held it towards the little man in the pentagon.

Verl looked at the straw, then back up at Arax questioningly.

"We teach him to fight," Arax said. "If any see him ever, it is sure to say you'd be on your way to the arena for the making of him. And up there, I cannot help you. But here, this is the staff they'll give you. I can teach him how

177

to hold it, all the moves and thrusts and feints you'll need to
know to stay alive."

Arax offered the straw again, and Verl, grinning
thinly, made the little man reach for it.

The piece of straw in the little man's hand darkened,
became a wooden staff.

"Shorter, thicker," Arax instructed. "Hold it there
and there most times, hands not so close together."

The real piece of straw had fallen through the image
of light and air and lay across the pentagon on the floor.
The little dream Verl stepped across it and swung his staff.

~

"I am not a witch, Holy Father! Blessed be the
Nameless One, I am not a witch!"

Arnaby pitied the simpering nurse. Varina's sallow
cheeks were scarred black from facial whippings, her right
shoulder, showing through rips in her course flaxen
penitent's robe, was welted and fiery from a recent
branding, and her fingers, most painful of all to see, had
been boiled in hot oils and had melted together into thick
knobby lumps of flesh.

But Arnaby could do nothing to help her. He shook
his holy staff of bells and blessed the hearing room with
more of the acrid incense smoke as the Priest of the East
Wind asked her the same questions over again. It would
matter little what the boy-king's nurse said today. They'd
had orders for weeks to make her confess, and the queen
regent had lost her patience.

"Where is the Capsen Witch hiding?"

"I don't know, Father. Sure as the Black Spirit's
loving wings, I don't know."

"You covered the king's bed with this sheet, did you
not? This sheet embroidered with a Capsen's spider's web
to curse him with unholy nightmares!"

"No! To protect him from them."

"And who told you it would do that?"

"She did, my lord. I told you that. The Lady Ailil
did. The Lady Ailil."

"When? Where did you see the Capsen Witch?
When did she give you this sheet to curse the king with?"

Arnaby shook his bells, waved his incense burner,
trying to distract her. If he knew how to send her a message
not to answer without betraying his disguise as a Badurian
priest, he would. For weeks this simple woman had parried
all questions well on her own. But today more than ever
Varina looked tired, confused. Her dry blistered lips were
trembling.

"Years ago, my lord," she answered. "Years ago,
when she lived here in the palace with the old king–" She
stopped, whimpered once, cast a wild gaze around the court
room, her mouth opening and closing over wordless denials,
as if finally hearing the rest of his question.

After weeks of stubborn pride and denials, she had
trapped herself.

"Then you do admit she gave you this sheet to curse
the young king?" the high priest asked her.

"No, my lord! No!" She broke down, slumped
forward, visibly losing any last strength of composure that
had sustained her so long. "No, my lord. No." She ended
in a pile on the floor, weeping. "No."

The four Badurian priests, Arnaby among them,
descended the dais and surrounded her, shaking bells above
her.

"Child," the high priest said. "Let the Spirit enter
you, and repent. Confess the whole truth now, and be
forgiven. The Capsen Witch gave you the sheet to curse the
king with. You have been taken in, a servant of her evil
powers. Your soul flies with her at night. See with us this
truth and confess! Where does she hide by day? Where
shall we find her?"

"I don't know, I don't know."

The priests shook the bells over her. "To still deny
the truth condemns you--more than you know. Be warned.
You do not go from here today to more persuasion of the
body. This is your last chance, child, you will not be asked
again. If you yourself can be found innocent of witchery,
you will tell us now where the Capsen Witch hides and free
your soul from her bonds. But if you deny you know," the

179

bells rang over her, "you reveal yourself to be a witch in her thrall, and condemn your soul to eternal damnation. Do you understand this, child?"

"I... I... She used to speak of hills."

"Where?"

"I don't know where. Hills. West of Drespin."

The high priest got no more out of her. 'Hills' would not be enough to satisfy the queen, Arnaby knew, but he suspected it was all the poor wretch ever did know about Ailil and her people. Varina would be cast down to die as an unrepentant witch in the dungeon. Or if she survived that, maybe she'd be chosen to die quicker in the arena. Innocence had little chance to prove itself against this queen, Arnaby had already warned the Duke of that, two years before she'd beheaded his brother, her husband, the king. But now innocence--and ignorance both had even less chance to survive against her priests.

~

Invisible to anyone looking at him, Verl waited for the guardsmen's cage to descend. The prisoner they pushed out into the pit this time was a woman. Verl dove for her cup as soon as she hit the floor.

He had no trouble taking the cup from her before the mob attacked. To his horror, he discovered she had no hands, just fleshy webbed paws, no fingers to keep a grip on the cup's handle and fight him for it.

Clutching the cup, Verl stood, and within the safety of darker shadows beyond the mob fighting over her, he withdrew his illusion of invisibility from the minds of those around him.

Not far away, Arax and a friend stood waiting for the poor battered woman to be left alone so they could go to her, pick her up if she were still alive, and carry her over to Verl's section.

Verl added her cup to his hoard. Then he wetted some strips from a dead man's loin cloth with water from another cup, and waited for her to be brought to him.

~

The little dream Verl advanced on a rat, holding his staff up over his shoulder.

"More to the side. Hold it out ready now. Looser," said Arax.

The rat snuffled at a dung heap. It sat up, scratched at its shoulder with a hind paw, then licked whatever was in its front paw. Its teeth were sharp, its eyes beady in the dim morning light. It took no notice of its approaching attacker.

The dream Verl scaled the dung hill, stepping closer.

"Ready? Swing. Hard as he can. Aim for the head. Aim--"

Arax slapped his knee and burst into laughter. The little Verl's club had passed straight through the rat's long head, through its shoulder, chest, and out the other side, not even flicking a whisker on its snout. The rat kept licking between its claws, undisturbed.

"That rat didn't even see him, did he?"

Verl laughed too. "Apparently not." The little Verl flung his staff aside, and leapt up onto the hairy shoulders of the rat and raised his fist high in victory, then he dug in his heels to go for a ride.

"Teach you how to ride a horse now, too, must I? You mount from the other side, mate."

Both men were still laughing. The rat, paying no attention to its hapless rider, started snuffling off into darker shadows, going in the opposite direction from the one the little rider was trying so hard to steer it towards with a yank of its long hair. Their laughter was an uncommon sound down here in the dungeon; and it felt good to Verl, even more so to hear Arax laugh. For several mornings now, while everyone else slept, Verl's little man had trained and worked hard, swinging and thrusting his staff, changing it for a sword, an axe, a dagger. The pentagon was still scratched into the dirt beside Verl, a stick man in its center. Most everyone else in his group by now, having heard that Verl could show them their dreams, had come to him, and had sat before his pentagon, and had told him long stories of their homeland and their family, during the endless hours of daylight. Then Verl would sketch a different spiral shape in the empty fifth corner to reflect something that each one had

181

told him, and then staring down into the pentagon with them, he'd walk inside their memories, behind their words, and let them see images of just what they wanted to see of the world they had left behind them. But early mornings, when everyone else was still asleep, was private time, time separated out and special, for Arax, for Verl, and for the brave little dream fighter who rose up from the stick man for another hour of Arax's training and entertainment.

The rat disappeared into deeper shadows, and its little rider made of light and air vanished with it. Arax turned back to Verl, still chuckling.

"No, I tell you, I don't think that rat ever knew what hit it–"

He stopped, his attention caught by something just beyond the pentagon. Verl looked and saw the new woman from a few days ago lying close by, Varina, she called herself, she who had no hands and whose open wounds still needed constant care. She flicked her eyes closed, turned over, pretended she was still asleep.

Verl met Arax's eyes. The rat, an animal without human fear and imagination, may never have seen Verl's illusion of the little dream fighter, but unfortunately, Varina may have seen far too much of it.

~

Two days later, Varina was strong enough to walk, to take her cup and get her own water and food. She stood among the other prisoners waiting as the guardsmen's cage descended, not far from Verl, eyeing him. Then when her turn came, she went forward, pressed close to the cage, curling what was left of her fleshy right hand around her cup, and darted her other hand into the cage quickly to paw at the guardsman's arm.

"I'm ready to talk," she rasped. "You tell the High Priest that. Tell the queen. Varina's ready to talk, you tell them. I've seen true witchery. And I have proof of it."

Chapter 17
Lion's Hunger

Duke Rayid of Navarn drew his cloak around him and paced to keep warm. The summer sun beat down from a cloudless sky, taking the sting out of the brisk highland winds.

The Norgol Highland felt as raw and unexplored as it had in his youth. And despite his grey hairs now, he still responded to it like he had then, its wildness kniving cold, unnamed impulses through him. The giant-tossed boulders of granite, the rushing torrents driven by snow melt cutting through the black gorges, the high plateaus where the heather in bloom this one month of the year swept the horizons purple--Rayid closed his eyes and breathed the highlands in.

He spread his hands open to the wind. He imagined his fingers scratching down lion-claw rips through a doe's heart. No blame would speak back to him in this wind, no human pity that would weigh a doe's fear more than a lion's hunger. Life and death were indistinguishable here, existence undefined by human limitation.

If Rayid had no responsibilities, no inheritance from his father to uphold, no name to mold him to his people's expectations, he'd live here in the highlands.

Instead, his capital was along the peaceful shores of Lake Maynard and its long trade river to the sea. Comfort and a show of prosperity, not wildness, brought commerce and security--brought pride to his people.

And bought him their loyalty. His lion's hunger fed on them in luxury. Rayid lowered his arms and yanked on his fur-lined gloves.

He would do whatever he had to do. As he always had. To keep his word. To keep his country prosperous.

His lips pulled thin. To keep himself in power.

From the next cliff over, a shepherd boy sailed down to his flock in the pasture terrace below his village caves.

Rayid watched, always fascinated by the human kites the Morris cliffmen had been using here for centuries, sailing down to their pastures or cornfield terraces or the river below. When Rayid first put on his crown, leaving his father's deathbed and his brother's greater share of Norgondy behind him, he had entered his own newly partitioned-off country of Navarn through Moxie Pass here in the Highlands. And coming out at its head among the cliffmen, seeing for the first time the wonder of their sails, Rayid had defied his counselors' warnings. He'd laughed at their fears, harnessed on a cliffman's sail to his arms and back, and *flew*. Twenty-four years later, he still remembered the wind against his cheeks, and the first frightening blur of red, yellow sandstone mixed with splotches of grey brush as he dropped fast before the sail caught hold, and then, the quick jerk up, and the floating down, the sailing-- *the flying.*

In the past few weeks, leading his army home from Norgondy through the pass, he glanced up often at those treacherous cliffs while his captains, fearing ambush, scouted through them. Leaving the worrying to them, Rayid wondered instead what it would feel like to sail down from those towering heights.

But wild impulses were not something he could give in to, nor something he could admit aloud to anyone else. That first flight twenty-four years ago ended in a broken leg on an unskilled landing. He had been the show of decorum, rationality, power and mercy ever since.

"Friend Rayid."

Barzolf's voice came quietly from behind him. It warned Rayid not to move when he felt a great muzzle sniffing up the back of his leg and thrusting itself into the palm of his left hand.

Rayid turned slowly to greet the hermit's dog first, submitting his gloved hand to the dog's continued inspection. He had no doubt that if the dog had not already recognized him, he would have been attacked before Barzolf had a chance to call off his dog.

"Hello, Daxid," he said. Half wolf, half Morris shepherd, with the thick red and black coat of a mountain

184

dog, Daxid thrapped its tail back and forth against its sides in response.

Rayid scratched the dog's ears and nodded a greeting to the stargazer beside him.

"Your dog's as wild as the highland winds."

"He'd say the same of you."

Rayid met the glint in Barzolf's granite grey eyes. Years ago, Barzolf was the one who'd fitted the kite harness onto Rayid's shoulders. The stargazer was the one man Rayid could never hide from.

Barzolf rested his hand on Daxid's back. "Anyone else who comes for a star reading, I have to keep him chained up. But he does allow me your visits once a year. We expected you yesterday."

"We hurried to get here. But we missed the solstice by a day."

Barzolf glanced up at the sky, already reddening with the lowering sun. "It's going to be as clear as last night. The midsummer shower of stars was heavy, but there should still be a few stars speaking tonight."

Rayid looked up too. Each midsummer, the flurry of falling stars lasted for three to four nights. It was held to be the most portentous time to consult a Morris stargazer. Not that Rayid believed Barzolf's predictions any more than he'd believe the dream interpretations of an Eller Island dreamwalker or the smoke-enhanced illusions of a Capsen tellerwoman---not that Rayid believed anyone's sight was closer to seeing the future than anyone else's, but he had made a life-long study of all the diverse beliefs among the peoples of both Norgondy and Navarn. On a practical basis, doing so made the traders he dealt with from the various competing routes each feel like he agreed with their ideas intimately, and that kept them willing to favor him with their friendship, their most honest prices, and their best secret information on their neighbors. On a more personal basis, he had become intrigued by the similarity of beliefs and magical symbols of the three main descendants of a legendary people from the southern continent called Lakemen. Barzolf's cloak was embroidered with the five star constellations, the yellow stars connected by red threads

185

that outlined the same five symbols that an Eller Island walker drew in his dream pentagon, and that a Capsen tellerwoman wove into a puzzle spell tapestry--or indeed that shone onto the inlaid bear claws from the Capsen-designed stained glass windows in the court room of the Norgon king where he'd grown up as a child. Or, so Rayid assumed. In truth, he'd only seen four of the claw circles lit with the magical symbols each year, one each at the solstices and equinoxes. But he'd never seen the fifth design, the spiral of forgetfulness, shining down onto the fifth circle. That absence had always kept him more intrigued by the puzzle of the connection between the symbols and the three ancient cultures.

The wind stung colder; evening was approaching. "That's what I was counting on, to still be in time to see stars falling again tonight, so you can tell me how much I shall be charged for Morris wool next year." He grinned at his friend. It was for friendship and Barzolf's rare ability to unmask Rayid's deceptions that kept Rayid returning to him each year, more than any belief in his predictions. Still, and Rayid had never discounted this, Barzolf had predicted his marriage, the year of his twin sons' births, and the month, three years ago, of his family's death.

"Come." The stargazer put a hand to his shoulder. "You can help me install that new lens you had made for my telescope before night falls."

The two men started walking to Barzolf's cave, its entrance framed by a wall of adobe darkly painted and dotted with bright constellations. Before they reached it, a warning call of a Morris shepherd horn blasted through the air. Two horns answered it.

Rayid and Barzolf detoured to the edge of the cliff to watch perhaps thirty shepherds, old and young alike, grab staffs and crooks and sail down to their flocks on the terraced pastures below their cliffhouses next hill over.

"Wolves?" Rayid asked. He'd never seen so many Morris cliffmen answer the warning of the horns before. He glanced down at his own army camped in the river valley far below, building their evening fires, undisturbed by the commotion above.

Barzolf's answer was quiet, disheartened. "Not wolves. We've had new visitors every week this past year. Look." He pointed to the sky. A large bird—no, Rayid corrected himself---not a bird, its wingspan greater than any bird he'd ever seen, was diving down towards the cliffs. Tawny, massive, it had the claws and wings of an eagle, but the head of a mountain lion. When it reached the flock of sheep, it hovered and swung its forked tail. A lamb fell beneath it. The monster roared and lifted up into the air.

Two shepherds sailing past the eagle-lion stabbed their staffs at it, but the monster took no notice. One of the shepherds got tangled in his ropes. His sail unbalanced, he landed hard on the rocks near the cliff. Struggling to rise, he slipped, tumbled down to a lower terrace. Other shepherds, already landed, circled the fallen lamb and raised their staffs and crooks, and started slinging rocks up into the air. One shot arrows. Barzolf mumbled a chant.

The lamb twitched its legs, tried to raise its head, then stopped moving. The eagle-lion roared in lust and dove down towards it again, claws extended. Shepherds beat at it with their staffs, shot rocks, arrows at it as it dove between them. Undaunted, it grabbed the lamb's limp body and flew off.

"Nothing stops it," Barzolf said.

"And it's–"

"A garug. At least matches the old legends of one."

Rayid nodded. He'd never seen one before. He had heard stories of other farmers closer to the Black Hills seeing garugs often. "Those new priests who've taken over Norgondy call those monsters their god, their 'Winged One.' They're killing all people who don't honor it."

Barzolf turned rock-stern eyes at him. "More fools they," he said.

Despite himself, Rayid shuddered. What he'd seen and heard the last three months traveling through Norgondy, he'd never forget. Beliefs of other peoples may intrigue him, but the zealotry and assuredness of these Badurian priests had created a power he'd never encountered before. If it spread into his land, it would be as unstoppable as their god. "I thought garugs were black."

187

"Some are." Barzolf grunted and pointed to the sky again. "Here comes another one that is."

They watched the second attack, the shepherds just as helpless to stop it as the first. "Their gods are hungry tonight," Barzolf said.

~

"Hallo! Freyshin, Master Freyshin." Crel banged two pots lids together as he searched through the tilemaker's workhouse and tool shed, calling for the old man, his daughter, or his two apprentices. In the workhouse, tile molds lay stacked and ready. In the yard, chickens scattered at his noise, but an old sow and her brood rooting near the mound of a several days old smoldering kiln ignored him. Beyond the kiln, the great brick oven for glazing was cold.

"New pots for old. Spoons a three-pence. Hallo?" Crel's boots sank heel and toe into the sandy clay as he yelled across the centuries-old digging pit behind the maker's yard, but still no answer. Freyshin's boat was pulled ashore on the river bank. His town wagon was parked by the barn, but no horses were around.

Crel stopped banging the pot lids and started back to his hutwagon. Twice a year Wiss and he would spend the nights here as guests of Freyshin and his daughter on the outskirts of the port city of Sonachin awaiting passage to the Eller Islands at the end of their circuit. With no one home, Crel would have to find an inn in Sonachin tonight. It would not be the first time on his long journey home that the houses and shops of Wiss's regular customers had been deserted.

Passing the brick oven, Crel slowed, looked again. The grate was slightly open. It had been closed when he'd first passed by it.

He walked over, pulled down the lid.

"Well, hello, Giln." He grinned at the apprentice hunched inside the barrel of the oven and offered a hand to pull him out.

The lad, several years his junior, clambered out, his cheeks, apron, bare feet blackened with soot. He glanced

188

around the yard in terror. "Are you with the priests? Have they come back?"

"Hold, hold. I got Jesser with me, that's all. You remember Jesser?... What's happened here, Giln? Where's Master Freyshin? Or his daughter Mistress Sylvan?"

"She's been taken. Folks called her a witch. Master Freyshin, he fought it. Taxman and guardsmen came with the priests, told Master Freyshin hand over his silver, they'd listen to her again. He gave them all he had, and went into town this morning to sell his horses. They came took her away in a cage yesterday. The taxman now says Master Freyshin has more taxes due, and they'll cart him away too, if he can't pay."

"They took her yesterday, you say?" As he listened, Crel started leading the frightened apprentice to the pumphouse to get him stripped, cleaned, and calmed down. He'd heard the same story more and more often in other towns along his route home. Taxmen had come, and so had the Badurian priests. And tradesmen Wiss and he had once called friends and customers had no money left to buy his wares. Too many of them had been accused of witchery, either by a frightened neighbor wanting to lay the blame on someone else, or by a greedy neighbor wanting to "buy" the tradesman's holdings.

Giln faced him with eyes as black as the soot on his cheeks. "She's no witch, is she, Crel? She's no witch?"

Crel set his pot lids down, and started pumping out the water before he answered. "I don't know, Giln. The priests say we shouldn't know any witches. We have to believe them these days. So I wouldn't admit to knowing anything about anyone they call a witch, if I were you."

~

Duke Rayid lay on the cold rock shelf, one arm under his head, the other across the dog's back. Earlier they'd viewed four of the planets through the telescope with the new lens Rayid had had his spectaclemaker cut for Barzolf. A few minutes ago, the two of them had rolled the ancient telescope back to its niche inside the cave. It was time to watch the whole wide dome of the night sky. Rayid scratched the dog's ears and listened to the stargazer name the constellations.

Summer solstice on a moonless clear night, and all five of the major constellations were visible. The five that controlled his destiny, Barzolf always told him, or that controlled his dreams, the dreamwalkers of the Eller Island would say, or that gave him the illusions that could shape his understanding of reality, as Ailil the Capsen tellerwoman had explained to him in their youth. Whatever god in the time before time that had played marbles and scattered the stars at random across the sky, men saw patterns in their clusterings, men saw meaning, saw stories meant for them. Rayid had heard the stargazer's stories before. How Mora the Spider boiled her children and fed their stew to her husband. When he choked on their bones as she told him what he ate, she laughed and licked her fingers. On her first taste of guilt, she could never stop swallowing, until she swallowed her fingers, her tongue, her lips, her neck, until she swallowed herself inside out and all that was left of her was the black speck of guilt no larger than a widow spider. And that god of antiquity cast her into the northern sky where the three brightest stars formed the triangle of her head, and the eight stars encircling them, her legs. Or by joining the eight stars from leg to leg, the pattern drawn of her constellation by the Eller Islands dreamwalker was called her web of guilt.

Opposing the Spider to the south were the nine bright stars that formed the Arrowhead, the path of right. Among the Capsens, that constellation was called the Bear's Head instead, and just in recalling that name, Rayid added the five stars to it that completed the bear's body, and the two patterns shifted back and forth in his mind, both present, both as real. Curious, he always thought. He may not believe the stars held meaning, that each star alone or in clusters had been placed in the sky for his benefit, but once a constellation was pointed out to him and named, he could not deny he saw its pattern. He could even see two constellations at once, as here, the Path of Right, and Alred's Bear, their patterns shifting in his mind as fast as he could think of their names, but he could never see the stars singly again, unjoined, insignificant, no matter what he believed. Perhaps that was the contradiction-- the denial and the acceptance-- that kept pulling him back here year after year on the solstice to hear Barzolf speak. Rayid sat up, uncorked the jug of hot mulled wine and took a swig, then passed the jug to Barzolf.

"And there, to the rising moon," Barzolf said, "Zaire's Sword. The seven, its silver shining blade of vengeance, and those four just above the horizon--the red, two blues, and the brightest diamond--its jeweled hilt. And, as in all, two meanings in its thrust. The blade that cuts down enemies, champion of justice and power; or the edge of sorrow that kills you, the slaying words or deeds that destroy those you love most."

Rayid stared at the Sword pointing towards him, seeing again the meteor that came straight through it three years ago before his wife and sons died. In his youth, his father had taken the Sword constellation as his sign on his standard, had paraded it each Harvest Festival, had called it the sword of peace.

"And countering it to the west, to the setting moon, Lorn's Harp, that plays the song of gifts, of all music, all arts, all crafts, of the magic that flows in and out of the hands of all makers. There is a pride in giving. The danger for Lorn," Rayid felt Barzolf's eyes on him, piercing through him, as he passed him back the jug of wine and repeated, "the danger for Lorn was in the giving for the taking, in wanting to feel the satisfaction and pride again, wanting the acclamation. To see a star fall through Lorn's Harp can mean you'll give all that you are for love, or that you'll be blessed by others loving you, or the converse, that for money, or fame, or greed, or hunger, you'll sell yourself."

Rayid chuckled, saluted the jug to the stargazer before taking a sip. "That's what I like about your prophecies. You can make them match everyone. Every situation." He corked the jug, passed it back.

"Those people full of contradictions especially," Barzolf said, still watching him. Rayid lay back down, scratched the dog's back.

191

"People full of contradictions are those I find most interesting," he answered finally.

"Your sons were born under those stars. You were blessed in their love. And in the love of your people..."

"But...?" Rayid asked him.

"But, my friend, you would ask me or anyone you love to step off that cliff if you saw it to your advantage. And there's such in you, we'd do it trustingly."

Rayid's fist curled around thick strands of the dog's hair. "An asset for any leader. Me, if I had what I wanted most, I'd live alone here in the highlands. Unencumbered. I do what I have to do for the welfare of my people. I ask of them what I must, for their benefit."

"Or for yours, my friend. Or for yours."

Rayid gazed in silence at the harp in the sky. His wife had said the same thing to him once, that he used her. And so he had, in marrying her, as much as she had ever used him.

Barzolf went on quietly after a moment, "And the fifth house of stars, above us. Always there, and never seen. The spiral of forgetfulness. Only in forgetting yourself, can you find your center, your soul. The center of the universe, written in the space between the stars."

Rayid looked up at the constellation hardest for him to see, but inescapable to tear his imagination away from when he did. Two spirals of stars meeting in the faint blue star Solon. He had seen their pattern on Barzolf's robe, the fifth symbol of power he had never seen formed by the fall of lights through stained glass windows on the fifth circle of the bear's claw in his father's court room floor. He'd had the constellation pointed out to him many times, he could see the first two circles of stars making a figure eight easily when he looked for them. The other circles spiraled outwards farther and farther as his imagination imposed the pattern upon them, joining star after star into the circling and the circling. All the stars joined in, that one there, and that one there, each part of a wider or smaller circle he had not seen before, stretching outwards east and west to the horizons, the myriad of countless stars, the whole universe patterned from the parts. The two halves of the cosmos spiraling away from each other yet touching in the center, in the one faint blue star overhead. As he stared up, scenes of his life, recent and old, disconnected, no story to them, no decision made from them, flashed in star after star to him, spiraled away from each other in his mind in two swirling circles, the good, the bad, the loved, the hated, his beliefs and denials present and forgotten, joined in random order to one faint star inside him. His father's face as he cut up the map of Norgondy, and handed him, the younger son, a small realm of his own. Ailil's face without the veil, her hair spread around her on the grass as she reached for him. The rush of colors the one time he put on wings--the kite of the Morris shepherds onto his shoulders--and flew. The laughter of his baby sons. The betting of his courtiers, his crowded harbors full of merchant ships, the hanging of an innocent soldier to keep the peace. Star after star, unconnected in reality, oddly juxtaposed in his memory, lost in their spirals dancing away from him, each alone meaningless, insignificant, becoming joined, meaningful inside him. His brother's wife beautiful and gentle, queen regent of Norgondy now, her child sat on his brother's throne--his father's throne, the land his father once split up to give him his own small share. Garug monsters tore into the flesh of a lamb, shepherds flew down to the lamb, fought for it. Garug priests in black robes pilloried a village woman they'd called a witch, stones thrown by her neighbors tore into her flesh. In his disguise on his way home from his old homeland, he could not save her. His young nephew sat screaming on his father's throne, squirming away from the sight of Rayid's brother's severed head in a jeweled merchant's casket. His people of Navarn were at peace, haggling over the price of the merchant ships' wares crowding the gangplanks and quays. His father's people, his brother's people frightened and dying, persecuted.

Barzolf was speaking quietly. "It's almost first dawn. Time for the stars to start falling. Do you have your question to ask of them?"

His young nephew Laird sat squirming on his father's throne. Priests in black robes stood behind him, circled Rayid like vultures, like eagle-lions, and tore into his flesh.

"Priests in Norgondy have made a god of a garug, and now hold the land in their thrall," he said. "What will come of it?"

The answer was there, unspoken but certain, as soon as he uttered the question. And confirmed by the sudden flash of five meteors falling out of the east through the constellation of Zaire's Sword. The longest, brightest meteor trailed across the whole sky, through the soul of the center, passing the blue star in the Spiral of Forgetfulness, and not fading until it reached the stars in the strings of the Harp. Belief and denial, questioning and doubt dissolved into certainty. One word. One answer.

"War."

The stargazer was watching him. "War," Barzolf repeated.

Chapter 18
Shell Game

"Damn you, bear, hold still." Crel struggled to lace up Jesser's red leather performing jerkin, but she was having none of it. For Wiss, she had always sat upright, letting the old man slide the sleeves on with ease, then waited patiently, an idiot's open-tooth grin on her face as she watched Wiss lace her up and tie a jaunty yellow scarf around her neck. But for Crel, she stood on all four legs, her rump jammed up against a corner of her cage, and swayed over him, banging loudly against the bars, while he crouched on the hay under her trying to lace the black leather thong through the last upper holes and tie it.

"Jesser, stop it!"

In response the bear lay down on top of him. Not hard enough to squash him, but certainly hard enough to make her point.

Winded, Crel waited, one side of his face dented by the tough sharp reeds of hay, the other side of his face pressed down by the bear's shoulder. Even a sweat-soaked horse smelled better than bear at close range.

"Jesser," Crel pleaded.

The bear grunted, content with herself.

"Wiss, do it for Wiss," he murmured from under her, then he closed his eyes. "I need your help tonight, Wiss."

Jesser lifted herself gently off Crel, nuzzled her broad cold nose into the crick of his neck, then sat upright obediently.

"So that's it, is it?" Crel stood up, stretched his sore back as he dusted himself off, finished dressing her quickly. "You help me, and I'll make sure to call you Jesserwiss tonight."

The bear lumbered to the front of her cage and pawed into the high nest of hay she built for herself every night. Curious, Crel followed, and found buried in the center of the nest Wiss's black tinker hat.

"I take it it's a deal, then," Crel said. "I'll pin this on and you can wear his hat tonight." He pinned the square wool hat on tilted to one side of her broad head, then scratched her small ears as she snarled back at him. "But you have to promise to do your best for him tonight, do you hear me? ...Come, I'll get something else for you."

He led her outside into the tilemaker's yard, ducks and chickens scattering at the approach of a bear.

Crel waited for the chickens to settle again, then he ran at them, clapping his hands, shouting, chasing them. Frantic, they beat their wings, squawked in terror, two of them managing to lift themselves off the ground for a few feet. They left behind a trail of feathers. Crel chose two long tail feathers from the red and yellow rooster.

Jesser whuffed at them curiously when he showed them to her, then he pinned them onto her hat.

"Couldn't be more beautiful, Jesserwiss. You'll be the prettiest bear in town tonight."

Crel chose two long black tail feathers for himself, chained Jesser to the back of her cage to wait for him, then climbed into the hutwagon and opened Wiss's old stenciled trunk, its painted clan bears, turtles, herons all but faded into the wood. The performer's tunic Wiss always wore when he took Jesser into towns lay folded inside. Capsen clan colors, half green with thin yellow stripes, the other side of the tunic, midnight blue to midwaist, then below the belt the colors switched. The breeches, tight-fitting, were one leg green, one blue. Crel had lengthened them and taken in the sides of the tunic during the long nights between towns on his journey here. Tonight, for the first time, he decided to wear the black jester's mask instead of his tinker's cap. It felt oddly appropriate.

He checked the props for Jesser's tricks packed inside the burlap sack, then shouldered it and took Wiss's accordion off the wall above the trunk and went inside the tilemaker's shop.

"Did you decide which key?" he asked the tilemaker.

The tilemaker shook his head, held out three of the copper keys Crel had brought him that afternoon from his hoard of scrap metals. Most of the keys he had salvaged from the ashes of the Drespin boarding house over three months ago. Copper always being in short supply in his trade, he had taken whatever he could find made of it, and there must have been at least two copper keys for every room and lock box of the boarding house among the ashes. He'd never considered he might find use for one of them as a key.

"These are the closest," the old man said. Two of them were very similar in the cut designs on their heads, the third was plainer and shorter. "The taxman wears it hanging on his chest on a gold chain, so I got a fairly good a look at it. It had a similar design as these two, I think, but shorter."

Crel took them in his hands. All three had similar grooves for the lock, but none were exactly the same key. The two longer ones were definitely heavier.

"I don't see how you get a key to match a lock just by looking at it."

Frowning slightly, Crel shrugged a shoulder, then chose one of the longer keys. He slipped it in his pouch. "I'm hoping that all I need is one to look right. Wish me luck, Freyshin. And tomorrow, if all goes well, you'll have your daughter home.

~

Crel rode into town, facing backwards on his white pony, playing the accordion, leading Jesser on her chain. She walked upright, swinging her head from side to side, growling and snapping at the onlookers if they got too close. So far, so good. The more ferocious she looked, the more townsmen came to see her, Wiss had always said.

Even so, he watched her closely, and jerked on her chain if she took a sideways step towards someone. Wiss may have always trusted her, but Crel never completely did. He had no fear for himself, he'd grown up handling her. If she killed him one day, well then, she'd kill him. In the meantime, there was something about her foul, stubborn fights with him that he loved as much as he hated. Perhaps...perhaps he did believe the Capsens enough when they claimed that Wiss's spirit and those of his three wives had each joined with the bear's when they died, taming

197

some of the wildness out of her. On long nights alone these last few weeks, Crel had talked to her sometimes as if she were Wiss.

But here in town among strangers, Crel would just as soon she did growl at everyone, keeping them a safe distance away from her.

When they reached the town square, they circled the merman fountain twice before stopping in front of Sonachin town hall with the tavern in its cellar where the guardsmen, priests and town magistrates had been drinking. Most of the dignitaries came out and joined the crowd. The tax collector with the key around his neck was among them, Crel was gratified to see.

Crel drove a stake into the ground and hooked Jesser's chain to it. Then he motioned the crowd in closer in a circle around them, just out of the reach of Jesser's chain.

She danced in a wide circle at first to his music. Even with the chain, whenever she got close to the spectators, the ladies and young children would gasp in terror and cringe away from her, and their men would laugh at them and broaden their shoulders. For good measure, Jesser snarled at the crowd every few steps and showed her pointed teeth. When Crel stopped playing the accordion, he handed her a battered tin plate that she took in her teeth and circled around with it. The crowd clapped quietly and threw in a few coins that she tried to catch with the plate. Someone also threw in two apples.

Crel gave her time to eat the apples, while he asked for three volunteers. He chose a guardsman, a fisherman, and a nervous young lady being shoved forward by her laughing lord.

"Can you read?" he asked them. "Jesser can." The bear growled on cue at her name. The young lady giggled nervously and edged closer to the guardsman.

Crel handed each a tin platter, one painted blue, one yellow, one green. On the face of each was a large black number. Crel read the numbers aloud for all the spectators. "You have two, sir, stand over there. You have three, my lady, stand over here and show the crowd. And you, lad, this is the number five. Stand on that side, and remember the number."

"Jesser," he said. She growled and finished crunching her second apple.

"*Jesserwiss*," he said. This time she looked up at him, then moving slowly, slowly, she sat up on her haunches, and waved a paw at him.

"Jesserwiss, find the man with the blue plate. Blue, Jesserwiss. What number is on it?"

The guardsman held up the blue platter, and Jesser ambled over to him. The guardsman stepped back a step as the bear got closer. Jesser stopped within a foot of him at the end of her chain, stood up as tall as he, and opened her jaws and roared two times.

The crowd applauded, and the guardsman, his fingers clenched white around the platter, lowered it and stepped back among them.

"Good girl, Jesserwiss." Crel tossed her a dried eel from his sack. "Now Jesserwiss. Find the yellow platter. *Yellow*. What number is on it?"

The young fisherman held the yellow platter up in front of his chest like a shield. Crel had full view of his Adam's apple moving up and down just above the platter and below his rough beard, the fisherman swallowing his fear constantly. But he stood his ground better than the guardsman did when the bear approached and roared five times in his face.

Silence at first, as the crowd waited for the sixth loud roar that never came, then the applause and cheers came heavier than before. As Wiss had always said, tell a crowd what to believe they see, and they'll see it. Crel had told them the bear could read the number, a feat many of them could not do. What he had not told them, Jesser knew the colors of the platters, not the numbers written on them, and she'd been trained for years to growl the right number of times for each color.

"Jesserwiss, find the green platter. Green, Jesserwiss. What number is on it?"

As Jesserwiss came, the lady edged closer and closer to Crel. He put a hand on her shoulder to steady her, and she raised up the platter. The young lord who had pushed her into the circle to volunteer looked frightened now, and he held a hand on his rapier at his side.

Jesser growled three times, and the crowd shouted and threw a fortune in apples and talents. The lady herself, now that it was over, spun around to Crel, her face aglow.

"It's true, it's true, it is the number three!"

As he took the platter from her, he nodded, then held out a dried eel to her. She looked down at it and back up at him, then glanced over at the scared lord, his hand on his rapier, but he hadn't moved a step towards her to save her. She smiled back at Crel, straightened her shoulders and took the eel from him. She stepped closer to Jesser and gave her the eel.

"She likes being scratched, just behind that right ear," Crel said, as he stepped beside her. The lady glanced at him and nodded, her eyes brimming with tears of appreciation and pride. She lifted a hand and scratched the bear's ear.

"Thank you, my lady." Crel bowed to her and led her back to her lord.

"Now, Jesserwiss." He clapped his hands twice in the center of the circle next to the stake, and the bear stood up to him. "I want you to find something round. Round, Jesserwiss."

That was easy. There was an apple a few feet away, and Jesser sat down by it and ate it happily.

"Good, girl. Now find something yellow, Jesserwiss. Yellow."

This time the bear walked around the circle looking at the crowd. She stopped in front of an old woman wearing a yellow shawl and poked her nose towards her. The old woman froze stiff, and still stood frozen after the bear returned to Crel.

He gave her another piece of eel.

"Okay, Jesserwiss. Find something shiny. Something *small* and *shiny*, Jesserwiss." He emphasized the words, hoping she'd remember them. It was not something Wiss had often asked her to find. "Shiny, Jesserwiss. Shiny."

The bear sat looking at him, cocking her head sideways. Then she roared at him, went and found another apple and ate it. The crowd, waiting, started murmuring.

Crel held out a whole long eel. "Shiny, Jesserwiss. Find something small and shiny."

The bear lumbered to her feet and started walking around and around the circle, twice. Then she stopped in front of the taxman, the copper key shining on his chest under the lighted street lamps.

"Good, girl!" Crel said. "Good girl. Bring it to me."

The taxman's hands clasped over his chest and he stepped back into the crowd of guardsmen. Jesser growled, and opened her jaws towards his hands.

"Sir, sir." Crel opened his hands appeasingly. "Let her borrow it. She won't swallow it, I assure you."

"I... No."

"You'll get it back, good as new. I just want her to show you another trick. What do you say, everyone?"

The crowd agreed uproariously, and the guardsmen and town mayor around the taxman both urged him to give the bear the key.

"You can take it off the chain. She'll bring it back to you. I swear it with my life."

The taxman met Crel's eyes. Then his cheeks reddening, he fumbled the chain loose, held out the key to the bear. Jesser picked it up gingerly in her teeth from his palm and brought it to Crel.

Crel reached into his sack and took out his last three props, the top half of tortoise shells, identical size, their green and yellow patterns slightly different. Their edges had been filed smooth through the years to slide around better.

From his pony, Crel unhooked a small folding table. With his back facing the crowd, still unstrapping the table from the pony's side, he slipped a quick hand into his pouch, and pulled out the copper key inside it between two fingers. Wiss had taught him the shell game as his trick with Jesser for years, but sleight of hand was the old man's specialty. Wiss had always enjoyed these nights performing in the towns, and he'd always worn the mask saying a small dose of larceny was in his blood as a Capsen. Crel had often wondered if his trade as a tinker during the day was only his excuse to keep traveling with his bear and tricks at night. Still of all the things he'd learned from the old man, he could only hope he'd watched him often enough to keep the key hidden.

He set up the table in the center of the crowd, and placed the three shells on it. He held his hand out to Jesser for the taxman's key. Freyshin had been right, the key was shorter and lighter than the one in his other hand. Still if luck stayed with him, the taxman would never notice. The design on the head did look similar.

"Now watch carefully," he told the crowd and Jesser as he lifted the shell on the left hand side and slid the key under it. "I know you all have seen this trick before, but my bet is, the bear can choose the right shell the key is under while more than half of you can't. So everyone, watch my hands. Sir," he nodded to the taxman, "you especially. Now I used to have a partner who played the accordion and sang a song with the crowd, trying to distract the bear, and she still chose better than half the crowd!" He'd started sliding the shells around, quicker and quicker, as he talked. It wasn't the bear he was trying to distract, but the crowds. The slight differences in the three shell patterns as they slid around fast actually made more spectators confused at the end, trying to remember which was the correct pattern. "So, who's the best singer here? Could you start a round for me? "The Rig of the Cutty Main," that's always a good one. And if everyone sings and she starts dancing to it, so much the better!"

The full round, short, but repeated three times gave Crel all the time he needed to keep shifting the shells around. Jesser did start stomping one foot then the other to the tune, but she never took her eyes off the shells. Most of the crowd though kept watching her as much as the shells, hoping to see her start dancing.

The taxman never took his eyes off the shell with his key in it.

The song ended and Crel lifted his hands from the shells.

"Ready? You vote first. Everyone clap who thinks the key is under this shell?" He pointed to the left shell, and perhaps half the crowd applauded.

"This one?" The middle shell, and fewer people clapped.

"The middle one, yes," the taxman said gruffly.

Crel nodded at him. "We'll see. And who says this one instead?" More than half applauded, all who hadn't voted yet, and many who already had. Crel had always found that amusing, but he kept his face expressionless.

"Jesser, which shell is it?"

The bear came over to the table and nosed over the shell in the middle, always the shell in the middle, always the position he left the right shell, and out fell the key.

Crel nodded to the taxman. "You were right!" He picked up the key in his left hand, closed his hand around it, and went over to him, and handed him a key.

For a breathless second, the taxman frowned as he looked at the key and felt the weight of it, maybe. But the rest of the crowd was cheering and Crel turned quickly away and handed Jesser the battered tin plate to pass around.

"Pay well, pay well. To buy her more apples and eels from you, of course!"

He packed up the shells and platters and apples and coins into the sack and folded up the table. He glanced behind him only once and saw the taxman sliding the key onto his chain. Crel breathed a sigh of relief and kept working.

Later he hitched up the pony and kept the bear chained to her stake near the fountain steps after feeding her. Then he joined the guardsmen, taxman and town magistrates in the cellar tavern below the town hall until the wee hours of the night.

~

Leading a bear through the narrow corridors and stairwells of Sonachin town hall in the blackest hours past midnight was not the smartest idea Crel had ever had. Still a guardsman had watched him pull up the stake and lead Jesser and his pony out of the square, going home, he told him. When Crel doubled back through side alleys, the guardsman was still in front of the town hall talking to another guardsman. There was no way Crel could leave the bear outside with the pony in the shadowy alley beside the hall without fear of her being noticed.

When he reached the tresor's room, he found it locked. He was glad now he brought Jesser. He had her rock her full weight against the door until the lock gave way, and it opened.

"Stay here," he told her, just inside the shadows of the room, "and don't let anyone in." He lit a lantern on the wall above her with his small taper.

He found several lock boxes similar to the one Freyshin had described. One did have the royal crest of Norgondy on top. He slipped the taxman's key into the lock and it clicked open.

Inside, silver and copper talents, paper credits, deeds to ships, shops, land, and a long tally sheet showing who had paid what. Another sheet listed those condemned by priests as witches, and a list of their property that had been confiscated—half to their neighbors who had accused them, half to the crown. No wonder neighbors had turned in neighbors in every town Crel had traveled through in the last two months, if the priests had been there first.

He heard a noise outside. Quickly he checked the tally of taxes due again to find Freyshin's name, grabbed twice the amount listed, enough he hoped for Freyshin to get his daughter a new hearing before the priests, and started to close the box.

Then, he paused, silver still glinting inside under the lantern light. Flexing his fingers, he grabbed just one extra coin. He wore a jester's mask tonight, but he was a tinker, not a thief. He locked the box and left the extra coin and key under it for the taxman to find in the morning, his payment for lending him the key.

He almost made it down the last stairwell when he saw torchlight shining on the walls ahead. He blew out his candle, and tried to turn around. But Jesser was behind him and she growled when he shoved her, trying to turn her.

"Who goes there?"

Trapped between the bear and the guardsman coming up the stairs, Crel raised his hands and went on down. His wild plan to save a friend when, as a rule, he never got himself involved in anything had worked so surprisingly well tonight, that he was beginning to believe he might actually get away with it. But now, his luck had run out. He was caught at the worst possible time, his pouch full of stolen taxes.

In the last few months, he'd seen innocents accused as witches imprisoned, enslaved, burned and beheaded, and their property added to the priests' taxes. He could only imagine with each step he went down what would happen to him, guilty as he was. He grit his teeth and stepped into the torchlight.

He was immediately greeted by the guardsman's sword at his throat.

"Who–?"

A flurry of fur and blackness interrupted him as Jesser shot past Crel charging at his attacker.

Shoved aside, Crel fell backwards against the steps jutting hard into his back. By the time he got to his feet, the bear was on top of the guardsman squeezing his arms against his sides in a hug that could kill him, and her teeth were at his neck.

"Jesser!" Crel tried to pull her off, to stop her. She had never killed anyone before, he would never trust her again if she did.

She growled and backed away only reluctantly.

The guardsman was unconscious, losing blood through teeth marks in his shoulders, but he was still breathing, still had a pulse.

Crel stomped out the torch beginning to catch fire on the rug where it had fallen, then pulled Jesser away and ran.

~

The sun had been up for hours and the captain of the Desra Day was ready to set sail, but Crel was still dockside, pacing up and down in front of the guard house, waiting for his papers to be signed and a writ of passage to be authorized. It was definitely time for him to get home to the

Eller Islands and get a legitimate passport signed in his own homeland, rather than one forged by a Capsen count. It was getting increasingly difficult to explain that no, he was not Capsen, he was not of the witchtribe, his former master had been, and he'd inherited his trade when his master died near his homeland a year ago--yes, a year ago, see the date? Signed by the old king--that's long before the Capsens were enemies of the state.

This morning he was more nervous than ever waiting for his passport to be stamped so he could get out of town.

Jesser, Esra and her mule colt, the ox, and the two wagons had been loaded in the ship's hold since before sunrise, and the sails were being unfurled. The merchant captain of the Desra Day had given him only a few more minutes to board if he wanted passage too. Crel believed him, especially when the merchant mentioned that if his cargo sailed without him, it would become the captain's property to sell in the next port.

Crel stuck his head back in the guard house, but the sergeant at the desk waved him away. The door behind him was still closed. "No word yet," the sergeant told him.

Back outside, Crel kicked at a coiled rope holding a bobbing skiff against the dock, and glanced back up at the Desra Day. The main sail was already down and the yard arms were being secured.

He heard his name called behind him. Freyshin's apprentice Giln came running up the dock to him.

"I thought you were gone! Master Freyshin said to tell you to get out of town quick. He paid his taxes off fine, and still had enough to get Mistress Sylvan a new hearing set before the priests this afternoon. But when he was in town, he heard more news. The taxman discovered his key didn't work. He found the real key beneath his box, then counting, found money missing. They're searching for the bear handler who came into town last night—but the priests are saying they won't find him. It was a demon they said. Half bear, half man, sometimes two, sometimes one. When the guardsman woke up, he said he'd been attacked by a man who changed into a bear, right there before his eyes, and that's the story that's spreading. Some say they don't believe it, but Freyshin, he told everyone he could, that he believed it, and the priests are agreeing now, looking for more witches and demons everywhere!"

Crel shook his head, listening. "I'm trying to get out of here. I just haven't–"

"Freyshin says now. Before people start remembering that you too have a bear. If anyone from town saw you here today–"

The door to the guardhouse opened, and the sergeant came out, Crel's papers in hand. "He said you can go. But you only have a few days left to get your passport changed. You'll have to wait a month in the Eller Islands for the new king to sign it, but since you said that's where you're from, he decided to give you time to get there and try."

Crel grabbed his papers and ran to jump on board the ship as it was pulling up anchor. He waved to Giln from the ship's rail and yelled back down to him. "Tell Freyshin I'll see him in a month when I come back through. I'll have a new supply of pots for him to buy by then." Anything else about a demon bear and the morning news, he left unsaid.

Chapter 19
Arena

Bells rattled.

On your knees, Arax had warned him. *Make sure you kneel and repent your sins to their black winged god. That's the only way to get a staff to defend yourself.*

Bells rattled closer. Verl clasped his hands above his head and raised his arms in supplication. "I believe! Save me, Winged One!"

The bells rattled above him. He could smell the burning incense that had permeated the air at his trial, the unbreatheable air so reminiscent of the stench of death and decay in the dungeon. The end of a priest's staff, the hem of a scarlet robe stopped in the dirt in front of him. His hands were pried open, and a staff was placed in them.

"May the Winged One have mercy on your soul," the priest said, then lowered his voice. "If you live, remember this." The priest tapped Verl's finger against an indentation on the staff.

Verl squinted up, the glare of the sun stinging his eyes after his long months of imprisonment. He focused on the priest's face inside the black hood, and when he could see him clearly, his fingers clenched around the staff. It was the face of the fake Island dream interpreter. The face of the guardsman who had stood beside the queen disobeying her orders when the merchant duke revealed the skull of the dead king.

The priest barely nodded at Verl's recognition, then he stamped Verl's cheeks with the sign of the black winged god, and spoke aloud again. "May the Blessed One take you under his wings and protect you, my son."

Gripping his staff, Verl stood in front of the five other prisoners and faced the mounted guardsmen at the far end of the arena. He was barely conscious of the noise of the spectators. The sun was in his eyes, he watched it shine on the polished swords. He was aware of little else.

The master of arms signaled the trumpeter, and six of the guardsmen charged.

The rider on the grey warhorse in the center came directly at him. From where he stood in its path, the horse appeared monstrous galloping towards him. He could hear its labored breath and feel the thunder of its stampeding hooves. He saw the power in its broad chest, its muscles bunching, pulling right leg, then left leg forward. The wild flight of its black mane tossed up high in the air, and above the mane--the flash of a sword swung up.

Behind Verl, the other prisoners panicked, ran for the sides of the arena, two of them dropping their staffs. The five other guardsmen pursued them. Verl crouched, waiting for the grey warhorse, watching the sun reflect on the rising sword. *Choose your moment*, Arax had said.

The thunder of the horse, the spittle of its froth filled the air. At the last moment, Verl cast into the mind of the ' guardsman a full-size reflection of himself running to the left side of the horse towards the sword arm and raising his staff. At the same instant, he vanished from the sight of the guardsman and sprinted to the right side of the horse.

As the guardsman charged past the reflection of Verl and swung his sword, the image vanished. Verl could not maintain the illusion on the other side of the horse. Quickly, he recast it behind the horse's left rear. He made the image turn around, raise the staff again. His little dream singer illusion had grown up, become a gaunt, hardened fighter. His mornings of practice in the dungeon under Arax's tutelage, swinging an imagined staff at a unheeding rat had paid off. The guardsman shouted a war cry at the illusion of his escaped prey standing behind him, and tried to pull his horse around to ride him down again.

But the horse, as unaffected by Verl's mind tricks as the rats were, was trying instead to cut back towards the right towards the real Verl. Its rider cursed, yanked on its head towards the reflection he saw of Verl on the left. The horse frothed, strained against the reins, and reared up in the air. The guardsman pulled its head harder to the left, and it obeyed.

As the guardsman swung the sword again at the illusion, Verl circled with the horse, then came closer, and whacked the guardsman on the shoulder with the staff. He ran backwards out of the way as fast as he could.

The guardsman whirled around, then pulled his horse around, but he saw no one there. He whirled his horse back to the left, the horse snorted aloud, ears laid back, confused. The illusion too had vanished. The guardsman spun his balking horse again towards Verl, and this time Verl let him see him, staff in hand, breathing hard. He could not let the guardsman chase only his illusion very far or very long; he could not risk drawing too much attention from any spectator who might be watching, starting to wonder what was going on. As far as he knew, only this one guardsman could see his illusion. For the benefit of the spectators, he had to make his last minute dodges away from the charging horse and swinging sword look desperate and real.

The guardsman yowled in fury when he saw him, and dug his heels into his warhorse to charge Verl again.

And again Verl cast his reflection to go to one side of the horse, while, invisible once more to the guardsman, he ran to the other. The horse charged past him as the guardsman swung his sword. When the guardsman pulled back on the reins to turn him again in the wrong direction, the horse tossed its head in refusal of the reins, planted its forefeet and stopped, its hind legs skidding forwards, its head lowered stubbornly against the straining pull on the reins, its rear end bunching higher. The guardsman went sailing over its head into the dirt.

The trumpet sounded, the first charge was over, one pass was all the mounted guardsmen were allowed. Verl had survived the mêlée longer than he had expected.

The guardsman stood up, yanked off his helmet, and glared at Verl, fury and darkness in his eyes, as he came closer. Then he went to his horse, yanked up the reins, remounted and rode off the field.

Verl turned slowly, finally, looking around the arena. He was the only prisoner left alive.

He watched the priests descend into the field.

~

Arnaby watched the singer fight. The duke had told him the singer could seem to vanish right in front of him. Duke Rayid had said to watch for him, recruit him if he could; as a royal hornblower, he could be a major source of information. Arnaby had inquired around from time to time, but he had not expected to find the singer in the dungeon.

The duke said he was more than a simple dream interpreter. Arnaby had discovered from asking at Singerhalle that Verl was born first son of a village shaman from the Eller Islands. He had the power from his ancient bloodline to form more illusion than just disappearing, Arnaby suspected, watching him in the arena. Seeing him stand waiting for the oncoming guardsman, seeing an instant of blur like a heat wave surrounding him just before he ran forward to one side of the horse while the guardsman sliced his sword through nothing but air on the other side of the horse, then chased his horse's tail.

Luckily, Arnaby didn't think anyone else had seen that instant of blur like he had, nor anything at all suspicious in Verl's actions today that might condemn him for being more magical, more heretical than a simple dream interpreter. For it was the singer being nothing more than a dream interpreter that would save him.

As for the crime that had sent the singer to the dungeon, Arnaby in his guise as a priest had convinced the queen that if Verl survived his trial by ordeal in the arena today, then that would be proof that Verl was innocent, that the hornblower from Navarn on the next horn hill who had been hung as the duke's spy was the only guilty one, and that Verl had not been involved. It had helped persuade the queen of course when Arnaby had told her that Verl was a dream interpreter and her son, the king, needed him.

When the guardsman was unhorsed, when the trumpeter sounded the end of the first mêlée, Arnaby rattled his belled staff.

"Let the day be over," he said to the High Priest of the East Winds who questioned him in surprise for interrupting the holy trial. "There is only one prisoner left,

211

all others are dead. There is no need for a second charge.
And I have here," he pulled a scroll out from under his robe
and handed it to the High Priest, "an order from the Queen
Regent asking that this prisoner be freed if the Winged God
saved him today. What better proof that the Blessed One is
protecting the life of this chosen man as his own, than that
the horse of the very guardsman sent to challenge him goes
wild and uncontrollable near him? The Winged One worked
through the horse to save him! It is a miracle we have just
witnessed! And just" --he gestured at the scroll-- "what the
queen has been praying for, an answer from the Merciful
One to cure the king of his nightmares. This prisoner is a
dream interpreter, he has admitted that. But he is no witch
or sorcerer, he was never sent to the dungeon accused as
one. Indeed the only one to accuse him of such heresy is the
demon's nurse, a condemned witch herself, the very one the
demon instructed to hex the king with his nightmares. She
knew only a god-sent dream interpreter could cure the king.
That is why the nurse accused this prisoner of having demon
powers that would bring him here to the arena today, to kill
him. Instead, he lives! The God in his holy mercy and love
of the king has saved him! He is innocent. More, he is the
God's chosen one."

The High Priest read the queen's orders briefly.
"Then we shall question this prisoner. If the Winged One
has indeed chosen him for the king's salvation, we shall
know from his answers."

~

As Verl watched the priests descend towards him, he
remembered the fake dream interpreter-priest tapping his
finger against the indentation in the staff. *If you live*, the
priest had said, *remember this*. He felt for the indentation
and looked down at the staff. It was carved in holy prayers
and blessings of the Badurian priests, many of which Verl
had studied in his last years at Singerhalle. The fresh small
cut that indented the wood marked the beginning of a
prayer. *Descend your wings upon me, fill me with your
glory, grant me your sight. I am your vessel, I am your
chosen one. Badur.*

212

Verl fell shaking to his knees in front of the high priest, his expression, his voice as full of shining awe and gratitude as Singerhalle training for dramatic performances could make them.

"Glory be to the Winged One! I felt him descend upon me. He has *chosen* me, *saved* me!" Tears rolled down Verl's cheeks, he kissed the priest's robe. "He told me, I shall be his vessel. I shall be granted his sight. Teach me, lord father, what I can do for him."

Chapter 20
Painted Smiles

"Water to fire, hot earth to blood." Merind murmured the ancient formula as she swirled her boarhair brush into the pot of bright red paint. Liquid quicksilver from roasted blood-of-the-earthstone had been added to fiery brimstone to make the black of earth's first night. When that black mud was heated again, it made blood paint.

Blood. How appropriate. She painted the dress of the lead shepherdess on the giant mural encircling the Bear Clan Inn of New Drespin not the green of Capsen morning, not the yellow of veiled evening, not even the white of the midsummer sun overhead, but the bright vermilion of blood that had first been as black as primeval night. She was coloring not life, not joy and promise as tradition called for in the march of the Capsens following Alred out of the wind-swept midlands into their promised land; she was coloring death. The bloody massacre of her friends around her as she sang on a Springing Eve to save only one couple became a twisted red ribbon lacing up the dirndl's bodice. The bloody mucus and pulp of Orist's eyes being squeezed out before her became the bright folds and darker shades of the long red skirt as the shepherdess strode forward into history, her white lambs gamboling around her. Caris's face blistering, the scratch marks bleeding, as she poisoned herself with yew twigs, sacrificing herself so Merind and her other friends could live, became a red kerchief tied gaily around the shepherdess's crook.

No one else may ever know the meaning of the red dress on the clan's new town mural--Merind would certainly never tell anyone. But she herself would never look up at it without remembering every sword thrust, every rape, every suffering of her people under the new king's tyranny. Tears gathered at the corners of her eyes, and for the first time since Springing Eve, she let them come.

She dabbed harder into the can of blood paint, mixed it in with white and yellow until it turned to a rosy flesh, and then she gave the shepherdess Caris's smiling face.

"Red?"

Merind swiped a tear off her cheek as if swatting a fly, then she shrugged down at her mother who was climbing up the scaffold. Ailil's progress was slow. She carried her own heavy set of paints and brushes in a sling hanging off one shoulder, and, making her load heavier and more off-balance, peeking up over her other shoulder was Merind's baby brother strapped to Ailil's back.

"It's a bright color," Merind answered as she took her mother's paints from her and set them down while her mother hung up Eris in his pack on the scaffolding behind them.

"You gave Alred the face of a tinker," Ailil said, studying the life-size fresco of the legendary hero leading the march into history.

Merind finished painting a cheek blushed by sun and hope-filled youth on the shepherdess before she answered. "That tinker has the same two marks, the greater and lesser bear claw wounds on his sides. Your people believe he is Alred come back to life to save them. Let them. Following him, fighting back would be far better than staying here with you, holed up in this forsaken hellpit."

Ailil didn't answer at first. She mixed her colors and began to paint. She chose one of the already traced-in Capsen artisans who had designed the stained glass windows for the throne room of Alred's new-found patron, King Edoff of Norgondy. A few feet beyond Ailil, a widow of a slain Drespin glassmaker worked lovingly on the fresco of another of those famous artisans from two hundred years ago. At the time, Edoff had ruled the land in peace and tolerance, and it was he who, in delight of his new rainbow-filled throne room, granted Alred's people the Capsen valley for all eternity, a homeland finally of their own.

Eternity had proved short-lived. Ailil kept her voice too low for the widow near her to hear. "You may have rarely agreed with me, Merind. And less so now."

215

Merind swirled her brush into the blood-red paint and gave the shepherdess a thin smile. "I'm not staying here," she said.

Ailil darted a glance at her. "I never believed you would. From the moment you arrived, bringing a list of where your friends had been sold, you've not kept your intentions a secret from anyone."

"I'll rescue them one by one. Alone, if I have to." Cricket calls, long promises made beside a river, Merind knew what kind of power she would have alone. It would never be enough, not for the revenge she needed. She could make illusions, nothing more. She set her brush aside, turned around. She clenched the scaffolding and looked out across the ancient crater that had become all that was left of the Capsen world.

The mist-shrouded lake filled more than half the bowl. Trapped along its narrow shores, a dozen new towns rose against the red and black lava cliffs. Merind dug her fingers into the soft pine of the scaffolding, heard crickets mocking any pretensions she'd had that night, any plans she'd made.

A white blur in the sky descended. Merind watched it come closer and form into an ungainly stork. It drifted down to a chimney two houses over and laid a stick on its mate's nest.

The crickets mocked. She heard them, felt them sawing across her veins and sinews inside her head, inside her heart. A stork on your roof was a sign of fortune and stability, a promise of a brighter future.

She turned back around, embittered. She'd agreed to survivors hiding here in the mountains. But not to this permanent rebuilding, not to this total acceptance of Capsen defeat.

"When I came," she said, "I thought there might be some here who'd want to help me save our friends who've been captured, who might still be alive and suffering. That is, if you'd give any of my volunteers permission to leave."

"Permission to be slaughtered?"

Merind stared back at the mother she barely knew.

216

"We can't stand against an army, Merind. Here, our people are safe. We can survive, until times change."

Merind held her breath, held in a mounting rage. "Staying here won't make those times change."

"No. But any Capsen captured outside these hills, neither you nor I can protect. From what I've heard most recently, the priests are in control of the country now, and the horrors you've seen committed by the guardsmen under orders from the queen will be nothing in comparison. The queen only wanted Henrik's son and me killed, and our people no longer a threat to her. The priests want more. They want our beliefs dead too. That means all of us. Had a priest been with the troops that massacred our people and burned Drespin, neither you nor any of your friends would have been left alive to be sold into servitude."

Merind's pulse throbbed like cricket calls hurting louder and louder through her. "I'm not staying here," she repeated, stiffer than before, and turned to leave.

Her mother caught her arm, held it. "I know." Merind saw the look then in Ailil's eyes above her tellerwoman veil. There was a determination in them that Ailil did nothing to hide.

"Inside my trunk downstairs in my room," Ailil said, "you'll find a scroll. I want you to take it with you when you go, take it to Duke Rayid of Navarn, ask for his help. He'll remember me." Ailil released Merind's arm and turned back to the mural.

Merind watched her mother color in the glass puzzle pieces on the rose window the artisan was designing. She recognized the pattern; he was cutting the window that would shine the winter sign, Zaire's Sword, onto the floor of the king's throne room. *Zaire's Sword*--that could cut through your enemies, or that could cut through to your own truth. "Why?" Merind asked. "Why did you allow this happen? How could you let her do this to us? To you? To your own baby son?"

"Let who? Queen Felain? She is the queen of Norgondy now; that's why. Would that she were our only problem."

"Priests or no priests, she is the murderer of our people. She's raped your daughters, killed your sons, and you, you could have stopped her, long time ago, you could have stopped her. Before any of this started happening. Henrik would have never allowed the priests to take control of his realm."

Ailil paused only a moment, then started painting again, without answering. Merind went on, in a torrent of words, asking questions she'd never dared asked of a mother she'd rarely seen, of a mother who was the beloved idol of her people.

"Her son's a mere puppet!" A few feet away, the widow stopped painting and looked up at them; and beyond her, a young husband and wife had stopped their work on the mural to glance at them too. Merind lowered her voice. "Her son's a puppet, no more a king ready to sit on his father's throne than Eris here is, shitting in his papoose. Less ready. You at least never beheaded their father."

"Nor yours," Ailil said softly.

The crickets went silent, and Merind no longer heard her pulse. "What?"

"I met Henrik in our youth, Merind. He had three children. One before he became king."

Merind opened her mouth, but no words came out. She glanced at her baby brother gurgling at her, then back at her mother who had set her brushes aside and was watching her now.

"He never knew about you, Merind."

"I've always been told you never knew my father's name. Just a stranger at a Springing Eve dance."

Eris gurgled again, louder, and punched his arms around, as if he had always known.

"Well, now you know differently," her mother said. "I lived at court with Henrik, only coming here to have you. But I was a counselor to him, not his wife. He did ask me to marry him, but I never would. If I had, all our lands, twenty years ago, would have been lost, become property of my husband and the Crown. I would have dispossessed all our people, we would have given up all our freedom to be who we are.

"In time, Henrik married Felain instead. He needed an heir, he was told. I gave Felain my friendship, and I never gave her reason to be jealous of my friendship with Henrik. But all the years she was barren...she started blaming me, believing I'd cast a spell on their marriage. After her son was born, she only got worse, more hysterical than ever, seeing assassins around every corner, hearing slander from every mouth, until Henrik could take no more and sent her away. When the Badurian priests came to see her in her castle on the coast, they found somebody all too ready to believe anything they said. You say I could have stopped her years ago? I never wished her harm. And so instead, her army shot Henrik with an arrow, and captured him. I had to run, I had to save our son. But when I came back to find Henrik, she was having him beheaded."

"I never knew..." Merind could think of nothing else to say.

"We learn to keep our secrets, we tellerwomen especially, you and I, weavers of dreams and lies. But I'm telling you this now, Merind, for a reason. You're not only a tellerwoman who can shape illusions that men believe are more real than what is there, you're heir to another power too. You're Henrik's daughter. You have a choice to make. One I never could."

Merind met her mother's demand a long moment, then she nodded. "I'll leave tonight. I'll take your letter to the duke. But then afterwards, I'm tracking down my friends."

"One last thing, Merind. I know you have as strong a power as I do, if not more, to shape what men will see. And to control that power, I know you've learned enough not to believe in your own illusions. But remember too, when Orist taught you to paint years ago, he taught you another wisdom of our people. To not only stand from the outside looking in at what you've created, but to put yourself inside your painting, and look back out and see yourself reflected, to see yourself for who you are, as others will see you in it. You gave the shepherdess Caris' face. You gave Caris a red dress. What does Caris see now when she looks back at you? When you make your choice of who

219

you want to be, will your friend here on this wall still recognize you?"

Merind gazed into Caris's painted eyes, her flushed cheek, her blood red lips. The crickets were silent, no longer mocking her. Their rhythm pulsed subliminally through her, a constant, triumphant sawing now. She was Caris's friend, her sworn avenger. And she was Henrik's daughter too.

She answered her mother. "What's happened to our world cannot go on. We have to stop it. For Henrik's sake. For all our people's sake. And to do so, I will make my brother king, if I have to. Or die trying."

Little Eris gurgled louder than ever, and batted his fists around in the air above his papoose.

~

Ailil watched her daughter descend the scaffolding, her brow knitting slightly under the green lace hood of her veil. She could be playing a dangerous game, she knew; Henrik was not Merind's father.

But as long as Merind believed he was, then Queen Felain would finally have the fate she deserved.

Her frown dissolving to a smile, Ailil hummed the Capsen summer growth song to Eris in his papoose as she finished her section of the fresco.

~

Verl felt a lifetime away from the dungeon. He poured oils of wintergreen, rosemary, beebalm into the hot bathwater and lay back in the marble tub and closed his eyes. The steam curled around him, he could feel the heat of it seeping into his cheeks. The heady combination of the scents intoxicated him, and the hot spiced water found aches he never knew he had and soothed them away. The water pressed into his shoulders, his back, his thighs–his toes! he could feel every single toe. He wiggled them, and felt the water flowing around them. He lifted his hand out of the suds, water sparkles dripped from it. He spread open his fingers, incredulous. If he had died in the arena, if this were his dream of death in the Ellison Fields, then that could explain this feeling of timelessness, this sense of floating, this denial of every memory of a prior life.

When the bell tower struck three bells, he lifted himself out of the priest's tub, dried, shaved, and put on the silk tunic and leggings the spy priest had laid out for him.

Arnaby walked in as he was tying his sleeves.

Arnaby handed him a velvet cap, and nodded in approval as Verl positioned it. "You've cleaned up well. Looking at you now, no one would guess there was even a shadow of you fighting for your life this morning."

Verl paused, his fingers still smoothing the hair below the cap. He noted a slight emphasis in Arnaby's words when he had said "a shadow of you." He didn't know how to react to Arnaby, how to trust him. He knew Arnaby had disguised himself as a guard who had disobeyed the queen when the duke came to her court, allowing the duke to escape with his life. He knew Arnaby had been at his trial every day as a priest. He knew Arnaby had given him the clue that saved his life in the arena this morning when the high priest came down to interrogate him. He did not know whether this priest, if he were a priest, had seen anything Verl had done in the arena that would make his words "a shadow of you fighting" be more meaningful than they sounded.

Verl turned to the mirror, saw a reflection of a courtier looking back at him. He answered with a courtier's wary duplicity.

"That was a different man this morning." He straightened the tunic of the courtier in the mirror. "Not me at all."

"Whoever he was, that was quite a conversion he had afterwards."

Verl met the spy-priest's eyes. They were dark, shadowed by his hood. "He was fortunate, he had holy guidance telling him what to do and say."

Arnaby grinned. "His fortune one day may depend on him remembering that."

The priest went to his cabinet, and took out his incense burner and lit it. The sickly sweet, pungent stench of the smoke reminded Verl that the air in the priest's room

221

while he'd been bathing and dressing had been blissfully free of the holy incense that permeated the rest of the palace wherever the priests walked. Another sign that Arnaby in private was no Badurian priest?

Incense in one hand, Arnaby grabbed his belled staff propped against the cabinet and pulled his hood farther down over his face. "Come," he said. "We'll talk further on your...conversion another time and--" he glanced around significantly, "another place. Your services are needed now. You are a dream interpreter, your father was a Village Father on the Eller Islands. The king has been having nightmares. Follow me."

~

Crel's coracle bobbed gently in the river. The midsummer sun, just setting in the west, cast an vibrant glow around him, making the sweep of the willow leaves greener, the long tall wave of the reeds oranger. A bull frog croaked. A crane stretched its long neck toward the line of salmon traps across the river, watching the wild bobbing of the closest one to the shore. A large salmon had just snagged in it. The crane waded closer, arched its head, then jabbed down at it quickly, but came up with nothing. The weave on the baskettrap was too fine for more than the tip of a beak.

In the coracle, Crel sketched the poised crane onto the back of a piece of birch bark. All day long lulled by the water, quiet conversation and laughter with his twin brother, yet instead of relaxing, he'd found his hands needed to keep working. Yesterday, Crel had brought a copper vase to emboss with river scenes, but the bobbing made the knife scratch stray marks, ruining his design. Tomorrow morning, while Clayl worked his nets, Crel would emboss a copy of the crane he was sketching onto a new vase.

Lissiv, his brother's new wife, came through the golden field of flax and stopped among the reeds along the far shore, waving her long blue and red plaid kerchief at them. Smoke rose from Clayl's stone hut on the hill; dinner was ready. Crel set his sketch and piece of charcoal away in a canvas pouch behind him and picked up his paddle to go help his brother empty the laden salmon traps into the bottom of their small round coracles. He whistled as he paddled with the current toward the closest trap. He'd be here a month waiting for his new traveling papers to be sent to the capital and returned with the new king's signature on it. A month of tranquility and rest in his island homeland still as quaint in belief and time-lost ways as it ever had been, a haven still blessedly forgotten by the terror of witch burnings and new high taxes scourging the mainland.

As Lissiv ladled out three bowls of fish stew, she mentioned the merchant ship that had brought a Norgon guardsman into their village today. He'd asked for stories about men who could change into bears, and recorded any other beliefs and stories anyone would tell him, paying a copper talent for any new wag-tongue gossip. The laugh was on him, Lissiv said, jiggling her apron pocket. Islanders were not prone to selling their histories and whale songs to strangers, but the women of the longhouse had taken turns today making up a batch of wild tales to sell to that seagoose mainlander.

"Brother Crel, you're not eating very much tonight," Lissiv said.

~

The spy priest took Verl to an anteroom near the king's chamber. Stepping into the room was like walking thirteen years back in time. The whole room had been transferred into an Eller Island dreaming hut down to the last detail. The walls had been laid with white stone, and the lone window opened to sea breeze. The door from the inside was roughhewn island cypress and a log of the fibrous cypress served as the one bench. A fire had been started in the giant clam shell in front of the log, and to one side of it lay a basket of saw reed and a whale skin pouch of crushed numbstool for sprinkling on the fire to produce the hallucinogenic stabbing smoke. Just thinking of the smell it would make, Verl could remember the comfortable sleepiness of his father's hearth.

To the other side of the fire were the drawing stick and a circle of smoothed sand waiting for him to make a dream pentagon. And beyond the sand lay the dreaming mat.

Arnaby tugged on Verl's sleeve and pointed to three vials of face paint on a rock shelf beside the door: the red, black and gold of the death god's mask. Verl met Arnaby's eyes and nodded a thank-you. Arnaby left the room, closing the door softly behind him, leaving Verl alone with his memories.

Verl painted his face as his father had, the last time he had seen him. Vicious, stern swirls of black, sharp lightning strikes of gold. Closing his eyes, smoothing the paint onto his cheeks and high brow, he felt tempted to shave and tattoo his head in god symbols too, and to put on a white linen robe, using a turban as a belt, revealing his shaven head for the ceremony. He needed no mirror; like instinct, his fingers became his father's fingers painting on the frightening swirls, the wide black lips, the red-stained teeth. Show, he knew from his years at Singerhalle, the show of how he looked and acted here tonight would create half the effect he wanted, bringing the dreamer under his power and suggestion. The other half would be the smoke.

Verl knelt on the cypress log, and added three hands of saw reed, one hand of numbstool to the low fire, and started chanting his father's words. Again. Three hands of saw reed, one of numbstool, chanting; again. The smoke billowed, gagging him, little rose high enough to escape the narrow window. His father's hand, younger than his father's hand, smoother, long musician fingers, held the drawing stick. He saw the black stick jut up through the smoke, followed it down, saw the hand draw the pentagon in the sand, all five symbols in its corners, no hesitation making the one he never knew how to make, the spiral of forgetfulness at the top. He knew the symbol now, by instinct he knew it, or by practice, his father's hand knew it.

His consciousness, his being, stepped inside the dream pentagon and waited. His body still chanted above him, red, black, gold god paint swirled on his face.

The cypress door creaked open and the seven year old boy king entered. Verl's father lifted his long musician's bony finger and pointed to the dreaming mat.

In the heavy smoke it was barely a heart beat before the young king was asleep. Verl saw him asleep on the mat through eyes still open on his chanting body above him, but Verl saw him small, awake, looking around him lost inside a tunnel of blackness through the smoke, a shining spark of light seeking him where he stood inside the pentagon. Verl's hand scratched a tilted crown below him in the pentagon, then he stepped into the tunnel and took the young king's hand.

Together they fell through darkness, swirling stars, lightning flashes, blinding light, and landed on the cobblestone streets of Norgarth outside the city gates near the port. Young Laird tried to pull his hand away, shake his head no, and Verl heard him whimper. Very gently, firmly, Verl pulled him forward past the docks to a small blue cove ringed by a white beach and dark cliffs. Laird's hand slipped out of Verl's grasp and reached for his sword. Wave after wave of the ocean came in, each cresting higher. White sea foam splashed on them, stinging cold against their cheeks. Up out of the sea foam rose a head, crystal white, a blue light shining through its vacant eyes and its laughing, sallow cheeks. "Father," the young king whispered and raised his sword.

The head of ice looked down at them, and as he opened his mouth to laugh a heartier laugh that boomed with the crash of a sea wave over them, Verl recognized the old king too.

In fury, the young king beside him stormed into the laughing mouth, and with Verl beside him, whacked at the teeth of ice that clattered louder and louder with each maddened swing. Old Henrik laughed aloud with the booms of a crashing waves, and then bit down, and closed his mouth upon them.

From inside his eyes of ice, Verl and Laird watched the next giant wave swallow the beach, the city, palace, tower gates and all.

Verl stepped back out of the dream pentagon. The boy-king was crying on the mat before him.

"Rise, King Laird, it is over," he said softly and held out his hand to the young boy. "We go to your mother now."

Each step closer to the throne room, Verl heard his choices echoing on the flagstones. To tell the dream as he had seen it, or to tell the safer lie they wanted to hear.

He had no intention of getting sent back to the dungeon.

He bowed before the queen regent and the young king on his throne. A circle of priests stood nearby, Arnaby among them.

"Good news, your lady. King Laird has no more to fear. His dream is frightening to a seven year old, unable to see its promises. He'll be a great king as he grows older, greater than the father he has defeated, his face and bravery will replace his father's memory in the hearts of all his people. And like a great tide sweeping over and swallowing us all, he will live forever in our tales."

Chapter 21
Bear Man

Jesser wailed. It was an ear-splitting sound Crel had never heard her make before. It echoed off chalk cliffs, resounded around the cove, and ebbed and grew again with the crash of the waves as the sleek Islander whaler lurched into them. With each high lift and splashing fall of the boat, the bear skidded across her cage. Her hay and blankets removed before the voyage, her claws scraped uselessly against the iron floor, and her rump and shoulders heaved into the iron bars every time she lost her footing. And as the next wave, then the next, splashed over the bow of the boat and whipped the bear's snout with stinging salt spray, she raised her head towards the sky and, in terror, wailed.

"Peace, Jesser. We're almost there." Crel kept his voice low, his words simple. But as the bow rose again, the bear stomped one hind foot then the other, and shook her fur dry in the cage above him, drenching him all over again. His whaleskin cape covered him from neck to boots, but left his face unprotected, and the sour taste of brine and wet bear fur lurched in choking, unswallowable waves inside him. "Peace, Jesser." Trying to comfort the bear had no more effect on her than if he had yelled curses at her to shut the hell up.

Yelling curses at her might have had a better effect on him, though.

Still, the concern and pity on his twin brother's face every time she wailed implored Crel to at least sound like he wanted to help her. His brother and the other two islander fishermen had their hands full fighting the waves and steering the boat past the rocks into the cove. Crel pushed against the rocks and tried oaring in rhythm with them, but he'd had little experience in what he was doing and the oar in his hand was useless if not a hindrance when he stroked too early or too late. The only thing he could do to help the fishermen was to take care of the bear-- and yet he had not the heart to tell his brother the truth: there was nothing he

227

could say or do now to quiet her. The Eller Islanders, in all their simple ways and quaint beliefs, had a deep faith that animal spirits would respond to men, their brothers. If Wiss indeed still lived inside the bear as he'd claimed he would-- which in all but long lonely nights beside the campfire Crel doubted--but if he did, that might be one thing, but the bear herself had never on her own responded to anything Crel wanted her to do. Not when *she* wanted otherwise.

And she clearly now wanted to wail her guts out to the sky. A splash of salt water crashed into her eyes again.

"Hush, Jesser. You're all right." He crooned to her. For the sake of his brother's concern, he crooned to her. Clayl's face was physically a mirror of his own, but Crel felt none of the pity in his twin's face now. Not when Jesser was making such a damnable ear-shattering noise.

"*Peace*, Jesser." She shook more water onto him.

The cage was latched onto the deck of the shallow boat. Her cart, upended was latched on top of it, the wheels latched to the sides of the cage. The boom of the single sail barely cleared the cage and the cart beneath it. There was little room left on the whaler for the four men, and no room at all for Crel's tinker wagon and other animals, all of which would have easily fit in the cargo hold of a merchant ship.

But Crel could not have waited for a merchant ship. He'd had to get the bear off the islands immediately once that guardsman came and started asking the villagers if anyone had seen a man with a bear act. Or worse, if anyone had heard stories about a man turning into a bear. An islander, a brother of the whale, would never tell a mainlander the truth of his beliefs, Crel knew that, and so had never feared the Badurian priests taking interest in them. But now, his presence had put the islanders in as much danger of being accused of witchcraft and false beliefs. He'd tried warning his family and friends not to make up far-fetched stories to match the guardsman's tale of a shape-shifting bearman, but laughing in their longhouses and taverns, joking about the mainlanders' credulity, they still insisted their stories could hide Crel. Within a day, he realized there was no way he could stop them from telling their outrageous stories, short of leaving the island and getting the bear away. He couldn't wait a week for a merchant ship.

And so, for the first time, the bear was not riding in the dark blind comfort of a cargo hold. Instead, she could see the sea splashing up waves and wild froth at her, and, drenched and wailing, the bear was definitely not pleased with what she saw.

"Shh, Jesser." Crel wished to the Goron he could tell her to sit down and shut the hell up.

~

Once past the rocks, the ship sailed more calmly into the protected cove. The keel came to rest in the shallow water a few yards from the sandy beach. The men jumped out and started unlashing the cart and the cage. Crel opened the cage. "Jesser," he started, thinking after all her commotion, he'd have trouble coaxing her out.

But the instant she saw her freedom, she bounded past him, crushing him against the cage door. She landed in the water with a splash, and then, as if she were the happiest bear in the world, *damn her*, never one to wail outrage at the sky, she started playing in the water, slapping at the waves, trying to catch the curling breakers in her snapping jaws, then rising on her hind legs, she waded out into the waves, deeper and deeper. The sea was no enemy to her, her fear of it completely forgotten.

In relief, Crel unloaded the one thing he'd stowed in the back of the cage, Wiss's old trunk, all evidence of the bear act taken safely away from the island. When his traveling papers signed by the new king would finally come next month, his twin brother could dress himself in Crel's woolen tinker jacket and breeches and take the next merchant ship to Sonachin harbor where Crel, after hiding the bear in the woods south of town, could go meet him and collect the rest of his belongings. The port captain in Sonachin who had signed Crel's papers to go to his home island to await his new passport could be the first to sign the new papers that Clayl, dressed as Crel, would hand to him, and the captain would never know the difference between them. There would be no reason for him to be suspicious,

229

no way to connect the tinker Crel with the bearman they were seeking, and Crel would be free to move on.

"Now, ye have all the money ye be needing to get yerself a new ox to pull the cart, ye sure?" The cage was back on the cart, and the other two fishermen were back on their boat anxious to set sail before low tide left them beached for the night. But the two brothers were delaying their parting. This last month was the most time they'd spent together since Crel had been sold in apprenticeship to Wiss at age twelve.

"More than enough," Crel assured him. He was in no more hurry to see his brother go, but he could see the other islanders measuring once again how far out the tide was getting. They would never call Clayl over, never interrupt them, but they were worried. "Go," Crel told his brother. "You need to."

Clayl hiked up his whaleskin cape and untied a sack hanging from his side. "Lissiv packed up a roll or two for ye. She'll have my ear all night long if ye won't take it."

Crel nodded gratefully and tied it to his side. "Thank her. Thank you. Keep her hearth lit well, and her flax fields sown full and golden. And above all else, tell her not to tell another wild tale of magic and false spirits to any mainlander who comes asking. It's not safe times for that now."

His brother gaffed. "Mainlanders have no sense to know what is true and what is true."

"Promise me," Crel said, holding his brother's shoulder. "And have *her* promise you. Now go, before your friends have to wait the night out on the wrong side of the sea."

Clayl nodded. "Peace of the whale's dreams go with ye, brother. I'll see ye next month."

"Peace of his dreams with you, too."

Crel watched them set full sail past the rocks, then he picked up the shafts of the cart and lifted the yoke to his chest. With the cage empty, leading Jesser on her long chain, he could pull the small cart himself until he found a farmer willing to part with an ox or a mule. He could only hope in the mean time that Jesser would be willing, every

230

once in the while, to go in the same direction he wanted. He pushed the sailor's striped stocking cap Lissiv had woven for him to one side of his head and whistled to the sea wind as he started pulling.

~

That evening, with Jesser chained at full length to a tree near their campfire, Crel waited patiently beside a rabbit run deeper in the woods, sling shot pulled and ready. He had already killed two coneys, enough to feed the bear, now he wanted one for himself.

A twig snapped behind him, and Crel glanced around.

Nothing but trees and bushes. He felt no breeze, but a branch on one of the bushes was moving.

He was well off the road. Whatever was in the woods with him should be nothing to worry about, except maybe a cougar or wolf interested in him, attracted by the smell of his catch. And, more wary than he, rarely wanting a fight, sudden noise and arm waving would drive most cats or wolves away. Hand to his knife, Crel turned quietly back to the rabbit run, alerted now, listening to the woods around him more closely.

Another step on crackling timber. This one too loud for any stalking animal.

"Who's there?" He rose, spun around in time to see a leg clad in leather, pint-sized, disappearing behind a tree.

Crel darted to the other side of the tree, caught hold of a youth, dirtied-faced, maybe eight or nine, a short bow slung across his back. The boy tried to squirm away from Crel's grasp, and screamed.

"Hey, hey, hush there." Crel loosened his hold, but he didn't release him. "I'm not going to hurt you. Where'd you come from? Why were you spying on me?"

The lad stuck his chin up bravely, quit yelling. "You're him, aren't you? I saw your bear."

"Him?"

"*The Bearman*. Are you going to change into him now? Are you going to eat me?"

231

Crel opened and closed his mouth before he could answer. But his grip on the lad's arm tightened. No way could he let him go now. He raised his other hand, denying everything. "I have a bear on a chain back in my camp. She does tricks for me. I don't know what else you're talking about. We're new to this area, never done a show around here before. Maybe you're talking about someone else. Another bear act. Who is it you took me for?"

"The Bearman. He can change into one. Be a bear, or be a man, or be both, side by side. The many in one. His name is Crel."

Crel's breath stopped. "Where'd you hear that?"

The lad stuck his chin up higher. "Not many know his name. But we do."

Crel glanced around the woods. "We?"

"The Bearman's Men. My father's band. The tilemaker told us his name." The lad lowered his voice, nodded as if telling a secret, and squinted his eye. "But the Bearman might just eat you if he catches you."

Crel sorted out the lad's answers. "The tilemaker?-- Come here," he said more sternly than he intended. He shook his head in consternation, and pulled the lad with him around the tree.

When the lad pulled back, fear again in his widening eyes, Crel gentled his grip and his voice. "Come."

He led the lad to his catch of two coneys. He lifted them up. "Do you see these? These are what my bear eats. I was going to have one too, if you hadn't made so much noise and frightened the rest from coming out. Neither one of us eat children."

But Crel never convinced him, he didn't think, though he tried all the way to his father's camp. Highwaymen, forest dwellers, refugees from the inquisition; in hovels made of peat, in lean-tos made of willow and hide, in tents made of patchwork quilts hung loosely over low branches; hunger in their eyes, suspicion in their whispers, lies behind their welcome. Such was the band of the Bearman's Men. Freyshin, the tilemaker, his grey beard grown long and thorn-ridden, recognized him and stood up from the fire.

232

"Crel? Crel!"

The tile-maker's golden-haired daughter peeked out at Crel from behind a tent-flap.

"What's happened to you?" Crel breathed.

Irony was in Freyshin's crooked smile. "Welcome! Come, sit down, my friend." He raised an expansive arm towards an empty boulder near the central fire pit. A lone wispy trail of smoke vanished up beyond the tree-tops, testament to the camp's one luxury. "My friends, my friends." The tilemaker spun around him in a circle, his arms held out wide to everyone. "Our leader has come. This is Crel! The Bearman."

~

"Impossible!" Crel said, alone with the tilemaker and his daughter in their hovel. "I refuse."

"You can't. We need you. We need the stories about you. It's our one way to fight back. The priests are starting to believe there is a shapeshifter god, the Bearman, the enemy to their god."

"How...?" Crel shook his head.

"It didn't need much embellishment at first. The story of your miracle escapade in Sonachin spread quickly, some people believing it, some of us taking advantage of it. I, for my part, never told anyone otherwise. And since then, you've been spotted everywhere, stories coming in from all over the realm. A Bear appears here; a man in your jester's mask there. Sometimes two, three appearances on the same night, from towns and villages leagues away from each other, and another taxman loses the priest's tithings he's collected that day. Maybe he loses a share too of the king's taxes, but those he'd have to pay back. Sometimes it's your own band of men dedicated to your service who've relieved him of his funds. But sometimes, it could just as well be," the old tilemaker lifted his mug of ale in salute, "the taxman himself who dips his hand into his locked treasure box, and when he comes up short, why" --the tilemaker shook his mug and oohed as if he just saw a ghost, then winked at Crel-- "the poor man had barely escaped with his life from the ferocious jaws of the Bearman, who was stealing the holy funds from him, to hear him tell about it. Some stories of your powers have become truly amazing."

Crel could only shake his head again, staring into his emptied mug. The tilemaker's daughter rose and refilled his mug. She met his eyes, smiled. Pretty, he thought, even in rags. He was glad she lived, saved from the fire or the dungeon, glad she had survived undisfigured. What small part he'd played in that night's deed to save her, he was not sorry about. ...Just about the consequences afterwards.

"It's only been one month," he objected. He took a deep swig of the ale.

"One month, and a saucy song flies far and wide from the beaks of gossiping jays."

Crel threw up a hopeless hand at his inability to stop any such stories now. The girl smiled wider at his gesture and met his eyes.

"I never thanked you for saving me," she said.

"My pleasure," Crel said, then appraised her look and saluted his mug to her. But even as he accepted the promise of a later, greater show of her gratitude in the tiny extra lift in her lips and quick nod, his own smile faded. It was not her face he saw, not the challenge in her smile revealed once and only once below a dropped veil that he remembered from three months ago. He'd never found Merind again, not yet, but that witchwoman still haunted him, and it had been so with every girl he had met since.

He turned back to Sylvan's father. "Only one month," he repeated. "One month."

"One month, and you're a hunted man now everywhere. Even guardsmen have their tales to tell about seeing you, pursuing you, almost catching you, before you turned into a giant bear and attacked them. Every time they need a convenient alibi for losing a prisoner or two. Your bands of followers are growing everywhere. With a simple jester mask and outfit, or sometimes maybe a bear's growl, or a scrape of a bear's claw carved into a tree trunk, and it's becoming easy to release whomever we want," the tilemaker guffawed, "right after the guardsman pees in his pants and runs in fear of you."

"Surely–"

234

"No, you're right, not always so easy. But we're learning how to get the most steadfast disbelieving guardsman distracted by your sudden appearance, or evidence of it. And once he starts chasing after you, or someone disguised as you, he leaves his post clear and we come in. Whoever pays enough to have someone saved by you, it's most likely become possible for us to do it. After all, it's usually less than our client would have to pay the taxman or the priests to reconsider his familyman's guilt. And sometimes, all it takes to pay us, is someone who truly professes to believe in you instead of that Badurian devil god. You'll find there a quite a few of us who do, who believe in the stories we ourselves made up"--his grin was ironic again--"if we tell them often enough. Come. I'll show you something."

The tilemaker opened a long wooden box at the back of his hovel. Inside was a row of hand-painted tiles depicting the legend of the Bearman who came to Sonachin, first as a jester with a dancing bear, then as a figure in the dark treasury room opening a chest of gold that glowed like magic shining up into his face, then of a guardsman capturing the masked jester at sword point, then of the jester transforming into an avenging bear and attacking the guard. The final tile was a simple design of a bear's claw. Five long claw marks sunbursting away from the pad of the paw. Underneath each tile were stacks of other tiles, maybe four or five under the first few, but under the last two tiles, the one of the changed Bearman attacking the guard and the one of the bear claw design, the stacks of tiles were almost as tall as the lid of the box. "This is what I do these days. Once a week, I slip back into town to fire and glaze them. I bring all the tiles I can away with me, and paint them here, showing the truth of your legend to all who want to know."

"The truth?" Crel held his breath and his annoyance in.

"The truth is what people believe. Or what someone tells them they believe. And here," he gestured around him widely, indicating the Bearman's camp, "I've become the one doing the telling! These last two tiles, these, whenever the deed is good, whenever we need evidence that you've

235

been somewhere, saving someone, or stealing back our stolen money, these are left where they're sure to be found." He shrugged. "They've actually become my best sellers. I get orders for one every two to three days. After all these years, you've made my fortune, my friend."

Crel closed the box lid gently. "Why? What made you leave town? What brought you here, to this? Your clay pit and shop, Freyshin, have been in your family for generations."

Freyshin was silent a moment, then nodded at his daughter. "I thought all was worked out too, when you left. But then the next day, a devil of a guardsman came around asking questions. He's the only one I'll give credit to for having the intelligence to think for himself. He wanted to know how it was that I'd suddenly had enough money to pay off my taxes, and then enough to buy Sylvan's release from the priests, when I hadn't had any money left the day before, and when, the night before, the exact same amount of funds from the taxman's lockbox had been stolen. Had I perhaps known anything about a so-called Bearman?" Freyshin shrugged his hands admitting defeat, and shook his head. "He was connecting too much, and Sylvan and I might never get away from him. I told him I'd sold my pit and kiln to my neighbor who'd been wanting the land for years. He wanted proof. And the next day I had to make good my claim and give him a copy of the deed that sold my father's land to my neighbor." Freyshin looked away to the dark wall of his tent hovel and was silent for longer than he had been before. "Considering the price my neighbor bought it all for, he's quite inclined to be generous now, enough to look the other way on a moonless night when I slip back in to fire up the kiln to make more tiles.

"And yet still, that guardsman, he kept questioning me, kept demanding to know if that's where the ransom money came from." Freyshin met Crel's eyes, raised his mug and swilled the last of his ale. "I couldn't risk Sylvan's life again, staying there, or anywhere else but here. Simple as that."

～

Back in his own camp, Crel lay with his hands behind his head, staring up at the stars. A few feet away, at the end of her chain, Jesser was snuffling, scratching, snuffling under a fallen log. No telling what she had found.

The patch of sky above the clearing was shell-strewn crowded with stars. That constellation there, that was part of what the Capsens called the Hunter Bear, the first constellation Wiss had pointed out to him years ago, one of the easiest ones still for Crel to identify. Five stars in a semi-circle, a sixth and a seventh brighter stars, hidden now behind a tree, would be about...there, haloed by their arc.

How anyone could make a bear shape out of those seven stars, Crel had never understood.

He propped himself up on an elbow, pounded open a few walnuts from a stash he'd collected along the road from the cove today. He clicked his tongue to alert Jesser and tossed her a couple, then popped one into his mouth. "Fine mess of my life you've made for me now, Jesserwiss. You wouldn't believe what I was told tonight."

He lay back down, folded an arm behind his head again. ...Who's to say those two stars over there, those four stars making a long box there, and that one too, that faint one, who's to say they couldn't be added to that arc and make instead a join-the-dot stick man hung upside down? Who decided these constellations anyway, who's to say which star has to belong to which? He popped in another nut, chewed it. Damn. Who'd ever want to spend their lives making pictures and stories out of stars? Scattered dots of light. "Wiss," he said aloud to the bear, as if his old master were still inside her, "you never told me something. Why I have to see in stars what someone else did? Call them what someone else did who died centuries ago." The stars were prettier when he didn't know what to call them. When he could just see them as stars, not as something else.

Patterns, he supposed. Constellations were patterns. That was what Ailil had said in that cave. Men always had to look for patterns, always had to solve a riddle out of everything around them.

Or else make one up when there wasn't one there. He hadn't been able to escape that cave himself without

237

trying to see some kind of pattern in the jumbled mix of five symbols. Without trying to make some kind of order out of them. His answer to their riddle had finally been to paint *damn!* on the five waiting lines, and Ailil had laughed.

But to see stories in stars. To believe them important in your life. To believe they'd give answers to you.

Years ago, when he was still a young boy, he'd grown out of looking for shapes in shifting clouds. But at least clouds kept changing, kept giving him new ideas, new answers when he needed them. The shapes and patterns that someone else claimed seeing in stars hadn't changed for centuries.

He pointed up, renamed the constellation he had just made up, the join-the-dot man hung upside down from the tree. "Damn you, that's your name now. Damn You." He pointed to each of the four stars of the body: "D. A. M. N."

Then he laughed with no humor left, sat up, and hung his head into his hands.

A few moments later, he sighed, leaned forward, added a stick to the fire, watched it spark.

"Tell me, Jesser." She grunted, raised her head. "When you look up at the sky, do you see anything besides dots of light? Shiny stones scattered by an avalanche maybe?" The bear twitched an ear, then ignored him and started digging again. "Well to tell you the truth, I don't see much more either."

But some people must. Generation after generation. They told the same stories, pointed out the same constellations, kept believing that someone else's pattern, someone else's answer could affect their own lives.

"Freyshin said much the same thing tonight, Wiss. Truth, or what most people want to believe is true is what someone else has told them to believe.

"And you know what's the worst thing with what he said? Freyshin admitted he's now the one doing the telling! Telling everyone to believe I, we -- We're some kind of legend." He ran a hand through his hair, squeezed his head tight. "Ah, the Goron... I'm as damned as that hanged man up there. He's trapped me in a lie, Wiss, one I may never get free from."

238

He shook an accusing finger at the bear. "It won't be the first time I got trapped though. The first time was your fault. Your brother, Orist. Asking me not to tell his people I was not their great leader Alred come back to life. In exchange for that, for keeping my mouth shut--for keeping a bear with me-- I got to take over your wagon, take over your trade. It would have taken me years to build up my own route...

"I trapped myself, I guess, that time. But this time--

"Wiss, what can I do? People want lies, want legends to believe in when they have nothing else. Orist as much as said that. Freyshin tonight too. They want to make a legend out of me, some story seen in a constellation, grasping at a promise they see in shifting clouds--

"Shifting clouds." Crel chuckled, then shook his head. "Yeah, I can play that part. You taught me well, old man. The law of the road for merchants. If I want to stay in business and be left alone to do so, tell whoever's in power, I'm loyal to them. Loyal to whatever new king rules the realm. Well there's two kings ruling me now. One sitting on the throne in Norgarth, one here in the woods all around me, making up stories about me. And I, their shifting cloud. Easy as a shell game, you and I. We'll be what they want. Be what they think they see." He picked up a walnut shell, showed it to the bear. "Look. I'm here, see? You and I, trapped inside this shell they've made for us. They call us the Bearman. And they'll follow us, around and around, following their phantom legend they've made of us. Then one day, look." He swirled the nutshell around in the air as if shifting its position, then turned it over. "Gone. Empty. We're no longer there. Once I get my wagon, when I no longer need them hiding us, we'll be on our way. No...no wait." He pointed the shell at the bear. "They want to follow us, then one of them still can, follow me not us. Bring you in your cart half a day behind me. No one would ever know you were still with me. And no guardsman looking for a bearman will ever look twice again at me. Yes!" He nodded his head, threw the nut shell into the fire. "May work. May work indeed." He pitched the last nutmeat to Jesser, lay back down, crossed his arms behind

239

his head, looked up, and grinning sardonically, began to whistle courage to the hanged man above him.

~

Three days later, Crel was invited to his first Bearman trial. "Not that we ask anything of you, friend. But so you can see what we're doing for you."

What they were doing for him? Or what they were doing for themselves, Crel felt like asking. But he kept his irritation to himself and followed the tilemaker through the woods.

The path was not easy. The woods grew thick and overgrown. Hanging tendrils and vines spider-webbed his view. Close twigs and branches scratched his arms and poked in at his sides. At each turn, Crel eyed every tree trunk for a notch, every bush for stripped branches, for some kind of landmark he never saw that told the Bearman's Men which abandoned deer trail to follow. It made him nervous that he never saw one; he glanced back, found that he could not see five feet behind him which way they had come. He'd lived half his life camping in forests along the roads of the realm, but here, he'd be lost on his own; he could not find his way back if he had to. The woods had never felt so dark, so unfriendly around him.

Freyshin held a sticker bush branch aside for Crel to pass under. As Crel took hold of the branch, he snapped it deliberately off. He would make a trail himself if he had to.

But at the snap, Freyshin whirled back and stared at him through a mask plastered in green leaves. Only his black, unmoving eyes showed the man behind the leaves. Crel sucked in his breath and shrugged an apology behind his own borrowed mask. He would not mark their path again. He dropped the twig and went on.

The nine other men and women ahead of them wore the same mask of leaves, and all but their leader were dressed in black tunics and leggings that had been painted with swirls of tan, gold, green dyes, camouflaging them remarkably well in the dark woods. The leader of the Bearmen was dressed instead in the alternately striped and checkered colors of a jester. Blue, red, yellow. Not the

240

Capsen colors of yellow, green, blue fields that Crel had worn that fateful night, but wearing a jester costume, whatever the colors, said all it needed, Crel assumed. The leader had become him for the day, the Bearman in person. How many other highwaymen around the realm were also wearing a jester's tunic that day, with faces hidden behind leaf masks, or furry bear masks, or simple black masks as he had worn, Crel feared to wonder. What deeds they were doing in his name, impersonating him, or the legend they had made of him, still daunted him.

And yet what deeds, what atrocities they said they were fighting against, the witch burnings, the arrests of townsmen, merchants, landowners who couldn't pay their higher and higher taxes, whose properties were stolen, their families ruined if not condemned as heretics by greedy or frightened neighbors—no, Crel could not blame his new friends driven into brigandage. And if nothing else, he did have one commanding reason himself to support them: if the king and his new priests weren't stopped soon from arresting, burning, impoverishing all of Wiss's old friends and customers, Crel would have no one left to sell his wares to.

Crel kept his mouth shut, his eyes open, and kept walking. He'd be loyal to whatever new king ruled his realm—be the "king" man, bear, thief or legend. Merchants could afford no other creed.

They came to a stand of tall aspen. Their bright quivering leaves rimmed with sunlight lightened the mood of the forest and chased away its gloom and oppression.

Until Crel passed through them and saw beyond them.

A small dip in the ground past the stand of aspen had been burnt clear of underbrush. The tree trunks walling the burnt clearing had all been seared black as well, and only the patch of grey sky above brought any light into the area. A dried creek bed, a lumpy black line of soot-covered pebbles marking it, ran its course through the clearing.

The Bearman's Men spread out behind the burnt trees around the clearing and waited.

Within minutes, a brawny middle-aged man, clean-shaven, blindfolded, was led into the clearing. From the look of his brocaded vest, black jacket, shiny boots, he was no pauper. His guide in an executioner's black hood and mask silently untied his hands and removed his blindfold, then he left him standing alone beside the dried-up creek.

From behind a tree close to Crel, Freyshin cupped his hands over his mouth and made the low throaty growl of a bear. From a tree on the other side of the clearing, a growl answered him, then from another tree around the circle came another growl, and then another. The man started turning slowly, eyeing the wall of trees surrounding him.

"Who are you?" one tree asked him, in a low throaty voice.

"Why have you come?" asked another.

As the man turned slowly, looking for the voices, seeing nothing but burnt tree trunks, the leader of the Bearmen in his jester outfit and mask of leaves, stepped quietly into the clearing. When the man, turning around, saw him suddenly there with him, he gave a start. But he quickly recovered, straightening his broad shoulders and clearing his throat, then he stepped forward and lifted a hand to greet the bearman.

"You. You, my good man. I have come asking for your help."

The bearman said nothing, he stood quietly regarding the man through his mask, not lifting a hand to greet him.

From the surrounding trees came the voices. "Why are you here?" "You are not a poor man." "What do you want of me?"

The client chuckled, spread out his hands good-naturedly to the bearman. "I do say, you put on a good show here. But I assure you, all these theatrics are not necessary for me. I am not of faint heart. I am here for a business deal. I'll pay well for your help."

Silence followed his words. The bearman stood quietly regarding him.

The stranger straightened his shoulders again, stood stiffer. "I am Captain Howet of the merchant ship Red Bell.

It is true, I have had good fortune and fair winds all my life, I have never been a poor man since I went to sea, until now. The Bell has been taken from me, all my cargo and property impounded for taxes and high penalties, the guardsmen say. Stolen is more the word. Without your help, I am ruined. But I come not asking only for me. A passenger of mine has been arrested for treason. He told me his cargo was of Cosian silks. But he failed to mention his two chestfuls of snow bear fur from the outer islands. All trade in bear fur, indeed in all furs resembling bear, have been outlawed by the Priests. There are bearmen I am told who wear bear masks, and the trade in bear skins have suddenly rivaled the prices paid for silk, if you can find the right buyer. I'm sure you can appreciate, my good sir, what I'm offering. Word on where to find his shipment, to keep or to sell or to use however would best meet your advantage. All I want is enough funds from it to buy back my ship and crew, impounded and fined for transporting him. I have ten days to find the funding to pay the fines before my crew is hung, as warning to other shipmen. Four of those days have already passed."

Howet was not the Bearman's men usual client. In a quick conference after hearing his story, three of the party spoke against helping him. The loss he was facing was a business loss, not a personal or emotional loss, and he was not someone they could trust easily, if it was to his advantage to sell them out, would he? they asked. Four others wanted to save his crewmen from being hung, and they and another of the women in the party wanted the money, silk, and furs the venture promised. Freyshin, a merchant, like Crel, like the Red Bell's Captain, like the leader of Bearmen band, claimed Howet was a victim of their enemies just as they were. The high taxes, the outlawing, inspection, and confiscation of their goods to pay for the guardsmen's wars and the priests' incense burners were also hurting their countrymen, merchants and customers alike. The Bearmen had a chance now to send a stronger message to the queen that the country was fighting back.

Crel listened. Freyshin could sound convincingly noble and concerned when he spoke to the band, Crel had noted that. But Crel also suspected Freyshin wanted the money and furs more than the justice. As for himself, when he heard the captain's story, he'd been remembering how lucky he had been that the guardsmen at Drespin had not discovered the wounded Capsens hiding inside his wagon. Whether the sea captain knew what was in his cargo or not, Crel could sympathize with him for getting caught. There but for the luck of the Goron stood he. Only difference would be, not being as rich as a captain, he wouldn't have fared as well, he would have more likely shared the fate of his crewmen getting hung.

The leader of the Bearmen agreed with Freyshin. "This captain says he came to deal with us. Perhaps he is willing to offer more. He wants his ship back; if we help him, then maybe this fight of yours, Freyshin, can be carried by our new ship all over the realm. Wherever we might need to go."

Including, Crel realized, picking up his brother and his tinker wagon in a month.

The next morning Crel wore his jester outfit and mask as he took Jesser with him into the Bearman camp. He carried with him a sackful of tin and copper sheets he had pounded smooth and flat over the night to pass out among the Bearmen. His participation had not been expected, they told him; they could fight their own fights in his name, he did not need to get involved.

But for this raid, this time, they would be fighting by his rules instead.

He passed out a shiny sheet of metal to each of the Bearman raiders.

Chapter 22
Dardin Canal

"Don't move!" the merchant captain said.

Crel glanced down at the sketch taking shape on the back of one of the captain's sea charts. "I'm not," he answered. He lifted his tankard of dark Sonachin ale, and saluted the captain, then took a draught. "Not moving a breath. Just refilling myself. How's it doing?"

"If you stay still long enough, we might be finished by morning." He shaded in Crel's high cheekbones, then started on the low, round neckline of the boatman's red and white striped chemise that Crel was wearing. The captain charcoaled in a few of the stripes.

Crel shook his head. "My brother will be wearing an islander tunic, lime-bleached linen, high neck buttoned across, from his wife's flax fields and loom. You've seen them surely. No stripes. Red scarf usually. Or else his whaleskin cloak, if he's just come in from fishing." The captain quickly colored the shirt solid black and changed the neckline. "Let me see what you have," Crel said.

The captain slid the sketch around on the table for Crel to see. Crel moved the oil lantern that the tavern keeper had brought over for the captain to use and stared down at his twin brother's face. His own face, he reminded himself. Clayl's wife told him she couldn't tell the two of them apart, except for the hair. No reflection in a pool of water or in a polished shaving tin had convinced Crel she spoke the truth half as much as the captain's black and white sketch.

Crel handed the sketch back and nodded. "His hair's lighter. He's the farmer fisherman our father was, out in the sun all day. His hair's more flaxen, like his fields. Mine's copper."

The captain rolled up the scroll, slipped it into his pouch. "You're the tinman. Copper for the tinker. He's a flax farmer. Shouldn't be hard to remember. And you want

245

him paid for your stay, and your tinker wagon brought to you in the next port south of here."

"In a month, yes. When I bring you the purse to buy back your men and ship, I'll bring you two silver talents extra. One for him, one for you."

The captain lifted the lantern and shone it in Crel's face. Crel sat motionless as the captain studied him. Then the captain set the lantern down and thrust out his beefy hand. "Aye. Our deal's made. You bring me my money back in time, I'll find your brother. It's a rare good thing to meet a man you can trust these days. I'll be here day after tomorrow waiting."

~

It had been a long day, and Crel needed to be down on the docks before dawn. He wouldn't have time to return to camp and make it back before then.

He counted out his money, kept aside three silver talents and a few coppers, and bought himself a loaf of bread and one third of a bed upstairs. He bought a candle as well to light up the room and wished he had not.

He threw open the shutters to release some of the stench. How people could live like this, he had never understood. Like rats scrambling over each other. Rarely in his life had he slept in a town. When Wiss and he had stayed with friends and fellow tradesmen along their circuit, the workshops and kilns they stopped at were like Freyshin's, always on the outskirts of town. And even there, Crel would pull a pallet outside near Jesser's wagon before he'd sleep inside confined by walls. He only truly felt comfortable in the wide open country at night, a campfire glow limiting the world. In a crowded town, even by daylight, the clamor, the confusion, the constant needs of people everywhere oppressed him.

One of his bedmates tonight was already snoring heavily, mountains of filth rolling up and shaking down along one side of the bed, hordes of flies resettling with each snore. Crel blew the candle out and lay down on the stiff mattress. Straw ends poked through the worn cover into his back.

He tossed, turned, slapped at flies and bed bugs, rarely slept. By twelve bells when the third man, reeking of ale and vomit, joined them, Crel could stand the press of humanity no more. He climbed and rolled over the mountain, elbows and fists pummeling into him, knees kicking him off, and a sleep-disturbed growl that could match Jesser's any day, keeping him moving quickly. He figured it was a preferable route to going across the vomit. He dressed and went downstairs.

He drifted along the wharf of Sonachin, tempted more than once to jump in and wash the filth off. The moon-lit crowd of dead fish and refuse bobbing against the boards below in the rising tide restrained him. It was not very foggy tonight. He hoped it would be more so tomorrow. The success of his plan counted on it..

Sailors and shoremen were playing a lonely dirge on a harmonica and two accordions in the shadows of a warehouse. Seeing his outfit the shipping company had given him this afternoon, too short for his arms and legs, but brightly striped, they waved him over as one of their own. He pulled two bales of hemp together and stretched out beside them. He offered them some of his bread and he listened to them tell new tales of the Bearman.

It had been easier than expected to hire himself on this afternoon with the shipping company. The canalman's boy had quit the day before with rumors of the Bearman murdering and eating youths and barmaids in every dark corner of Sonachin, which, according to the tales Crel was hearing tonight, had become as dangerous as the lone, deserted bends in the canals and rivers near the upper forest, the Bearman's more usual haunts. The canalman had been desperate to replace his boy with anyone, and he'd hired Crel on the spot, barely glancing at the papers Crel had forged for himself this morning, and asking surprisingly few questions. His boat had already been commissioned to take the priest's load of confiscated goods from the merchant captain's ship to the realm's oldest university and library in Solenzia on Dardin Lake, seminary and stronghold now of the Badurian Priests . Crel's timing could not have been luckier.

247

Crel lay back on the soft bales and closed his eyes as he listened to the sailors and shoremen. He'd thought the stories the Eller islanders were making up about a shapeshifting bearman were wildly incredulous–they were nothing compared to the stories he heard here tonight.

Tomorrow, he'd give them a new story to add to his growing legend.

~

The fog did come in before dawn, but it burned off by midmorning. Crel had been warned by both Freyshin and the merchant captain that progress would be slow, but he had not expected it this slow. The canal boat had not even reached the first ascending lock bypassing the rapids. His own cobb pony pulling his tinker wagon and the lazy, dull-witted tarney oxen pulling Jesser's cart could have made the same distance in half the time. But this one single towhorse was pulling ten times the load he could have pulled by wagon. Cargo was cheaper and quicker to ship by canal boat--if you were a wealthier merchant and had more to sell than would fit inside a tinker wagon.

The barge was loaded with cargo from more than just the merchant captain's ship. Three guardsmen rode on the crates, playing cards and drinking. The canalman steered from a platform on the back of his boat and shouted orders to Crel on the towpath with the horse. And in the bow of the boat, in the position of honor, seated on a scarlet padded chair Crel had latched onto the deck this morning, and shaded by a matching black-fringed parasol, napped the fattest priest Crel had ever seen. He remembered the mountain of the man snoring in the bed last night every time he looked over at the folds and bulges in the priest's voluminous black robes. The priest must be twice the size as the man last night.

Past the second lock and towards late afternoon, a barefoot lad sat on the far bank, his feet dangling in the water, fishing. The priest, awake now, and fanning himself with a white feather fan, waved a slow blessing on the lad. One of the guardsmen shouted over to him, asking if he had caught anything worth eating. The lad held up two catfish and an eel, and the guardsmen cheered and jabbed at each other. Their journey had been idyllic, a fine respite from the fear and paranoia inciting the city of Sonachin where the threat of murders and vandalism became dark reality for the guardsmen on duty there. The more people talked about the murders and rapes of barmaids in the formerly quiet sea port, the more murders and rapes seemed to happen. Here today instead, assigned to protect one priest and his treasures through the reportedly more dangerous countryside where bearmen had actually been encountered, the three guardsmen had found the day slow and uneventful. One offered to buy the fish from the lad; another wanted to buy his pole and bait instead; and all three of them laughed happily with each other. No one but Crel knew the lad's identity.

And Crel, recognizing the bearman leader's young son, glanced back after the canal boat passed to see the lad hold up an unlit candle and a piece of tin, a signal to Crel that all were ready and in place up ahead.

~

The first sparkling lights went unnoticed. Only Crel saw them falling on the water ahead of the canal boat as no more than glints of lazy sunlight. They proved his idea could work; he was relieved to know that much. The bearmen hiding along the trees reflected their candlelight into dancing lights upon the water with their strips of polished tin and copper he had handed out to them yesterday. But there was no fog to diffuse the lights, and the guards were too busy playing crossjacks and the priest had fallen asleep again. No one but Crel saw them.

Then the bearmen started shining a few lights closer to the boat, onto the boat, onto the crates, onto the men, onto their cards, and by evening when they approached the fourth lock and the fog had encapsulated them, no guardsman was playing cards and the priest no longer slept. The little pins of light shone will of the wisp around them and eerily through the fog rising before and behind them, trapping them in their spell.

Crel spoke softly. "It's said foxfire lights are seen whenever lost souls escape hell."

"Aye," said the canalman. "They carry the lanterns from hell with them."

"I never seed them afore anywhere but far up ahead of me in the mist. One night afore a battle I seed them. Most the men died the next day." The guardsman's face was blanched pale as he looked around him, sword drawn.

"No. Never afore were lights on us like this," said another guardsman.

"Invoke your god, Priest. Keep us safe," said the third in a stronger voice than his companions. He was standing up, turning all around, sword in hand too.

The priest started chanting, calling on the Winged One to descend upon them and protect them.

A bear growl coming thunderously through the fog interrupted his chant.

Bless you, Jesser. For once, bless you. Crel hadn't realized they had come this close.

The guardsmen gripped their swords tighter. "It's the Bearman! The hell lanterns come with the Bearman!" "Or the spirits holding them have." "Pray, Priest. Blessed be the Winged One, Blessed be the Winged One. Save us!"

"Hallooo!" shouted a voice from above. "Who goes there?"

"Sawyer, is that you?" shouted the canalman. "Open the gates, let us in quick!"

Two tall lock gates loomed ahead in the fog. The lock keeper operated a saw mill at this site, and so had built the first deep locks on the canal, Crel had been told.

"Head for the gate on the left," shouted the voice from above.

"Take the strawfeeder up," the canalman yelled to Crel. "When we get through the lock, we'll bed down in the mill tonight. These devil lights will be gone by morning."

True, Crel thought. *We'd better be.*

For good measure, Crel looked around at the dancing lights nervously. "Praise be the Winged One, protect me!" he said. He unhooked the towrope from the horse, tossed it

250

over to the boat, and led the horse up the hill through the eerie lights and swirling fog.

"Hurry, lad," a guardsman yelled behind him, as the lock gate started opening.

When he reached the top, he was out of sight of the boat below. Freyshin and the Bearman band were there, tin and copper plates cupping the lit candles in their hands. Jesser was in her cage beside the mill, Freyshin's daughter beside her. Jesser growled aloud in greeting to Crel, and Sylven opened the cage. Confronted by a charging, grunting bear, the poor horse beside Crel reared and neighed in fright, its terror loud enough to carry down through the fog to the boat below.

"Lad!" the canalman shouted up. They could hear the priest chanting again.

Freyshin winked at Crel as he handed him his jester's guise and mask. Crel hand signaled Jesser, and she stopped, stood up, and obliged with a louder growl. In concert, Crel screamed a death scream.

"Lad!" came the shout again. Then, silence.

The lock gate opened fully. The bearmen positioned themselves around the top of the lock, lying down to be unseen, candles and tins hidden. Then slowly Freyshin turned the winch that lowered the gate's towrope down to the boat. The winch needed oil, it creaked mournfully through the fog.

"Take the rope!" Freyshin shouted down.

The boat entered the lock and the gate closed behind it.

Then in the basin between the two gates, twenty feet below, it sat waiting. Silence. No lights. Clear of fog. Waiting.

Finally, the canalman shouted up, "Sawyer, let in the water! Get us out of here."

His voice echoed up the walls.

And hundreds of will o' wisp lights started flashing, jumping down the walls, searching for the voice.

"Winged One, save us!" whispered one of the guardsmen, his words carried up through the well. The priest began chanting, his voice unsteady.

251

His clothes changed and mask on, Crel tossed one of the boy's catfish to Jesser, and after a brief swallow, happy with her pay, she obeyed Crel's signals and stood up on the platform above the well of the lock and began to dance, growling softly. The moon broke through the fog above her and outlined her to the men below.

The priest chanted louder than ever. Crel peeked over the edge. The priest stood up, his fat stubby arms upraised, calling upon his god. He pointed suddenly at the bear. The guardsmen stood behind him, swords ready.

Crel gestured to Jesser and she growled.

The priest shouted his god's name and pointed up. The lights flashed and found him. And found the bear. Crel gestured, and Jesser roared.

The priest shook his arm at Jesser, pointed, chanted, lights flashing on him, on his hands, his sleeve, his robe, his shoulder–then he suddenly stopped mid-chant and clutched his chest. Jesser roared on cue. The priest collapsed onto the deck of the canal boat.

A guardsman scrambled over to him. "He's dead!"

"Dead..." the others repeated, looking at the lights on the walls around them, the bear above them.

Crel signaled and Jesser left the platform. He threw her a meal of apples, the second catfish and the eel; and as she sat down and ate them contentedly, he took her place on the platform.

The lights all flashed upon him. In the jester outfit, the same he had worn that night he had taken her bear act into Sonachin and started their legend, he pointed down to the men on the canal boat trapped below. They were hushed. The Bearman had shifted shape before their eyes.

"It is a shame your priest has died." It was. Crel had not wanted that. "His god has no power over me. It might be well to remember that. If you do not wish to join him in death, you'll do as I say. You have something that belonged to my friends, and I want it returned."

Freyshin threw an open crate tied to the rope over the edge, and started turning the winch to lower it.

The men below caught it and started loading it as directed, first with the priest's treasure box, then with the bear furs, then with the other unopened crates.

When the bearmen had finally hauled all the cargo up out of the lock, Crel stood among them, arguing with them softly, but adamantly. From the priest's treasure box, he'd counted out the merchant captain's fines he'd been taxed for shipping the illegal furs unbeknownst to him-- according to what he said–and left the rest of the tax money in the box. Of the cargo, he would allow the bearmen to take only the bear furs to make into their costumes in future raids--more than enough fortune to pay them for the night's deeds. He was no thief, he reminded himself. No thief. And the bearmen band of highwaymen wouldn't be thieves in his name either, at least in his presence. He was taking back only what did not rightfully belong to the priest, the confiscated money that the merchant captain needed to save his men from hanging tomorrow and to buy back his ship, and the bear furs that should belong to no one.

The bearmen in the end took much more than Crel wanted them to, and all the rest of the money, but not everything at least. As they melted away into the forest, Crel took the towhorse for himself and hitched him to Jesser's cart. He left a silver talent from his own purse hidden inside a discarded harness. It should be more than enough to pay the canalman for his horse.

Then, just before he left, he pushed the heavy lever that opened the water sluice into the lock from its sister lock. By the time the boat would rise high enough for the guardsmen to escape, all trace of the bearmen would be gone, and he in the other direction.

~

A month later, Jesser stowed safely in a camp in the woods, Crel waited on the docks of Marriend, the first port south of Sonachin, for the merchant captain to bring him his tinker wagon and his papers from his brother as agreed. A week later, the captain still had not come.

Crel went from the next port to the next port and back again towards Sonachin. *It's a rare good thing to meet a man you can trust these days,* the captain had said, before shaking his hand on their deal.

Indeed, Crel thought. Indeed it was a *rare* good thing.

In Sonachin, posted on a tree just south of town, Crel found a flyer. The picture sketched of his brother was on it, the same sketch the merchant captain had drawn of Crel. The reward money offered for the Bearman, as it called him, had been crossed off. Handwritten across the flyer, "The reward has been claimed. He's been found, hiding out as a fisherman on Eller Island. The Bearman is dead, Sonachin is safe again. Praise be to the Winged One. Long live our glorious king."

Chapter 23
The King's Picnic

King Laird was turning eight. His week-long celebration would culminate tomorrow with his formal engagement to the three-year old granddaughter of the High Badurian Priest. Little Lady Charain sat beside the king now, more prim, quiet, daunted than Laird ever was.

Behind the royal couple sat the ten other companions of the king, all under age twelve. And to his left on the floor, knelt Lord Foundling, Laird's whipping boy since birth, allowed to watch the pageantry and puppet shows today too.

Before the last puppet play, while the jester changed her backdrops, servants uncovered the lanterns around the room. In the flood of lights, Verl blinked awake. He hadn't slept much lately. He knew most of the twenty, thirty courtesans in this music chamber on an intimate basis. As dream interpreter for the court the last three months, his services had been a novelty at first. But five weeks ago Lady Gentian had come to him with dreams of her lover, and from then on the news spread. Descending into their dreams with them, Verl was forced to share whatever images, desires, physical feelings the ladies experienced. To have such dreams interpreted had quickly become the court's most popular diversion. A new bowl of powders-- ground mandrake root, cinnamon and myrrh--was now kept filled and waiting for a dreamer to add to the fire herself to insure she would have the dreams she wanted. Verl had made his fortune within a week.

But lately, it seemed, he was getting paid more in keys than in coins. His dungeon walls may have changed, become brighter, softer, more tiring, but just as dangerous. Most of the lords and gentlemen of the court were outside in the halls this afternoon as every afternoon, winning and losing estates and holdings at crossjack tables and backgammon, but they all knew him now by name and reputation, and not a few of them had come to his dreaming

255

room out of curiosity and suspicion. Many of the men stayed, requesting the mandrake powders, but luckily most of them still paid in coins, not keys.

Verl stifled a yawn, glanced around at the ladies, caught a few of them eyeing him back. Lady Gentian arched a suggestive brow at him above a fluttering fan. He had not been fool enough yet to use anyone's key. His refusal had the unexpected result of his clients returning to him more and more often, night and day now, demanding he share another mandrake dream.

Laird, up front, twisted around in his velvet throne, and gestured something to the two lordlings behind him. The three boys hooted aloud, interrupting the whole room. Verl saw the queen regent raise her chin stiffly. Laird saw her disapproval too. He gestured as if he were slashing a knife at her throat, then he laughed louder with his friends. Beside him, the thin bony shoulders of Lord Foundling sank beneath his tunic. He wore the same outfit as the king's, but in opposite colors and in coarse linen not silk. Knowing what awaited him for Laird's behavior, Foundling kept his head facing forward at the curtained puppet theater, not saying a word.

Hooded and silent, standing over the queen regent and frowning down at her in suppressed annoyance, the High Priest nodded towards her son. He would be speaking to her again privately, but their meetings were no secret to the court.

And no secret to Verl.

Queen Felain had come to his dreaming room two weeks ago. No warning, no knock. She closed the door behind her. Verl rose from grinding his powders, and made a quick bow, the pestle still in his hand.

"My lady."

She walked around the room, inspecting it, not acknowledging him. She glanced down at the dreaming mat along the wall, toed at the ashes in the fire pit below the scorched clam shell, sorted through his collection of keys, already carefully ribboned and labeled with the names of his clients that day, and shook the smaller bowl of coins by the door.

She spun around to him, the crinoline and silk in her long gowns rustling.

"Why are you not a Singer?"

"My lady?"

"You apprenticed at Singerhalle. One of their most talented, I am told. You ended up a hornblower, then a prisoner down in my dungeon, and now here. You never took the chain of mastery of a Singer."

Verl squeezed his hand around the stone pestle before he could think how to answer. "I never earned the chain. I tried to play a dream I'd had for my masterpiece. I failed."

"A dream." The queen crooked a corner of her lips. She glanced down at the fire pit and the bowls of powders beside it. "I hear you mix your own incense. This room is one of the few in the palace not blessed with the purifying air of the priests' holy incense."

Verl leaned down, set the pestle back into the mortar. "Arnaby brought me here first for your son's dreams. He is a Badurian priest, yet he had arranged this room like an Eller Island dreaming hut, in every detail, including the islander powders. I've been following his example ever since. I assume the priests have not disapproved."

She met his eyes. "I would be careful, dreamer, not to assume anything. The walls in this palace have eyes and ears, even into here." She glanced over at the dreaming mat. "It might be wise to remember that. Does this Priest Arnaby counsel you in his faith?"

Verl drew in his breath. "We have talked."

Felain nodded in approval of his answer, and glanced at the walls again. "You can be careful. Do you believe what the priests tell you, dreamer, or do you still hold to your islander beliefs?"

"Blessed be the winged God," Verl answered.

Felain looked down at his clenched fist at his side, and Verl, reddening, loosened it. "I see," she said. "Laird needs someone who can think for himself. Not just repeat what the priests say. Laird will start coming to you three hours a day for his lessons."

"My lady?"

257

"You taught my son not to fear his dreams. I thank you for that. Now it is time to repair the damage you have done. I wish my son to fear no one, but no ruler should grow up not fearing himself. You shall teach him what the priests cannot."

"My lady—"

"The priests have charge of the grandest library in the realm. And teach only from the books they approve. You, dreamer, you trained at Singerhalle, and learned the traditions of all the land, the beliefs and languages of all the people. This too is what a king should learn." She held his eyes. "The false as well as the true, shall we say? So he can stand on his own someday and know the difference."

Verl bowed. "I shall be honored, my lady, to try and teach him all I learned."

She gestured down at his powders, the fire shell, the dreaming mat. "But not here. He'll come to your chambers at four bells every day."

Verl nodded.

"Do these work?" she asked, pointing down again at his incense powders, holding her hand open for one.

Verl bent over, picked up the ladies' bowl and placed it in her hand. "They seem to. For everyone, it's a little different."

She smelled the powders. "Cinnamon. Myrrh. What's this lighter tan?"

"Ground mandrake. Your ladies keep bringing it to me."

"My ladies say they enjoy coming to you." Felain pinched some of the powder between her fingers, releasing a fresher stronger waft of the combined scents, then sprinkled the dust onto the fire below. "How do they work?" she asked.

Verl watched a white flame spark up and sizzle higher than the shell. "The myrrh helps bring on the trance. My other powders, down here, will help you sleep too. And cinnamon helps make dreams vivid and compelling."

"The cinnamon is for remembered passion," the queen said.

Verl watched the fire burn lower, nodded. "For some the memory of passion, for some the hope of passion future. And for others, I think they bring their dreams with them. Or what they wish they had in their dreams."

"Are they ever disappointed?"

Verl shrugged. "It is their dream. I can only follow them into it, see what they see, try to say what I've seen—"

"Feel what they feel, I've been told. Every touch, everywhere they're being touched. And what does the mandrake root do?"

Verl shook his head. "They claim it brings the strongest memories, the strongest passions. If that's what they believe, then perhaps that's what's most real to them. And wishing it so, their minds centered on it, the dreams they want seem most likely to come."

Verl bent to pick up another bowl of incense. "If you wish, my lady—"

Before he finished, she reached out the bowl of incense she held, tipped it over and poured it all onto the fire.

Verl watched the fire flare up, sizzle, spark madly. "My lady—"

The room was starting to cloud with smoke already, the burnt cinnamon, the myrrh strong enough to choke. "We shall see," Felain said, "if it works."

~

The clatter of silver on silver behind Verl broke through the memory, brought him back inside the music chamber. Bottles, the jester's aid, stood beside the puppet theater, joking with his young audience, introducing the next play, teaching them a new song. Verl knew the tune, but the words were different from the Capsen song he knew. It was not a song he expected anyone else in this room to know, few even in Singerhalle would recognize it. But it still surprised him that Jing the jester would dare use any Capsen song at court. The servants were closing the silver lanterns, dimming the lights again. The High Priest stood beside the queen, no longer looking down at her.

Seeing the queen, Verl shifted uncomfortably in his seat. The queen's dream that day had certainly been the most powerful, the most violent he'd ever entered. He swallowed, darted his gaze away from her.

Three seats beyond her, he saw the back of a Singer in blue, wearing the gold-linked chain of mastery and the silver of a court singer around her neck. Verl recognized the black curls that escaped her hood. Eleidice. *"Why are you not a Singer?" the queen had asked him that day...* "Will you show me your dreams?" Eleidice had once asked him, her long dark brown fingers opening his to a piece of charcoal in his hand. He was glad she had become a court singer. In just over a year now. Years, years ago, in another lifetime, another dream, his fingers stretching hers, taught hers to play the lute--

"Why are you not a Singer?" the queen's voice in his mind demanded again, more stridently, more insistent for his attention. *"Why not a Singer? Why just a dreamer? Why?"*

Verl crossed his arms tightly, closed his eyes again, and yielded to the memory.

~

Through the thick, hypnotizing smoke, Verl guided the queen by her elbow over to the dreaming mat, fearing she might fall before she reached it. Then he hurried back to his powders and squatted. He had not had time to mix in his other powders yet, nor to chant--he'd done nothing to help him counteract the smokes himself, nothing to help him concentrate enough to enter her dream instead of one of his own. He threw in some crushed numbstool and saw weed directly into the fire as she had, and started chanting. Magic words, nonsense words, --no, numbers only, counting one, two, three, no chance for stray thoughts, four, five, six, concentrate, don't think, not even this much, hurry!, seven, eight...

He plunged into the cold, dark tunnel between their minds, searching, concentrating just enough not to follow the images his memories flashed at him, just enough to remember where he was going. When he found the one

260

flickering spark before him that was not his own, he tunneled towards it, and entered her dream.

She was already moaning, moving, with weight heaving down on top of her, pushing in.

Her eyes were closed. Verl saw the darkness with her. Sparks flashed against their eyelids that brightened, then dimmed again. Strong arms viced around her; her nails dug into naked pumping shoulders. Verl's fingers curled around the sweaty skin with hers.

"I'll make you a son tonight, Henrik," she whispered. "Ailil has promised us."

Harder, she thought, *harder*. She didn't say it.

An image of a mandrake root formed, maybe from Verl's memory, its two long roots opening wider as he cut his knife into it. She spread her legs wide, wrapped them up around Henrik's back to receive him deeper. Verl felt the gorging, the tightening, the shifting in his own loin. Felt too the thrusting from inside as she did, the soft sliding back, the sudden thrust again. Felt the back of his tongue sliding back and forth against the soft roof of his mouth, pushing in, pushing, the closest he could compare. And the soft pleasing numbness in front of his ears that spread in quick rivers through him. Felt the sparks stinging against his eyelids. He had not often played the violin, but the slide vibrating the string inside his loin was there, and the pluck, pluck, pluck on his lute, its deeper vibrations, sharper, softer. He was a tightened string, shivering, waiting for each next thrust.

"More," she whispered. She reached up, pulled the thrusting neck down, bit into it. Verl tasted the coppery tang of blood. And more blood. More.

The blood kept coming. Filled his mouth, choked his throat, spewing out, choking him, choking her. "Henrik--" she gasped. She flashed open her eyes, saw the bloody severed neck of the husband she'd had beheaded thrusting above her.

She screamed, *screamed!*, Verl may have screamed too. They couldn't move; trapped, they couldn't push the body off. And there, when she could finally turn her head, there standing beside the bed, his white teeth gleaming his

laugh surrounded by his long white beard, was the High
Priest of the Badurians. He pointed his bony accusing finger
down at her with one hand. In his other hand, he held up the
freshly dripping head of Henrik.

Felain screamed. In terror, for her, and for himself,
Verl fought free from her dream.

He stumbled to her side, shook her shoulder, called
her name. Then he rushed to the small chamber window,
flung open its shutters, pulled up the pane. He leaned out,
heaving in the fresh air, calming himself, clearing his mind.

Then finally, the room emptying of smoke, he turned
around. The queen was sitting up on the mat. She stood and
met his look.

Verl swallowed, wandering what he could say.

"Don't bother," she said. "I am no seven year old
child too frightened to face my nightmares. And then to
deny them by asking if they could mean something else.
Just...I ask you. Help my son learn to never give anyone
such power over him. I've made that mistake twice now."

Verl stared back at her. *Twice?* Once to a husband,
he realized. And once to the priests that had helped her kill
him.

"Don't tell anyone what you have seen here today,"
the queen commanded. "And I shall allow you to live."

~

Verl could hear his pupil's sharp laughter now,
jeering at the puppets louder than anyone else in the room.
The unruly young king threw a cherry pit at the girl peasant
puppet on the stage and laughed again.

In a shrill swizzle voice, the puppet scolded him.
"For shame! For shame! To subject your subject to torture,
sir! You've mussed my pretty red hood."

The puppet started humming the same child's
counting song that Bottles had taught the king and his
friends before the play. The puppet bent over and put
flowers into her basket. The top of a black furry head
popped up behind her as Verl started nodding back to sleep.

A scream jerked him fully awake. Little Lady
Charain, until now sitting so calmly next to Laird, pointed at

262

the furry puppet head that kept hiding behind a tree each time the girl puppet turned around.

"There!" she cried. "Over there!"

The king, for once being chivalrous, sat up straighter and reached over to his distraught little fiancée and patted her arm. "Don't be afraid, Charain. You watch. I won't let her get eaten. Will I, Wolf?"

An angry growl and a shake of a furry puppet head answered him. The girl puppet started picking flowers again. Off to the side of the stage, a puppet dressed as Laird, wearing a golden crown and riding a white horse, cantered into view. He waved a sword as long as the puppet to the audience, and the children cheered Laird's name.

But when the girl puppet in the red hood stepped up close to the tree and the black furry arms snatched her and spun her around to the ground, it wasn't a wolf humping over her, but a bear twice the little puppet's size. The girl puppet screamed, Lady Charain screamed, and Laird and his friends and all the lords and ladies in the room went uneasily quiet. The bear growled and began ripping up the body of the girl puppet.

The King Laird puppet galloped bravely to the rescue. He dismounted and whapped the bear with his sword.

"Unhand the maiden, you dastardly beast!"

The bear rose up, towered above the king puppet, and the audience was silent, except for the frightened whimpers of the king's three-year old fiancée. Rumors of an ogre called The Bearman haunting the woods of three northern sea provinces had reached the court a month ago. Several units of guardsmen had been sent out to track the ogre down, but few had returned. Taxmen had been waylaid and robbed by bands of highwaymen grown more bold than ever, and reports claimed the Bearman's spirit led them all. Holy Badurian Priests were not immune from the ogre's attack either, their god, apparently, giving them no special protection. But all reports of priests' deaths and disappearances coming in from the hornblowers every few days had been kept quiet by the Regent and the High Priests.

Verl, hearing the horns, knew of them, few others in this room did.

But the threat of the Bearman killing the king's guards and his good people was no secret to anyone in the court.

The Bear puppet turned around to the king and growled. It had the face of an ogre, half human, half devil with the long black snout and bloody sharp teeth of a bear. The king puppet stepped back a foot, swung his sword. The bear swiped it aside.

"Now!" said Bottles, sitting inside the shadows beside the puppet stage. "Now, my lords and ladies," he said to the children, "sing! Sing! He needs your song!" In his pied silks, Bottles crept quickly to the side of the king's throne and squatted among the children, and started to sing the song he had taught them.

"Hurry," he urged as the Bearman circled the brave little king puppet, and with a growl, swiped his crown off. "Louder! He needs you. Tell him what to do."

The children began singing with him, some shouting more than singing.

>Demon bear, Demon bear, comes to town
>Frightening children all around
>Counting One, Two.
>Save us Laird!

The tune was indeed the old Capsen counting song about a dancing bear that had always intrigued Verl, but the words, now that he could hear them better, had definitely changed.

>Hero king, hero king, swing your sword
>Winged God, Savior God, help our lord!
>Counting Three, Four
>Kill the Bear!

The children had joined hands and were counting louder every time the king puppet struck the bear with its silver sword. Some of Laird's companions in the second row were rising in their seats to see better.

>Hero Lord, swing your sword, kill it dead
>Bleeding bear, dying bear, off with its head
>Counting FIVE

264

The Bearman's Dead!

As Bottles and Laird's companions shouted "five," the king puppet swung the sword mightily at the bear's neck, and the furry ogre-faced head went flying off into the audience. One of the young lords caught it, and tossed it to his friends. The king puppet drug the heavy bear carcass to the edge of the stage and heaved it over onto the floor as the lanterns were being opened again around the room. To the approval of one of the older boys who went to pick the carcass up, a red bloody paste squirted out of the headless neck when he squeezed it.

As the court left the music chamber, Verl lingered, watching Jing the jester and her assistant Bottles dismantle the puppet stage. He still wondered about their song, and finally he approached them.

Jing's long white hair hung in braids down to her waist and curled in two giant loops back up. Her hair perhaps had never been cut in her sixty-seven years at court where she'd been found as a naked baby inside an iron pot down in the kitchens one frosty morning, the rumors said. Her lips were painted in a blue smile, and each cheek was tattooed with a star, on her left cheek a yellow star, and on her right a red star. The tattooed stars were still bright but cracked by years of laugh lines stretching them. They crinkled more out of shape as she squinted up at Verl through her horn-rimmed spectacles. She stood less than half his height but she was still as thin and agile an acrobat as her delta monkey Gal, who was now busily unpacking the puppets Jing had just packed away.

"Ah," she said to Verl, recognizing him, "the dreamer who doesn't sing. Or is it the singer who no longer dreams?"

Verl's hand tightened into a ball at his side. One by one he relaxed his fingers. He had no idea what she knew about him. Or how. "I've heard that song before," he said. "About a bearman coming to town. You've changed its words."

Jing cocked her head at him. Then she took off her spectacles and polished the thick lenses with the hem of her tunic, put them back on, and squinted up at him again. "I knew Lollander," she said. "He told me about you. Is he dead now?"

Verl caught in his breath; then he glanced away.

"I see," she said. "Sing a lolly. --Gal!" She snapped the monkey's leash tied to her side. "Put those puppets back." She nodded back up to Verl and answered him. "I heard a child's song once. I changed its words about a bearman. You saw a child's nightmare. And you changed its warnings. King Laird becomes a hero twice now and sleeps peacefully at night. And we both are still alive and well-fed in his court. While Lollander died in a dungeon. Sing the lolly. Hold a holly. He used to make me laugh when we were young, in the old king's father's court. Times were different then."

Jing pulled Gal to her, and the monkey jumped up into her arms and wrapped a braid of her long white hair around its neck. The monkey's small hands pulled on the ropes of the braid like it was driving a team of horses, and bared its teeth in glee. Watching them, Verl clenched and reclenched his hand.

"Lollander was like a father," he said.

She took off her spectacles and looked up at him without squinting. "He saw music in you, he said. Me, I'm just a storyteller, a jester, I play with puppets. And I have a monkey who rules me." She put her spectacles back on. "But I control a monkey's world. Those who believe in our stories, in our songs, live in a world we create. Isn't that right, Singer?"

Jing turned her head sharply, and looked to Verl's left. Verl followed her gaze and saw Master Singer Eleidice standing behind him.

Eleidice nodded. "So we like to say in Singerhalle, Lady Jing." She smiled, then slowly met Verl's eyes. "Hello, Verl. We waited for you to come try out for your masterchain again this week. You never came."

Verl bowed his head. He paused a second, his head still lowered, composing himself. Close up, Eleidice had grown taller, more mature, and she smelled of the cloved oranges hanging in her pomander. And he, for a year now, had never dared hope he would speak to her again. "My

266

lady," he said, straightening. "I...am no longer a Singer. I haven't played the lute since you last heard me. I have a new life here at court now."

"Do you?"

The monkey chittered and pulled on the reins of Jing's tresses. "I have work to do," Jing said. "Perhaps we'll meet again, dreamer. And talk more then about old friends."

Jing pried Gulls' hands away from her braid, and released the monkey to the floor. Then she went to help Bottles fold back the wings of the stage. Two servants were carrying the dismantled backdrops away.

Eleidice slipped her long dark fingers around Verl's arm. "I hear you have made a new name for yourself here, Verl. You told me once that your father saw into dreams. Now I hear," she tightened her fingers briefly around his arm, "you can too." She loosened her grip and Verl watched her hand drop. "How much would you charge an old friend for showing her how you do that?"

~

He didn't interpret her dream. She didn't ask him to. Once they got into the privacy of his dreaming chamber, all they did was talk about old times, old friends, and the news over the past year from Singerhalle. Luckily that's all they did. Or maybe not so lucky. He watched her from the edge of the crowd as she sang on North Beach for the king's picnic, and wondered if he did regret not sharing a dream with her yesterday. Or if he regretted even more never allowing her to get any closer to him than that. She had been willing, he knew. Years ago, as well as yesterday. But she was a Master Singer. And he never would be.

Closing his eyes, Verl listened to her sing, and heard the echo of his youth when he first heard her quicksilver voice sliding the words of her songs into his being. Her voice had been beautiful then, during their long sessions together when he was teaching her the chords on her lute. But listening to her here, he knew with a sad, proud certainty that her voice, grown mature and deeper now, no longer belonged just to him. She enraptured her royal

267

audience so today that her flawless playing of her lute tremored and rose and receded in her song's background as unnoticed as the waves crashing behind her. All he had ever had a talent for, himself, was for playing the lute, never just the singing. He opened his eyes, saw even Laird and his young friends still sitting silent, mesmerized by her voice.

Verl left her crowd and wandered down the beach. He could still hear her when he stopped and looked out at the waves. Sandpipers skittered in and out of the waters in front of him, and farther out, a gull dove for a fish. The last thing he had told Eleidice before he left Singerhalle–he remembered that last evening vividly, looking out at the waves, hearing her sing—the last thing he told her that night was about the seagull that pecked the eyes out of his puppy when he was a child.

The seagull lifted up from the water triumphant, a silver fish hanging from its beak. Two squawking gulls flew in, tried to steal its fish.

He toed at the sand, made a small hill, stepped it down flat. Eleidice had made him promise yesterday that, at the least, he would go get his lute someday, try playing it again. Perhaps he would. Someday.

He saw a clam shell half-buried in the sand. He picked it up and washed it off. Hand-sized, it might make a more authentic bowl for his incense powders. He led a different life now, he hoped she had seen that, he was not a Singer. That life was beyond him.

Just as she was.

Her song ended, and he walked farther down the beach searching for another right-sized shell.

Later when Verl returned to the king's birthday picnic, Laird rose and motioned him over.

"Dreamer, I want to show you something. See if you can see it too." Laird waved his friends and an approaching guardsman away. "No, just my tutor. No one else comes."

Verl followed the-boy king over a cliff to the south of the beach. Laird pointed down. "There. Tell me what you see."

Below was the port of Norgarth, the city, the palace, the delta beyond. And from this height, Verl could see most of the curve of the coast to the end of the bay. Then, Verl realized that Laird was pointing closer, to the coastline just below them. Looking down, superimposed on the bay, he saw it too. This was the scene from Laird's dream, the view from which the giant head of ice would first be seen rising up from the sea to attack Norgarth.

The boy king was watching him, expectantly. "This is it, isn't it? From right there, that's where I'll save the city? That's where I'll defeat my enemy and become a hero forever!"

Verl drew in his breath, but still didn't tell the young king what his dream had meant to him.

"So it is, sire. Right there."

"I'm going to build a post here. A watch tower. A secret watch tower! Just so I'll have the first report when that head comes sailing in. And you know how I know where to mark this spot? Look up there. That cave, see? Mostly hidden behind that bent-over cypress. But from this angle, right here, you can just see the mouth of the cave. I knew that cave was there, that's what I and my lords came up here looking for this afternoon, though they didn't know it. But you, I'll tell you, because you know what else we will see from here someday coming out of the sea."

Verl did finally see the black edge of a mouth of a cave. Perhaps, like all boys, Laird craved a chance to go exploring. That encouraged Verl, a way to relate to him. He hadn't found many in their afternoon lessons yet. "How did you know that cave was there, sire?"

"Only I know it, and my father did, and his father before him. Though it did my father no good to know it. He told my mother, and she told our army, and I was here with them when he came out of that cave trying to escape the city, and this is where we caught him. He told my mother about it, but not for sure where, but he did tell me, and if I hadn't shown the priests where, we wouldn't have caught him, and he wouldn't have been beheaded. So I've been thinking. I don't think I'll tell my son someday how to escape the palace. There's a tunnel from my chamber right down under the city, and it passes right through the pauper's pit in the dungeon, so I'd have to empty the dungeons out first, just like he did, crazy men were everywhere, attacking our armed men circling the walls of the city just to get to free of that dungeon."

"Just to get free of the dungeon? Yes, I can see someone doing that."

"Yes! You came from there, didn't you, dreamer? The guards said those men, in rags, or all naked as pigs in a mire, kept running towards our swords as if they didn't care if they lived or died after being down there."

Verl looked down at his young charge. "No, I suppose they didn't."

"Tell me, dreamer. Do you think I should tell my son someday or not? I don't want him to lead guards here to capture me. But how will he escape someday if he doesn't know?"

"I...I don't know. That is a dilemma, sire. Perhaps...we should talk more about it later as we...get older." He said it distractedly, looking back up at the cave, glancing around, taking landmarks. He had never imagined a secret way back down into the dungeon. He wondered if Arax *was* still alive. Sing a lolly, Jing had said. Hold a holly. Lollander wasn't alive, because of him. But perhaps Arax still was.

Laird nodded his head, making his own decision as imperiously as any eight year old suddenly would. "Yes. I think I will tell my son someday. But not that crypuke Charain. Even if I do have to marry her when she gets old enough to have a son, I'll not tell her anything. In fact," he smiled with a sudden inspiration that chilled Verl away from his private thoughts, "I think, after she gives me my son first, of course, I think I shall just have her beheaded first, before she can think to behead me."

Chapter 24
Harvest Moon

Sunshine spilled down the southern slopes of the coast range, sweetening the best grapes still left on the vine until first frost. In the villages, men from twelve to fifty-four competed in foot races and archery shoots, and in playing lutes and tambours for the women who sang and danced in the great wine vats. King Grape, either a white donkey or in some villages a white ram fed during the night the dregs of last year's wines and crowned this morning with wreathes of grape leaves and nuts, pulled a cart laden with apples, squashes, and sheathes of barley and rye. The festooned beast, left to wander drunkenly through the crowds, was often entreated by young virgins in white lace shifts to come taste their brimming cupfuls of first wine. If a maiden were so lucky as to be nipped in the fingers or nudged in the breast by King Grape, she would be ensured a good marriage dowered with the village's best harvest next year.

Every Badurian priest in Norgarth county wandered through the hills today, visiting as many villages as they could, blessing the grapes by shaking their belled staffs over the white donkey's back when it peed its good fortune and by chanting prayers of thanksgiving to their winged god who, they preached, empowered this humble beast as its holy messenger this one day each year. Once a witch or a heretic had been publicly stoned or burned in a village in warning, and other disbelievers carted away, conversion of the rest of the villagers was encouraged with gentler means, absorbing the older beliefs into the new.

In Norgarth, Harvest Moon was celebrated with wilder abandon, as if the city of the refined was making up for its loss of country innocence. Masked balls were held in every square, drunken parades in every street. Each was led by the citified version of King Grape, a nude man painted white wearing an ass's head and tail. This King Grape was more than willing to approach any woman, virgin or not, to taste her wine and nip her offered breast. If given the opportunity to hump her beast-like in the street, the parade would encircle them and bray for them. A new custom, gaining popularity in the last two years, many of the marchers also shook belled "holy" staffs over them.

King's Court was deserted by midday. Even the guards and servants were outside partying in the streets. Or at least Verl thought he had the Audience Hall to himself as he waited for Arnaby to come. The spy priest had left Verl a note in his basket of labeled keys last night saying he'd be in the Hall today at noon. Instead of a signature, the note was signed with the Badurian chant *Descend your wings upon me. I am your vessel, I am your chosen one.* The phrase had become a code between them.

Verl had come early, curious to watch the fall of colored lights from the stained glass windows in the ceiling form a pattern in the third white circle of the bear claw mosaic on the floor in front of the throne. As the mechanical clock in Imperial Square tolled the midday bells, a knife shape with a blood-red tip merging into a blue blade with a shining diamond hilt aligned perfectly in the center of the white claw. The Edge of Sorrow, his father had always called the similar pattern tattooed on the left side of his shaven head. It was the third symbol of the whale's dream that created man, the third direction dreams flowed in their forewarnings of your life to come, the simplest symbol his father had taught Verl to draw when making a dream pentagon. In Singerhalle studying other languages and legends around the realm, Verl had learned the Morris stargazers called the same symbol shaped by a constellation of red stars, blue stars, and the brightest diamond star: Zaire's Sword. The double-edged sword of vengeance, the blade that struck down your enemies, or the blade that struck down your best friend with a killing word or deed.

Verl raised his palm over the circle on the floor to intercept the falling lights, to catch the blade in his hand. The pattern formed brokenly, the red bled more across the blue. Verl wondered what the Capsens called the Edge of Sorrow, they who had built this hall with its sunburst-like bear claw tiled into the floor and with its spectacular ceiling and walls of stained glass windows that bejeweled the hall with dazzling colors. That the pattern of a red and blue knife blade formed so perfectly in the middle circle of the claw could be no accident.

He turned his hand sideways and caressed his fingers through the stream of colors. Twice before when he'd come into this hall, he'd seen two other of the five sacred symbols of life. At sunset on the Springing, the day the merchant Duke presented Felain with her husband's head, the Web of Guilt entwined its delicate labyrinth on the left circle of the claw. And the morning after Verl interpreted Laird's dream, the summer solstice, his first official day at court when he received his keys and sash, he'd glanced down to see the irony of his choice of how he'd interpreted the boy's dream---to ease a child's nightmare, or to save his own neck?---mocking him in the second circle of the claw, the lights shining down on it forming for that half hour of summer dawn the Path of Right. Had his lie been his Path of Right? It had imprisoned him here as Court Dreamer, watched by queen and priests and jealous husbands, in a gilded illusion of luxury and freedom from his dungeon. And that lie had led him here today, on Harvest Moon, to the Edge of Sorrow, to the coming blade of winter, in more danger than ever. He released the pattern of lights from his hand and watched it fall again onto the floor.

A orange and purple slipper, a silver bell hanging from its hooked toe, planted itself over the circle covering the pattern.

Verl drew in his breath, glanced up quickly. He had thought he was alone.

But no one else had come into the Hall except Jing the jester and her monkey. Gal leapt onto his chest with a squeal, clambered up onto his shoulder, and choked its tail around Verl's neck. Verl reached into a side pouch, pulled out a nut for his chiding friend, and nodded to Jing. In the weeks since Laird's birthday, he'd run into Jing and Gal almost every day. For the monkey, Verl kept a pouch full of nuts; for the jester, he kept his wits clear, his words guarded. He was never quite certain of her loyalties. She could be fascinating in her observations that were as twisted in their own way as Lollander's words ever were. In that way, she had become his one link to the beloved old man. Jing was the closest he had come to making a friend he could speak honestly to here at court. Or perhaps, because of that, she might be his most dangerous enemy.

Verl nodded a greeting. "I thought you'd be outside today, dancing in the wine."

"King's Udor's carriage horse stepped on my toe when I was young. I'm older now."

Verl paused, not seeing the connection. "This happened at a harvest festival?"

"Did it?" Jing handed him her monkey's chain, then grabbed his arm as she bent one knee up and took off her belled slipper. The pattern of colored lights broke across her naked foot as she held it up between them. The blur of red light bled crookedly down the toe to the swelling of blue light at her ankle.

"Your foot must have hurt," Verl said.

She put the slipper back on. "It does now when the weather changes. Or when it gets cold and wet. The doctors tell me it's gout. All I know, it doesn't help to dance in cold, squishy grapes. I'll wait to drink the wine tonight." She set her foot back down square upon the bear claw circle. "I came in here seeking a festival of lights instead. And you? Why are you in here, young buck like you in the height of your rutting season, instead of out there leading a parade?"

In spite of himself, Verl blushed. Silently, he handed her back Gal's chain. The little monkey jumped onto the back of the dwarf's head, wrapped its arms around her neck, and taunted up at him with its head just topping hers, its mouth opened wide into a toothy grin.

"I like the lights in here too," Verl said. He looked around the deserted hall glistening in the full sun. "It's not often you can come in here when no one else is standing around breaking up the patterns on the floor that the stained glass windows make." His gaze settled for a second on her foot covering the bear claw circle. She removed it; he glanced up and saw her peering at him, the monkey above her head laughing toothily.

"I've never stood near a carriage horse," she said.

Verl opened his mouth, closed it. "But you said—"

She cocked her head sideways. The monkey held onto her neck and went for the ride. "I've lived in this court as long as I have because kings don't hire fools to tell them the straight truth. And you, Dreamer who's not a Singer, I thought you knew something of not telling all the truth either." She raised her hand and turned it palm upwards in the stream of falling light. "When I first walked in here, I saw your fingers playing harpstrings of colored light."

Verl met her eyes, said nothing. The gesture she described was something he'd found himself doing from time to time, but not consciously, not since the dungeon. Still, even now as he remembered, his fingers started twitching again. He clenched them into a fist to stop them.

"Did you hear their music?" Jing strummed her fingers through the shaft of light.

"No." Then another memory twisted inside him, and he added very softly, "Music is in the eye of the listener."

"Hi lolly, hold a holly! That sounds like something Lollander would say! I shouldn't forget, you have a history of believing fools will tell you a truth that's straighter than their words. He and I learned as children in here how to build a kingdom full of lies. The wise look for the deepest meaning in what you say when there is no real meaning. And the wealthy pay you best if they think they can find a hidden truth behind your twisted words, which of course must mean," she winked, "they're as wise as the wise to hear a meaning in your madness. I became their court jester, he their hornblower. Why'd you kill him, Singer?"

The question took him off guard. Then, slowly, surprising himself, he admitted something he never thought he would. "I didn't tell the guards the truth. I alone decided not to send the queen's orders to kill a man. I let them blame the both of us, and then kept quiet as they arrested Lollander as well as me."

She nodded, her mouth set firm. "You kept quiet, and so kept alive." Jing sighed, raised a hand to her monkey. Gal grabbed it and slid down her shoulder to hug her as she hugged it back. "Hi lolly, hold a holly," she said

275

softly. The monkey pursed its lips out wide to kiss her twice noisily on the cheek. Then chittering, bored with its show of sympathy, its scolding echoed through the empty hall until she released it. Gal jumped down and did two somersaults on the glittering floor.

The monkey stopped mid-flip, started patting at the floor as if to catch the colors. It screeched when it looked at its empty hand.

After a merciless moment of watching the monkey, Jing shook her head sadly. "A witch told me the same thing in this hall once. That men will look for patterns, deeper meanings, all the harder when there are none. We used to play a game in here of connecting these dots of colored light into pictures---animals, weapons, spider webs, whatever we'd see---and then tell each other their stories. Of course, she wasn't a witch then, just a daughter of the realm I tutored with Udor's sons."

Verl watched her. It was not the first time Jing had told him something as dangerous to say out loud as what he had just told her about his guilt. Still Edge of Sorrow, precipice of winter: Decision time. It was what Verl had come to meet Arnaby for, to choose a side. The Badurian priests may have tried to rewrite history, and may have condemned to dungeon or death in the last year any heretic who spoke of a different past, but the truth must come out. No one past the age of ten could have truly forgotten that the Capsen witch Ailil had fostered in this court, had grown up with Henrik and the Duke Rayid before she became Henrik's royal whore.

In return, Verl told Jing what he knew of the time before the Capsens were called evil.

"Her people built this hall."

The old jester nodded. "She told us that." She toed at the bear claw circle between them. The double-edged sword of lights was already looking jagged, starting to break apart. "Will I see you in here at Midwinter, Verl?"

Verl glanced at the fourth bear claw circle, met her eyes. So it was true, and she saw them too, she who had tutored Ailil. A Capsen legacy in a kingdom built of lies. "I wasn't sure. Until today. These are more than random dots of light. They do connect into shapes, don't they?"

"Patterns, yes. That keep returning and returning. People who see them will look for meaning in them. Special guidance. Even when you claim there is no such thing, you can't help looking. You still want to believe someone else, something else will tell you a deeper truth. So, hi lolly, Singer," she winked at him again, "learn what we learned in here. If you create a pattern, someone else will believe whatever you tell them it says. That's the power any teller, any dreamer--any fool has over you." A hint of Badurian incense smoke wafted past them, and a belled staff clicked against the tiled floor. They were no longer alone. Jing finished in a whisper. "Or any religion."

His back to the approaching priest, his curiosity about the bear-claw circles stronger than caution, a question was suddenly important to Verl. He pointed quickly to the fifth circle, and asked in a low voice, "And that one, have you ever seen that one?" If he guessed right, that should be the fifth symbol, the spiral of forgetfulness, the design he could never remember having seen to know how to draw it in his dream pentagons. He had drawn it that one time for Laird, yes. But that was different. That had felt as if his hands had moved of their own volition, as if by instinct, as if they were his father's hands. He had never since been able to remember the spiral he had made. If she knew it, if she had ever seen it...

Jing narrowed her grey eyes behind her spectacles at him, then gathered her monkey to her. "I'll be in here later this afternoon," she mouthed.

Then looking up past him, she jingled her belled cap and stomped her belled slippers and started to croon aloud to quiet her monkey's warning scold. *"Fiddle Fi Fence. You smell anon scents Of the Winged One's incense, little Gal. T'is all, t'is all."* She chucked the monkey under its chin. "Greetings, Brother Arnaby. Your smoke blesses me, but I fear my monkey has a lost soul. It makes her cough. I'll take her outside."

After she left, Arnaby lowered his priest hood and chuckled.

"You asked to meet, Verl. Does this mean you've made a choice?"

Verl tightened his fist, glanced around the room. "I've found a way to free my friends."

Arnaby said nothing at first. Then quietly, "Are you sure?"

"I've been there twice to make sure the way is still open. Will you help me?"

"The price will be high."

"I've made that choice. That much of a one, at least."

Arnaby nodded, put a hand to Verl's shoulder. "Come walk with me," he glanced around the hall, "to where we can talk about your friends' conversion more privately, my son." He lifted his priest hood back on. "I'm on my way to the Delta. I have a ship to bless."

Verl looked at him askance.

"I asked for this mission on purpose. This ship's crew has never been blessed during a festival. Come. You may find the journey there profitable to your endeavor with your friends."

~

The Delta had its own version of Festival parades. Stiltwalkers on the longest bluest stilts—those who performed the most daring spins and jumps—were the chosen leaders, and as leaders, they wore sinuous white eel skins and the great leering heads of a ghost shark. Seven other stiltwalkers from the settlements followed each leader's antics across the harvested rice paddies. Other stiltwalker parades wended out past the windmills and dikes into the mudflats beyond to where distant fishhuts built on stilts stood guard over boats bobbing in the bay.

By mid-afternoon, and only half a league outside the city gates, Verl and Arnaby rode donkeys down the wide boardwalk that crossed the mudflats to Port Norgol during high tide, stopping every few minutes for the day's busy traffic. Carts laden with wine barrels from the hills were hurrying to the ships to be the first new wine sold and exported. Milkmaids in high laced caps argued with wives

278

in blue knit shawls as they led their own slow parades of belled cattle and sheep up and down the boardwalk in both directions. Groups of eight children pulling mudrunner sleds of large rounds of Delta cheese and playing the fife and drums crossed the boardwalk at every sloping entrance from the mudflats below, leaving thick trails of the slippery mud in their wake. For each passerby who asked for a blessing of the Winged One on Harvest Moon, Arnaby recited a chant and raised his belled staff, delaying their progress to the docks even more. It had been the slowest half league Verl had ever ridden.

Waiting for Arnaby once again, Verl picked up a clay shark head lantern off the buckboard of a milkmaid's wagon. He had seen many such lanterns at a distance this afternoon, some made of gourds, some of baskets, some of real shark heads. The eyes and mouth were hollowed out, and the candle inside stood waiting in a pool of fish oil. Come nightfall, bright beady shark eyes and sharp-toothed leering grins would haunt the Delta by the thousands, as the black spirits of ill will and ill luck, Idi and Odi, would be dispersed with the oily smoke. Verl set the shark head lantern down and glanced over at the nearest heap of refuse and fish heads, one of the many such heaps out on the mudflats that would be set ablaze tonight too, the thick black oily smoke obscuring the harvest moon but purifying the land and chasing away all loose dead spirits before the long winter months when Idi and Odi would return. Black smoke, Arnaby had said, rising from the heaps immersed in fish oil, while the foul-smelling incense in his holy burner gave off only the pure white smoke of the Winged One's blessing. The spy priest had pointed out the difference with a chuckle when no one could hear them.

Finally reaching the docks in Port Norgol, Arnaby boarded and blessed the three merchant ships moored there, boarding the Red Bell last. After Arnaby chanted his blessing and waved his incense over the Bell's coiled ropes and furled sails, he and Verl were ushered down into the captain's cabin for "an offering." As the door clicked shut behind them, the merchant captain looked up from his maps to greet Arnaby. His smile became a frown at the sight of Verl.

He held up his hand for silence, tapped out his pipe, and rose to lock shut the two port windows before turning around for an explanation.

"Don't worry," said Arnaby, taking off his priest's cloak and sitting without being asked, "he knows I know the Duke, and he's told no one else"—he glanced at Verl—"yet. If nothing else condemns him to hang from the gallows beside us, that already has. He's come to ask us a favor, Howet, and in payment," Arnaby reached across the captain's desk for two pieces of saltwater taffy and handed one to Verl, "he'll owe us more than just his life."

Verl took the taffy stiffly, but he remained standing by the door, listening, saying nothing.

"What's the news about this Bearman?" Arnaby asked the captain.

"I found him. Or someone claimed to be him. He doesn't quite accept it yet himself. He won't be useful to us until he does. He had a twin brother though. I handed the queen's guards the Bearman's picture, told them where I'd seen someone looking like him. When they got through with the brother, and more than like, his village too for harboring him, I'm sure whatever they left for the Bearman to find will finally convince him he has no more abiding love for his sniveling queen and baby king. We'll have him on our side, Arn, beholden to the Duke's aid, easily."

Chapter 25
Navarn

The sky was leaden. Sullen clouds rolled down the hills beyond the teeming harbor at Lake Maynard. Winter lay not far behind.

Merind pulled her woolen Morris cape around her and kept walking. She was not alone, and that had not made her happy. But Duke Rayid had insisted she take an escort with her. For appearance's sake here in his city, if for no other reason. In gritting silence, Merind had acquiesced, but it had not taken her long to leave the tame festival parades and market stalls in the stately Guild Hall plazas behind her and stroll among the shoremen on the docks instead.

Today, as most days she'd been in Navarn, there were as many merchant ships from Norgondy in port as there were ships flying the Duke's flag. Merind bought salted anchovies on rolls for herself and her companion; and they paused in the shade of a warehouse as they ate and watched shoremen crating wagonloads of furs. More shoremen were busy wheeling the crates aboard a ship bound for Sonachin in the north of Norgondy. *The Pine Bough*, she read on its stern.

Salt upon the salty. Merind scrunched her mouth as she swallowed, and washed it down with ale. She stared down at the roll, took another bite.

Some of the furs still had heads attached. If bear heads, they were folded as is and packed in a separate crate. Other furs, the heads were hacked off before the pelts were loaded. Bear furs, as well as any other furs that could pass as bear, Rayid had tried explaining to her, had become the season's most in-demand commodity, selling better than wheat, apples, or wool. With his lips pulled thin, not hiding his insincerity from her tellerwoman perception as well as he thought he was, he'd gone on to say it was perhaps the most help he could give her people in their struggles against the Norgon queen, "mother of his brother's son, after all."

His farmers were more than happy providing him with foxes, lynx, wolves, bear, anything hunting their flocks, eight pence a head, for him to sell the furs, two talents a pelt, to any merchant brave enough to risk selling the contraband, ten talents a pelt and up, to outlaw bands already amassing against the Norgon queen and her priests in the northern provinces. And some merchant captains the Duke trusted most, he'd told her, had started to spread the Bearman cult to bands of highwaymen and refugees along the western and southern shores of Norgondy as well, planting new seeds of revolt, organizing new Bearman bands that would spread the demand for the furs they used as disguises farther and wider. New markets were opening every day, the merchants were getting happier, and the actual war Merind wanted him to help her start and the troops she had begged him to send may never be necessary. Let the queen's regency fall from within. Then he'd come help her and her mother clean up the spoils and put her baby brother on the throne. The duke's lips pulled thinner when he said that, and Merind, more certainly then, did not trust him.

She still wanted the troops herself though. She'd memorized the list of where the last thirteen of her captured friends had been sent as enslaved workers, she spoke it as a litany every night before she fell asleep. She was wasting her time here if the duke promised her no real help to go save them. Gave her no real power to take back the crown-- she crunched the last piece of roll in her hand--*to take back the crown as was her birthright*. Hers as much as her baby brother's! Henrik had been her father too!

She swallowed that last crunched piece of bread and finished off her ale. She did have one more secret she could tell the duke to convince him.

Merind detoured on the way back to the Rayid's palace to watch a reveler climb a scaffold built atop the gate tower, the highest point in Norval City. At the top of the scaffolding, a Morris shepherd waited with a huge silk kite to strap on the young man's shoulders. A pile of hay at the bottom of the gate was being raked high after the last youth's "landing."

More Morris cliffmen were trying to train the next five youths how to land safely; but it would take more than a festival afternoon to teach them. Two days ago, Merind had ridden out into the hills beyond Lake Maynard with Rayid, and watched ten units of guardsmen, two hundred men strong, training not only to land safely, but to circle in the rising air and fly higher, then twist and turn until they could land standing up on a target, releasing their kites from their backs with one quick hand, drawing their swords ready to fight with the other.

And this was a duke who said he was not training his troops for war?

~

Merind stood on the scaffold, the harness buckled tight around her shoulders. But not too tight, the shepherd advised, she still wanted to her arms free to control her kite. She listened attentively to his instructions, frowned only briefly when he shook his head at her long skirt. But the men below had taken her coins, sent her up without a word about it.

"Is there a problem?" she asked.

The shepherd's lips were stiff, a lie from someone who did not like lying. "No, my lady. Be sure to fall into the hay."

"And the skirt?"

He met her eyes.

"I want the truth."

"Then I'd advise my lady to climb down the way she came up."

Merind nodded, and took off her robe and underrobes down to her drawers and tunic. The wide skirts puffed into a sail of their own on their way down, and landed in the center in the hay stack.

"Better?" she asked. The crowd of spectators below was growing larger.

The grizzled shepherd shook his head, but this time with a grin on his lips.

"Remember keep the ropes even. Don't pull down on any harder than the others. The secret is to sail down. You're soaring on the wind like the eagle."

"And to turn?" she asked. She tested twisting her shoulders. "I saw your men in the hills doing this."

"No, no!" He straightened her shoulders. "You must go straight down, land in the hay."

"Give me a reason," she said.

He rubbed his beard, assessing her, then he squinted his eyes in approval. "Were we in the hills, I would teach you. Along with my own daughter. But not here. No wind here to ride. Just enough to float down on safely."

The first few seconds were the hardest. The fastest. The giddiest. She wasn't sure if she were laughing or screaming. She did know she had to fight to keep her arms straight, to keep her arms wide out and even, to keep her silk kite straight above her head where it could billow up, catch the most air, so she would not plummet hard as an arrow as she'd seen so many of the men do. *Arms straight*, the shepherd told her, *don't pull to either side*. The blur of colors, the sickening blur, too fast, *arms straight, arms straight*.

Then, mostly down, she got jerked up, and the great taut fabric billowed upwards straining against its ropes, catching the air, slowing her down. Slow, not slow enough, not the controlled slow peaceful descent she'd watched in the hills, but slower, not the plummeting arrow, slow enough to land mostly on her feet, before she sank as ignominiously deep into the haystack as most of the men, her outstretched arms finally trapping her from sinking farther.

Shepherd youths were helping her out of the haystack, unharnessing her shoulders, one meekly handing her the rescued skirts. She looked back up the tower to the scaffolding and the shepherd saluted her from on top. She raised her arm in triumph, and thanked him with a wave.

Her crowd was cheering.

~

284

By four bells, Merind charcoaled in the final details of a sketch of a guardsman flying off a cliff. She blackened the kite above him, shaped it to look more like giant wings. She glanced over at the sundial centered below the library's observatory. The tall rod extending from the north pole of the brass astrolabe would have pointed its shadow directly at the fourth number on the floor, if the duke's owl wasn't perched atop the rod, casting its odd shadow instead.

Merind shooed her hands suddenly at the bird and imitated its cry. Startled, the fat old owl screeched back at her and lifted its wings to fly off. Then, as always, indolence overpowered any instinct the bird had of fear—overpowered any natural sense the bird should have had at all, Merind had decided---and it resettled its wings, hunched its shoulders, and turned its neck slowly around to blink disdain at her, before falling asleep again.

But it had spread its wings out wide enough this time for Merind to see the bone structure better. She began to hum a Capsen victory song as she copied the bend of the joints and emphasized the long sweep back of the wing feathers she'd drawn on the kite.

Satisfied, she compared her sketch to that of the garug monster drawn to Rayid's careful description last week. Half-lion, half-eagle, with a scorpion-like curled forked tail. It was the beast the Badurian priests worshiped as their god, Rayid had told her. The beast in whose name her people were being hunted, massacred and burned at the stake as witches.

She hummed softer. The guardsman's body filled out in her mind's eye, rounding up out of the paper. His face blackened, his nose lengthened to a feline snout, his legs stretched down into eagle claws. She saw both images, the guardsman flying under kite wings on the page, and the drawing greying in her mind, starting to leech off the paper into the filmy illusion of the guardsman hovering above, shifting into a lionbird. As the hovering monster darkened, it slowly became more solid than air. This was a new creation for Merind. She took the time to make it look real. She hummed a new note, higher, stronger. The ropes to the kite pulled up through the sketched guardsman's shoulders, attached instead to the monster's shoulders. They pulled tighter, shorter, pulling the wings up with them off the page.

Winged, free at last from the paper, the hovering image roared. Then it tipped its wings on a thermal and rose, circling upwards on the air ever wider until it soared around the room.

The garug-guardsman landed quickly on top of a bookshelf as the door to the library opened and Duke Rayid entered the room.

Merind stopped humming, folded her hands over her sketches on the desk, and waited.

~

Crel wandered through his boyhood village on Eller Island. Two out of every three houses were burnt to the ground. Most of the houses left standing were vacated. Loose shutters and doors swung woodenly in the wind blowing salt and sand off the beach. Doors hurriedly shut, blinds quickly lowered in the three or four houses still occupied whenever he approached them. His warning someone still lived here.

He looked behind once to see a young boy's soot-covered face peeking out at him. A rough hand grabbed the child back and the blind fell flat again.

The brick hearth at the smithy still stood, a few scattered tools and nails, all broken, lay in the ruins. Crel picked up Yarisol's iron sign among the ashes, dusted it off, propped it up against the anvil. Yarisol had always been so proud of his work. On the hitching post outside, another "Bearman: Wanted Dead 5 talent Reward" poster flapped the sea merchant's sketch of Crel's own face staring back at him. Crel yanked it down.

Across the street, the women's long house where the wives and daughters of the village wove their woolen and linen cloths, their brightly colored sea designs prized throughout the realm, where they argued and laughed and gossiped about their husbands to each other and bore their children and watched them play, was burnt to the ground. In the center of the scorched earth and timbers was a funeral pyre, blackened arms and legs still jutting out. One in every ten residents, he'd been told. Crel dreaded what he'd find at his twin brother's house.

His pulse quickened when he saw the house still standing. Hope against hope, knowing better, but even the shutters hung straight. He ran forward down the lane through Lissiv's flax fields. Perhaps...perhaps, so far on the outskirts of town, they'd been spared.

He slowed when he saw her flax was unmown, overgrown. Her fields should have been harvested by now.

In front of the house, he found a stake driven into the ground with Clayl's body, half-eaten by crows and rats, bound to it. His brother's head had been hacked off; dried blood smeared the open blade of the scythe Yarisol had forged for them for their wedding. A wanted poster blackened with blood had been nailed into Clayl's chest.

Crel heard footsteps behind him, cracking the grain. He swung around, saw the blacksmith approaching.

Yarisol stopped an arm's length away, stared at Crel's beard, his sailor's stocking cap, his hair dyed black and unclipped. "Crel?" Crel's yearmate, foster brother to Clayl, his boyhood friend would be one of the few men who would recognize him, no matter what he wore.

Crel swallowed tightly, couldn't think of a word to say. He bent down, picked up the scythe, tried to hand it to Yarisol.

Yarisol shook his head. "It be yours. Now."

Crel dropped his arm, still clenching the staff. Indeed yes. And it had more bloody work to do. A sea captain who'd betrayed him. Guardsmen, a unit—a whole army of them, if necessary—who had done this. Capsens may have wanted Crel to be their legendary Alred come back to life to avenge them. Refugees and highwaymen may have wanted him to be their shapeshifting Bearman god in whose name they stole back their taxes and killed their torturers. But it was the guardsmen themselves who had honed him, who had shaped him into a weapon here. Crel hefted the scythe to his shoulder, closed its blade. The Bearman, in his most frightening incarnation the realm had ever imagined, had been forged.

"Lissiv?" Crel asked, glancing back at the house.

"Taken," Yarisol answered. "All our wives be taken. Sold in the mainlander markets. Mine too."

"Then first thing we do is bring them back."

Yarisol nodded. "All of us left be ready to go, if ye tell us where. Crel--" He reached out a sudden hand to Crel's arm, gripped him with the strength of his hammer. "Crel, none of us told the guardsmen when they came that Clayl be not you. None of us told them a thing."

Crel looked back at his brother's body bound to the stake, then met the terrible question in his friend's eyes. "I don't think anything would have stopped them, no matter what you said. You are not to blame." His fist tightened around his scythe, seeing instead of Yarisol's face, the sea merchant across the table from him drawing his sketch, shaking his hand with their deal. "But by the whale's dream, I do know who is."

~

Rayid closed the door behind him, barely looked over at Merind. He strode to five paces in front of the desk, held his arm out straight. He clacked his tongue twice to the owl and called it by name. "Tychobrav!" The bird opened one eyelid and cast a baleful look at Merind. Then it twisted its neck around to face the duke, lifted its great wings and swept towards him, its wings flapping the air.

Merind memorized the motion.

"I thought we discussed what your behavior would be in this city," the duke said, without looking at her. The bird landed on his arm and wrapped its talons around the leather band he wore. "You can wear your tellerwoman silks stripped down to the last one, or none at all, dance naked through the halls of this palace for all I care. But out in the city, you'll keep your skirts on. My people have expectations I'd like them to maintain. It keeps them in control."

Merind said nothing. Rayid untied a leather pouch from his belt. She watched it squirm, then began to hum softly again. Rayid immediately riveted his eyes on her, she tilted her head, grinned back. He unlaced the pouch and pulled out a mouse. She clacked her tongue twice. "Crisis!" she called.

The sound of wings flapping in the air came from behind Rayid. He glanced back. The garug-guardsman swept towards him, around him, hovered in the air above the mouse, stung it lifeless with its tail. It landed on the duke's hand, bit off the mouse's head.

Rayid met her eyes with steel in his. Then still facing her, he looked out of the corner of his eyes at his owl instead, and fed the still-squeaking mouse to his owl, whiskers and all.

"You are a witch like your mother," he commented.

"Did you expect otherwise? I have need of an army." Her hum changed note. The garug monster gripping his bare hand with its claws shifted into a kite-flying guardsman. The guardsman released the kite as it settled to the rocks behind him. He drew his sword and saluted the duke.

Rayid laughed heartily. "Clever child." He shook his arm and his owl took flight back to its roost. Then he swept the guardsman and rock image off his hand with his other hand. "Clever. Presenting fascinating possibilities." He went to the desk, moved her hands, inspected her sketches. He nodded. "All right. You can have a few men to help you go rescue your friends. But in disguise. I don't want them found out. I don't want it revealed who sent them."

"I want more."

His eyes swept up at her.

"You say I'm a witch like my mother. I am also my father's daughter." She saw his reaction, heard the sharp intake of his breath. So, he knew too. "My mother told me. As Henrik's daughter, I want an army to take back his crown." He frowned slightly, oddly, at the mention of Henrik, perhaps he had not known, it looked like he was more surprised than before. She smiled faintly, Rayid could hide his reactions from most people, but not from her. She hummed again.

The air grew hot around them. The garug-guardsman rose up on a current, circled the duke's head.

289

Another garug passed him. And another. Then ten, twenty, two hundred strong, circled the room. "An army to take back my country from the bitch queen who's destroyed it. And from her army of priests who call their monsters gods."

Rayid rocked back on his heels and watched the monsters circling. Then he narrowed his thick black brows at her and nodded once firmly. "Take five of my men now, to help you find your friends. Then, when the time comes," he glanced up again, "we'll see about making this army of yours real. If—" he met her eyes, "you can."

~

Alone that night, Rayid consulted his astrolabe, positioned his telescope, shuttered the lanterns. He focused on the sword constellation, the bright red star at its tip. The sword of truth, Ailil had called it, when she first showed it to him as children in his father's palace. The constellation at its zenith tonight during the fall equinox. The sword that cuts down your enemies, or the sword that cuts down your friends with the bitterest truths between you.

Ailil.... She had first kissed him that night, showing him the constellations, telling him their stories, mired in her Capsen myths.

Rayid refocused on the blue star overhead. The star always overhead, at the center of the universe. The star at the center of the spiral of forgetfulness, the fifth symbol he could never quite remember. He could never remember either which stars connected to form the two spirals circling away from the blue star in the center. In Barzolf's company on his stargazer hill guiding the Morris shepherds, or in Ailil's company all those many long nights ago, he could see the spiral of the stars. He forgot them every other night in his life. Forgot or ignored them.

He had hoped he had forgotten Ailil too. Or had ignored that she had forgotten him.

Rayid uncovered the lanterns, took Ailil's message from his pouch. Reread it, frowned.

Why now? he wondered.

He took it to the desk, added it to Merind's sketches. "She's like you, you know," he said softly to the night.

"You should be proud." He folded the sketches and the message away into his pouch. He laughed to himself. "Do you know she flew? Put on kite wings today first time she had a chance? Same age I was when I did.

"Ailil!" Rayid stretched his fingers on the desk, leaned forward on them, screamed the tellerwoman's name. "What game are you playing here? What are you doing? Why would you tell your daughter she was Henrik's child? And then... Then send her to the one man who would know it was a lie."

After a moment, Rayid sighed, snuffed out the candles, opened the window for the owl, and left the library. If her own mother lied to Merind to use her as a weapon in her war against the Norgon queen, did that not give him permission to play along--or keep quiet as if he were--but in secrecy, use her too, for his own best interests instead?

Their daughter had come up with an interesting way to make his flyers look more like the garug gods of the Badurian priests than even he had planned. Clever, she was. Clever. She might indeed be useful.

Chapter 26
Spiral of Forgetfulness

The sun was setting past the ramparts of Norgarth into the western sea. The glass dome observatory on the palace rooftop glittered with the blazing colors. Verl had the impression he had stepped into one of the kaleidoscopes the toymakers peddled on market day.

As he walked around the room exploring, he realized that much of the glow came from reflections off the five stained glass windows on the palace rooftop. Those would have to be the same rose windows that jeweled the throne room by daylight. If so, he stood above the throne room now.

The walls to the observatory were panels of lightly colored glass. Verl counted: five panels each of red, orange, yellow, green, blue, then red again, twenty-five panels in all, interrupted only by the iron door that led back down a steep circular staircase squeezed between the palace wall and the bell tower.

Verl had never guessed an observatory was up here. From the square below the palace, even from the rooftops of Singerhalle, the parade of statues of kings and gargoyles around the roof of the throne room must hide the dome from view. And during his months living in the palace, he had heard no one speaking of an observatory.

The glass dome above was clear to the heavens. A brass telescope in the center of the room slanted up towards it, its lenses covered. There had been a small telescope at Singerhalle, but nothing so ornate.

He stepped closer to the telescope and reached out a hand to dust it off. As he did so, Jing's monkey leapt from his shoulder onto the barrel of the scope. Gal screeched and slid off as her sudden weight snapped loose the brass clasp holding the scope in position, and the scope swung upright.

"Gal!" Jing reprimanded. She gathered the monkey to her on its chain. "You asked about the fifth symbol, Verl? I think this will be it."

The jester knelt between a brass astrolabe centered on the floor and a second set of two flat wheels. The larger wheel below was toothed to turn slowly. When Verl noted it, Jing pointed to a set of gears below the astrolabe and to a rod along the floor that connected, she explained, to the mechanical clock in the bell tower next door. "Every week when they reset the clock chimes, they're turning these gears, never knowing it."

Verl looked at her questioningly.

"Ailil brought us up here when she was a child and showed us how it worked. Henrik and Rayid came often after that. No one else knew or, maybe, just didn't care anymore and forgot about it. After Henrik died, and the priests took over, I've had no reason to show his son yet." She met Verl's eyes. "He'd be more destructive in here than Gal. And what the priests would do to a secret room built by Capsen lore and magic, if they knew it was here— Hi lolly! If you want to risk your life in the dungeons again telling them about this observatory, you can. Just leave my name out of it. At my age, I'm quite content to live out my last years in the peace and lies of luxury."

Jing pulled out a long kerchief from her jester's pouch and wiped dust from the top wheel, uncovering the inscription and designs etched into it. "I think this is your Spiral of Forgetfulness."

If the design she pointed to was indeed meant to be a spiral, it was no wonder Verl had never remembered it as one. But it was a design he had seen tattooed on his father's head. A design he'd also found scratched on a rock face on top of the hornblower's hill. And seen once too in a Morris stargazer book at Singerhalle above the caption: the Birdfoot Star. If a spiral was a wound spring pointed towards him, he could almost see how the design might match. Or two spirals, perhaps, side by side, circling away from each other. Four broad curved rays narrowing to points jetted from a blue circle in the center. On each side, two of the jets curved towards each other. If continued, the circles formed by the two jets would narrowly miss. As in a spiral. On the other hand, the design still looked more like an owl's footprint in the sand, as the book had described it.

The design etched below the birdfoot spiral was a constellation of stars Verl recognized. The pattern of nine stars he called the Arrowhead, the symbol of the Path of Right he drew in his dream pentagons. Added to the nine were five more stars making in total the constellation the Capsens called The Bear. Lines joining the stars completed an outline of a bear.

Verl glanced over at the astrolabe. All five constellations were etched in red showing their position among the stars, one to each of the four winds, and the fifth, two adjacent spirals of stars, circled a blue star in the center.

"Ailil read the inscription to us, years ago," Jing said. "But I can't tell you what it says, I don't read Capsen."

Verl read the inscription. He'd been trained in all the languages of the realm at Singerhalle. But one of the Capsen words was new to him. "Garug?" he asked Jing.

Jing shook her head. "A mythological beast, I think. At least I've never seen one. A cross between a lion and a bird, Ailil said."

Verl pursed his lips and then read aloud. "When the lionbird steps from the fire, the land will move. The sea will storm, the harvest rot. When the Great Bear wears a crown, princes die. Beware the Birdfoot Star."

Verl looked back at the bear constellation and the spiral of stars etched above it, crowning it. "When the Bearman wears a crown, eh?"

Jing was watching him. "From the counting song of Capsen children, yes. And this wheel below counts too. 198 teeth in it. In the fifty years since I first came up here, it's moved fifty teeth."

"198?" The number was familiar. He calculated back. "That's about how many years ago Alred led the Capsens out of the desert of the Midlands. And when they came here, and King Edoff granted them a valley of their own, that's when the Capsens built the throne room for him. In appreciation."

"And this observatory," Jing added.. "Perhaps...in warning instead? Touch here." She traced a finger along the design of the birdstar spiral. Verl copied her and discovered that the lines of the etching went through the top wheel.

"When Rayid was here," she said, "he and Henrik took off the top wheel once. There's a hole in the bottom wheel right about here." She pointed just below the spiral. "In the fifty years the wheel's been turning, the design above has come closer to the hole beneath it. Next year it should be right above it."

Verl frowned at her.

"I climbed up into the rafters of the throne room once, just to see. When I was younger, of course. There's a small window in the ceiling that never lets light through. It should be right below us now, in the center of the five rose windows outside."

Verl retraced the design of the birdfoot star spiral, memorizing it. If what Jing had said was true, then next year the fifth claw circle tiled on the floor before the throne would be filled with this symbol.

He rose, looked out a red panel to the west at the setting sun, the silhouette of the city towers darker now. One year. The bearman. A lionbird.... The winged one of the Badurian priests perhaps?

Princes die. He clenched his fist. He'd already cast his fortune in with Arnaby and that merchant captain this afternoon, both spies for the duke, both plotting the Bearman's brother's death and blaming Laird's forces to get the Bearman, whoever the unfortunate soul was, on their side. Verl would be dealing with those two spies too, for their aid in freeing his friends in the dungeon tonight. But he had no ill wish towards Laird, no wish to see him die.

His gaze settled on the silhouette of the dungeon tower, the three dark strips at top its only windows. He could clearly see for the first time from this height where bricks had been added to narrow the windows—so no witch could fly out at night, except as black smoky sludge, the stories said. He scoffed. There had been no witches in the dungeon that he'd ever met. Just friends falsely accused---

His eyes riveted suddenly on the harvest fires starting to dot the delta beyond the dungeon tower. Like so many shark eyes. Or like the evil sparks of foxfire. What had Arnaby said? About white smoke, black smoke? Idi and Odi, the delta spirits of ill will and ill luck, were being driven off tonight in that thick black smoke rising from fish oil-drenched bonfires.

Verl turned on his heel back to Jing, ready to go. He had an idea now how to conceal his friends' escape, and he needed time to get it ready before meeting Arnaby at the ship tonight.

~

Behind closed doors of his dreaming chamber, Verl mixed incense powders and oils, trying to find the combination that would make a towering billow of thick black smoke. He finally decided fish oil would have to work, if he could send enough men from the ship for it.

He dropped a whole mandrake root onto the fire. Grey smoke, not white enough. Strong enough to make him sleepy though. The root shriveled until it looked like the bones of a burnt man. Or an animal. ...*Or a god?* More pieces of his plan fell into place.

He still needed a tower of white smoke to be conquered by the black. After trying several more powders, he remembered Arnaby lifting up his incense burner. The Badurian holy smoke was white, Arnaby had laughed, while the evil spirits of Idi and Odi fled away in black smoke.

Verl should have reasoned it out sooner. The holy smoke itself would be perfect.

Verl kept little Badurian incense oil in his room; he never used it if he could help it. The halls of the palace stank of its foul odor, but his chamber had a window he could open whenever a priest visited and he had to use it.

Verl sat on his heels, gazed at the fire. He'd need a quantity of the priests' oil that might be impossible to find. Unless.....

He stood up, went to the nook beside the door where the week's assortment of ribboned keys were kept in a bowl. For once, the ladies of the court would have a visitor tonight.

He emptied the keys into a pouch and tied it onto his belt. Then he went to a shelf behind the dreaming mat where he kept his vials of powders and oils. He took down a narrow leather case and opened it. Inside, cushioned in blue velvet, was a Singer's pipe he'd found last market day. Silver and thin, it looked like a flute. With the attachment screwed on, it could even play three notes, disguising it. A Singer was trained in three weapons from his earliest days at the Singerhalle: his music, his knowledge, and his blow pipe. The blow pipe was usually the first of the three the youngest apprentices enjoyed mastering, much to the dismay of some of their instructors' arms and legs. Verl had bought the pipe thinking Laird might find it fun. But perhaps not, and undecided, he hadn't shown it to him yet. A blow pipe was not meant to kill, only to put an enemy to sleep long enough to escape. Laird wanted weapons that would kill.

Verl's gaze strayed back to the center shelf.

Unlike most Singers, he knew poisons that could make a blow pipe a killing weapon, had some of those poisons on this shelf. But he never would have told Laird that. Nor he would ever consider using them himself, not even tonight. Singer training was too ingrained in him. His training had ended up ruling his actions in the dungeon-- he'd become a healer there, not a killer--and if there, he'd be ruled by it anywhere.

Still...

He picked up one of the vials of poisons, started twisting it around in his hand. He wasn't a Singer. He had to quit telling himself that he was.

Finally, he shook his head, set the vial back down. He couldn't risk taking a chance tonight. Even if he were tempted...*even if he were*...he wet his lips, shook his head again, his training might still make him hesitate. And hesitation could be deadly.

When he set the vial back down, heard its thud on the wooden shelf, an odd sense of relief swept through him. It surprised him. He hadn't known he had any beliefs, any dreams left in himself to be relieved.

Verl set to work, finishing quickly. He unscrewed the flute end from the blow pipe, and slipped the pipe section into his tunic. Then he added the stonefish spikes

297

he'd bought as darts in Port Norgol today to a second pouch on his belt. The sting from a stonefish's spiked fins were slightly painful but quickly effective without having to add any drug. Many a stiltwalker who took off his stilts to check on his rice had stepped on a stonefish lurking in the mudflats. He'd be found hours later blissfully asleep, and upon awakening would report wild, vivid dreams, full of bright swirling lights and tingling music. The stonefish spikes made darts Master Singers would approve.

The spikes did have a problem, though. After multiple stings, some people could become immune.

Verl frowned at the possibility, and double-checked it in a book. The immunity could wear off in time, you had to keep continually being stung. He closed the volume softly, glanced back at the vials on the second shelf. It was unlikely that anyone inside the palace had been out in the mudflats recently enough to have developed an immunity.

But tonight was no night to take a chance. He opened an empty vial and mixed inside it the sleep of ground mandrake, the dreams of crushed numbstool, and the calm of myrrh. Still nothing strong enough to kill, or so he hoped, but he would have them with him too, just in case.

He slipped the vial into his pouch with the stonefish spikes and left for Port Norgol.

~

The crescent moon was peaking above the cliffs and the stars were out in full when the Red Bell anchored in the cove below the cave to the dungeons. It was a bright clear night, with a low fog bank still far out at sea. Half a dozen dinghies rowed ashore, their lanterns swinging heavily as they rode the waves in. Two were filled with the merchant's men who would scour the shoreline for more seagull feathers. Several birds had been caught already as they followed the ship from Port Norgol. Half a burlap sack of feathers had been plucked before the greedy gulls learned to not dart in so close to the fishing nets. Four other dinghies were full of sailors who would follow Verl into the cave, carrying three barrels of fish oil and the half sack of feathers. Each of these men carried a weapon, and none of them, from the look of them, would have any hesitation using them. Verl would have to make sure none of them would ever find their way through the tunnels any farther than the dungeon.

He unhooked the dinghy's lantern and stepped ashore.

The cave barreled inwards through the cliff. Gloomy and moist by day, its brick walls seemed narrower, shorter, darker by night. Verl tensed with each footfall and murmur of the men behind him. He had explored this tunnel twice before, but always alone.

The tunnel forked, and Verl motioned the men to silence. His heart thudded; he could not quiet it. No one could hear them, he kept telling himself, ten feet below the ground, but knowing the fact did not make it feel true.

They were below the gates to the city now. To the left, the tunnel led to a large unbricked cavern, and a dead end. To the right, stone steps climbed up to the pit of the dungeon. And past it....past it, according to Laird, the tunnel continued up to the king's bedchamber. A secret escape route for the kings of Norgondy.

Verl hoped he could find the second door leading out of the dungeon. He'd found a map drawn on the floor of the cavern from Laird's description and had memorized it, then recovered it in moss. Twenty paces along the wall to the right, then a dozen bricks up.

Verl nodded to the sailors and started forward. Fumes from the fish oil were getting strong in the close quarters. His breath came in strangled gasps; and as they climbed onwards, the lanterns jerked odd shadows of the men following him, closing in upon him. Footfalls on stone, their labored breath, the dull slap of their swords and axes echoed around him.

It was relief when he came to the end of the tunnel. At the top of the steps was the stone door he'd never tried opening. From behind it, he could hear the unearthly howls and tortured screams of nightlife in the dungeon.

The door did not open easily. A half hour passed, maybe longer before two hardened seamen pushing on it made it budge. Then it creaked, and swung backwards on its own, almost knocking the men off the top steps.

If the nightly screams of the dungeon had brought back nightmares to Verl, the sudden silence when he entered it, lantern in hand, was more terrifying. Everyone was watching him, startled; but he knew it would not take long for the gangs to attack.

The sailors, their axes and sabers drawn in one hand, the barrels and burlap sack of feathers used as shields in the other, crowded in front of him.

They weren't enough to stop the surge.

Two of the prisoners pummeled forward, then ten, then fifty. They broke one barrel, fish oil splashed up, the slimy streaks glowed in the lantern light like silver fish escaping. Feathers flew from the gunny sack. Then blood spurted. A bearded head sailed up above the crowd, and the sailor in front of Verl sliced his axe through the air again.

Amid the confusion, Verl closed his eyes, felt the sea within his veins lurch sickeningly. He forced himself to sway with it and, concentrating on the rhythm, went invisible.

Then carrying the lantern, which he'd kept visible, he stepped beyond the sailors, over a body, shoving his way, and being shoved, and punched, and battered, through the mob.

On the other side, a few steps beyond everyone, he heard a woman scream with terror, louder than all the fighting. He turned, everyone seemed to turn, and he saw her point, others pointing now, screaming at the lantern, floating, it must look like, through the air.

The dungeon went eerily quiet again. Most everyone down here had been accused of witchery and heresy, but they were more frightened of him than he was of them. He recognized one of the gang leaders, still here, still in blood lusting power. The brute stretched his muscular, sweaty, blood-smeared arm out in front of him, and crossed his second and fifth fingers, a child's sign of protection against the evil eye.

Verl laughed aloud as he walked onward. His laughter in the eerie silence bounced off the walls of the dungeon pit.

He stepped over a dead prisoner, dead a few days from the smell of her. Rats, flies, undisturbed by his passage, kept eating.

In the center of the dungeon pit, everyone still watching the lantern, Verl dropped the illusion from their minds and materialized in front of them.

The immediate effect was as he had hoped for. His magical appearance still kept them far away from him. But for how long it would, he was unsure.

Verl held up his hand, spoke quickly. "If you want out of here, if you want your freedom, you will do as I, The Bearman, say! My men will step aside, let you out that door. But first, I need your help. To make your escape good. To make your escape a mystery to the guardsmen. I want a dung heap, here." He pointed down, swept his arm around him. "Piled as high as we can make it. I want all the dead bodies we can find, bones, or just dead yesterday, piled on top of it. And you. And you and you. Gather up all those feathers. Work quickly, work quietly. And then we'll all be free to go."

The dung heap started, Verl spotted Arax sitting cross-legged by the wall, watching him. Verl nodded, and Arax waved back, rose, and came to him.

Verl slapped his shoulder and embraced him. "You old bearfighter! You're still alive!"

"Aye, and half ye auld gang still be here too. What is this? Ye call yerself the Bearman, now?"

Verl lowered his voice so no one else would hear. "It's the name of a new ogre in the realm believed to be fighting the god of the priests. If anyone from here gets caught, they'll claim the Bearman released them."

Arax pulled at Verl's tunic sleeve, the silk blackened with grime, blood, and fish oil. "Well, new name or no, ye've gotten yerself into some finery, since I seen ye last."

Verl unlaced a pouch of coins from his belt and tied it through a hole on Arax's shirt. "Aye. And there's more coming for you too."

Arax met his eyes. Even in the dusky light, there was a plea in them, a hope that countered Arax's gruff beard and powerful build, and a fear that struck Verl to his core. "Is it true?" his friend asked.

"That you're getting out of here? That you're going home to your frozen isles? Yes! Or wherever you want! But I need your help tonight. Meet me over there to the right of those sailors at the door."

When Arax left him, Verl went to the two barrels still full of fish oil. He directed a sailor to empty one of them onto the dung heap. Most of the prisoners were already streaming out past the sailors into the tunnel, the heap in the center of the pit as high and foul as Verl had asked for. Several of the prisoners, Verl noted, were clutching their tin cups in their hands as they passed him. Their one treasure, their one bond to life they'd fought to the death for here in the dungeon. What value those tin cups would have for them outside, Verl did not even want to try to guess.

The stone door was bricked on this side to match the rest of the dungeon walls. The second door would be too. Starting from the corner of the opening, Verl paced twenty steps to the right along the wall. He was counting the twelfth brick up, searching with his fingers for a latch hold, barely felt it, when Arnaby came up behind him.

"We wait," Verl said. "Until everyone is gone. The sailors too; I don't know them well enough to trust them. In the meantime, we'll need that empty barrel to take with us."

As they waited, the sailors from the beach brought in another sackful of feathers. They emptied it on top of the dungheap. "You sure now it's as you want it, lad?" they asked Verl before they left.

Verl nodded. "Bring a boat back at dawn to take my friend with you on your ship."

~

When Verl and Arax reached Laird's chamber in the palace, Verl stepped inside the room first, alone and invisible, his blowpipe loaded with a stonefish spike.

302

The boy-king was asleep. The guardsman posted for nightwatch sat in front of the fire playing a solitary game of gammon. Verl went up behind him and aimed at his neck.

The guard gasped out loud. Verl glanced nervously back at the boy-king. Laird turned over in his sleep, but he did not awaken.

Counting every drawn-out second, it took almost a minute for the guard to collapse and fall asleep. Verl checked to make sure he was still breathing, then he carefully turned him over to face the hearth, his back to the rest of the room, and recovered the dart from the guardsman's neck.

Then finally, he pulled back the tapestry from the wall hiding the secret door panel, and motioned Arax to come in. Verl went to work quickly, pouring most of the gilded urn full of holy incense into the barrel Arax held for him. He was careful to leave enough oil that the urn wouldn't be noticeably empty for a day or two.

Then, sorting through his pouch of labeled keys, he chose Lady Ellis's as the closest chamber down the hall, and motioned Arax to follow him. It may take them another hour or two to fill the barrel full of the priests' holy oil. Time was not on their side.

~

The dungeon was greying when Verl lit the dungheap with his lantern. It was almost dawn.

The two of them circled the fire, fanning it to keep it growing. Then the fish oil poured on top caught fire, and the flames soared. The black smoke rolled from the flames in thick ugly billows, choking the men, filling the dungeon, then swirling upwards to sludge out through the slits of the windows.

Pressing wet cloths to their noses and mouths, and between gags and coughs, the men howled and bayed like wolves or dogs in pain, and roared at the top of their lungs like bears.

Then Verl and Arax ripped open the barrel of holy oil and heaved it on top of the roaring fire.

303

The fire sputtered a moment, then the flames leapt anew, higher, hotter. The sweat and heat burned Verl's cheeks and forehead, and dried his lips and throat. They'd made the dungeon a brick oven, and even through the wet cloth, it was hard to breathe. He howled, howled as loud as he possibly could. His chest hurt, burning from the inside.

The black smoke greyed, then patches of white smoke swirled up with it, then puffs of white, all white, floated out through the windows. The stench was nauseous, burnt flesh, burnt dung, and both laced with the foul incense of the priests' oil. His throat, his chest, his stomach muscles kept gagging, kept wanting to vomit, but there was nothing inside him but scratching scorched air. He howled, weaker, but he tried, had to keep trying.

They ripped the top off the second barrel of fish oil and threw it onto their bonfire. Then gagging, running, they left the dungeon without waiting to see if the black smoke would rise again.

The door swung easily and quickly shut into place. But not before the smoke followed them out through the tunnels. Gagging, coughing, running blind, finding their way with their hands, they finally outran it, and collapsed, coughing, at the mouth of the cave, breathing in long painful gasps the cool muggy air of morning fog.

Sailors, two men each, helped them down to the beach to the dinghy bobbing in the fog. "We'll meet again!" Verl promised as Arax boarded with the four sailors.

Then Verl took the reins of the horse Arnaby had brought for him and mounted quickly. He still had one final job to do tonight before the morning bells rang.

~

The sun was rising. By its first good light, the hornblower stood at the stone table outside his hut, transcribing yesterday evening's scroll of news and court orders into horn notes.

Invisible, Verl walked five paces behind him and aimed a dart at the back of his neck.

304

The hornblower swatted at the sting. Two of the guardsmen he'd encountered in the halls had swatted too before collapsing. Verl stood quietly waiting.

The hornblower started writing again, then cocked his head, scratched the back of his neck. He found the dart, pulled it out, looked at it, spun around. He must have been stung before, he seemed to recognize the stonefish spike for what it was, thin as it was, short as it was, he didn't assume it be a stinger from a bee as most people would--it wasn't a bee he was looking for.

"Who's there?" he shouted. He started running for the boulders and the copse of trees behind Verl looking for someone. Verl had to step back out of his way as he passed him. "Who's there?" the hornblower shouted again.

Immune to the stonefish, had to be. More than a minute had passed. Verl took out the vial of numbstool, mandrake, and myrrh oil mix and dipped another spike into it, reloaded his pipe, and waited for the hornblower to quit running.

He shot him in the arm.

The hornblower's hand went to it, spun around to Verl's direction. "Where are you? Who are you?"

Verl stepped back, started running sideways, as the hornblower ran towards him. The hornblower couldn't see him, but maybe he could hear him.

Verl stumbled over a rock, made it roll forward. The hornblower picked the stone up. Verl shot another dart dipped in the oil at his shoulder.

The hornblower ran towards him, staggered, then he tumbled over in front of Verl's boot.

Verl waited a moment, then he turned the hornblower over and listened to his chest.

His heart was beating slowly, his breathing was very faint. But he was still breathing. Verl sat back on his heels and dropped his head, catching a deep painful breath in his still burnt chest. The hornblower had taken two dosages of the oil and three stings of stonefish spikes. Verl could only hope it wasn't too much. The hornblower was just asleep, not unconscious, never to awaken. *Please let it be so*, Verl prayed to whatever real god there might still be in the world.

305

And if—when—the hornblower did awaken, how much would he remember? The guards would never know what had happened to them. This hornblower might.

Verl still wanted him to only be asleep.

He rose heavily, then climbed the stone platform to the mouthpieces of the two long mountain horns, one shorter, higher noted than the other. He unrolled his own transcribed message and sent it out:

"The Bearman released his witches from the dungeons of Norgarth. A feathered messenger from the Winged One tried to stop him. The holy messenger lies in ashes. Beware! the Bearman and his witches prowl across the land. Beware! The Bearman comes. Lord of the Winged One, Lord of the Nameless One, save us all!"

Verl had one final thing to do before the morning courier came. He climbed down the platform and went back to the hornblower's side.

The bells in Norgarth started chiming as he carried the hornblower to his hut--chimed longer than the first hour of day, he noted as he paused to listen. The town was alerted then, they knew something was wrong. The smoke may have been spotted, the rumors already started, perhaps even the guards were already descending to the dungeons and finding them empty. Verl quickened his pace.

He placed the hornblower on his cot, covered him, made it look like he was still asleep from last night.

Then, knowing he should go, Verl glanced over to the second cot in the shadows of the hut, his own, when he had been here last spring. Covered now in wooden boxes full of scrolls and other items this hornblower had stowed there.

He had made a promise to Eleidice that he would get his lute as soon as he could. He had spoken without believing he ever would.

He dug it up hurriedly from under the cot. In its case just where he'd left it, planning to never touch it again

A lot had happened since then. Many decisions made, and as many broken.

He recovered the hole, then cradling the lute case under his arm, went to his horse.

Chapter 27
The Chosen One

Invisible, and as quietly as possible, Verl opened the door to his bedchamber. The night was finally over.

Then, his heart skipped a beat. One of the queen's guardsman sat beside his bed, tapping his foot.

Verl stepped back quickly, started closing the door. The guardsman looked up at the movement, then came to the door, looked up and down the hall, frowned. He started to close the door, then stopped and sniffed the air. He cocked his head in puzzlement, probably smelling smoke, fish oil, dung, horse sweat, Goron knew what else Verl had on him.

Verl stood frozen, his heart pounding too loudly. The guardsman stepped farther out into the hall and frowned up and down it again. Verl slipped into the bedchamber behind him. The guardsman closed the door, and Verl stood trapped, waiting.

Men were outside shouting, running up and down the streets. Confusion reigned everywhere this morning. It had made getting back to the palace easier than Verl had hoped.

The guardsman went to Verl's window, pulled back the shutter, watched the commotion for a few minutes. While the guardsman had his back turned, Verl set his lute down hurriedly inside his wardrobe, took off his boots, and grabbed himself a fresh set of clothes. He was already halfway out the door again when the guardsman turned around, saw the door reopened. The guardsman marched over. "Someone there?"

Verl ran down the hall without looking back. He was invisible, but he could hear his stocking feet padding against the flagstones. He did not stop running until he reached his dreaming chamber a hall away from the throne room.

Someone had been inside the dreaming chamber too since he left it; he saw the tip of a boot print in the ashes by the firepit. But nothing else was disturbed. Verl changed clothes quickly. He only had a little water in the wash basin he used for cleaning his vials and pestle. He splashed it on him, it was barely enough to wash off his hands and face, but it would have to do. He tore open the windows, leaned out, tried shaking ashes, grime out of his hair. He considered throwing the dirty clothes out the window too, but in the end stashed them under the dreaming mat. He'd figure out what to do with them later . He glanced around the room, the vial and spikes he'd taken with him were arranged as before, and the blowpipe back in its case looking like a flute again. He started to leave the keys in their nook too, then thought better of it, and pocketed them. Whoever had come in here might have noticed them gone. Then, composing himself, he walked back down the halls towards his bedchamber. He snuck from shadow to shadow, but otherwise he was in full sight of anyone who cared to look.

When he opened his door and found the guardsman still waiting for him, he caught his breath, as if surprised.

The guardsman stood stiffly, looked down his nose at him. "Verl, master of dreams, you have been reported missing. Your presence was required by the queen and high priest at first bell this morning. They are in the west wing hall waiting for you. This way, please."

~

"My lady." Verl bowed before the regent.

Felain looked up from a table map of the realm. Two guardsmen stood with her, one pointing down at the map. The high priest was on the other side of the table, listening to him. Three other priests, including Arnaby, stood in a huddle near him, conferring. Several lords and ladies aroused by the morning's clamor milled around the room.

The queen barely nodded acceptance of Verl's bow. "You were gone from your room last night, Dreamer."

Verl stiffened. He had one chance. His hand went to the bulge in his pocket, as if hiding it before answering. "Yes, my lady."

"What do you have in that pocket?" the queen asked, seeing his hand.

"I.... Nothing. I'd rather not say. It's a private matter only."

Felain came around the map, held out her hand. "Show me what's in that hand, Dreamer. Or show the guards."

Verl nodded as if forced to and slowly pulled out his collection of labeled keys.

Felain took the keys and sorted through them, reading their labels; then she laughed softly. "So, this is where you were last night. Tell me, is there a key for every lady in the palace here? I know there's been a competition for whom you would visit first." She looked over at her ladies in waiting, all of them with their attention fully upon their conversation. "I'm curious. Which one?"

Verl glanced over at the ladies, glanced back. He swallowed, shook his head. "I'm sorry, my lady. I cannot name her. I might compromise her position, if I did."

Felain laughed louder, handed him back the keys. "You are a prize! Most men would not consider that, not until they had a jealous lord coming after them. I've no doubt you'd be the talk of the court, any other day. But something else happened here last night, Dreamer, far more important. Do you know what it was?"

"I've seen everyone talking in whispers, my lady. And yelling outside. But I've been told nothing yet."

"There's been an escape from the dungeon. Ah, I see that brings back memories for you. There was a great fire inside it. Burnt bones and feathers as if from some giant beast. And nothing left of the witches but smoke, the townsmen tell us. And you know nothing of this?"

Verl opened, then closed his mouth, speechless a moment, wondering what he could say. It was the same reaction, he hoped, he would have had if he had known nothing. He glanced back over his shoulder at the ladies of the court again, as if seeking encouragement from one of them. He shook his head, shrugged. "When I was in there, your majesty, I heard, saw things I never want to remember. Witches flying around at night–" he swallowed, crossed his fingers in front of him to ward off the evil eye. He saw the head priest start to make the same sign with his right hand. "At least, that's what I think I saw. I can't swear to it. I heard them, I heard something. It's so dark and terrible in there at night. I stayed away from them, just trying to survive. Blessed be the Winged One, I did."

The high priest came closer, lacing his fingers together in front of him. His thick white brows furrowed as he stared at Verl. "You, Dreamer, you survived the trial in the Arena by the grace of the Winged One, claiming you were his Chosen One. *Chosen* for what, do you think?"

Verl inclined his head in a show of respect to the priest. "By its allforgiving grace, my lord, I believe the Winged One must have chosen me so I could be its humble instrument, interpreting its blessing upon the king, so all here could know it had sent his royal highness, not nightmares, but dreams of greatness in his sleep."

The priest studied him a long uncomfortable moment. Verl knew the high priest resented Verl tutoring Laird in matters outside Badurian teachings.

Finally Verl inclined his head again. "As indeed, the Winged One continues to bless me, my lord, allowing me to see the dreams of those who come to me. The queen can attest to that. I am but the Winged One's grateful servant."

The queen narrowed her eyes at him. It hardly mattered if she believed he had any faith in the Badurian god or not. He was not the only one in her court who spoke the words the priest wanted to hear. A kingdom built of lies, Jing had called it.

Felain changed the subject quickly. "Why we sent for you, Dreamer, you were a hornblower. The high priest has told me he's not sure what the horn message sent out this morning said, but he had a report that someone heard the notes for 'bearman,' 'dungeon,' and the blessed 'Winged One, Nameless One.' Perhaps you heard them too? Or perhaps," she nodded at the keys, "you were being too entertained to hear them? Those words were not in the message the courier delivered to the hornblower last night."

"I ... must have been still asleep, my lady. I never heard the horns this morning." He clenched the keys. It

310

would matter if she suspected he was lying to her. Arnaby was right; he could not risk staying at court any longer after last night.

The queen turned back to the map on the table, moving a marker that represented her forces in the northern provinces. She spoke without looking up. "The priests want to send you away on a mission, Dreamer. They tell me it's necessary to take you away for a while from Laird's side. I am not sure," she looked up at Verl, "I can agree to let you go."

Arnaby stepped forward, picked up one of seven furred markers that showed where the major encounters with the bearman bands had been reported. "My lady. We must find out what this Bearman is. We can no longer be at its mercy, waiting for it to strike" – he set the marker down on top of the walls of Norgarth– "wherever it pleases. If indeed this Bearman came to this city last night, past all the guards, we need to find out how to stop it before the panic it leaves behind destroys us all. Peasants and merchants are outside in your streets already packing up, escaping the city, leaving looters behind them. This is only the beginning. Your guards alone cannot stop this Bearman, they can barely control the looting. You must let me go with your royal tax assessor when he leaves on the morrow. For all appearances, I'll travel as a itinerant priest, spreading the holy mercy of the Winged One throughout the villages of your northern provinces, and bringing them hope and word again of your support and good will. But out there among the people, I shall also have the chance to spy for you, finding out whatever I can about the truth of what this Bearman is. If, that is, I have someone with me who can speak the languages of all your peoples. This dreamer has been trained in many languages, I've been told. I need him; your country needs him. Along the way, I promise to you, my lady, I'll take his majesty's tutor to the library at Solenzia where perhaps he can find more books to help prepare your son for taking the throne one day."

The high priest stiffened and frowned sternly at his brother priest's suggestion that he'd take Verl into the realm's central library that was now the monastery and seminary for their priests. But that was the precise suggestion that would convince Felain, and Verl saw her straighten and smile slightly at the high priest. This was not the first time Verl had seen Arnaby play the two of them against each other.

The captain of the guard who had been pointing at the map when Verl entered nodded, as if the issue of Verl had already been settled. "Then, priest, you'll want to start looking here first. This small island off Sonachin harbor. One of the Eller islands where the tinker reported to be a Bearman was killed. From there, canals go to the library at Solenzia. This is where the first priest was murdered." As the queen and priests gathered around the map again, listening, making plans, forgetting him, Verl headed quietly for the door. He was almost knocked down by a courier running breathless into the room.

The courier knelt before the queen, and doffed his velvet cap. "My lady! The hornblower is dead. Died in his sleep. He could not have sent any messages this morning! But, my lady, Singerhalle has found someone who could interpret what the horns sent out this morning, whoever-- or whatever--sent them." The courier handed the queen a scroll.

Felain read the horn message, blanched. The high priest took the scroll from her, read it, and gripped it hard, almost crushing it.

He turned on his heel to Arnaby. "Go, brother Arnaby. Go now! Take that dreamer with you. Find out whatever you can about this Bearman from the gates of hell."

Chapter 28
The Bearman Lives!

For as long as Merind could remember, it had rarely snowed in Drespin. And never so much as it did here in Sorenzia.

She pulled off a mitten and caught a snowflake on her fingertip. More delicate than lace. No pattern the same, Orist had once told her.

She grimaced. There was no meaning in its uniqueness, no importance, until this one snowflake was added to the multitudes that blanketed the farms and cities and shut down the world.

The snowflake melted and Merind pulled her mitten back on. She would add an army of multitudes behind her one day and do the same. Shut down Felain's world. Shut down the inequities. Shut down these trade markets that bought and sold people like cattle.

Another oxcart with sled runners on its wheels scraped across the stone bridge. This time a child no more than three was in the wooden cage. Would that she had the money to free them all.

"Make way!" A guardsman shoved her back a step with the threat of his sword. Traveling in caravan behind the cart was a taxman and a priest with his unholy retinue. The child could surely not be a heretic. Someone sold to the next city along the taxman's route perhaps and traveling in the safety of his company. Merind closed her eyes and turned away with the possibility of another answer. Or someone sold to the taxman himself by the boy's father to pay his taxes.

For the next several hours, Merind wandered in and out of the half-timbered shops built on top of the bridge. Most were print shops and book copiers; a few were cloth merchants and inksellers. Two of the three water mills anchored below the bridge's arches made the paper sold throughout the realm. Whether the paper mills came first to Sorenz Valley, or the Library on the island across the bridge was built first, was a chicken and egg question. The river that powered the mills was fed by the Norgol plateau to the east. The wild loneliness of the plateau that backdropped the spires of the island inspired the student woodcutters to some of their greatest works. And the torrent that flowed past the island nine months out of the year was consistently deep and plentiful to keep the students supplied with paper which was rare and expensive elsewhere in the realm. The valley made a natural setting for both a library and rich mills.

The mills were closed for the winter now, as was most everything else. Snow covered the narrow valley of flax fields and mulberry groves for as far as Merind could see. The only sign of life beyond the bridge was the slow cold billows of smoke rising above the grey row of silk worm farms along the western bank of the river. The giant factory hearths were keeping the worm eggs dormant until spring.

A few weavers who were owned by the shopkeepers were still working. Merind could hear the clack, whisper, clack of a loom in the back of a haberdasher's. She ran a hand along a smooth bolt of brightly dyed silk and compared it to another bolt of much coarser linen. Most of the flax grown here would never become linen, the shopkeeper told her—his excuse why his linen was so poor-- most of the flax would be used to make paper instead. He tried to turn her attention back to his fine silk, but it was not what she had come to the market for today.

The third industry that had grown up around the Library of Norgondy was active only during the winter. The so-called Labor Fairs, the buyers and sellers of people. Some claimed that unlike the slave auction in Elkhorn in the south of Norgondy, Sorenzia only dealt in buying and selling the contracts of indentured workers needed on the mills and farms. But Merind knew there was nothing of free will in Darine's contract of servitude being auctioned off today at five bells.

Finding a small dressmaker's shop at the end of the bridge, Merind bought a bright linen tunic and a warm sheepskin cape for Darine to wear home. Darine was the last of the thirteen Capsens captured that night in Drespin who was still alive and whom Merind had not freed yet in the last few months with the help of the duke's five men. Darine's "rescue" would be the easiest of all--and, perhaps, the most demeaning, they had only to buy her from the slavers. Every time Merind thought those words, "buy her from the slavers," it made her angrier at Felain.

She crossed the bridge to the island and sat down at a long trestle table beside the blazing hearth in the Town Hall Cellar. She ordered a piping hot glass of spiced apple wine and a plate of pinenut sausages and waited for the duke's men to join her.

Next table over, a group of students sat around a blue-collared raconteur who was performing a reading from a book. An ever present Badurian priest listened closely to make sure what was read was not heretical.

Merind's wine arrived just as a Norgon guardsman swaggered down into the Cellar, disrupting everyone's conversations. He started passing around freshly printed posters and handed one to Merind.

"Have you seen this man?" the guardsman asked the room. "I have. Keeper, an ale!"

As the keeper poured him a mug from the giant oaken barrel, Merind slid the poster around on the table to look at it. Blond hair, dressed in the red scarf and cap of a fisherman . . . but his face was that of the tinker who had brought Wiss's body home. Crel, his name was. The poster called him the Bearman. It was a copy of an old wanted poster that warned justice had been served, the original Bearman had been executed.

"I tell you I've seen him!" the guardsman repeated then swigged half his ale. "And he's not dead! I was there that day we nailed him to the post and cut off his head with his own sickle. Four months ago that was." He took another swig. "Then two nights ago, I saw him again. He attacked our unit in broad daylight. Sickle in hand, black-cloaked, like a demon returned from the gates of hell. What he and his men didn't kill, in bear shape he came back and killed us all. The priest, the tax man, all dead!"

The priest rose, motioned to some men in the corner to surround the guardsman. "Come, my friend. You're deluded. These bands of brigands who call themselves bearmen are dangerous and crafty, yes. But they only dress the part. And soon, by the Grace of the Nameless One, and by the courage of our fine men like you, we'll catch them all. Come, now." The priest nodded to the two men holding the guardsmen's shoulders and they started guiding him back up the stairs.

"No! I tell you. No!" the guardsman shouted before being pushed out the door. "It was the same man! The same man we killed! This Bearman's *not* human. He does not die!"

~

"Darine's on block number three," one of the duke's guardsmen whispered to Merind as he sat down on the bleacher beside her. Arrangements had been made and they carried enough talents in their satchels to outbid everyone.

First up, an old man with one eye patched behind his heavy spectacles. His hands were curled up with arthritis. "Forty years spent as a book artist and designer of fine woodcuts," the fairman said. "On his way to the debtor's prison. He can still work your ledgers. You can have him for what he owes in taxes. Do I hear a bid?"

A silk farmer offered a half-hearted bid, a miller's agent raised it. Neither was high enough, the fairman announced, and the warden led him away in chains.

The next drew greater interest. A young woman, a scarlet-haired wholesome beauty, standing stiffly straight; but her eyes were vacant. Merind had seen that same look that night in Drespin Hall on the captives repeatedly brutalized. The empty stare of someone no longer living, enduring only. If it was so hard to see this stranger on the auction block, how much harder would it be to see Darine standing up there next?

"Gentlemen, a rare find! Look at her hands." The fairman nodded to the warder, and the warder lifted up her hands to show off her long nimble fingers. The woman yanked them down and clenched them beside her. "And spirited too! The hands, gentlemen, of a true Eller Islander weaver. Her work, I'm told, is a marvel to behold. What value would she add to the products of your looms? What new fine weaves will she teach your young workers? And young and healthy enough too, plenty more years inside her to bear a dozen daughters to add to your rosters!"

Several traders went forward to inspect her closer. One among them wore a black cloak and leaned on a staff. "What's wrong with her then?" another one asked.

"T'is well you asked! Honesty is our policy in all our dealings, as well you all know. You saw the stubborn streak in her a second ago. This one I'd keep under lock and key for a year or two and guard her well. She was the wife of the one who was first called the Bearman. She'll take a stern hand---"

Before he said more, the room erupted. The trader in black had edged forward till he stood between the girl and the warder. He pulled out the head of his staff from under his cloak, flicked open a lever, and the long curved blade of an islander sickle flashed out, stopping just under the warder's neck. At the same moment, every door to the Fair arena swung open and in swarmed men dressed in bear furs and bear masks, wielding swords, axes, and bows, maybe fifty or sixty of them. With little contest, they surrounded and disarmed the dozen guardsmen on duty, and then ten bearmen archers aimed at the traders on the bleachers.

"Everyone stay calm, and you won't get hurt," the man in black said, his sickle still just grazing the warder's throat. He flung his hood off, and Merind could see the profile of his face.

Crel.

"You," the tinker said, scratching the sickle slightly up the warder's neck until he was forced to raise his chin higher. "Release her. Now."

Some of the traders around Merind had copies of the wanted poster the guardsman in the tavern had been passing around the city, telling his story to anyone who'd listen. Merind saw the traders unfolding the posters, comparing the face, and heard them starting to whisper, "It's the Bearman himself!" "T'is true. He never died!"

As the warder shakily unlocked the woman's manacles, the keys ringing leadenly, the far door pushed open and all the prisoners were herded in, released from their cages by more brigands in bear masks. Darine, in a mended grey shift, was pushed in among them, looking bewildered and terrified.

Merind rose, shoved her way down the bleachers. Ten arrows pointed at her, and before she reached the floor, the duke's men grabbed her by the shoulders and pulled her back.

The commotion distracted Crel. He glanced back, then froze, recognizing her.

"We must go!" shouted one of his men, coming forward, grabbing the woman down from the auction block, pulling her past Crel.

Crel shook himself free of his stupor and raised his arm to his men. "Come on!"

The bearmen herded the freed workers out the back door, Darine among them. Casting one last glance up at the bleachers, Crel followed; then the archers started edging backwards towards the door, keeping their arrows trained on the crowd.

Slowly the guardsmen, then the crowd in the bleachers bunched forward, ready to give chase. Merind whispered to the duke's men four words: "the fire at Maori." They nodded and followed her, slipping behind the crowd and over the side of the bleachers. One of the men grabbed a lantern off a post and handed it to Merind. She leaned over, picked up several straws off the floor, and lit them in the lantern's flame. She laid the lighted straws among the rushes at the corner edge of the bleachers and started to sing softly. The straws leapt up into a small fire. The song made it look higher, wider than it was, starting to spread fast. Only a few in the crowd would need to see it to panic everyone.

A trader on the bleachers screamed, "Fire!" The few traders closest to him came rushing to stamp out the illusion, but most of the crowd went running for the far doors.

They didn't get far. The bearmen must have bolted all the other doors from the outside, except the one the bearmen archers were blocking, training their arrows on anyone following them.

Merind weaved her hands over the small real flames, then started tamping them out with her foot as she sang louder. Fire had always been her most natural element. The flames had burned their image indelibly into her mind by now. She no longer needed to see them. There was enough power in her memory of them to thrust the vision she wanted of a growing fire into the minds of everyone in the hall to see. The real fire died as an illusion of a blazing inferno, floor to ceiling, spread along the wall towards the archers. Pandemonium broke out as the crowd scrambled, yelled, and shoved more desperately to escape to the far doors again.

Merind gestured, and the duke's men hurried after her walking calmly into the wall of fire. Merind had freed four of the Capsens around the realm with the same illusion of a blazing fire wall, the first one at the Maori silver mines; and the five men had become accustomed to trusting her word that it was illusion only.

The bearmen archers had backed away from the fire they saw approaching, but once outside, they still pointed their arrows at the door. Crel stood with them, waiting. Merind kept singing to concentrate on the illusion.

Crel turned his head sideways, looked at the fire through the corner of his right eye. Merind wasn't sure how much of her he could see instead of flames, but he knew to try.

"Hello, Tinker," she sang softly, standing in the door still inside the illusion. "We want to come with you. You have a friend of mine."

The archers glanced at Crel nervously, hearing the words coming from the fire. "We?" Crel asked.

"I have five men with me. I can't talk long and keep the fire going."

"Can you keep it going from out here? If so, you can come on out, and I can send my men on."

Merind stepped out the door and the duke's men came with her. She nodded at Crel, then turned to face the door and, weaving her hands, sang louder again.

Crel motioned his men on with the duke's men. When they'd slipped away, he touched Merind on her elbow and guided her backwards towards the end of the building. Then Merind stopped singing, and together they ran for the bridge through the snow storm.

They escaped over the bridge landing climbing down four rope ladders. The archers came last, and brought the ropes with them. At the bottom of the bridge, they followed the support out around onto the ice then back under the bridge into the first of the abandoned mill traces. The archers swished the rope ladders behind them to erase their footprints.

The bearmen had prepared their escape well, Merind noted. By the time the alarm bells rang in the city above and the guardsmen were trampling up and down the bridge hunting for them, the released workers and the bandits were all safely huddling inside a huge empty vat in the middle millworks which had been closed for the winter. They waited silently until the dead of night, then as the snow fell covering their tracks, they walked across the frozen river and up onto the west bank. Keeping to the trees they followed the road to the seventh long grey building along the river, a silk farmer's factory.

A sympathizer, the farmer claimed as he led them down into his cellar. He scurried among them, wringing his hands, bringing them lanterns, blankets, bread and cheese, incessantly talking. He welcomed the bearmen, yes indeed, and no man would keep their secrets more. His taxes were too high, they were ruining him. He'd had to sell out his own grove of mulberry trees last year. He would have to purchase mulberry leaves for his worms this next year at market price, to try to stay in business for as long as he could. How he could, he didn't know. Unless, that is, the bearmen could help. After everyone had settled and were starting to eat, Crel handed him a large sack of pilfered taxes.

Then the tinker came over and sat down among the freed prisoners.

He met Merind's eyes, but neither spoke. He pulled a blanket over the shoulders of the young woman he had freed. She was Lissiv, the wife of Crel's twin brother, Merind had discovered talking to her. It was Crel's brother whom the Norgons had killed, mistaking him for the Bearman.

"Crel," Lissiv said, reaching up to clutch his hand on her shoulder. "Little Jere, they took him this morning and carted him away."

Crel gripped her hand at the news; his face looking grim, determined. "I promise you, Lissiv, I'll find him."

"He's only three. He's only.... He was so frightened." Lissiv lowered her head; her shoulders shook with broken sobs.

"Blue wide eyes?" Merind asked. "Wearing a ragged shift that was once white with sailor red?"

Lissiv looked up at her, nodded.

"I saw him," Merind said. "He was in the company of the taxman and many priests."

Crel's eyes went haunted. He rose, and went and talked to a group of his men.

When he returned, Crel squeezed his sister-in-law's shoulder. "Get some sleep. We'll be gone before morning. If all goes well, we'll have Jere back in a few days."

Crel looked over finally at Merind. "I met your mother," he said.

Merind nodded. "She told me," was all she said back.

Later that night in the dusky red light emanating from the fire in the factory oven, Merind and the duke's guardsmen stood waiting by the stairs as Crel and his men and his sister-in-law were getting ready to leave. "We're coming with you," she told Crel. "Perhaps we can help you find the boy. They took the east road."

What she didn't tell him was why. Now that she'd found that the leader of the bearmen was someone she knew, Merind had found her army of multitudes.

～

For the second night in a row since they'd left Sorenzia, the Bearman's son's constant whimpering interspersed by loud screams for his mother awakened memories inside Verl that he'd thought he'd buried years ago. Listening to a long pitiful "Mammam!", Verl squeezed his eyes shut against an unbidden image of his own mother's face when he'd told her his naming dream.

His shoulders hunched into hard knots as he leaned back against an unforgiving tree in the Baskong Forest. Verl hadn't been much older himself when he had been sent away from the Islands the next morning, only a few short hours after telling her, not a tear in his eye. He'd set sail full of hopes and promises, believing himself already a man, and forgetting so soon that he'd never see her again.

But then, he hadn't been sold away from his mother and carted off in a cage like this child had. If Verl could, he would buy the child himself, then go back to Sorenzia and buy his mother too, and set them both free. If he could. If only he had not sworn to Arnaby to not say a word that might break their disguise. If only he had not sworn to sound as if he too were in full support of the plan brewed up by the priests and guardsmen of Sorenzia to trap the Bearman, using his son as bait.

That the child was not the Bearman's son, but the son of the Bearman's brother's wife by the Village Father before she'd married the Bearman's brother---all this according to Arnaby's network of merchant spies---made no difference. Arnaby still expected the Bearman would come hunting for the child, and the duke's spypriest still intended to meet up with the Bearman when he came.

Verl held out his half-gloved hands to the fire, the long protruding fingers stiff and red from riding all day through the icy wind. He was only now beginning to feel the sting of the fire through his fingertips. He brought them to his lips and blew hot steamy breath on them, then wiggled them towards the fire again. It was as cold here under the trees tonight, but the wind had died down.

The boy screeched again. Nerves and muscles inside Verl's back and shoulders slammed him against the tree trunk and made his outstretched arms start jittering, as if he'd been strung as sensitive to the child's screaming by now as lute strings tuned too tight. He balled his hands into fists and crossed his arms to control them.

He was not the only one who had reached his breaking point. "Someone shut that brat up!" the captain of the guard ordered. The captain barely glanced up from his game of crossjacks as one of his men rose.

The guardsman stopped a few feet from the fire, bent over the unit's gear, and picked up a horsewhip. Verl's breath caught. He cast an accusation at Arnaby for ever having asked his forbearance; then he broke his word and stood up.

"Let me go, Captain. Try to settle the boy first, if I can. I speak his language."

The captain eyed him. Verl was accompanying the priest as a translator, the captain had been told, but Verl hadn't proved himself yet as anything more than an unwanted mouth to feed and another body to kick awake in the morning. With a shrug of dismissal, the captain grunted assent and waved his man back to their game of cards.

From his own pack of gear, Verl took out his lute case bound in extra leather wrappings to protect it from the cold. He had only tried playing the lute once or twice in the last few months since retrieving it. He dusted the sprinkling of snow off, unwrapped the case, and cradled it under his arm. He grabbed an extra blanket as well and went past the covered sled, the boy's cage by day, to a second fire, and beyond it, to the giant tree with the cavernous hollow in its trunk, the boy's cage tonight.

Verl nodded to the two guardsmen sitting dwarfed by the tree trunk, sharing stories and a skin of ale. Some of these Baskong trees were so huge that if forty guardsmen sat shoulder to shoulder around one, they wouldn't surround it.

Verl bent his head to enter the hollow trunk. Once inside, he had to stoop, his shoulders brushing the jagged heartwood. He edged to one side of the opening to let more firelight in, but his eyes still had to adjust. Not even forest fires could kill these giants, or so the legends claimed; but most of the interior of this one had been charred where a fire had tried to gut it. Outside, Verl had grown accustomed to the bright night of fire and full moonlight reflecting off the snow banks along the frozen river and off the silent horde of the ghostly tree trunks that soared to the stars. In contrast, it took him a moment to see more detail of the child's face than just the small circle of the darkness watching him.

"Hello in there," he said.

Silence. Fear pierced through the child's silence louder than his screams.

Verl spread out the blanket, leaving enough corner for the boy to cover himself if he wished; then Verl sat down on the blanket and opened his lute case. Not saying a word, he tuned the strings. The chamber of the tree around him deepened their tone, but the briskness in the air tinned them. He listened to the notes and readjusted them, then paused, and laid his hand across the strings, not daring yet to play. Hopes, dreams, illusions of flowers and lights, everything he had once tried imaging with his music was finally destroyed in him—he had killed a man, that hornblower with his blowpipe after all, he had told himself repeatedly in the last few months, every time he had touched his lute. He was definitely not a Singer now, not a peacemaker, never could be again.

When Verl finally began to let his fingers play, he played simply, without a Singer's flourish, without well-practiced art. A lullaby from the Eller Islands, the music only, not trying to make it magic.

The boy shifted in the darkness, and his tan pudgy fingers clutched around the edge of the blanket. More than likely his mother had sung him this song, just as Verl's own mother had. The boy was young, maybe three or four at most. His eyes were wide and dark and bright, reflecting the light of the fire beyond Verl. His hair was the coppery yellow of an islander fisherman.

"Do you have a name, lad?"

The boy pulled the blanket up to his nose and hid more behind it.

Verl closed his eyes and stretched back into his past, trying to remember other songs from the Eller Islands that Singerhalle had never taught him. A work song for the first seeding day of Spring, as simple a melody as the first. Children not much older than this child sat in the woven baskets on their mothers' backs and tossed a handful of flax seeds onto the ground as they sang along with their mothers. Slowly the blanket came down from the child's face.

"I bet you'd like a friend," Verl said. "Someone you could teach these songs to." Verl cupped one hand on the blanket in front of him, and, concentrating, cast upon the hand a reflection of himself dressed in Singer Blue. The image of the tiny singer from the dungeon plucked a silent string on his tiny lute, an action Verl had never tested making him do before. Then he looked up at the dark eyes peeking above the blanket again.

"He's a secret though. You mustn't tell anyone about him. He's just your friend. No one else's. Promise?" Verl took away his hand, and the tiny singer doffed his silk cap and bowed low to the boy. "Promise?" Verl repeated. The tiny singer put his hand on his hip, and tapped his foot impatiently at Verl. Verl cast his voice into him, squeaking it a tone or two higher, and the tiny singer scolded Verl in the deep Island vernacular. "He most assuredly do! Be all the seagulls knowin' better'n you if ye'd think once to doubt him!" The tiny singer scrambled across the blanket and knocked on the hard mountain that was the boy's knee. "Be that true, or be that true, me lad?"

The child released a slight giggle. He squirmed his hand out from under the blanket, palm up to the image of the singer, and the singer, nodding haughtily at Verl, hopped on, and from there, onto the child's knee. The singer positioned his lute and strummed his strings as Verl played softly for him. A jig this time, to celebrate the salmon run. The little singer tapped his foot to the music; then, as he strummed faster, Verl tried making him dance the jig. But the steps were complicated —happily so, and the child giggled aloud when the singer slipped and fell. "You then," the singer said, tapping his foot impatiently again. "You do it for me, you teach me the steps again. Sometimes ye be knowin', lad, a son must teach a father to remember."

As Verl played softly, the boy danced the jig with two of his fingers on his knee while the singer tried copying him. For Verl, trying to keep the image responding while he was playing even the simple notes was like patting his head with one hand and rubbing a circle on his hip with the other.

325

And often, like a released puppet on a string, the singer would stumble over his feet and fall to his knees again, and each time the child would laugh louder.

"No! Like this, like this!" the boy finally said. He jumped up in the center of the tree hollow and danced the jig himself, teaching the little singer to copy him. The next time the singer fell, the little boy tumbled with him, laughing gleefully. He rolled over and landed beside Verl's foot.

Verl softly set the lute aside and held open his arms. After a moment of looking up at him, the boy scrambled into his lap and held on.

"I want mammam," the boy said.

Verl nodded his head on top of the child's head. "I know. But you have to be a big man now. Make her proud. And here," Verl lowered his hand to the blanket and the little singer hopped on. He slipped the image inside the side pouch of the child's tunic. "Whenever you need a friend, he'll be there with you. You may not see him again, and no one else ever will, but he'll be there with you. I promise."

~

By dawn, Crel finished hammering a body shape out of a sheet of tin. He greased it with goose fat, poured a bucket of water over it, tossed a handful of metal shavings on it, and waited for the water to freeze. As cold as it was this morning, it did not take long for the ice man to take shape. He drank hot root brew that Freyshin brought him as he waited.

"Where are they?" Crel asked.

Freyshin shook his head. His beard was sprinkled with the falling snow and his breath blew out clouds of fog. "Camped just inside the Baskong. Why they're taking so long to get here, I don't know. Unless they're waiting for us to attack."

The tea burnt Crel's lips and made him notice the sting of the wind on his cheeks. He took another sip. "A trap?"

"They might think so. Too many priests among them. They might all be guardsmen instead, concealing

326

swords under their scarlet cloaks. But we have a surprise or two waiting for them ourselves." Freyshin nodded at the ice man taking shape, torso and head only, no arms, no legs. The thin layer of ice was shining, catching the first rays of the sun that filtered down through the clouds and the canopy of tall trees. "Do you think it will work?"

Crel finished off his mug of tea. "We'll see. Did you bring a cloak?"

Freyshin took the mug from him, dropped it into his burlap sack, and pulled out a black hooded cloak that matched the one Crel wore on raids in size and color but instead was of the thinnest light-weight silk. The wind snapped it out full-length like a flag. He bundled it into a ball and handed it to Crel. "The snowmen are looking good. The men have already made a row of them dressed in furs and bear masks, with bows and arrows in hand, blocking off the river just beyond the bend. Real enough I swear I was ready to enlist them into our ranks of bearmen."

Crel chuckled. They'd use snowmen as decoys before. No matter how many times the snowmen were shot with arrows, they still stood standing, "fighting back." He wasn't the only bearman the legends were calling immortal. Freyshin was right. People could believe anything they saw, or feared they saw. And the greater their fear grew, the more they could be made to believe what they saw. "Let's see if this thing will work," he said.

It was a struggle to slide the tin out from under the ice form. The layer of ice was thin, but it had rings of thicker ice from where Crel had dented the tin mold slightly. These rings should give the ice man enough strength to hold its form until it melted, but the rings were what made pulling the tin out more difficult. The right side cracked, and the crack broke into a wide hole at the bottom of the back, but when they set the ice man on a slat of pine, he stood upright from his waist up. They dressed him quickly, tying the hood tightly enough to cover most of his face, but loosely enough to suggest that he had a neck.

Finally Freyshin stood back and nodded in approval. "Better than I thought."

Crel frowned at it and shook his head. "So far."

327

They lifted the plank with the ice man on it and fit it over the bench of his tinker's hutwagon. Crel had found the wagon still intact, hidden under a haystack in his brother's barn last fall, and in the months since, it too had become a part of his legend. Many a foggy morning, Crel had dressed in his tinker wools and had driven his black wagon across the path of a party of taxmen and priests just before the bearmen attacked. Other times he had Jesser cross the road on her hind legs in front of the doomed party instead, or else she would appear to the survivors afterwards. And his third incarnation as the shapeshifter Bearman was when he joined the fight himself, dressed as the reaper of death, his fierce sickle thirsty for the taste of guardsmen blood to avenge its tasting of his brother's neck.

Today there would be more guardsmen to fight. And this time, the prize was the life of his sister-in-law's son. Jesser could not stand in for him; she was mostly asleep for the winter, back in their camp deeper in the forest. There was no waking her without getting clawed. Today instead an ice man driving his wagon would be the first shape the Bearman would take before the fight.

The hole in the back of the ice man happened to be the right size to slip the coach lantern inside the hollow form.

"Wait," Freyshin said. From his sack, he took out a thin package. He unwrapped the rawhide around it and showed Crel. It was one of the newer tiles he had made of the Bearman. With stars above her head and sparkles of foxfire below her, it depicted Jesser with Crel's face demanding the cargo from the canalboat trapped in the lock at Dardin Mill. Freyshin slipped the tile under the ice man, next to the lantern.

They heard a bear growl downriver. A closer growl answered it. The caravan of priests and guardsmen who had caged little Jere had been sighted.

Crel met Freyshin's eyes, then he hurried to hitch up Esra. At the last moment, he lit the lantern and turned the flame up high. What part of the head that could be seen under the reaper's black hood shone eerily, an effect Crel had not anticipated. He jumped onto the wagon beside the ice man and drove Esra out onto the frozen river; then he cracked the whip over her head hard and yeehawed at her to drive her into a canter before jumping off and running back into the woods, dragging a switch of pine after him to conceal his trail.

Freyshin was waiting for him. He had left open the door of Baskong heartwood that matched the scorched hollow of the giant tree near the river road. Their band had first attacked from this stand of trees on the river bend last fall. The tallest trees here were all survivors of an ancient forest fire. Over the past few months, the bearmen had built their hideouts in the hollowed trees, fitting them each with a perfectly camouflaged door that sectioned off a part of the interior. There was a large knobby burl in this tree's trunk that faced the road, with peepholes drilled through the burl, and an arrow slit carved to look like a jagged crack splitting the burl.

Freyshin had pitched his burlap sack behind the heartwood door, and had his bow and arrow in his hand, ready. Crel took one last glance at Esra slowing but still ambling toward the caravan of sleds and horses and priests already rounding the bend in the river.

He grabbed Clayl's sickle, and ducked into the cramped nook beside Freyshin, and closed the camouflaged door behind them.

~

Verl had reveled in the two-month long stay at the Library in Sorenzia. During that time, Arnaby, with orders from the queen, interviewed all survivors of encounters with highwaymen, whether the highwaymen were bearman bands or not, and inspected the growing contraband of furs, tiles, arrowheads, and other evidence of the survivors' stories kept locked away in the vaults under the Library. The spy priest spent every morning praying for salvation from the bearman scourge with the Badurian priests who had converted the university at the Library into their state seminary. Then he spent every evening meeting in secret with his network of merchant spies, passing along the descriptions of the bearman raids to other bands of bearmen around the realm for them to copy. And occasionally in the dark of night, he passed along the key to the locked vaults as well.

Meanwhile, Verl's official task, when not needed to interpret for Arnaby, was to search through the censured books and manuscripts for written accounts of the bearman attacks for the queen's edification, and also by her orders to search through the books in the great Library of the Realm for any reference to pre-Badurian history and culture that took his interest to help him teach King Laird. After his months imprisoned in the dungeon and in the court, Verl felt he had found his side gate into paradise.

Many a day he spent sunrise to sunset lost to the world among the stacks and stacks of books. At nights his dreams became haunted by pages of scrawled words as his fingers twitched in his sleep flipping the pages over faster and faster. He woke early each morning starved to read more.

Then, five days ago, Arnaby had told him to pack up, they were leaving. The Library that day loomed over him with stacks of unread books.

Many of the books he had read and couldn't bear to part with, he'd bought from the bookcopiers. Two mule loads of his treasures were in the caravan with him today. Many had pages of censured passages ripped out, or huge sections were simply left blank by the copier, but Verl also had a bundle of scrolls of his own careful notes, all ostensibly written and sealed for the king's use only. One scroll contained every reference he could find to the recurrence of the bird-foot tailed star over the centuries. On another scroll he'd recorded any information on the designs and myths behind the five symbols of power among the Morris stargazers, the Capsen tellers, and the Eller Island dream interpreters. A third scroll, the only one he opened for the head priest's inspection before leaving the library, claiming the other scrolls were all the same, spoke of the history of the land around the realm wherever the bearman attacks had occurred.

Five of those attacks had been along this road to Malla through the Baskong Forest. He knew more details of this forest now than he'd ever learned at Singerhalle. The height of these giants was legendary, the girth of their silvery trunks celebrated in no less than three songs that every apprentice Singer learned to play. But the silence here, that he might have mistaken for the silence of winter, was noted in every account he'd read of the forest, regardless of the time of year. He recognized from his reading too the scarcity here of undergrowth that hid and fed animals in other forests. Except for the tall reed stalks along the river banks spiking up through the snow, only a few small patches of clovers or ferns covered the forest floor between these trees. Their thick canopy kept the sunlight to themselves, and very little else could compete. Aside from an occasional bird in the tree tops, too high up to hear, or the slugs and mosquitoes in the summer, or the rare mouse, no animals had ever been spotted here. No deer lived under the Baskong trees, no wolf, and certainly no bear.

So the first bear growl Verl heard startled him. Most every attack by bearman bands started with bear growls; and so every guardsman and priest in the caravan had been warned to expect to hear them for the last two days. But in the dead white silence of riding through the Baskong forest, the suddenness of a bear growl startled him.

Verl was not the only one glancing at the wall of trees around them nervously. After the fifth growl, the captain of the guard called a halt and sent the twenty of his men not disguised as priests into the woods to search for bearmen. Verl leaned forward in his saddle to dust the snow off his horse's mane between his ears as he waited.

The guardsmen returned, reporting no movement anywhere. Nothing but trees. And silence. They'd searched through every scorched hollow in the nearby trees—where they would have tried hiding---but they found nothing in them.

The caravan moved on, and the growling began again.

Around the next bend, they saw a covered tinker wagon weaving towards them across the frozen river. The driver in a hooded black cloak sat ramrod stiff, not controlling the pony.

"Ho there!" yelled the captain of the guard.

The driver's face was hidden under his long hood, but Verl could swear he saw it glowing. A tune taunted at him, a line from a ballad of a dead lover who "walked the halls of Ambrose with eyes of glowing embers."

Verl shook the refrain away. This was not a song, not a story. The dead did not walk again. The eerie growling must have had more effect on his nerves than he'd anticipated.

"Ho there!" the captain yelled again. "You, identify yourself! Wake up! Your horse has gone off the road."

The wind tugged at the driver's cloak, but he did not move, did not answer. The captain motioned to two of his men to go wake him.

The pony halted as the two guardsmen approached it. But before they reached the wagon, the driver started swaying, crumpling down onto the seat as the wind whipped at the loose folds of his cloak. Then a stronger gust ripped the cloak off and flew it up above the wagon like a huge black crow, leaving no man on the seat behind it. All sign of the driver had vanished.

Another bear growl rumbled from very close behind him; and Verl felt the cold of the wind on his cheeks chill through him more than ever. The ballad of the dead lover drummed in his head again.

His hand on her neck was cold, his kiss on her breast was frozen.

The halls of Ambrose were sated, she was the one he had chosen.

The wind dropped the cloak, tumbled it, lifted it again, then flattened it across the ice. One of the guardsmen dismounted to pick it up.

The other continued to the wagon and retrieved something from the empty seat. Then he climbed into the hut from the back and searched it too as the caravan waited. When he returned, he handed the captain a tile. Bearman tiles were often found before or after an attack in this province. The cook at the Library had a collection of them, and was tiling his oven with them.

"There was nothing else on the bench but the coach lantern, empty of oil, and some broken-through ice that someone had sat on."

The captain took the tile and pitched it to the ground, breaking it. He glanced around at the trees, his face fierce, determined. He turned in his saddle to his men. "All right. This is why we came. Draw your swords, make your bows ready."

Then the captain shouted a challenge to the trees. "Bearmen, highwaymen, wherever you are! We know you're in there. I give you this one chance to surrender. We're escorting these priests to Malla, and WE'RE TAKING YOUR SON THERE TOO. We'll fight our way through the gates of hell to get them there. You won't scare us away with your tricks."

They rode on, rounding the next bend, then stopped, confronted by a line of bearmen stretching across the road and the frozen river, all aiming arrows at them. The bear masks they wore were fierce, with beady-eyes and long white teeth in jaws frozen open into snarls. The growling surrounding the caravan crescendoed, became deafening.

The captain ordered his bowmen to the front and his cavalry ready to charge. Everyone else jumped off their horses and circled the wagons for protection. The unit of guardsmen disguised as priests stood guard on the outside of the circle.

"Make way!" the captain ordered. "Lay down your weapons or die!" When the line of bearmen did not move, the captain signaled and his bowmen sent a volley of arrows. Each bearman standing before them was struck true, once, twice, or three times in their chest, but none of them fell. The thick bear pelts they wore must have protected them; yet even so, some of the arrows embedded deeply enough into their hearts that they should have killed them.

That was the last Verl saw before an answering volley of arrows rained down upon the guardsmen and priests. Men around him started dropping, gasping, screaming in pain. The man next to him fell silently. Verl knelt beside the child's cage and reached his hand through the iron bars to comfort him. The boy huddled in the center, trembling, his face ashen as the blood splattered up in the air around him.

No arrow struck the cage, and Verl pressed closer to it.

Then the captain came and yanked the boy from the cage. He lifted the child, kicking and screaming in terror, up in the air above him. The rain of arrows stopped.

The captain strode out onto the open ice, circled around with the screaming boy above his head. Verl followed behind them.

He glanced once over his shoulder as he followed the captain. The line of bearmen were being hacked in two by the swordsmen on their horses, but some of the bearmen were still standing, arrows riddling their bodies. Everywhere else was silence, everyone else watching the captain and the boy.

"Do you want him?" the captain shouted to the trees. He pulled out his knife and aimed it at the boy's throat. The boy's wide eyes froze on Verl's face watching him over the captain's shoulder. The boy was quiet now, too terrified to cry.

The captain circled with the boy again. "Come out and get him, if you want him. Alone. Or he dies." The silence of the Baskong forest was his only answer.

The captain turned to Verl standing behind him and handed the boy and the knife over to him. Then he drew his sword. "Come out and fight! And we'll let the boy go free. And your men too."

The boy clutched Verl around the neck so tightly that it became hard to breathe. The air was silent, waiting; the wind biting cold.

"I'm coming out," a voice shouted from the bend in the road behind them.

~

In the hidden corner of their hollow tree, Freyshin grabbed Crel's arm. "You can't! It's a trap. They'll kill you, and the boy too."

Crel met his friend's eyes. "If I die, do what you can to save him. But this...may be the only chance they'll give

334

him." Crel slipped the two plates of the tin body form he'd used to make the ice man over his shoulders, fastened them, covered them with his long black cloak and hood, then reached for his brother's sickle.

~

Verl watched the Bearman walking towards them over the ice. His cloak flapped around his legs in the wind, and the curved blade of his Islander sickle was opened. Its steel glistened viciously, reflecting both the sun and the snow. Verl held the boy against his shoulder with one hand, the knife in the other, and waited for the Bearman to come close enough. Even a bear growl now would be a break in the tension.

The captain raised his sword. Verl waited, watching the Bearman walk closer. He had memorized the boy's face last night as the boy fell asleep on the blanket before him, and had practiced it then. He hoped he could make the illusion look real, it was more complicated and took more concentration than anything he tried doing before.

The Bearman lifted the glistening sickle in the air, ready to swing it. Clutching the boy, Verl stepped back from the captain's side, and vanished from the sight of the Bearman. In the same instant, he cast an illusion into the Bearman's mind of him still holding the boy and still standing beside the captain.

The Bearman circled the captain, eyeing the captain, eyeing the boy he saw being held beside him. "Let him go," the Bearman said. "And we'll break off the attack on your men, let you go free."

The captain smirked and circled with him "Oh, we'll let the boy live, I'll keep my word on that. He's too valuable to me, I'm being paid too well for him. But you, and your men will hang till the vultures tear your bones dry. I promise you that too!" The captain signaled to the caravan, and his men disguised as priests dropped their robes and drew their swords. They surrounded the Bearman and the captain. Verl slipped back farther behind them, still staying close enough to cast his illusions into the Bearman's mind.

The Bearman, eyeing the circle of guardsmen surrounding him, shouted a war cry "Clayl!" and swung his sickle at the captain.

The captain countered him with his sword, half the length of the sickle's handle and blade. His steel knocked the blade aside. As the Bearman lifted the sickle to strike again, the captain twirled in towards him and brought his sword down hard on the Bearman's chest.

The sword ripped through the cloak, then thudded and rebounded, hitting armor. The Bearman stepped back to strike again. The captain still recoiling from his thrust barely twirled away in time to counter him.

The child twisted in Verl's arm to start watching, whether drawn by the clash of steel, or by the Bearman's shout----an Islander word, Verl realized, an Islander name he'd had time to recognize now, a name he had known as a child himself, without the manly "l" on the end. Clay, his year-mate had been called. He would have become Clayl. Verl stared at the Bearman. His breath was cold, the boy's arms around his neck was choking him. The Bearman had had a twin brother, that captain had told Arnaby.

"Crel!" the boy shouted, when the Bearman's face was turned towards him. "Uncle Crel!" Crel. The name of the twin had been Cree. Before the "l." The boy who had been as a brother to Verl, who had grown up on his father's hearth. Images from his naming dream that night started playing before him. The bloodied Islander scythe. Crel's face, his father had identified to him in his dream. A guardsman of the Realm raising a sword above him—

"Crel," the boy shouted louder. The Bearman looked to where he saw the boy, turned instead in confusion to the sound, and in that instant exposed his left side under his raised sickle. The captain's sword thrust through what must be a gap in the armor, and blood splurted out, freezing as it puddled on the snow.

The captain pulled his sword out from the Bearman's side, and the Bearman fell to his knees, crumpled over onto his back, and lay on the bloodied snow and ice, dying, his sickle fallen beside him. As in the dream. …As in the dream.

Verl stared down, barely breathing, barely aware the boy in his arm was screaming, struggling to get free. "Crel!" the boy called.

A swordsman rode up to the captain. "They were snowmen!" the swordsman yelled. "That's all they were. Snowmen! We've cleared our way through."

The captain looked down at the dying outlaw, then at the tumbled snowmen and line of bear masks and furs littering the frozen river and road ahead, then at the boy and caravan. Shouting was coming from the forest, arrows were starting to fly again. The captain sheathed his sword, grabbed the boy from Verl, and shouted orders. "Then away! Now! We don't have time to stay and fight. Not when we still have our prize here. And this one," he kicked at the Bearman's moaning body, "is what we came for." He raised his voice and shouted to the trees. "You hear me, Bearmen, your immortal leader's dead!"

The guardsmen and priests ran for their horses, mounted them, and lifted their wounded onto the wagons amid the volley of arrows as men in bearfurs and swords, a hundred men strong, came running out of the forest at them. The captain pitched the boy into his cage, and signaled his men to escape.

The caravan didn't stop running until midday, half a league away, no longer being pursued. Verl's head felt still in a daze, the world rushing around him, half in dream, half in visions of blood and snow and screams. And dying men lying beside a bloodied sickle.

Chapter 29
Sacrifice

"There be truth, and there be truth," cawed the
Pelican.

The boy Ver dipped his hand into the conch shell
filled with goose fat. Then he held his greased hand out
towards the Pelican. The Pelican's beak was wide and deep
enough to swallow him whole, and Ver tried to keep his
voice from quivering. He knew a man stood inside the
Pelican mask and feathered robe that towered before him,
but he knew a deeper truth stood before him too—it was the
spirit of the Whale's friend, the Pelican, who was cawing to
him with a man's voice. *"Not all truths be True,"* he
answered as he'd been told to say.

*"Daughter of the Goose Moon laid an egg and gave
ye life. She taught ye that you are her gosling."*

The Pelican reached into a cauldron and pulled out
a black sea snake. The snake hissed, and whipped its body
around the hand holding it, then lashed its tail out to whip at
the hand again. Its fangs and mouth were white as sea
foam, and its tongue was black and quick.

Ver stepped back a step, but he did not run from the
gods. *"There be truth, and there be truth,"* he answered, his
voice catching in the back of his throat.

*"The Goose Moon's truth be not your truth. The
long sly brother of the Whale swam up through her stormy
waters and crashed through her cliffs to change ye from a
goose's egg."* As he spoke, the Pelican swam the snake
through the air then thrust it seven times towards Ver, at his
thighs, shoulders, eyes, and heart. The snake hissed and
whipped furiously each time it came close. *"He left the
memory growing between your legs. Then he left ye to let
her teach ye for seven years. Tonight he swims back to his
brother's risen call and he whispers to ye the secret to your
soul. You are not a daughter of the Moon. Die, and be
born again, a Man."*

In terror, Ver watched the snake swim towards his outstretched hand. He swallowed the hot dry air of the bonfire's wind, then obediently, he turned his hand over to offer the soft side of his wrist. "I die to be born again a brother of the Whale."

The strike was quick, not the long painful sting of a blue jelly's tentacles. Ver swayed on his feet and saw the world whirl around him.

His yearmates, shadows in the dim moonlight, crowded to him. Through the haze, through the yellow smoke rising from the fire, Ver identified Cree grabbing his wrist first. "Brother of the deepest sea. My life for yours." Cree sucked the first spewing foam of poison out and spat it at the fire. Then Ver's hand was grabbed again and again as he teetered on his feet losing consciousness, until all seven of his yearmates had sucked his wound clean.

Verl stared down at the blood splattered on his wrist. He had not remembered the nightmare of his initiation week for many years. Only during his first few years at Singerhalle would he wake up in a cold sweat still hearing the Pelican's cawing voice and the hiss of the snake. Curious once, he had looked up the snake in his master's book, an indil sea snake, not as deadly as the banded sea snake, but to a child it would be. He suspected the village elders had milked it first. Even so, of the eight yearmates, three did not live through the next five days to enter the dreaming hut and become a man. Islanders believed in harsh, demanding gods. As a child, Verl had too, and it had taken him years of studying songs and legends of other people to convince himself that a heaving sea storm and a hissing snake's bite were not proof of a god's will.

But all that had ended years ago. Verl wiped the blood off his wrist onto a strip of bandage and finished wrapping the soldier's wound. Then he knelt beside the next bleeding soldier.

An ear torn off by an arrow, his left side gushing blood, the soldier's stench was unbreatheable. Verl gave him a stick of numbstool to chew to dull the pain, then wrapped his head gently. Then he tore off the bloody tunic. An arrow had pierced the soldier through the bowels and green spew and intestine were bulging out through the skin. Even in the best conditions, the man would not live much longer. Verl pushed what he could back in and wrapped his side with wet cloth, then he went on to the next guardsman. The guardsmen unit had a healer; but at Singerhalle, Verl had had as much training in the healing herbs as most apprentice healers had, and Verl had readily offered his help when the captain finally let the caravan stop to tend the wounded. Several men had died already who might have lived if they'd been treated quicker.

Next man over was a priest. He turned his head when Verl knelt down beside him— *Arnaby*. So this is why Verl hadn't seen him after the arrows started flying. And why the spy priest hadn't done anything to stop the Bearman from being trapped, as Arnaby had planned to do. He must have fallen in the first exchange.

The arrow in the spy priest's chest was broken off, but it had pierced his heart and lung. From the look in his eyes, Arnaby knew there was nothing Verl could do for him. If he took out the arrow, he'd only kill him quicker.

Arnaby grabbed his wrist as Verl wrapped his chest. "Promise–" he started to say, then he coughed up blood and turned his head away.

Verl released the wrist gently and enclosed the spy priest's hand a moment in his. Blood oozed out between his fingers until he could not see his own knuckles. He lifted his hand off and spread his long fingers out as they dripped with blood. The dream images swarmed around him as they had all morning. *Cree grabbing his wrist first, sucking the poison. Ver grabbing Cree's wrist first and doing the same for him. They'd been as brothers then, pledging their lives to each other in the act.*

Hollow promises. They'd been only children. All that had happened so long ago it had been forgotten.

Verl tied the bandages around Arnaby shoulders and gave him numbstool to ease the pain. Arnaby opened his mouth as if to say another word. He gasped and choked on his breath. Verl nodded. "I promise."

Arnaby stared up at him and Verl knew he knew his promise was hollow. Verl didn't know what he was

340

promising, especially to a man he owed his life to, but cared little for. But perhaps the words themselves could comfort a dying man.

Arnaby turned his face away, and Verl finished knotting the bandages. *In his naming dream, the dying body that Verl's fingers were bandaging had been Cree grown to a man beside his bloodied scythe.*

Two more wounded men were all Verl had left to see. More moaning came from the row of men on the other side of the tent where the guardsman healer was still working. Verl finished bandaging the last priest---a slight leg wound, he'd heal quickly—then Verl glanced over at the healer. His back was turned, wrapping a patient's shoulder. Before the healer could turn around, Verl pocketed three strips of fresh bandages, a pouch of numbstool, and several pinches of salts and unguents from the healer's supply bags from where they lay opened in the center of the tent. Verl was not finished yet. Not according to the dream.

Verl nodded to the healer when he came over, closed his bags, and shouldered them. Together they started to leave the tent. Other men would come load the wounded onto the wagons for the long trip still to Malla.

On his way outside, Verl paused over Arnaby. His gasping and coughing had stopped, and his eyes were staring blankly. Verl closed the eyes and pulled the priest hood down over the head.   Arnaby was not the only one already dead.

Verl found the healer wiping his hands and tools in the snow. The captain of the guard was talking to him, asking how soon they could move on.

Verl grabbed a handful of snow and washed his hands too. "I'm staying," he said. "Until tonight. I have a friend to bury. Arnaby was a court priest. He deserves to have his rites chanted over him."

The captain gave Verl the same appraisal he had the night before when he'd offer to quiet the boy. As if the captain were surprised Verl was there at all until he spoke. The difference, this time it looked like he was ready to say no.

"I'll catch up with the van tonight. My horse was limping on the last turn. He might have taken a stone or got some ice caught, and I'd like to check him out too. Walk him slower for a while."

At that, the captain gave Verl the same dismissive shrug he had the night before. "See to the horse then. Make sure to return him safely to us by tonight. We have others you can ride if you need to cut one out for yourself."

At the horses, Verl lifted his roan's leg, and pried off the hard leather pad that protected the soft parts of the hoof from the ice. With a hoof pick, he dug behind the studded winter shoe as if finding an ice ball embedded there, and replaced the pad. Then he saddled another horse and tied on the pouches from his pack. Glancing around to make sure no one was still watching him, he slipped the medicines into one of the pouches. He loaded his mules with his books to go on ahead with the guardsmen. If nothing else guaranteed that he'd catch up with them tonight, now that Arnaby was gone, the books would. As well as the fate of the little boy.

...Now that Arnaby was gone. For the first time in his life, Verl realized he was on his own, with no one telling him what to do. He could disappear, never come back, and no one would notice him gone more than the loss of two missing horses.

It was an odd thought only. A taste of freedom that didn't make him feel any differently.

Or perhaps it was the dream haunting him that wouldn't let him feel differently yet. If he made the dream come true, if he went back to heal the Bearman, what good could it do him? The rest of the dream had never come true, never made him a Singer.

Verl tied the lute case onto a mule, then paused as he pulled the knot through. Perhaps now with Arnaby gone, he would need a claim to who he was among the bearmen or among any traders he might encounter. He glanced around; no one was watching. He shielded his hands with his body and opened the false bottom of the lute case. He took out the signet ring and a golden talent he'd hidden there almost a year ago.

The ring gleamed, catching the sunlight. Seeing it, Verl grimaced. He polished the ring with his gloved half of his fingers. The duke's crest shone brighter, and Verl felt the wind bite his cheeks. Wearing this ring, if he ever needed to, would not necessarily mean he was betraying his king. Not if he were still careful of his words and actions. He felt no loyalty to the duke's dead spy priest. And certainly none to the merchant duke he'd only met once. To a little boy, perhaps, son of the Bearman's brother, he felt some loyalty, some responsibility. And, in extension perhaps, to the boys he himself and the Bearman once were. But to the Bearman's enemy, the boy-king? His own protégé?... No, he decided, no, he was not betraying him, not choosing sides against him with this ring. He'd simply learned enough in the past two years to lie when he needed to. To the king once already when he'd left his court. And now to the spy priest as he lay dying, promising him nothing. Verl pocketed the coin and ring and sent his mules on with the guardsmen.

After the caravan left, Verl dragged Arnaby's body out onto the ice and built a cairn of dried grasses over him. Before lighting it with his lantern and oil, he pulled off the spy priest's cloak and his rings and pocketed them too. Not choosing sides, he reminded himself.

Just making use of whatever lies he could to survive. Jing would be proud of him.

~

Verl walked his horse among the corpses. Out on the frozen river he'd found only the blood and scuffling marks from where the Bearman had fallen. Crel was not among the bodies on the road either.

Verl looked around at the silent trees. "Hello!" he shouted. "I have medicines! I've come to help."

No answer.

"I'm Crel's brother. I dreamed once he would need me to heal him."

A tall figure dressed in a bear mask and furs stepped onto the road from the trees. He carried a bow with an arrow nocked and pointed at Verl. "Crel's brother is dead," he said.

"I was his yearmate and friend. We grew up as brothers."

Another figure in a white cape and fur glided out from among the giant trees. "If he has medicines, bring him." The voice was feminine, with the soft rhythmic accent of a Capsen. Verl, noting it, said nothing.

Within minutes, bearmen had circled him, bound his hands, stripped his horses, and searched through his pack and pouches. They blindfolded him and pushed him forward.

Verl stumbled and slipped on the ice, but he allowed himself to be shoved. Blinded, he focused on the voices around him, on the shuffling, on the crunching of twigs as they left the road and entered the forest. He listened intently, seeing in his mind what his eyes could not see more vividly than he would have expected he could. *Music is in the eye of the listener, Lollander had said. There be truth and there be truth, cawed the pelican. In a kingdom built of lies, Jing would laugh.*

The wind no longer slapped against his face and he smelled wood burning Rough hands let go of his shoulder, and Verl stopped.

The air was slightly warmer on his cheeks, and a sensation of closeness, of having bounds, with people crowded tightly around him, told Verl they had gone inside. A hut perhaps, or more likely a hollow of one of the giant trees. For an instant, the sensation of his space being bounded reminded him how it felt being invisible, expanding outwards, bound by the walls of the dungeon. He swayed on his feet with the sickening memory and swallowed a rise of bile. One of the rough huge hands caught his arm and steadied him.

He heard his pack being opened, and someone sorting through the assortment of medicines. The calming cinnamon-and-earth smell of numbstool mingled with the heartier smell of wood and the slight stinging smell of an herbal astringent. "Crel?" he asked. Someone must have already worked on him, given the telltale smell of astringent.

344

"Asleep," answered the Capsen woman.

If she were the one who had cleansed Crel's wound with the astringent, then she must be a tellerwoman, a healer among the Capsens. Verl thought all tellerwomen had been killed or captured in the last two years. All that is except the Capsen leader Felain had wanted to capture most. Ailil, the mother of Henrik's second son.

Verl turned in the direction of her voice. "Will he live?" he asked in Capsen.

The room went dangerously quiet. Then the tellerwoman answered in Norgon. "He'll be glad for the numbstool."

"I can give it to him when he wakes, and check his wounds then," Verl offered, in Norgon.

"You can help."

She wouldn't trust him to be alone with Crel then, or, perhaps, to do anything at all for him. "I came here to help. I've been trained in healing at Singerhalle. I didn't come here to kill him."

A deeper resonant voice, thickly accented, an Eller islander, spoke behind him. "You said you were a yearmate."

A flat statement, with no belief in it. Verl turned in the direction of the challenge, and answered in Eller. "We pledged as brothers of the whale. That be my truth. Why I came back."

The huge rough hand yanked off his blindfold. A mountain of a man, with the burnt red face of a blacksmith, vaguely familiar, stared into Verl's face. The mountain stepped back. "Who be you?"

Before Verl could answer, a woman gasped, seeing his face. "You!"

Verl looked over at a second woman. Dressed in a brightly designed linen smock, black woolen leggings, and a heavy islander shawl, she stood in the background against the heartwood of the tree. Verl recognized her too, and his heart sank.

"Your son is all right. I need to get back to him quickly tonight, make sure he's not afraid--"

"You! *You!*" The islander woman rushed forward, and swung a fist hard into his right eye. Verl staggered back a step, and she punched at him again. No one made an effort to stop her. "You were with the priests! You be one of the ones who took him from me!"

The blacksmith grabbed Verl's shoulders from behind, letting the boy's mother continue to pummel him, not letting Verl raise an arm to protect himself. "Please, lady. Please. You are...Cray's, Crayl's wife...I didn't know that then."

She stopped mid-swing, nursed her fist with her other hand. She spat at the ground. "Where be he? Where be my son?"

The blacksmith still had not released him. His right cheek swelling, Verl shook his head crookedly. "I need...to get back to him. He's with the guards. He has no one to protect him now. He's been...crying for you. Please! Let me help Crel. Then I can go back to him. The priest who I was with, who took him from you, was not your enemy. He was on your side, helping other bearmen. He's not... he wasn't a priest. The Duke of Navarn's spy in disguise. That man there," nodding his head at the man in bear furs who had met him on the road, "that man has his rings in his hand to prove it."

The strong arms of the blacksmith swung Verl around to face him again. "I asked ye, who be you? How do you know Crel? How did you know Crayl's name?"

"I was their yearmate–"

"*I* was their yearmate."

Verl caught his breath, stared up at the mountain of the blacksmith. The face *was* familiar. If a yearmate in the same village, he would have to be the son of—what was that blacksmith's name?

The Capsen tellerwoman spoke from behind him. "This is the Duke of Navarn's crest on this ring."

Verl turned his head slightly towards her voice. "That would be the ring the duke gave to me. The others belonged to his spy–"

"You're a spy for the Duke of Navarn?" asked the deep voice of the bearman.

"No, no. He asked me to spy for him. I refused. I—"

Lie if you can, Jing's voice whispered. *Lie and survive.*

Verl shook his head. "I was working for the queen then. I was the hornblower at Norgarth, on my way to give her news of what had happened at Drespin--"

The room went deadly quiet.

Verl grimaced, then went on, condemning himself more. "The duke met me in the market, asked me to spy for him. I could not, and still keep my oath I'd sworn to the king."

Everyone was staring at him, not saying a word. *There be truth and there be truth,* mocked Jing. *In a kingdom built of lies, cawed the Pelican.* ---There'd been seven of his yearmates with him that night facing the Pelican's ordeal. Who was his friend who'd snuck back to the village to bring them nails from the smithy for the raft they had to build the next day? His face puffing red as he ran out of the woods into the men's secret cove? Yaris–

"Yarisol! You're Yarisol."

The blacksmith released Verl's shoulders. "How know you that?"

"I'm Verl. Your yearmate too. Son of—"

"Horl. The village father. You left that day. We were never to speak your name again."

"You're a spy for Queen Felain now?" the tellerwoman's voice was still laced with death.

Verl faced her. "No," he answered as coldly, surprising himself with the rise of emotion at her suggestion that he could be. Singer-training, he controlled his voice, started over. "No. By her order, a friend and I were taken to the dungeons when I would not send her message to kill the duke when he left Norgarth. I would not spy for him; but I did not betray him either. But I did betray my friend, he died in the dungeon because of me. Because of that, you can believe me, I will never betray my oath to another friend. Not to my boyhood friend Crel and tell anyone of my meeting with you. Nor," he met the tellerwoman's icy blue eyes, "will I betray my oath to King Laird either and join your fight against him."

"Not choosing sides or not getting involved are luxuries you don't have, son. No one does anymore." The bearman's voice had softened. "But it took the death of his own brother to convince Crel this has to be true now. Perhaps you two were fired in the same mold."

The bearman took off his bear mask. "Name's Freyshin." He stepped aside, gestured behind him. At the back of the tree's hollow lay Crel on a bloody padding of horse blankets with a burlap sack covering him. A lantern hung from a nail in the heartwood above him. He was sleeping fitfully. Pain twitched in his face and drool seeped from the corner of his moving lips. "If you can help him, I won't stand in your way. But I will have a knife in your back if you make any move to hurt him. I made the same deal with this witch here. Now I have you both watching over each other's work. Making sure there is no harm done to him by the other."

The tellerwoman stiffened, but she nodded and knelt down beside Crel. She pulled the burlap sack off to show Verl. Crel's ribs were wrapped in bloody rags. "Bring me your unguents and bandages," she said.

Verl knelt beside her and helped her remove the bloody rags. He felt the barely contained fury in the tellerwoman's stiffness so close beside him; and he followed her instructions. But he inspected the wound himself and she let him. She had cleaned the sword cut well, and it wasn't as deep as he had feared. He fingered the area gently. Wherever the hole was in Bearman's body armor, it must not have been wide enough to let the sword in at an angle to hit anything important. One rib was very tender, and Crel cried out in pain in his sleep when Verl touched it. The tellerwoman quickly rolled a numbstool head into a softened mound and placed it under the Bearman's tongue. Not as effective as chewing or sucking on the hard, woody stem of a numbstool, but Crel wouldn't choke on the pulp as he slept.

Crel had been wounded before, Verl noted. Both his sides were scarred with deep bear claw markings. The sword had pierced a long welt of the larger clawing. Verl ran his fingers over the welts, and glanced at the tellerwoman.

"I didn't let him die then either."

"He's lucky you were here to stop his bleeding today too," Verl said, trying a smile.

She didn't respond. They spread the unguent and rewrapped his side with the fresh bandages.

Verl didn't stay long in their camp afterwards. But he did stay long enough to talk to the boy's mother and to learn a special song from her to sing to Jere that night. And long enough to promise he'd meet them in the woods outside of Malla in two weeks with word on how to rescue him.

When he left, the bearmen blindfolded him and led him back to his horse.

~

Eleidice had come from Malla, Verl remembered, as the ferryman rowed pass the stately homes of the town's prominent citizens. Long and narrow, some five stories tall but only one or two rooms wide, the brick mansions were pressed between their neighbors. Each had wrought iron balconies and carved marble friezes more ornate than the last. At the end of the peninsula jutting above the tall reeds of the marshlands, was the only home with precious dry land left around it: the mayor's palace. Eleidice had been born in that palace, a daughter of the mayor and a countess, the wealthiest, most refined student at Singerhalle. With the most refined, beautiful voice, even when she first arrived, a miniature lady at nine years old. Yet she'd looked upon Verl, her section leader, as her hero then, more enchanted by his music than by all her gold and jewels. Verl clutched the boy's hand beside him with the memories.

Behind them, the southwest shore of the marshlands was crowded with the blackened hovels of the factory workers squeezed between the iron gates and smokestacks of the coal and iron works of the master armorers and swordsmiths. To the north and east bordering the desolate marshes loomed the dark cliffs that traded men's lives for its riches, or so sang the lays of Old Miner Jold. Eleidice was the only student who had never laughed at the lays. More curious, she grew eerily quiet and left the room whenever the other legend of those cliffs was sung on dark wintery nights.

Verl followed her once and asked if she were well. Her face, strained by candlelight, looked back at him, haunted, and he never asked her again.

Eleidice had never returned home to Malla, and claimed she never would

The dream of every other young student at Singerhalle was to someday make the pilgrimage here to the dark cliffs of Malla to try to see the dragon for themselves. As the apprentices grew older, more experienced, they learned the stories were legend only. There was no such creature as a dragon.

Verl pointed out the cliffs to little Jere, and told him to watch for the dragon flying out of them tonight.

The ferryman cast a hardened look at Verl, then glanced down at little Jere. "Youngest one yet," he grumbled. He spat at the water in the canal dug free from the marsh grasses, the only access to the peninsula, and poled forward with his long oar. "You couldn't pay me enough to do what you do."

"Shut up, old man," said the captain of the guard. "You took our fare well enough. This lad deserves whatever he gets. He was a criminal's son."

The mayor was red-haired, short, fair-skinned. Not Eleidice's dark-skinned father. The mayor bartered with the taxman for the price of the boy. The town had paid ten silver talents to buy him. The captain of the guard had bought him for only three, Verl remembered, but he translated the deal for them, made no comment. The mayor spoke Norgon, as most educated men did, but he claimed not well enough.

The town's taxes to the crown came to eight talents. The mayor counted out the taxes, crossed out the names on a long census roll he checked with the taxman, and handed over the purse. The mayor's own taxes and that of his three aldermen came to five talents more. He opened another purse of ten silver talents the town had collected for the boy, gave three talents five to the captain for buying the boy, paid the taxes of five talents, then kept one talent for himself, and slid the remainder change over to the taxman with a nod. "Two weeks tomorrow, full moon, the dragon comes out. You'll know where to find him."

Verl left confused. When the ferryman rowed the guardsmen back to town, Verl offered to buy him an ale.

He discovered what he had feared. The town bought a child every year, but not to work in the mines.

Later that evening, the captain, chuckling over his ale, swore Verl to secrecy, paying him two pence of his take in the boy's purchase to keep his promise. Then he whispered to Verl the rest of the fate awaiting "the Bearman's damned son."

~

"The townsmen of Malla bought Jere to sacrifice him to the dragon," Verl told the bearmen, and Merind, and Jere's mother hiding in the woods outside of Malla. The bearmen had arrived a day late, moving Crel northward slowly as soon as he could travel. Crel lay in front of the fire propped up on a pallet, bear furs covering him, listening.

Jere's mother covered her mouth with her hands to stifle a cry. Then she broke and started sobbing into her hands. "No—"

Verl touched her arm gently. "There is no dragon. It doesn't exist. But the townsmen of Malla, the peasants, believe it does. They've been told for a century their own children will be eaten, if they don't feed it once a year. Only the mayor and his aldermen know the far uglier truth. They get to keep a share of what the town pays for the child."

"Full moon, end of the week, you say?" asked Crel

Verl nodded. He drew a map in the dirt with a stick. "On the third hill, north end of the marsh. At the rocky shelf in front of the cave, half way up the cliff. That's where the taxman will come to get the boy, to take him to sell again to the silver mines farther north. After the townsmen leave Jere at dusk, he'll be alone for several hours

351

before the taxman comes. We can get him away then easily.

"If I hadn't been at that meeting, all you would have heard from the townsmen is that the dragon had killed him. End of the trail."

Merind took another stick, drew an outline of a dragon by the mouth of the cave on Verl's map. A dragon that looked more half-lion, half-bird, the Nameless One, with scales.

"Supposing," she said, "the dragon does decide to come out of her cave this year?"

~

Verl kicked the edges of one of the three-toed footprints impressed into the rock shelf outside the cave. To his left, half the rock face near the cave had fallen away in years past, exposing part of a skeleton of an extremely large creature turned to stone. He ran a hand over the rib cage. He had read accounts about fossils in the older journals at the library, but had never seen one. Whatever the creature was that lived here once, it was huge. Merind had suggested an ancestor of the garugs she'd seen in the east, perhaps. The skull was three times the size of a horse's head. No wonder the town of Malla believed in dragons.

The ferryman came up behind him. He laid a hand on the stone skull. "It's said the dragon buried her mate here centuries ago, and that's why she'll never leave this cave."

The ferryman passed Verl the jug of ale he'd been drinking. Verl thanked him and took a swig. "Tell me, have you known anyone who's seen the dragon?"

The ferryman snorted, took the jug back. "Not and lived to tell about it. Same with this poor child you've sold to the beast. If you can find him come morning, you can ask him. But I tell you, he'll be gone by dawn, nothing but his clothes left."

Verl tried not to look over at the pole where Jere was struggling against his ropes and wailing for his mother. The women of the town were taking turns laying sprigs of mistletoe around his neck and pine bowers at his feet, some trying to kiss away his tears, telling him to be brave. The town's Badurian priest and the five itinerant priests who had come in the company of the guardsmen with Verl were chanting their evening prayers and swinging their incense pots on the edge of the rock shelf that jutted out over the marshlands below. The last glow of sunset gleamed over the scene, turning everyone in the evening mist into slowly moving shadows of orange and sepia, all as surreal as dream people. Or as memories from a distant past where black sea snakes and dragon bones were unquestioned gods.

Jere cried aloud again. Verl squeezed his fist until his fingers dug into his palm. A young mother, her three children in tow, took her offering of mistletoe and pine branches to her priest to have them blessed.

When the sun finally set, the first half of this nightmare was over, and the townsmen of Malla started to leave. Some of the women, crying, looked back at Jere. Some of the children, clutching their mother's skirts and following, were crying as loudly as Jere by now in their fear of the night. Other children ran on ahead, shouting, playing hide and seek among the legs as everyone from town followed their mayor and the bell-ringing priests in a quickened pace down the hill. Their yearly duty done, all citizens had to be sure to be locked safe inside their homes tonight with their shutters pulled before the hunter moon arose.

Jere yelled to him piteously when Verl left, following the townsmen. Verl had only had one chance to whisper to the child in Eller on their way up the hill that he'd be back again later. If he could have spared the child from this night, he would have. But if he had tried helping the child escape any earlier, he realized now, the captain of the guard would have hunted them down relentlessly. Knowing the captain better in the last few days, he knew his obsessions, and Verl was certain there was no other way to free the "Bearman's son."

~

It was near midnight, the full moon overhead smeared by the thickening mist, when Verl followed the mayor, the taxman, the captain of the guard, and five trusted guardsmen back up the hill. When the taxman took possession of the boy, the mayor would get his papers stating his taxes had been paid in full. The actual exchange was made in person each year, lest one side not deliver.

The boy was still screaming; but there was also a rumble, a snarl, a growling, a stomping coming from the cliff above them as they got closer.

The captain drew his sword. "The Bearman's son! By all the fouled breath, these highwaymen never give up their tricks. Hurry, men! We've got them now."

The guardsmen jerked to a stop at the top of the cliff. The taxman and Verl almost plowed into them. The mayor trudged up behind them, puffing heavily. "What--?" the mayor asked, but he was quickly quieted. Through the mist on the rocky shelf ahead of them, a bear dancing on her hind legs was boxing at a dragon, keeping it away from the boy tied to the post.

Verl drew his knife, started forward. The captain tried to stop him, but Verl said, "I can get to the boy while they're still fighting."

Verl dodged Jesser. Not easily, during rehearsals, she always tried to come at him, growling surlily. She obeyed Crel's hand signals from where he lay hidden on his pallet in the cave; but she never behaved as willingly in winter, Crel said. Merind's dragon was easier to dodge. Verl just had to make sure not to run through it.

He reached Jere, slit the ropes binding him, grabbed him in his arms, and ran four steps. Then, on cue, the dragon's tail whipped him in the back and Verl fell, cradling the boy's head under him.

"Run!" Verl yelled to the mayor's group. He stumbled to his feet to take his own advice.

Then he fell again, flattened, as the dragon breathed fire. As it did, Verl and Jere disappeared from the sight of the watchers and rolled away from the illusion he left of himself and boy struggling to get away from Merind's flames. As he stood up, invisible, the dragon ripped its

354

lion's teeth into the illusion of his back and shoulders. The illusion of the boy squirmed and clawed at the ground under him, still trying to escape. Merind added pools of blood dripping from the dragon's teeth and splashing over both of them.

Jere screamed; Verl covered his mouth, made him stop, as if he had died at that instant. The scene look real, gruesome, Verl didn't let the boy see it. No matter how many times they had practiced in the last three nights, the dragon's feast was still hard to watch. But this time, this time, . . . more than just looking real, more than just believing what he saw, he felt the dragon's presence too. It was an odd, odd feeling. Whatever Merind was adding to her illusion inside his mind, he felt the presence of the dragon—and, he realized, of the bear. An awe in him of their presence he could not question, even knowing the truth of the illusion, he felt an awe in him of being . . . in the presence of *gods*. Verl shivered, his head and neck perspiring in the wintery cold mist; but he kept his part of the illusion as real as he could.

He heard commotion. The mayor and taxman had left, the guardsmen had not. The captain mustering them, shouting, coming to rescue what he could of the boy. If that was why. Verl could be charitable and assume it was. The boy was too profitable to him.

But Jesser heard the men, turned, and saw the flash of steel in their arms. The bear dropped to all fours and charged at the only enemy she had seen on the cliff. She hated swordsmen in red, Crel had said, ever since she attacked the guardsman capturing him that night in the town hall of Sonachin.

The captain stood his ground, the others ran. The long tooth of the sword swiped Jesser across her nose. She snarled and leapt, killing the captain with her first bite.

The bearmen carried Crel over to Jesser's side. He was not happy with her. This was the first time his bear had killed a man. She sat on her haunches wailing ungodly sounds at the sky, sounds that echoed, Verl was sure, into every peasant hovel and smug townhome in Malla. The bear's nose was scarcely bleeding, but she wouldn't let anyone close enough to touch it.

Several bearman came back from having trailed the mayor, the taxman, and the five guardsmen down the hill. "The mayor's dead," one reported. "He collapsed half way down. From fear, I'd guess. There'll be many new stories told of tonight."

Chapter 30
The Birdfoot Star

Ash had been falling for three days. The trade route to Norgarth along the Cerol Canyon had split wide open when the earth moved, and the river had been gushing over what remained of the road ever since. Crel's troupe of bearmen were not the only ones traveling south through the woods avoiding the main roads these days. It made encounters more common, more dangerous.

Verl dusted ash off a meadow starflower, the only one he'd seen blooming this spring. Crops were dying, turning brown, wilting as soon as they broke ground. The troupe had heard yesterday that a volcano had erupted along the coast to the west of them the day the earth moved, and five villages had been buried under either the lava flow or the ashes.

The gods were not pleased---that's what most everyone they met was saying. When the Bearman was killed in the forests of the giant Boskongs last winter, and his son was taken and eaten by the dragon of Malla—which was really the lion-bird, the Nameless One, didn't you know?—the Bearman's spirit had arisen as a god himself this time, at war with the Nameless One, and all her priests. The stories were no longer only whispered in dark taverns, for the priests could no longer enter every village and command that heretics who praised the Bear God be arrested. In two villages they passed last week, the Badurian priests had been stoned instead.

The Nameless One was a false god. Or so the usual story started. The queen regent had betrayed the crown, sold the realm to the devil whose priests had demanded more taxes than ever to imprison your neighbors and torture them. The old gods had had enough. The land itself was erupting, punishing the devil worshipers, purging itself of the evil one, and the northern provinces were in revolt. Or perhaps, argued a few of the priests and converted guardsmen, perhaps the queen too had been a victim, betrayed, as we ourselves were, by the false words of the high priests of the Nameless One. Take up your scythe, your club, your whale spear, follow the path of the Bearman! March south, march south, to warn her, to save the Boy King, to save the land from the anger of the true gods, before it is too late.

Or perhaps, argued the soft voice of the Capsen Tellerwoman, have you heard her speak behind her veils in your tavern or village square? it is the queen regent's fault for beheading our lord, our own true king after all. The Capsen Tellerwoman is the daughter of the great King Henrik himself, and so it may be true what she says.

Verl picked the starflower. From what he'd read in the old histories of other years when the Birdfoot Star came, volcanoes, dying crops, revolt, this could just be the beginning. He crumpled the only hope of new life he'd seen growing this spring, and let the petals fall from his hand.

"Verl! Verl! Come see!" Jere was running towards him from the creek, holding up a large catfish hanging from his pole. His mother was following, laughing, trying to keep up. Her hair was tied back in a yellow scarf, and she was thinner now. They all were.

Verl knelt down to Jere, took the fish. "You're a great fisherman now like your father was. He'd be proud." He stood up, met Lissiv's eyes. "Come," he said, placing his hand on the boy's shoulder, "let's take your fish and clean it, let your mother boil us a fine stew."

Verl added the herbs he'd collected to Lissiv's pot. He watched her stir it, and felt content. He could live like this. They could be happy here, just the three of them. Let the rest of the world die away on its own.

"I'm leaving tomorrow," he told her. "I've decided I've waited long enough."

Her hands paused; then she started stirring again. "Jere will miss your songs around the campfires."

"I promised the queen I'd return. I have the books her son needs to read."

Lissiv chopped an onion, added it to her stew. "Promise me," she said, "to tell Merind and Crel before you leave."

~

"The horns told Queen Felain you were dead, you said. Died while trying to rescue the boy from the dragon. You can't just return to the palace and become her son's tutor again."

Verl played his lute softly, idle notes plucked in response to the sparking fire. He used to equate notes with shards of light, each note a different color. The fire spat sparks of light briefly up towards the sky full of stars, but each spark was white, colorless, and they never reached the sky. Idle notes. No song in them. He nodded over to Crel. "I suppose I can't let her see me then. But I still have to go. I don't know if there's anything I can do to save Laird now, but I still have to try."

"You would stand against us?" Merind asked. Her eyes were dark, challenging him. The rest of her face was hidden behind her veil. She had started dressing in her Capsen silks again, almost a month ago, in direct defiance of the queen's orders to arrest all Capsens. Her tellerwoman veil rarely came off now, and townsmen they met along the way pointed and stared after her, some in shock, a few in admiration of her bold example.

Crel added a stick to the fire. "He's taking no side, Merind. Or trying not to, for as long as he can." He met Verl's eyes, nodded. "I would too, if I had the chance. But I have no fear that he'd ever tell the queen where we are. Nor who we are."

Verl vibrated a soft glissando that followed a spark up to touch the new faint star in the sky. That was the other reason he wanted to go back to Norgarth. To see Jing. To see the observatory again. "Tell me," he pointed upwards, "do you know what constellation that is?"

"That one? We call it the great bear. It's just coming into ascendance now," Merind said. "We have many legends around it. It's the constellation that leads our people. Why'd you ask?"

"The star crowning the bear's head. Have you seen that one before?"

"Not...that I know of. No."

"Watch it. As it gets bigger, if it does, and comes closer, take it as an omen for starting your war."

Merind frowned at him. Half her face hidden behind her veil, it was often hard to read her expressions now.

"Telling you that may be the most help I'd ever be able to give you and Crel. Whether I stayed with you or not."

Crel was still looking up at the stars. "The great bear, eh? Coming into ascendance. Those are the stars I once called the hanged man. That one there, there, and there. And that faint one can just add to the noose. Some omen that is." The Bearman sighed, leaned back against a tree. "Play for us will you, Verl? One last time. I envy you your freedom to walk away from all this."

Verl bit his lip, silenced his lute instead. He was not free. If he were, perhaps he would stay. He had more respect, more easy friendship with Crel than anyone he'd met since Lollander. But he'd sworn an oath to serve the king instead. Or perhaps.... He picked up a stick, began to draw a pentagon in the dirt. He was driven back to the observatory more because of his curiosity. That was not an easy thing to admit. Not to Crel. Not to the boy Jere, who did hold his heart in his small hands. His curiosity about that star, about what was going to happen when it came, to see it for himself, as selfish as that was, drove him more, and pushed away all other thought.

He drew the symbol of the birdfoot star, the spiral of forgetfulness in the fifth corner of the pentagon. He still didn't want to see Laird get killed. That was reason in itself to go, to do what he could to warn him. He drew his old design of a seagull in the center of the pentagon, and in its beak, as crude of a design of a starflower. He positioned his lute again, nodded to Crel.

"This is something I've tried to play all my life," he said.

Verl hadn't played the 'Song of the Meadowflowers' by Dellet the Younger in over two years. Not since he'd left Singerhalle in disgrace. Slowly he entered the song, the notes precise, but stiff and hesitant, not music. Not the rapture he always felt losing himself in it before. The only songs he'd been playing lately were country songs, simple songs that belonged to the people. Songs that made you tap your foot and dance, that made you laugh and remember, then drink an ale and laugh again. Songs of the earth, songs of the people. Not of dreams, not of illusions, not of lies.

Still...he wondered if he could make illusion with his music now.

He stared down at the pentagon he had scratched into the dirt. As he played softly, he entered the center until he stood smaller, smaller, inside the flower drawn inside the seagull's beak. His music followed him. Crescendoed down around him. His fingers fled faster across the veins of his lute, strumming him, shivering through him. He bent over, plucked the one starflower he had found in the meadow today and picked it up. The fire towered above him, bloomed into circles, sparked up, littered the sky with stars. The star he held in his hand flowered into circles, stretching him in all its directions, into seven long petals of golden-red fire.

Smoke thickened and stung his eyes. He reached for the fire to clear away the smoke, to shape the smoke into circles, into the seven long petals of the starflower of fire he held in his hand.

He smiled, smiled. The flower was real enough he could smell it, believe it, lemon and meadowlands in a spring that had bloomed around him in undoomed years.

But this year was doomed.

Verl crushed the flower in his fist, watched the sparks fall from it. He felt the sharp heat of fire, smelled the burn of flesh.

He yanked his hand out of the fire, empty, stared at it, his lips parting in disbelief. His smoke-stung eyes were too dry for tears.

"What in the Goron's hell have you done, my friend?" Crel was pulling him back farther from the fire.

361

Merind was wrapping his burnt hand in wet cloth. Verl's other hand lay flat across his silent lute strings.

Verl opened his mouth, closed it without an answer. He tried flexing his burnt fingers, but they stung too painfully to straighten them. It would be weeks before his hand would be limber enough to play his lute again "I was trying to make a starflower," he said, as if that could explain himself.

Merind met his eyes. "With your music? You stopped playing your lute minutes ago. Did you even know that?"

In a daze, Verl shook his head, not sure what he remembered, not when reality had ended and the vision of the starflower sure had begun. He let Merind finish wrapping his hand. "You sing when you make an illusion."

She paused, then gently, she tied the cloth around his wrist. "I hum so I will not lose my concentration. I could count instead, or recite the Wayford edicts. But I'm not singing a song, not trying to make music. Music that you've put your soul into like you just did on that lute is too deep a truth; it can't be used to force a vision that you want others to see. I know you never had the training you needed from your father on making illusions, but I thought you did know that. You play beautiful music. And you've learned to create very realistic illusions. But you can't do both at the same time. You have to decide which one you want to do."

"I saw a flower made of fire," Crel said quietly. "It was beautiful. But I've never heard you play like that before. It was even more beautiful. Reminded me of better days. Traveling down the road, just me and Wiss. I could even smell the meadowlands."

"Such music speaks to everyone separately," Merind said. "Lets us see our own memories in it. You play it, Verl, but it comes from someplace beyond you, beyond any of us, and draws us into it each in our own way. We're connected to you through it, but it's no good to use that connection to force us to see the shapes you're trying to make us see. We're filled with our own visions that the music reminds of, and there's no room to plant false memories into someone so lost inside themselves."

Verl stared at the fire. Music is in the eye of the listener, Lollander had always tried to tell him. Verl had only deluded himself all his life, only tried to play music to make his naming dream come true. He had learned to give himself to his music, but never completely. Full of its rapture, he had always tried to make it lie. And then had always failed. He pitched a pine needle at the fire. Then he lay his lute inside its leather case and put it away.

"There is one thing I've been wanting to ask you," he said to Merind. "In Malla, making that dragon—there was a music in it, of sorts. The dragon was real, even when I knew it wasn't. I wasn't just seeing the dragon. I was feeling its presence. I was certain of that. It was a god on that stone shelf with me. Two gods. I felt I was in the presence of Jesser as a god too. How did you do that?"

Her bright eyes were watching him over her veil, assessing him. Or challenging him. Unsure which, Verl looked down, clasped his lute case closed. There were times he did not trust her. Times he was unsure of her intent.

"Build a dreaming hut tonight," she said. "And look into my dreams. There's a spot inside most everyone's minds that can make us feel in the presence of gods. If you can find that spot, your power to make people believe your illusions can be unstoppable. Joined in a dream, maybe I can show you where it is. And how to use it."

~

Felain added a black furred marker onto the map of the realm in her council room. Another bearman band had been reported traveling southward, this one along the valley of Cerol River, less than a week away.

"This may be the one the witchwoman travels with, the horns said. I want it taken. You can kill any brigands you capture, and give their leaders to the priests. But bring that witch to me. No letting her get away this time, or I'll have you burned in Norgarth Square in her place."

The captain of her honor guard saluted. He owed his rapid advancement in the last year to the regent's increasing impatience with the army's failures. Three of the

363

northern provinces were in revolt, the priests' inquisition had angered her subjects throughout the realm, crops were dying as soon as they were sown, and earthquakes had ripped the land apart. After the last earthquake, a tidal wave had flooded through the streets of Norgarth, bringing disease in its wake, and leaving the Delta still under water, its refugees camped out in rags, filth, and rats in Norgarth Square. The Norgons blamed the regent for all their troubles. And she in turn blamed the captain of her guard.

"There is one other matter, my lady. A sea merchant ship was boarded yesterday down at the docks. Its cargo bay held a dozen crates full of bear skins. The captain himself with only slight persuasion told us where to look. His cargo's been seized and he's under guard waiting outside your door. He says he's ready to talk. This, my lady, may be the proof you've been waiting for."

The captain of the Red Bell was brought into the council room in chains. There was a gash on his right cheek and his trimmed black beard was ragged with dried blood. But he carried himself with dignity as he came forward and knelt to the regent.

"My lady, I left the Duke of Navarn's port a week ago, and sailed straight here. I loaded those crates full of bearskins on the duke's very own docks and brought them here to show you. He is the one selling furs to the merchants and telling us to sell them to your people, spreading the bear cult throughout your land to seed the rebellion against your young son, his nephew, the king."

The merchant captain raised his manacled wrists. "I came here to bring you proof. The duke plots against you. He's starting a war, and that, I assure you, is not good for my honest trade. I would have come without your guards' advice, or their chains, to tell you this.

"Locked in my desk in my cabin aboard my ship, I have a scroll. It lists instructions to merchants on how to contact bearman bands plaguing your northern provinces and lists villages in your southern and eastern provinces who also harbor brigands who might be trying to form new bands of bearmen. This scroll, my lady, was given to me during a private audience with the duke. I convinced him I would be in his service and he could trust my word. But it is you, my lady, and your son, my king, whose service I humbly seek."

"Captain, if what you say is true, you shall indeed be rewarded. Does the duke know you came here?"

"No, my lady. If any among my men report to him, I am unaware of it. But they did see me captured, and I put up enough struggle to make a good show for them. No one could report I came here to see you on purpose."

Felain turned back to the map model of Norgondy and picked up the duke's crowned marker from off his bordering realm. She squeezed the marker in her hand, strangling it, then spoke to her captain of the guard.

"Prepare the guard to march," she said. "We'll take Navarn before he takes us. How soon will your men be ready?"

"By midsummer we'll be at their border in full force. And may I say, my lady, this war will rally your people behind the king. They'll know now who his real enemy is, and they'll rise up in his defense."

The queen set the duke's marker back down in his palace in Navarn. "We shall see then how quickly he falls."

~

A bed of pine needles under a horse blanket for a dreaming mat, a fire pit lined by flat stones instead of shells, numbstool and saw reed crushed on top of one of the stones, waiting, Verl finished hanging two blankets from the roof of a quickly pulled together lean-to of pine saplings laced over two boulders. Then he went to tell Merind he was ready.

She was dancing with Jesser as a circle of men, women, children played tambours and drums or pounded stones against stones. Merind would twirl in close to the bear. As Jesser reached for her, Merind would twirl away, trailing a silk scarf across the bear's snout, laughing; and the bear would stomp heavily to the music after her, reaching for the scarf, opening her jaws to the sky and growling happily.

Verl sat down at Crel's fire. The tinker was busy hammering dents out of tin cups and spoons. He barely nodded to Verl, without looking up, without glancing over at

Merind dancing with his bear. Crel had argued with Merind two nights ago not to take Jesser out of her cage again without her chains on. The bear had killed that captain, he kept saying, the bear was no longer safe. Crel wanted no one else handling her. But Verl had still seen Crel hugging and whispering to Jesser in her cage as he fed her, and still had seen him walking with her into the words, his hand resting on her shoulders.

"I should write a song about Jesser someday," Verl said.

Crel polished at a spoon until it flashed in his hand in the firelight. "She'll kill someone else again someday. There's nothing to stop her now. I can't control her anymore."

Verl grinned. "I don't envy you, my friend. You can't control either of the two women in your life."

Crel glanced at him darkly, then over at Merind and the bear. He picked up another spoon, started bending it back into shape with his hammer and tongs. "I can't deny there's a certain..."

"Fascination for her? Be careful of her, Crel. Everyone else here follows you. But you, you follow her, whatever she says to do now."

Crel polished the spoon, set it aside, picked up another before he answered, without looking up. "A year ago, all I ever wanted out of life was to be alone with my tinker wagon and my trade. A night like this, out in the woods, just me and the animals and the campfire, and my world was complete. I've been doing what everyone else demands of me instead for a long time now. Why should she be any different?"

"She is."

Crel stiffened, then he met his eyes, nodded. "Yes. She is."

Merind went to sleep quickly on the dreaming mat, almost as soon as Verl added the second hand of numbstool to the fire. Through the yellow thick stabbing smoke, he let his mind tunnel towards hers. When he found the spark and drifted towards it, she stood holding the spark glittering in her hand waiting for him. Instead of entering her dream, she thrust herself back into his mind, hurtling the thread of his consciousness back through the tunnel with her.

He winced. Her presence in his mind withdrew a step. He saw her in her yellow silks, faceless except for her eyes watching him over the veil, one escaped wisp of hair lifting in the wind where there was no wind. "I'm sorry," she said. "I've not done this before. Not where I've met someone conscious of me inside their mind."

She lifted the spark of light, looked around. "This way," she said.

He followed. When the spark touched memories around them, the memories flashed open uncontrollably. As if walking through the Gallery of the Stairs in Norgarth Palace, picture after picture crowded before them. It made him desperate to hide; he felt he was revealing himself too openly. But it did no good to close his eyes; inside his mind they would not close. It did no good to tunnel away; she drifted beside him wherever he went. And as soon as he felt her with him again, the spark would immediately pull them back to where they had been, forcing his attention onward.

She seemed never to notice his panic. Or, thankfully, never to care. He tried to calm his breath, control himself. When he did, he heard music. A soft tune playing itself on a far-off lute, repeating scales, over and over, slowing the beating of footsteps across his mind, slowing the rhythm of his pulse, and finally, within seconds of their first appearance inside his mind, he relaxed, no longer fighting her invasion, becoming curious instead to look around and explore his own subconsciousness.

Flashes of light and dark clamored for his fascination. Scenes from his past in muted colors and foggy sepia sharpened into faces, events, some remembered, some long forgotten, each claiming they had once defined him. All were shards of himself, puzzle pieces that did not connect, but that somehow added up to the one single man he had always thought he was. A puppy at the beach; a seagull pecked its eyes out. Eleidice singing to his music; older she sang again in front of sea waves that sucked away the sand behind her. A cloud of arrows rained down upon him; a guardsman standing beside him was struck in the neck and fell against him. Shards of stained glass window colors shattered across a marble floor; a reflection of himself in Singer Blue on a dented tin cup raised a lute and played each color as a note in challenge to the lie he had made of his life. Deeper, ever deeper, less focused, greyer scenes drifted around them, from his dreams, and from the dreams of others.

Merind stopped and watched a giant head of ice loom out of a maddened sea.

"The king?" she thought to him. "My father's face?"

"Laird's nightmare," Verl answered her. He waited with her as the boy-king brandished a sword and charged into the leering laugh of the ice king's mouth and was swallowed whole. Laird's scream echoed around them.

They pushed on, deep towards the back of his neck. "Here," Merind said. She touched a tiny grey fold of bulbous mass with the spark she held in her hand.

The spark exploded around him, glowed through him; he spun around, his heart, his mind spinning higher and higher, looming brighter and brighter, his breath choking in awe. He exploded into sparks, he spun around in the presence of stars. He wept in the presence of gods.

And certainty. In the presence of a glorious, overwhelming certainty.

Merind sat on the dreaming mat, waiting for him, when he opened his eyes and stepped out of himself.

"Not everyone will have as strong a reaction," she said, her voice hypnotic, heavenly. "But most will believe they're in the presence of a god. When you touch that spot inside their minds with your illusion, most will fall in praise and wonder. Your god, any god you want to create, can enslave a multitude of believers. You have that power within you, if you choose it."

She paused. He trembled, in his awe still, or in his fear of what he heard. His skin felt cold in the night air, cold with the temptation.

She nodded. "You'll have that power within you when you make that ice head to trap the king."

The glory shed from him. In loud chinks of breaking ice, it crashed from dizzying heights. He plummeted with it, landed sitting stiff on the ground in front of an ebbing fire inside a makeshift dreaming hut. Reality tasted of sulfur and lead. "No," he whispered. Then louder, "No..."

She rose, started to leave. There was nothing angelic in her voice now. "It is your task in the war ahead. To capture Laird. He showed you how to do it himself. It is within your power to do so. He already believes it will happen. In creating illusions, it is belief that creates the reality. That's what created that certainty that you felt inside you. Think on it."

~

Verl strapped his collection of books and scrolls onto his two mules and said goodbye to Lissiv long before dawn. By sunrise he was half way up the hill to the west of the bearmen on his way to the coast when he heard the morning horns blow.

The location of a band of bearmen traveling with a witchwoman had been confirmed, the horns reported, and before first bell, two units of guardsmen had left the gates of Hoffer, less than league upriver, to overtake them. Verl pulled his reins up short and spun his mare around. The camp below was packing up, but they wouldn't leave in time before the guardsmen attacked.

Verl slid from the horse, tethered his two mules to a bush, then jumped back on and raced down to the bearmen camp.

"Run!" he yelled, skidding to a halt. "The guardsmen have found you!"

Men, women, children grabbed their closest possessions, what they hadn't packed yet, bows, quivers, swords, rocks, clubs, any weapon they could find, drove their carts, wagons, oxen, geese, mounted their horses and mules, and ran for the trees downriver. Amid the commotion, little Jere shouted Verl's name and ran towards him, his mother chasing after him.

"Grab him!" Verl yelled. He heard a rumble. An arrow whizzed past his arm. He spurred his horse forward, took Jere from Lissiv's arms, and gave her a hand up behind him, then headed for the trees. The rumble came louder; his horse reared and neighed in terror. Jere's arms choked around Verl's neck, Lissiv clung to his waist trying to hold her seat. Verl held on with his knees, clinging to Jere with one hand, and trying to spur the horse, shouting to control it as the horse reared again, and came down hard and lost its footing on the rolling ground.

It wasn't the charge of the guardsmen that had made the rumble. Stones were flying down from the side of the hill, the water in the river was roiling, splashing up, the ground was starting to split. Another aftershock, this one the largest yet. The horse rose from its stumble, screamed its terror, and bolted towards the charge of the guardsmen.

Half the men were busy trying to control their own horses, some had dismounted to safer ground, trying to hold onto the reins of their rearing horses, as Verl's mare rushed into them. Verl held on to Jere, death grip still on the reins and pommel. He could think of nothing else to do but vanish from the sight of one, two, he didn't know how many guardsmen he could strip the image of Jere, Lissiv, and himself from. That night in the dungeon, no one had seen him then, but that was in the dark except for his lantern, and he'd had time to plan. But here, here, no one was watching, he hoped, but the quake would end in seconds and then they'd be surrounded. A riderless horse, he could pray that was all they would see.

His horse reared to a stop as another horse in front of her reared up, screaming aloud in panic, pawing at the sky. When his horse came down, Verl bounced hard on the impact, and Lissiv did too behind him. Her arms around his waist slipped; she lost her seat.

Wrapping both arms tight around Jere, Verl swung his leg around and jumped down beside her.

Too late, too far, as she stumbled to her feet, she was no longer invisible, no longer inside his illusion.

But she was looking around for him, screaming his name and Jere's, she couldn't see them.

"Over here, " he shouted as he stumbled for his footing. Then the ground stopped shaking. As she ran for his voice, a guardsman saw her, raised his sword, and Verl saw it swing. "No!" he yelled. He extended his illusion, didn't know he could do that; she vanished, and the guardsman checked his swing when he saw her disappear. In her place, an image came to Verl's mind, perhaps from Merind's thoughts last night, perhaps from seeing her illusions in other battles. Jesser. As the guardsman swung again, the image of the bear rising up, snarling, batting her clawed fists at the sword, replaced the invisible Lissiv; then Verl reached her hand to pull her away, leaving the image of the bear for the guardsman to slaughter. The temptation, the instant of knowing, remembering, Verl touched the spot inside the guardsman's mind and the bear image's fury became that of a god.

The bear turned, rose higher, it snarled and swatted at the stunned guardsman stumbling away from it. So real, Verl felt the presence, so did others around him. The bear roared. "Jesser!" Jere yelled, recognizing her, believing her, knowing her to be the friend he'd hugged and petted. "Watch out!" Jere yelled, as the guardsman swung at the towering image. Jere wiggled from Verl's arms before Verl had time to react, and ran towards the image of the bear to save her.

"Jere!" Lissiv shouted, and she ran to catch her son, yank him back, as the sword came swinging, struck the bear, swung through the image, struck her instead in the chest, and out through her back.

She fell. Verl grabbed Jere to him and watched her fall. She was visible, she'd run forward too fast. In the next second, as soon as he realized it, she had vanished from sight again. Verl bent to her, dragged her body few steps away from the image of the dying bear. More men were stabbing it, making sure it died, and through tears, Verl released the image, let the bear god vanish before them all.

Verl knelt down beside the dying Lissiv, held her hand. He kept her invisible, but the blood trail from where he dragged her overflowed the ground and kept on spreading. He pressed his other hand over Jere's sobs, tried to keep his head buried against his shoulder.

They knelt vigil over her, keeping her invisible, long after she died, long after the guardsmen around them regained control of their horses, remounted them, and rode after the fleeing bearmen.

Jere was asleep in his arms when Verl finally stood and went to find his horse.

Chapter 31
Ice Islands

Verl gripped the ship's railing as a dolphin arced into the sky and dove through the ship's wake. The permanent grin on the dolphin's face as it swam beside the ship just below the surface, half rolled over, winking at him, was that of a god who could see into him and find him laughable. Here he was: a failure as a son, a failure as a Singer, a failure as a friend. His last act among the bearmen had been to abandon Crel, because nothing had become more important to him than his own curiosity to see a legendary star from the secret observatory above the palace of the king.

Yet instead, a twist of fate, a swing of a Norgon sword, and he'd become the sole protector of a little boy. Jere. He gripped the railing harder. He had learned in the last few days that Jere was the one thing he could not abandon. A child who still looked upon him with trust and faith.

The dolphin god dove again. On the Eller Islands, the whale was a god. Its first brother was a dolphin, and second brother, man. That made as much sense to Verl today, after all he'd seen this last year, as a mythological flying beast the Badurians had made into a god in whose wordless name they had burnt and killed a realm they could not convert. Or as much sense as an illusion of a god Merind, and now he, had created out of a dancing bear and a highwayman. An illusion to fight a delusion. A lie to fight another lie. This dolphin god instead came into his life only long enough to laugh at him, then it disappeared again back into the sea. A master god of irony.

Hand sliding along the yard ropes to ensure he wouldn't slip, Verl made his way down to the cargo hold where he and Jere shared a hammock. He eyed the crates of bear furs as he descended, the barrels of molasses to buy more furs, and the bundles of spices to buy blocks of ice. As fortune would have it, or as a wink of that dolphin's eye

373

would have it, when he and Jere had arrived two days ago in Rannisport, three ships were in dock but only one was ready to sail out — the Red Bell. He recognized her striped sails immediately and confirmed it when he got close enough to see the freshly repainted name on her prow. "Arnaby's dead," he told the merchant captain as soon as they were alone inside the captain's cabin. Verl related how the spy priest had died. But he said nothing about Crel, nor anything about Jesser or Merind. Verl had not forgotten that this merchant captain was the man who had betrayed the Bearman, getting his brother killed to goad him into becoming a legend. Now that Verl knew the Bearman was Crel, he would not tell the captain any hint about having met him.

On the other hand, the merchant captain had helped him release his friends from the dungeon, and had taken Arax to his village in the Orliand Islands. By this time tomorrow, the Red Bell would be landing in the Orliands again, where the captain would buy snowbear furs and berg ice with the molasses and spice. And where Verl would look at Arax's ice carvings. That had become his new plan as soon as he heard where the captain was heading. It would postpone his return to Norgarth by a week. Yet he'd still reach Norgarth two weeks ahead of trying to continue over land scorched, misshapen, and ruined by lava flow from the volcano eruption last month south of Rannisport.

Jere was playing hockey with the ship's boy, using potatoes as pucks. Few of the wobbling potatoes ever made it into the other boy's makeshift goal. Each time the ship swayed over a wave, the potatoes would scatter in the opposite direction they'd been hit. The cook would not be pleased that the boys had raided his sack of potatoes again.

"I saw a dolphin jump," Verl said.

"Where?" Jere's eyes lit with excitement as he ran for the ladder. Before they set sail from Rannisport, Verl had paid a sailmaker's wife a year's wage to take in Jere and raise him as her own. But when Verl had tried to leave the boy, the trust in Jere's eyes listening to his promises that he'd come back for him had lanced straight into Verl and trapped the lies in his throat. No, he would never abandon Jere.

Verl waited for the ship's boy to climb the ladder after Jere, then he followed the two boys up onto deck.

~

"It's taken me months to find out where you've been hiding." As he spoke, Duke Rayid hammered out a chunk of fosfar from the brilliant blue vein running through the tellerwoman's cave. "No one could tell me." He tossed the blue crystal up in the air, caught it, pocketed it. He met Ailil's silver eyes above her veil. "Then I realized myself where you'd come."

He walked with her out of the cave and gazed across the expanse of the lake and the bowl-shaped cliffs of the ancient crater surrounding them. Twenty-four years ago she'd brought him here, and for a summer month they'd picnicked on these shores, just the two of them, escaping the rigors and plotting and drudgery that court life had become for them as his father lay dwindling in his last long year of senility.

Over there on the east bank, below Dragon Gate's Pass, Ailil had taken off her veil for him, just as she had done when they were children. The grassy cove was replaced now by the shops and taverns of New Drespin, and he and Ailil had long since gone their separate ways.

"Why did you tell Merind she was my brother's daughter?"

Ailil barely glanced at him. "I'm sure you've guessed why."

"She and her bearman friend have raised an army of peasants and craftsmen behind them. Are you sure she'll yield the crown to your son when she wins it?"

Ailil stopped to watch a loon dive into the lake then come back up with a fish. "I plan to make sure she does."

~

"Bless the shebear faith! Here walks a sight I have not seen!" Before Verl had descended the gangplank, Arax had wrapped his arms around him and lifted him a foot in

375

the air. "And a wee one at your side. Who be this fine young lad?"

Verl had barely regained his footing, hand grabbing hold of the rails to right himself as soon as Arax set him down, before the huge man hefted Jere up over his shoulder, twisted him around his back, and twirled him upside down and around in front of him, the boy's frightened squeals turning to giggles and demands for more by the time they reached Arax's handcart on the dock.

Arax sold his load of snowbear and seal furs for two barrels of molasses and three bags of peppers, rosemary and sage. Then he took Verl, the captain, and Jere into his village to meet his wife. Jere rode on top of the cart and pointed the way.

The sun was high, the air frigid and fresh, the stony tundra a carpet of midget-size flowers—flowers Verl had not seen growing anywhere else this spring. Stunted windswept trees were budding, while patches of crusted snow still glistened in the crevices and shadows of every granite outcropping. Spring was just starting to come to the Orliands, but unlike on the mainland it *was* coming. Verl breathed in its freshness and his heart thrilled at the startled flight of a long-tailed pheasant their rickety cart passed. All Orliand ice shepherds lived on this southernmost of the ice islands, Arax told him. The islands farther north would be snowbound all summer long.

Arax's wife was hearty and broad, taller than Verl by several inches. She took the boy from Arax's arms and had him help her open a barrel of molasses to make what she called ice cream while Arax led Verl and the captain to an underground cave in the cliffs shouldering the village.

Verl pulled the fur cape that Arax had given him around him and admired the intricate ice statues of bears and elks. The light from Arax's torch sparkled off the facets and sharp edges of the carved rocks of ice and whitened the rounded curves of the animal faces. The second chamber of the ice cave was piled high with the true luxury commodity the islanders had to sell: ten blocks of iceberg ice. Verl waited as the captain and Arax bartered, then he helped them load two blocks of ice, each one half as tall as Verl, onto a sledge to take to the ship's hold.

Along the way, Verl told Arax his plan, and his big friend's booming laughter frightened away the black and white sea skimmers as they dove along the pounding shore. Their caws scolded loudly in protest as they flew away.

The next morning the friends were on an ice trawler skirting small bergs and growlers that had been corralled into a fjord of a northern island. As new bergs calved off the glaciers along the islands' shores and floated down the shipping lane toward the mainland, Orliand iceshepherds netted them and towed them into several of the larger fjords where they alone could quarry them throughout the summer. Only the richest courts and manor houses in all of Norgondy could afford serving ice confections and cold meats and gelatins.

"That one there, I'd say." Arax pointed to one of the larger small bergs slightly taller than the merchant ship and as long as the ship, easy to hide behind. The foggy morning sun glinted off sharp crags the color of green glass. It must be one of the bergs that had rolled over either after splashing into the waves as it calved off a glacier or while it was being herded, Arax explained. The underbellies of a few bergs became this stormy green when they'd trapped sea algae in their ice.

Arax flagged the sister trawler over. As both trawlers edged alongside the green berg, their large nets were swung over high across the ridges of the berg. Then Arax and a crewman from the other trawler jumped onto the berg and hammered in spikes to secure the netting. The berg started to roll back and forth between the weight of the two men, sending out waves that bounced the small trawlers up high and slapped them down. Verl gripped the railings to keep from falling as he swayed with the boat, feeling like the waves were still slapping inside him..

When Arax leaped back on board the ship, his smile was as wide as a pelican's, and he slapped the seasick Verl on the shoulder with a laugh. "We got ye a good one, my friend."

377

~

Crel focused the telescope on Merind as she jumped off a cliff. She drifted with the air currents, circling down as instructed, her wide black sail looking like wings above her, keeping her distinct among the gaily colored sails of the Morris shepherds. Through the stargazer's telescope from the next cliff over, Crel could see her triumph as she landed among the sheep in the pastures below. It was the first time in her six tries that she had landed on her feet.

Duke Rayid had not been pleased with Merind's decision to learn to fly, but she had insisted that knowing how herself would help her make her illusion that would transform the duke's flyers into looking more like the monster gods of the Badurian priests. Since arriving at the stargazer's cliff yesterday, they'd seen two of those garug monsters attacking the sheep. During the second attack, the duke's flyers tried helping the flying shepherds keep the monster away. The garug had paid as little attention to the stabs of the soldiers' swords as it had to the clubbing on its wings by the shepherds' staffs. It roared at the men, then whipped its long forked tail at an isolated ewe. The ewe fell a few seconds later, and the garug dove through the circle of swords and staffs to claim its prey, carrying it up and away in long scaly talons.

Merind had studied the monster through the stargazer's telescope and she made several sketches of it afterwards. To Crel, it was an ugly beast, lion's head, eagle's wings and claws, scorpion's poisonous tail, a mistake of nature, even more terrifying in person than Merind's illusion of one last winter when she'd made the myth of the dragon of Malla come to life. But Merind had disagreed with him. She admired the beast, called it majestic in its fearsome power as it braved any shepherd or soldier trying to stop it. The duke had nodded at her, understanding her better apparently than Crel ever would.

He sighed, swung the telescope back up to look at the last faint streak of white of the tailed star. Against the blue of the morning sky, it could be mistaken as a thin wisp of cloud if they had not been watching it since just before

378

dawn.   When viewed against the night sky, it had been bright, looking close enough to touch. He could imagine he saw remnants of the two jets of fire swirling away from it that the stargazer had shown to them through the telescope last night. Or perhaps that was indeed just a wisp of curling cloud.

He let the heavy scope swing upright into rest position. Barzolf came over and locked it in place, but just before he capped the lenses, the barrel caught the morning sun and cast a second miniature sun onto the rock shelf below. The bright image of the miniature sun was focused intensely enough to scorch a stray tuft of grass. Crel frowned and stayed Barzolf's arm, remembering something that he and Wiss had seen in an Axfeld traders' fair long ago. Crel slid his hand under the scope until he held the fiery sundisk in his hand.

He rubbed the heat of it away, then he helped the stargazer cap the lenses and roll the telescope back into the cave.

The stargazer's cave had a green glow to it. The duke had given Barzolf a fosfar crystal as brilliantly blue-green as those in the tellerwoman's cave. When Barzolf added the crystal to the fire last night, his cave became as bright as daylight inside. During the first half of the night, waiting for the tailed star to rise, they sat around the hearth bathed in the green light, cooking and eating and listening as the stargazer pointed out the night sky painted on the domed ceiling of his cave.

In the muted sunlight coming in from outside this morning, the painted ceiling was less vivid, but still discernable. Faint lines of ochre joined the stars together outlining the five major constellations. Each picture of an animal the lines formed, each pattern men had imposed upon the scattering of the stars, told a story. Or so Barzolf had said last night. Duke Rayid had chuckled at his friend, and amended him, saying that men had created meaning out of the patternings they saw in the stars, then lived under them, believing their stories real, believing their stories could influence their lives, and forgetting that *they* had been the original creators. Crel shook his head at both voices

379

from last night and answered them silently. In much the same way, men created gods out of bears and tinkers, and then believed them real. He closed his fist over where he had trapped the sunlight in his hand and followed Barzolf back outside.

The stargazer went to a stone table where he had been recording in his chronicles all morning. He carried with him a new set of scrolls he laid on the table. Daxid, his mountain dog, more wolf than dog, was chained under the table. He bristled and snarled as Crel approached. Crel stopped in his tracks; the dog rushed at him to the end of his chain and growled fiercely.

Barzolf jerked him back. "He's a friend, Daxid!"

The dog lowered its tail and sulked back under the table. It curled and lay down, resting its chin on Barzolf's foot. But it kept one eye half open and growled softly at every move Crel made. Slowly Crel retreated to the cave entrance. Jesser in a foul mood, caged all day, would be no more hospitable to a stranger than a hermit's dog.

The cedar frame around the cave entrance door was carved with five designs Crel recognized. They were the five patterns he had first seen in the tellerwoman's cave, the five symbols of the constellations, Barzolf had explained. The stargazer wore the five designs embroidered at random across his robe of stars. It was the first thing Crel had noticed about him when he and Merind had come with the duke to the stargazer's hill.

Crel and only a handful of his men had traveled with Merind and two of the duke's guards to meet up with her uncle. Crel's men were now training with the duke's men in the camps below while Merind sketched the garugs and learned to fly. The rest of Crel's band of bearmen had been left behind in Norgondy, where they, and an army of other bearmen bands all across Norgondy, were sniping at Queen Felain's forces, then running and escaping just slowly enough to be chased before vanishing into the hollow trees, hidden crannies and mat-covered holes in the ground that their compatriots had waiting for them. The tactic had succeeded several times in splintering the Norgon army as units broke off to give chase. That splintering had delayed the arrival of the full invasion force of the Norgons into the Moxie Pass for over a month now, giving the duke more time to ready his plans to meet them.

His plans. The duke's plans. Crel squeezed his fist.

A whole realm of bearmen believed they were following Crel's orders, but Crel knew he had little control over them now. It seemed he'd had little control over anything in his life since he had met Merind. Her uncle the duke was no better. And his network of merchants and spies, spreading the duke's orders from bearman band to bearman band in Crel's name, much worse. The merchant captain who had gotten his brother killed was one of the duke's spies, and Crel had not forgotten that.

Crel shook his head. If he wanted to stay with Merind, he'd have to forget it. Slowly he fingered the spiral design carved into the frame of the cave entrance beside him. Barzolf had called it the spiral of forgetfulness, and said it represented not only the constellation in the center of the universe, but it was also the symbol of the tailed star that returned to Colonium every two hundred years. Tracing the design brought back vivid memories of his long ordeal in the tellerwoman's cave, painting the five designs over and over, trying to make sense of them. He had believed then that nothing would be placed in random order, that the puzzle of Ailil's cave had to be meaningful, had to hold the key to his freedom. The lesson he had learned in that cave had opened his eyes, and had helped him survive this last year. It had taught him that not every event in the world had to hold a meaning. Not every group of stars in the sky had to form a pattern. And not every tale of a god had to be true. But people everywhere would always, stubbornly, believe they did, just as he had in Ailil's cave.

And just as the duke had said, it was belief in a creation---belief in a pattern, in an interpretation, in a country, in a god---that made the creation real, that gave the creations of men power over their creators. He was living proof of that, becoming a god to his followers. Even Freyshin, who had created his legend, would look upon him as a god now, from time to time.

Crel dug his fingernail into the four hooks crooking out of the spiral design as he retraced them. They did look remarkably like the jets of fire spiraling away from the tailed star that they had seen through the telescope last night. Verl had called the tailed star "the birdfoot star," and Crel had seen owl prints along sandy creek banks that had opposing toe marks pointing backwards that looked very much like this design. But Barzolf said among his people, they called the tailed star, and its design, "the Phoenix star." He said that unlike other tailed stars Crel had seen in his lifetime, this one with its great tail of fire would become so bright that some years it could be seen at midday. Since the tailed star had been visible so long already this year, Barzolf believed this year could be such a spectacular year.

If so, perhaps here was another chance to create a fear for the Norgon priests to believe in, and then use their belief against them. And perhaps that was just what Verl had intended.

Crel turned to the stargazer. " A friend told us we should time the final battle with the appearance of the Phoenix star."

The stargazer squinted at Crel, then he nodded slowly. "Probably a very good idea. According to the scrolls, the last time it came at the same time as the midsummer shower of stars, the night became a terrifying storm of falling stars. Let me see if I can find that passage." Barzolf opened one of the scrolls and started reading..

By the time Merind and Duke Rayid returned to the stargazer's hill, Barzolf had found what he was looking for, and he read aloud to all of them the description of the sky falling one night, in a storm of shooting stars, and about the mass suicides and panic that night, as well as the murder of the king the next day, all as portended by the coming of the Phoenix star.

A courier interrupted them. "My lord Duke! The Norgons are coming! They'll be inside the pass within the week."

. Crel opened his fist to where he had held the sun in his hand. He had two plans now---his own plans, not the duke's---of how *his bearmen* could fight the war, and he had less than a week to make his plans work.

Chapter 32
Moxie Pass

From the shadows of a cave, Jesser growled.
Crel raised his left fist, signaling for silence.
Jesser grumbled, but she lay back down.

Crel edged to the cave entrance, peeked out. He
doubted he could keep Jesser's attention much longer. If
the fog low over the valley floor didn't lift soon, her
patience would be gone. And with it, any hope she'd obey.

Crel opened his bag, threw her a fish. She sat up to
catch it, then ever so slowly, she turned her back on him to
eat it. She jerked from side to side as she turned, planting
one heavy foot after one heavy foot, making sure her chain
rattled aloud with each step. One more sign she was bored
with his silence game. She could be quiet when she wanted
to be.

The fog looked eerily orange, filtering thousands of
campfires beneath it. Over ten thousand men, the duke had
said. Most of the Norgon army was squeezed under the
cliffs below. What was left of the bearmen bands who had
lured the Norgons into the pass had camped in the Narrows.
They could escape from there into Navarn. But the duke
had ordered them to hold the pass while his own men circled
around behind the Norgons. It mattered little to the duke
how many bearmen would be killed: their "regrettable
sacrifice" would set the trap and win the war.

But in no way was Crel going to let his bearmen die.
Not if he could help it.

He opened the grilled door to the stone kiln Freyshin
had made and added a log to the fire. Inside the flames
were green and intense, one of the dozen fosfar crystals the
Capsens had brought to the duke for the battle sparked in the
center of the fire. A blast of hot air rushed out at Crel and
scorched his arms and forehead. He closed the door
quickly. The kiln was crude, more a bee-hive of ill-fitting
rocks cemented with mud. Freyshin had become adept at
building makeshift kilns on the road to fire his clay tiles to

leave around after every bearman attack. But building a dozen kilns for Crel in only three days had resulted in kilns that looked more primitive than ever, or so Freyshin had kept complaining to him.

The one task Crel had allowed Freyshin to take his time building was fitting in a chimney hole on top of each kiln. Using his anvil, Yarisol had hammered tin stove pipes for each kiln, while Crel spent his time polishing the inside of the pipes to a mirror-like sheen. Their first test was four nights ago. They lit the fires inside the kilns; then Crel angled mirrors atop the stove pipes to catch the firelight and send it towards the cliff wall opposite the cave. When all twelve beams of light met in one large brightened ball of light on the cliff wall, Yarisol joined on new pipes at the mirrors to encircle and focus the shafts of light.

In the mean time, the duke's spectacle makers had made a set of lenses large enough to cover the ends of stovepipes, the duke laughing at Crel's request. Two more rushed days followed, angling, adjusting, improvising before the final test; and then two nights ago, in the darkest hours, all twelve shafts of firelight were beamed onto the cliff wall to create an image like a giant snowman built of fuzzy snowballs that could be seen from the valley floor, and the duke no longer laughed.

"They work like Barzolf's telescope," Crel had told him. "Just inverted, projecting the light outward."

Crel had one last adjustment to make. Years ago Wiss had taken him to the traders' fair in Axfeld, where, as a young boy, Crel had been fascinated by images projected from a lantern onto a wall in a small room. The images he had seen floating around that room had been of ghostly animals and people, not just fuzzy balls of light.

Wiss later told him that pictures had been painted on glass covers over the lantern's holes, an old showman's trick. Crel had experimented with the idea over the years, and it had been inspiration for his masterpiece lantern he had given to Orist over a year ago. But when Crel tried painted slides over the lenses on his stove pipes two nights ago, all he got was a blur of dim colors on the cliff wall. The distance was too great.

But he didn't need color. Jesser was black.

Onto each lens of his stovepipe scopes, Crel added a shape of tin. The shadows projected onto the cliff wall retained the shapes much more sharply, in stark contrast to the snowballs of fuzzy light that haloed them. He recut each shape covering each lens, making one a part of a leg, one a part of an arm, one part of a bear's head, until, by yesterday morning, each joined perfectly; and the image of Jesser loomed over the valley floor.

Now they had only to repeat the image again tonight with the Norgons camped below. If, that is, this damn fog would ever lift. And if Crel could get Jesser to cooperate, to growl a bellowing growl that would signal all eleven men to uncover their lenses at the same time as Crel. If. IF. *IF!* Damn this waiting. Damn this fog that covered the Norgons below it. And damn Jesser for turning her back on him, going to sleep.

~

Duke Rayid crept gingerly along the side of the cliff. There had been a rock slide here recently, and he had to be careful not to dislodge any of the loose stones.. The fog kept him invisible, but any slip of his foot could give him away.

He reached the end of the slope of fallen rocks and found Captain Evers hiding in the boulders, watching for signs of Norgon movement through the thick fog. The captain gave him a thumbs up, all his men were ready.

Rayid continued down to the tree-lined creek bank, only yards away from the Norgon tents. General Nuce was knocking mud off his boot with a stick. The general looked up at his approach, but did little to mask his dissatisfaction. Nuce knew him well enough to be honest with him. Rayid appreciated that much about him.

"The fog, sir."

Rayid put a hand to his shoulder. "If it doesn't lift soon, we'll see no action tonight," he whispered back.

"I can still have a few men take you back to the main camps, sir."

Rayid shook his head. "I am where I want to be."

386

His general stiffened, then he looked out at the Norgon tents, close enough to spit on them. None of Rayid's officers had wanted the duke to risk coming into the pass tonight. Original plans were for him to oversee the war from the main camps, among the thousands of Navarns who, over the last few weeks, had hidden in the hills on Norgondy's side of the pass. Once the Norgons went into the pass, Rayid would have given the order to close in behind them.

Actually, according the general's original plans, very few of Rayid's men would have been needed at all inside the pass, only the best archers to help the bearmen hold the neck of the pass. A unit of twenty archers could have held the Narrows all day, leaving the full force of the Navarn swordsmen, cavalry and kite flyers to press forward, closing the death trap on the Norgons caught between them. The war had been won that way many times on their council maps.

Then yesterday, Merind's tinker had disrupted all their planning. The one contingency they could have never imagined.

Rayid glanced up the hill. Crel had not started his light show yet.

With this fog, he might never. Unfortunately, as luck would have it, the fog was already starting to thin in several patches. Rayid could see a crimson pennant with the black wings and belled staff of a Badurian priest flying over one of the tents nearby, a detail he could not have seen a few minutes ago. If the fog continued to lift, they may still be needing to save the tinker's hide after all before the night was out. Rayid could hear General Nuce's curses now if they needed to do that.

But the Norgon peasants followed Crel as their leader. Their revolution would fall apart without him. This tinker was too valuable to lose to his foolhardiness. And so, as of yesterday morning, Rayid had had to order Nuce to save the tinker at all costs.

Without saying another word, Nuce started knocking mud off his other boot. In their silence, Rayid gripped the pine branch beside him. Perhaps if he had paid more attention to what Crel had been doing all week, the situation tonight could have been avoided. But at first, other than providing whatever supplies the tinker asked for, Rayid had mostly ignored him. Whatever Crel was working on, his project had kept his men and him busy. And that thankfully had kept them out of the way, kept them from asking too many questions,. And that in turn had kept their followers willing to hold the pass, believing their orders still came from their own leaders, in their leaders' absence, never knowing the difference.

But then, yesterday, Crel had made a recognizable image of a giant bear appear on the cliff wall above the pass. And that would be what would get the young fool killed.

Not that Rayid didn't appreciate the man's ingenuity, Any panic or confusion among the priests and younger Norgons his tricks of light caused could be useful. But in recent months, Rayid had received more than one report of how seasoned Norgon guardsmen were no longer being fooled by bearmen tricks. It would not take such men long to question if those twelve beams of light were shining down from the image above, or coming up instead from somewhere below. And as soon as they questioned it, it would take the Norgons even shorter time to follow the twelve light beams to their sources.

And so the Duke of Navarn had posted an army of men to protect twelve peasant bearmen lighting fires.

Rayid gripped the pine branch harder. He heard the branch snap under his fist. He released it, watched it fall. Despite all his months of planning, little was left tonight that augured well for tomorrow. The uncertainty of war could make a man built of stone jitter the night before. Rayid closed his cloak around him against the chilled mugginess of the foggy night.

A low angered bear growl rumbled through the pass. The rumble grew quickly louder, splitting the night air, echoing from cliff wall to cliff wall all around them. Even expecting Jesser's signal, some primeval response in Rayid to hearing a bear growl in a pine forest at night scratched up his spine and urged him to run. The growl was more terrifying, more effective than he had imagined it could be.

General Nuce beside him muttered a curse. "There they are."

Five beams, nine beams, twelve beams of light blazed upwards towards the cliff wall above them. Through the thinning mist of fog, the specter of a giant black bear god took shape.

Then, directly over the cliff wall above the image, a patch of fog cleared to the night sky, and the tailed star, brighter than ever, flared into view from the valley floor.

~

Jesser's wail woke Merind. She hadn't been sleeping soundly tonight. Not with the birdfoot star shining brighter than the full moon for the last few hours. It had turned the tundra world of the highlands as murky orange as first dawn.

When she had fallen asleep, there had been only a few falling stars in the sky, no more than fell every summer solstice. Now a storm of stars was falling everywhere. It was just as Barzolf predicted, with the annual shower of stars coinciding with the coming of the Birdfoot star. But she had never imagined the majesty of it. The sky was on fire. It was like standing under a waterfall made of fire. Streaks of light shot down across the sky in all directions. One came at her close enough to hear it thunder and whiz before it faded, leaving the leaden smell of brimstone in the air. Merind raised her arms to the sky, spun and spun around to see it all.

She heard a shouting. One of the Capsen tellerwomen her mother had sent to help with the illusions tomorrow was screaming and running for cover under the rock outcropping. Others were leaving their tents and running after her, gesturing to Merind to come too.

But it was the shouting coming from below that stopped Merind. She went to the edge of the cliff, peered over. The fog was lifting. It had blanketed the valley floor all night, a rolling sea of white rimmed by dark fjord-like cliffs as seen from above. Now the light of the moon and the Birdfoot star were reaching into the canyon and brightening the cliffs walls to a fiery yellow and red, and the fog was dispersing enough that Merind could see the crowd of Norgon tents on the valley floor. She glanced over at the far cliff. Crel's image of a bear was impressive, even from this angle. But she doubted it could compete with the light of the full moon and the Birdfoot star shining upon it for very long. Judging from the alarm cries and bugling below, though, many Norgons had already seen it.

She hoped they could see this sky of falling stars too. For anyone not expecting this storm of stars, it would be a night of fiery hell they would never forget.

She heard another whiz of a falling star. As she ducked her head and ran for cover, she glanced back, and saw a fireball strike the cliff on the other side of the canyon.

~

Blinding light. The land lurched, and Rayid stumbled into the brambles, scratching his eyelid. The bear in the cave above began bellowing and didn't stop, the most ear-shattering, goron-awful sound Rayid had ever heard.

He scrambled to his feet, his face bleeding from the thorns. There were a few rocks tumbling down the cliff again, but the hillside had stopped rolling. A wisp of smoke or dust rose from a gash in the right shoulder of the image of the bear, and, background to the bear's bellow, he could hear the Norgons cheering.

He looked. Nine Badurian priests in their long scarlet robes stood atop a flatbed wagon only paces away from Rayid. A few minutes ago, they'd been chanting and waving their incense lanterns at the ghostly appearance of the bear image above them. Now instead they were brandishing their staffs into the air in jubilation. Rayid crooked his lips. A freak of nature, a tiny remnant of a falling star had lanced the image of the bear; and the priests were taking credit. Their god had answered their prayers. If their faith weren't so frightening, he'd laugh.

Worse, if the priests had any disbelievers in their crowd, and just minutes ago, Rayid had assumed there were many, it didn't look like it now. Even the captains who'd been ordering men to search the hills for the sources of the

390

beams of light had stopped and had drifted over to hear the priests.

The priests started chanting again, louder than before. Drummers beat drums to their cadence, and swordsmen began clanging their swords against their shields. Whatever panic the appearance of the bear on the cliff had caused was gone. The trick had backfired; the Norgons were tasting victory, having proof now their god was on their side.

The cliffs echoed the Norgons' uproar, and throughout it all, Jesser kept up her wailing. The gates of hell had screamed open, and it was the duke's own men who would be unnerved.

A Badurian priest rose up onto the buckboard seat above the crowd and raised his staff at the bear's spirit image on the cliff and shouted his curse. An arrow from the hillside above Rayid shot the priest through his chest.

"Fool, no!" Rayid mouthed. "Not now!" It could only have been a bearman, unnerved or not, none of his own men would have shot without the order to.

Killing the priest now had exactly the effect Rayid feared. Where only several units of men had been sent to hunt the hillsides for the sources of the light beams, now a whole army of zealot Norgons was charging for the hills. They would be swarmed. Dawn and the main force of his army could not come soon enough to save them.

~

Merind wove her fingers through the steam rising from her cauldron and chanted for concentration. This would be the most intricate illusion she'd ever attempted. She glanced along the cliff edge. In the predawn light, all eleven tellerwomen her mother had sent were chanting above their cauldrons, ready to help her. Spaced between them, donning their kite wings, six hundred of the duke's flyers were waiting to make their jump.

Overhead, the Birdfoot star shone bright white against the bluing sky, its tail long and beautiful. A few falling stars still flashed across the sky, but no other had come as close to ground as the one that had hit the cliff last

391

night.   As dawn got brighter, Merind could see the dark
hole in the rock face the falling star had made, cutting away
half the image's shoulder.   The image itself was fading, the
morning would soon be too bright to see it at all. She was
surprised Crel had not stopped beaming the image. Letting
it fade away would weaken its best effect.

The fighting below had already begun. Everyone on
the cliff edge beside her could hear the ring of swords
clashing and the screams of men dying echoing up through
the canyon. The soldier standing next to her, his wings
strapped on, gripped his sword in stern resolve to wait for
his order to jump, wanting instead to join the fighting now.

Merind wove her fingers faster, chanted louder, still
waiting for the sun to rise. The sky needed to be light
enough for her illusion to be seen.

She could see silhouettes of men on the opposite cliff
rolling boulders to the edge. Her mother had sent the
Capsens to create an illusion of an avalanche to add to the
panic of the Norgons. But Merind had told the tellerwomen
maybe later, if at all. She had trained the tellerwoman
instead to make the duke's flyers, dressed in black, look like
garug monsters for as long as they could. Merind's own
illusions faded away half way down the cliff, few of the
other tellerwomen's illusions lasted as long.

The sun fingered its first rays above the horizon As
it rose over the rolling heath of the Highlands, Merind raised
her voice to the shriek of a sunhawk then shot her arms up
through the steam, folding them inwards and curling a ball
of steam above her head. She spread her fingers wide and
floated the ball over the heads of the first five of the men
clustered around her ready to jump.

To either side of her, tellerwomen cast steam over
the first five of the flyers assigned to each of them. The first
wave of sixty black garug monsters leapt from the cliff edge
and soared downwards.

~

A falling star flashed a faint trail across the morning
sky. Three Norgons stopped in a clearing on the hillside and
pointed up. From where the star disappeared past the cliff,

black monsters soared out of the sky. As the flying monsters passed the cliff face with the faint impression still of the bear god glowering down upon them, the monsters transformed into men floating under giant wings, swords in their hands, ready to join their fight.

"Look!" one of the Norgons shouted. "Shapeshifters! The Winged One has sent us shapeshifters to fight for us!"

Has she you think? muttered Freyshin, as the bearman aimed an arrow through the trees at the Norgon and shot.

The soldier fell, his mouth still open, praising his god.

His two companions raised their swords and charged into the trees where Freyshin was hiding. He had time only to let loose another arrow before the Norgons were upon him. He would have liked to have seen the expression on their faces when the miracle fighters they thought their god had sent them started killing Norgons instead.

But he did die with the satisfaction of knowing that the Norgons had not yet found Crel's kiln, and perhaps now, with his having led the three who had come the closest away from it, they never would.

~

Half the morning gone and the canyon echoed ever louder with the clash of steel and the beat of war drums. Merind paced back and forth along the edge of the cliff trying to see any advantage one side had over the other. From this height, all she could see were mass movements of colors: the duke's army in the distance in blue and black bunching closer to the entrance of the pass, and the sea of Norgon soldiers in Badurian scarlet trapped below her. She tightened the harness straps across her shoulders. She had sworn to Rayid she would not make the flight down into the canyon herself. After making Navarn flyers look like the gods of the Badurians descending upon their own men— their own god against them— she was to wait, Rayid had told her, her job was finished.

It had been hours since the last of the duke's flyers had jumped off the cliff, and Merind was through waiting.

393

She could be no help at all from up here. She hooked the kite wings to her harness. Yet still, she did not jump. She slapped her side, started pacing again.

She stopped beside one of the tellerwomen stirring her cauldron.

"Still trying to make it look like an avalanche?"

The tellerwoman nodded. "It's what your mother sent us here to do. Just give us the word, and we're ready."

Merind looked over the edge again, then shook her head. "I'm not sure any of our illusions have had any effect today. Not for very long at least. There's just so many of them." She nodded back at the tellerwoman. "You helped me with the flyers. Now maybe I can help you."

She strode back to her cauldron, and added wood to the fire beneath it. As the steam rose, she began to hum. She let her fingers flow into the steam; she leaned forward, let the steam flow into her face. Her brow, her neck, her chin dripped with cooling beads of sweat. Sweat caressed her, steam caressed her, water and hot air caressed her. *Water to earth, earth to fire, fire to water, water to steam, steam to rocks*. She chanted the words aloud, and her fingers shaped rocks of steam dripping water. She chanted, deeper within herself. Fire had been her element always, she'd rarely imagined rocks before. But her mother could, her mother could.

She raised her voice, shouted an hawk's cry, a elk's bugle, a lamb's mew, shouted, and heard the crash of falling rock.

Up and down the cliff, the tellerwomen shaped the fall of tumbling rocks, boulders falling down mountainsides. The rumble vibrated deep inside Merind. She shook; the cliff shook with her, cracked beneath her; she felt the fall of rocks roar inside her.

She flashed open her eyes, surprised she could feel the illusion

The opposite cliffside was splitting apart tumbling down. So grand an illusion. This, if anything would panic the Norgons. She remembered the silhouettes she had seen at dawn of Capsens rolling boulders to the edge of the opposite cliff. The cliff edge cracked beneath her, she could feel it lurch. So inspired of her mother, or of the other tellerwomen, to use the boulders rolled forward on the opposite cliff for a model, to give their images shape. The cliff lurched beneath her again; she stumbled back, her cauldron tipped, rolled over, fell, cracked open.

This was no illusion.

Or was it? She could be fooled. Belief could do that to her. Even knowing it was illusion only, if the illusion were strong enough, powerful enough to be seen below, she would have to believe it too, have to feel what others were making—

There were men all around her. And women. Capsens, all of them. Tellerwomen. Rolling rocks, boulders, from the outcrropping they had slept under last night.

Merind grabbed a man's shoulder as he bent over a boulder, shoving it to the edge of the cliff. "What are you doing?" she yelled. The din, the roar of falling rocks drowned out her voice.

"Your mother's orders," he shouted back.

If the world roared or was silent, Merind no longer heard it. *"What?"*

The tellerwoman she had spoken to earlier brushed past her, helping to roll another rock over the edge of the cliff. "As you said yourself, Merind," she shouted, "illusion today is not enough. We're starting an avalanche. Here where the cliffs have had slides before."

"But my friends! The bearmen are down there too! They'll all be killed!"

The tellerwoman met her look, nodded. "Your mother is counting on that."

The cliffside cracked beneath Merind's feet again, wider than before. The canyon echoed with the roar of avalanches. Merind lost her footing. Others did too. Half the cliffside was splitting open and many of the Capsens were falling with it. Merind teetered on the edge only a moment longer, then grabbed the bars on her harness wings and jumped.

~

"Leave her!" Rayid shouted. "And come on. We need to go!"

Crel buried his head into Jesser's fur, hugging her shoulders one last time. Nothing he had done all morning had stopped her bellowing. Nothing had gotten her attention away from trying to claw her way into the mountainside. "Please, Wiss, if you're in there, keep her safe." He unhooked her chain from her collar.

"Come, man! No Norgon will get near her with that racket. She'll be safe! But they're coming, and we need to go. We can't hold them off any longer."

Crel nodded tersely to the duke, and stuffed his slingshot into his pouch. The morning had not gone well, the duke had said. The Norgons were swarming the hillsides and the duke's main forces would not reach them in time. The duke had split his men up, sent them to go take Crel's men stationed at each of the kilns into the Narrows, where they could hold off the Norgons until the battle raging at the entrance to the pass was won or lost. Rayid had come himself with twenty of his men to rescue Crel and Jesser, but Jesser, damn her, was going nowhere.

Crel covered the lens on the stovepipe and opened the door to the kiln, then ran out the cave to catch up with Rayid.

Jesser's wail changed note. Crel glanced back. She went suddenly quiet, motionless. Crel heard thunder and felt the rock beneath him move.

"Come on!" the duke's general yelled.

The duke grabbed Crel by the elbow, pulled him onward. There was sudden louder shouting, swords clashing closer, the Norgons were breaking through the trees into the clearing.

Too late to escape.

"Damn!" the duke muttered and pushed Crel back towards the cave. His men followed, made a ring around the entrance, keeping their duke safe. The Norgons charged towards them. Crel pulled out his slingshot. The ground shifted beneath him, rocks, boulders started falling. Ailil's tellerwomen making it look like an avalanche. Their illusion wasn't stopping the Norgons, some looked up, some got struck by falling rock, and fell. Crel shot another in the head, and twirled his slingshot again over the heads of the duke and his men. The thunder kept coming louder, more rocks, boulders, debris were pelting the Norgons and the duke's men fighting them. Jesser was not making a sound—

Only humans will see an illusion, Orist had told him. Trust what the animals see instead.

Jesser was crouched at the back of the cave, her chin flat on the stone floor between her paws, terrified. The cave shook, a tiny roar that was more a whimper came from Jesser.

"No illusion!" Crel yelled to the duke, pulling him back inside the cave. "This avalanche is real!"

He got maybe fifteen men inside the cave when the entrance collapsed. At least two more men were buried under the boulders as the front of the cave came down, he heard them scream. Then silence. The green glow streaming out the door of the kiln their only light.

Jesser began bellowing again, wilder than ever, and clawing frantically at the back wall of the cave.

~

Whole slabs of rock covered the valley floor. For hours, judging by the lowering sun, Merind had been climbing over them in a daze. The taste of dust was in her mouth, and the wind stung her eyes. Such devastation. She found nothing alive but a dog dragging himself up out of the rocks, his tail down but wagging uncertainly when she approached. He'd been following her ever since, limping on three legs. She didn't have the heart to send him away. When she looked at him, he cowered and hung his tail lower. When she turned her back on him, he followed again.

Conscience, Dead Soul, Guilt, she had many names she could call him, the Norgon dog that limped after her on three legs. How could her mother have ordered this? How? Or was this more than Ailil had wanted? Was this more than Merind had wanted? Death to the Norgons. But not like this. Not like this. Not to see it so.

A grey hand grasped upwards for the sky out of the rocks. Merind turned away from the corpse, kept climbing.

Half the cliffside she and the Capsens had stood on had fallen. A gaping chunk was gone from the opposite cliff, leaving orange and white rock scars where the bear image had once shone.

Towards evening, the duke's men found her. A few Norgon captains were with them, representing the hundreds of their survivors who had been fighting outside the pass when the cliffsides fell. A Navarn general told her the Norgons had laid down their swords and were ready to swear allegiance to her and the duke, the daughter and brother of the old king they had "mistakenly" beheaded. Merind nodded numbly; no one had found the duke yet, the general told her.

Men shouted from the east, seeing them. A few of the bearmen had survived in the Narrows, a few of the duke's archers with them. One came running over to them, the rest clambered up the far hill.

"They've heard a bear," the one reported. "They think it could be Jesser."

It was not until noon the next day they dug the bear, Crel, the duke and his men out of the cave-in. Everyone had frantically dug to reach them, Norgons shoulder to shoulder with Navarn guardsmen and the bearmen, all differences aside, all only hoping to find whatever life they could still find beneath the rocks.

That night, Merind finally coaxed the dog close enough to sniff at her hand as she sat and watched the duke and Crel come walking towards her.

Chapter 33
Ice Head

The tail on the birdfoot star was glorious. It had
been two days since the solstice, when the night sky was a
storm of falling stars and the tail on the birdfoot star had
splashed a trail of white across the early morning sky. The
tail was already growing shorter, according to Verl's careful
measurements in the hidden observatory. Yet still it thrilled
him to see it.

He adjusted the telescope and saw three jets of fire
curling away from the star separately from the tail. He
drew a picture of how the birdfoot star looked this morning
and added it to the notes he had made each dawn for the last
two weeks. Some mornings he'd seen four jets, making the
star look remarkably like the Spiral of Forgetfulness design
that had first appeared two months ago on the floor of the
throne room below. But still counting three jets this
morning felt exciting too.

Little Jere moaned in his sleep. He turned over on
his pallet by the door of the observatory. Soon Jing would
be bringing hot crossed buns and cheeses for them, and Gal
would be jumping on the boy to wake him up and play.
Jing had laughed at the two of them yesterday, saying it was
hard to tell sometimes which one was the monkey. The
monkey and the boy had become inseparable during the day,
most often playing chase the tail on the palace roof just
outside the colored glass dome of the observatory. Jing had
also started taking the boy down into court with her,
introducing him as a waif her monkey had found.

It was not an unlikely story. Refugees from the delta
floods and earthquakes this spring, and from a growing
plague of rats this summer had overcrowded the streets and
plazas of the capital, and many young children were being
abandoned at the steps of the palace kitchen by parents who
could no longer feed them. Queen Felain had ordered the
orphanages to accept all the children, sleeping four and five
to a bed; but the orphanages too became overcrowded. It

had become a good lesson for Laird, Jing reported, his mother escorting the boy-king daily to one of the orphanages to hand out food baskets himself. Verl wondered if Laird had grown patient enough yet to ride in the coach with his mother, let alone hand out more than one food basket in a week.

He winced. Often lately he felt a tinge of regret that he couldn't talk to Laird himself anymore. From the day he'd arrived back in Norgarth, he'd had to remain hidden. The court had heard of his death, killed by the dragon of Malla, and some still talked of it. The dragon had looked like the images drawn of the Badurian Winged God. It must have been a regrettable accident that had killed the king's tutor, everyone said aloud. Jing said that in private whispers, a few had started asking, what is really known of this Winged One?

Invisibly, Verl started slipping the books he'd brought with him from Sorenzia onto the shelves of the royal library, hoping Laird or his mother would find them. He wished someone else besides the priests were tutoring Laird now. The priests were never going to stop praising the boy for being the one who'd helped capture and behead his father. Until Laird was allowed to grow beyond that, he never would change. Jing claimed the boy-king was already too old to change; but in a few guarded moments while teaching him last fall, Verl had felt he had started to reach the child still inside him. Or at least, had started hoping he was.

He rolled up his notes, tied them, and laid them among the others in the corner beside his lute.

He had been teaching children most his life, he reflected, as his knuckles brushed against the lute case. First at the Academy, teaching the lute. Then Laird. Now, little Jere.

Verl smiled even thinking Jere's name and glanced over at him. No one had ever been so dear to him. With Jere, he had learned to love again, something he had never felt he would be capable of—or worthy of again, not since leaving the dungeon. Somehow even his music had changed since Jere had been with him, become deeper, truthful in a way he couldn't describe. He no longer tried to impress listeners when he played. No longer tried to control what others might hear in his music. No longer tried to control it at all, not with any of the art and flourishes he'd learned at Singerhalle. Instead music flowed into him and out of him like the feelings he'd learned from Jere flowed into him and back out towards the boy again. Even in playing the simplest song, he became who he most was when he played. No vision of meadow flowers guided his fingers now; he had learned to play himself. He expressed himself with his music, his responses to the world more adequately than he ever had in words. He could draw a likeness of the tailed star and add it to his other drawings as his testament of having seen it. But he could only play the glory, the wordless wonder of that white splash across the early morning sky in music. Letting it flow through him and out of him, and becoming in wordless ecstasy that much nearer to touching its truth.

And if—when—Jere clapped and sang along, or simply laughed in his eyes to the music, Verl would play for him again.

But he rose without touching the lute. He could only play in the dead of night or else in the crowded afternoons when High Court below was in session and no one would hear.

High Court... Their days were numbered here. Verl returned to the center of the observatory and fingered the writing on the disk of the great astrolabe.

By the dim light of dawn before the sun rose, he could barely see it. But he knew the warning of the Birdfoot Star by heart: When the star came, the land would move, the sea would storm, and princes would die.

And princes would die. Verl's fingers strayed. Did it have to be so? In becoming Laird's tutor, he had sworn an oath he would serve and protect his king. Not kill him.

As soon as he asked the question, he could hear Merind's soft voice in his head answering him, tempting him. *Your part in the war ahead,* she had said. Verl gripped his fist, shook her voice away. Laird was just a child. Not much older than Jere. From Jere, he had learned to love again--

Princes die, the warning said. Princes die.

The captain of the merchant ship The Red Bell had sent word three days ago that the iceberg his friend had carved was anchored half a day's sail away. They were ready, the captain said; they were only waiting for Verl's word to tow the berg into the cove where Laird had dreamed the Ice Head of his father would appear.

Your part in the war ahead, Merind's voice whispered again. Verl tightened his fist until his fingernails cut into his palm.

The berg was starting to melt, the captain had warned him yesterday. *"You need to use it soon."*

In the corner, Jere moaned again. He kicked his legs, running in a dream. Two little boys. They were different, Verl reminded himself. Very different. Not the same to him at all.

He wished he could believe it. Deep down inside himself, he wished he could believe it. *Your part in the war ahead.* Just being with Jere every day, watching him grow and change, made it more and more difficult to believe that Laird—that any child---had to die by his hand. Or rather, by his subterfuge. Knife in his hand or not, the end would be the same, and the blame, his.

First bell rang. The sun was rising. Verl opened the eastern door to the domed observatory, stepped out onto the roof. Any minute, the horns would blow today's messages. No news had been sent by the queen's army for three days now. Perhaps he had begun to hope—

He froze when he heard the horns. The queen had lost her battle. The priests had lost the war. The Duke of Navarn and the Bearman God had defeated the forces of the Winged One.

Verl could put off his decision no longer.

~

"My Lady," Verl said softly. He stood by the head of Queen Felain's bed and stepped into her dream. "You need to come with me. Your battle is lost." He took her

402

hand to help her up. In her dream, she rose willingly, as if floating to her feet. Then the dream swirled and blackened, and her eyes started fluttering awake. She pulled her hand away back to where she lay upon the bed.

"Who are you? What–?"

"A friend. You need to come with me. Quick. Before the guards and priests hear the news."

Her eyes flashed open. She could not see him. Verl touched her hand again, and she started to scream.

Verl immediately clasped his hand across her mouth, stifled her scream. "I'm trying to help you, my Lady!" She squirmed beneath his hand, struggling. Verl dropped his illusion, letting himself appear to her. "I am here. You know me, my Lady. You need not fear me. We need to go—"

Her eyes widened. "Singer," she mouthed beneath his hand.

He released his hand over her mouth, nodded. "Yes. Follow me, my Lady. I can—"

"You're dead."

Verl swallowed. "Call me a dream then. A ghost. I have come back to help you escape—"

"Guards!" Felain yelled. "Guards—!"

Verl clasped his hand over her mouth again, went invisible. She struggled beneath his hand, flailed her arms in terror. As Verl held her beneath him tighter, she reached for the bell pull and pulled. The door behind Verl crashed open.

"Your Majesty!--" Guards came rushing in. Verl released her, stood away. Felain sat up, pulling her sheet around her. She looked around the room, could not see him.

She shook her head finally. "Nightmare, must have been," she told the guardsmen.

As the guards left her room, Verl, invisible, slipped out into the hall with them.

~

"My Lord," said Verl. "It's come." He stepped inside Laird's dream and turned the boy king, dreaming of fighting in a tourney, around to face the sea. "Look, my lord. It's here. The Ice Head is attacking your people." As soon as Verl planted the suggestion, the arena, the bright tournament banners and the charging horses surrounding Laird on three sides became the beach, clouds and cliffs of the cove of Laird's nightmare.

The boy's sleeping form shook his head and he mouthed, "No, no..." but he could not stop the nightmare from returning.

Sword in hand, he stepped towards the crashing waves as the Ice Head bubbled out of the sea, grew larger and larger, becoming the head of his father. Slowly, in a trance, Laird started towards its giant laughing mouth.

"My Lord, I am with you. I promised."

"...Verl?" In his dream, Laird paused to look for Verl.

"Here, my Lord," Verl touched the sleeping boy on the shoulder. "Open your eyes, take your sword." Laird opened his eyes wide, and Verl put the king's sword in his hand and closed the boy's fingers around it. "It has come, my lord. The Ice Head is here. Don't be afraid. We must be quiet if you want to be the first to see it. Follow me."

The boy was halfway across his chamber when he stopped and raised the sword at Verl. "Are you a ghost?"

Verl pulled the tapestry aside to the panel in the wall leading into the hidden tunnel before he answered. "If you believe me so. Come, my Lord. I promised I would return when the Ice Head came."

~

Verl pulled open the trap door into the dungeon and shone the torchlight through. It was as Jing had told him. The pit was empty, flooded waist-high from when the tidal wave hit the city after the volcano erupted up the coast in the spring. The prisoners who had survived had been moved into cells in the upper floors of the dungeon tower. But most had not survived. Debris, dead bodies were left floating in the sludge. The morning sun streaming in through the three window slits high in the tower walls striped the dark water with three lines of incongruent sparkles, broken by the hump of another bloated body or heap of dung.   What might have been pretty elsewhere, the sun on the water, only added to the horror.   Verl had forgotten the unbreatheable stench of bodies left to rot.

He handed the lantern to Laird, hoisted himself through the door, then reached back into the tunnel for Laird and lifted him onto his shoulders.   He pulled the stone block on its runners back into place, hiding the door again.

With a hand sliding along the wall, he counted the stones as he waded through the sludge, the boy choking his arms around his neck, the lantern raised high, jerking the light around, until they reached the next hidden door.   Verl held his breath, but the reek permeated through him, through his pores and veins, and he could not leave the dungeon fast enough.

As he pulled shut the door into the tunnel that led to the cave over the beach, Verl saw that his hands were almost the color of the stones.   Black and slimy.   With the soot of the scorched stones from the fire he had built when he was last here and the "Bearman" had freed the dungeon, hopefully.   What else blackened his hands and breeches, he did not want to know.

He wiped his hands on his tunic, then set the boy king down.

"That stunk," Laird said.

"You have a royal talent for understatement, my Lord."   But his voice was hollow and Verl couldn't feel less like grinning.   "Come, we need to go."   He took the lantern from Laird and started down the tunnel.

But Laird did not follow.

"Why should I trust you?" he said.   "You're dead."

It was the first time Laird had hesitated since leaving his bedchamber.   His question was still the same, the distrust in his voice, stronger.

Verl unstrapped the king's sword he'd been carrying and handed it to Laird.   He held the lantern between them and studied the boy.   "What do you know of the dead?" he asked.

Laird's eyes widened.   He gripped the pommel of the huge sword until his tanned hands darkened.   In the harsh glow and thin shadows cast by the flickering lamplight, tight lines formed around Laird's mouth, as if he were squeezing his lips shut, fighting not to betray any reaction to the frightening question. He stood alone in a hidden tunnel at the mercy of a man he believed dead. "What do you mean?" he demanded in a shallow voice. In the last year, the boy king had indeed started to grow older, more cautious.

Verl held out his right hand, palm up. "Cut me," he said.

Laird retreated a step and frowned up at him. He looked taken aback. And suspicious.

"Do the dead bleed?" Verl asked.

Laird shook his head, no. He hefted the sword above Verl's outstretched wrist. He glanced up at the man who had once been his tutor and confidant. He withdrew the blade slightly and pressed it down instead onto Verl's index finger. He glanced up once more, and when Verl still did not react, Laird sliced a nick out of the finger, not ungently, but enough to make Verl wince.

Verl drew in his breath as Laird pulled away the sword. "Are you satisfied, my Lord? I swear to you, I am not dead." His finger bled his oath between them.

"Then why did they tell me you were dead?" Laird asked. "Why did they lie to me?"

The question trapped lies in Verl's throat. Everything he had planned to say to capture the king was lost.

Verl knelt down to Laird, searched his face more carefully than before. Not dear to him like Jere's, no, a monster instead, he'd help kill his father, had watched other men die in his name. But he was still a child; given different influences, he could still change as he grew, he was not old enough yet to deserve his fate. Or so Verl had kept telling himself for the last two months.

But Jing was right. Laird was growing up. His face pulled to a frown, his wide-set eyes sparked like black agates catching the glint of the lamplight, but they sparked from out of shadows cast by a deepening brow. His face was still open, still ready to believe, but it was not the simple child's face Verl had seen him wear a year ago.

Laird was starting to ask questions. And, more a man, starting to doubt the answers.

Verl nodded, accepting a grim reality. He would be as honest as he could. Yet Singer-training—more so, survival at Laird's court---had taught him that honesty could be a double-edge sword. With Laird older, he could use honesty to win the lad's trust again, the easier then to deceive him if—rather when—he must.

"On the Eller Islands, where I was born, the fishermen have a saying. There is truth, and there is truth. Or perhaps more to the point, there are lies, and there are other lies. Some are intentional, they distort the truth to gain an advantage. But others were never meant to be a lie. Do you believe everything the priests tell you?"

"I have...yes." Laird paused. "Later, in my chambers, my Lady Mother tells me something different sometimes."

"When she does, the priests are not lying to you, and she is not lying to you either. The priests believe what they say. Your mother sometimes has different beliefs. Sometimes, my Lord, you have to stop and look at the facts yourself, and decide what you believe is true and not true."

"That's what my mother tells me. When we're alone, after she tells me something different." He shook his head. "But this time, she and the priests and the counselors all told me the same thing. That you were dead."

"This time, the priests and your mother and your counselors were all told the same thing themselves—they were all told the story that I had been killed. Guardsmen saw me in a fight. But I didn't die, as they thought. When your mother and the priests told you that I was dead, they didn't lie to you, not from what they believed was true. But it was not true, what they told you, so in another real sense, they did tell you a lie."

The boy skewed his face at the contradiction, still with a child's clear logic, opening his mouth, scrunching his nose, starting to protest both couldn't be true . Then his eyes widened. His lips pressed thin and a deep frown furrowed his brow. In the dim light, he suddenly looked more like the coin images of his father than he ever had. Verl memorized that look to use later, went on.

"When I came back to Norgarth, I had to stay hidden because everyone was believing the lie that I was dead. Truth, my Lord, or what we believe is true, is very often no more than what we believe we see, or what others have told us they saw."

At that, Laird smiled. He straightened his shoulders and seemed to grow tall, certain. "There is truth, and there is truth," he said. "I see. And as king, what I believe is true will be what others will be told *is* true. The priests have always told me that."

The child's lips curled thinly. Laird had grown older; the monster, in whose name all power was justified, the monster that the priests—that wearing the crown---had turned the boy into, had claimed him. Laird was not little Jere at all.

Verl sucked in his breath, tried not to react. "There is more, my Lord. I've had to learn this last year that our eyes--that even your ennobled eyes--will not always tell us the truth of what is really there. I have a talent to lie, to change what people see. To change what people believe. To help me survive, I've learned to use that talent. As I will be using it again today."

"What do you mean?"

"I will be lying to you today, my lord. You may take this as my warning. It might be the only way I can get you to the Ice Head, as I promised. Watch." He vanished from Laird's sight.

Laird startled. He swung his sword around and around in the narrow tunnel, looking for him. "Where–?"

Verl ducked, then reached out quickly, caught the blunt edge of the blade as it swung past. "Careful! I am still here. You can hear me. But you'll be the only one who'll know that I am with you. Think of the powers that will give you."

As the boy's face transformed, brightening with the excitement of the possibilities of what Verl could do, Verl tightened his lip and released the sword. Laird believed now that he knew Verl's darkest secret, maybe even, watching his expression change, he was planning already how he, the king, would use him. In sharing his secret with his lord, Verl had proved himself a most loyal servant.

Your part in the war ahead, the memory of Merind's voice gloated.

Verl raised the lantern, letting it float visibly through the air above Laird, and led the way down the steps of the tunnel and out through the cave.

~

"Your Highness!" a chamberlain interrupted, bowing quickly. "The king is missing. We've searched his chambers, we've searched the palace. We can find him nowhere."

Felain heard nothing else. Servants were stripping walls, rolling golden vases inside Helvian tapestries. A lord of the chancery rushed past the hall, a casket of jewels under his arm. The High Priest, the captain of her guards, and the Lord Treasurer were behind her arguing where to spirit away the royal coffers before the duke's forces stormed the city.

Felain ordered the chamberlain to redouble his efforts, to send every servant through every hall, if need be. "Find him. I'm not leaving without him."

"Your Highness—" her captain of the guards tried warning her. She cast him a withering glance and he clenched his mouth shut and averted his eyes.

Not so, the High Priest. "We must leave within the hour, my lady, and you must come with us. Already the news of your defeat is spreading, and the people in the streets are blaming you—"

Blaming your god, she retorted under her breath. But they would all be damned for it.

No former supporters could be trusted now. The citizens in the streets would be quick to change loyalty to the winning side, and even quicker to claim they had always been secret supporters of the duke. And most certain of all, they themselves had never been believers in the false god that had led everyone else astray. She had seen the same thing happen when she and the priests had overthrown

409

Henrik. Within days, or hours, out there somewhere, some swaggart with a butcher knife and beer-bloated ego would call upon his followers to take action to prove their support for the duke, for his Capsen witch, or for the Bearman god instead. Within less time, no corner in these palace walls would be safe from some sycophant courtier ready to prove his allegiance to the new crown, and in the act hope to save his own position and prestige. He would have only one small boy and his mother standing in his way. And the priests.

She met the High Priest's iron-hard eyes. She trusted the priests least of all. She turned to her captain instead. "We will not leave without the king."

The High Priest tapped his staff on the tiled floor. The bells jingled as he spoke, punctuating his words. "You must, my lady. My priests and your guards can give us safe passage to our stronghold in Sorenzia. There in the library, we can await the arrival of the duke and petition for his mercy. The king is his nephew. All is not lost. But only if we leave quickly now. Your captain here and a unit of his men can bring the young king as soon as he is found. And you shall come with us, so your passage, my lady, shall not be as hard."

She shook her head. "I shall wait. I will not be separated from my son." She bit her lip. "Or is this your intent, my lord priest? To separate my son, the king, from my protection?" She gave a quick hand signal to her captain, then spoke loudly enough to be heard throughout the hall. "What have you done with the king, Lord Priest? Where is he?"

As her captain slid his hand to his sword and moved behind the High Priest, several other priests and guards came closer, surrounding them. The High Priest chuckled sadly, and shook his head as if in sympathy. "You are distraught, my lady. These are terrible times for us all. But by the blessing of the Winged One Who Shall Rise Again, we shall get through this tribulation together. I assure you of our loyalty to your son and to yourself–"

A voice behind Felain interrupted. "Your Highness! Your Highness!"

410

They all turned. A wounded guardsman, his side cut and bleeding, ran towards her, hand outstretched. "The tower—at the Cove. We were attacked. This morning, as we slept. All were killed, and I was left for dead—"

The Cove. Where her son had raised the tower to watch for the Ice Head. Where the Singer had confirmed the boy saw the Ice Head arise in his nightmare. Where Laird at age six had led the priests to capture his father escaping from a secret tunnel from his chamber in the Palace. *The Singer!* Who had come into her dreams this morning. She'd thought him dead, but if not---

She twirled around to the captain. "The Cove! That's where Laird has gone! Call your guards. It's treachery! Verl, the dream interpreter, has taken him there."

The High Priest grabbed her arm. "Come, my lady! We shall go with them, save the lad!"

They rushed out the hall. Guards, priests, Felain. "This way, my lady!" The High Priest led her, still pulling on her arm. "Quicker to the horses." She hesitated. The main gate was to the left. "Come. Servant's passage through the kitchen. You know the way. Come!" Priests crowded around her, pushed her forward with them. The guards were rushing down the hall to the main gate, the captain only glancing back at her. Abandoned, pulled to the right, Felain ran on with the priests.

They turned a corner, stopped. Priests surrounded her. Lantern light from the hall sconces lit the iron in the High Priest's eyes as he approached her. And lit the flash of silver and ruby in his hand.

"This is as far as you need to go, my lady. Now that we know where the king is, we no longer need you." He raised the knife. "And we can do the duke a favor—"

"Can you?" challenged the voice of her captain, as he came rushing around the corner, sword in hand, cutting off the head of the High Priest in one swing. Three other guardsmen followed him, and together killed the seven other priests. Felain pressed back against the wall, slight hand to her throat as she watched the massacre.

Breathless, she thanked her captain as he pulled the jeweled knife from the bloody hand of the High Priest. "I told you I did not trust him. Thank you, captain. I didn't think you'd come in time."

Her captain stepped towards her, shaking his head. "I'm sorry, my lady. I'm sorry that we didn't get here in time—" With a quick thrust, he plunged the High Priest's knife into her chest.

He released the knife and stood watching her fall, sliding down slowly against the wall.

"Guards!" she screamed. Her guards were here, watching her.

The captain leaned over as she sat looking up at him. Shadows and light stung her eyes. Her breast hurt. Oh, her breast hurt. She remembered her baby suckling them. Henrik suckling them. Henrik's laughter on their wedding day. Ailil's laughter as she danced with him. The captain moved his hand slowly towards her. Slowly, every movement in slow, slow motion. The captain had soft brown eyes, she'd never noticed. She tasted blood. In her dreams, she'd tasted blood, opened her eyes to Henrik's headless corpse as it made love to her, his neck throbbing blood all over her. It tasted colder than she remembered. It hurt. The Priest stood over her, holding up Henrik's severed head. The Priest was dead. It was the captain's hand, large, manicured. He pulled the knife from her chest, slipped it back into the Priest's fist. "Very unfortunate we didn't get here in time to save you, my lady. But I promise you this," he said as she fell over into the flood of blood on the cold flagstone floor, " I will find your son."

~

Seagulls cackled on the window sill. When Verl and Laird first entered the tower above the Cove, and found one man dead in his bed, this second in the next room still breathing, but barely, Verl had flung open the casements to let in more light, and in had flown the birds. They'd landed on the guardsman's chest, shoulders, cheek, and pecked at his bloodied neck before Verl could chase them away. They'd retreated as far as the window. Their raucous cries came like a warning.

Blood seeped from the guardsman's lips, and when he drew in each slow breath, his effort was halted and painful. Verl tore open the guardsman's tunic, tried to staunch the sword wound across his chest with the cloth There was nothing he could do for him, the wound was too deep. This morning, when Verl had sent Jing and Jere to tell the merchant captain to tow in the berg, he should have remembered that yesterday the captain had suggested killing off the men at the tower first to give them time to escape before too many troops and ships could be alerted. Verl had told the captain they could tie the tower guardsmen up, or silence the tower bell some other way, but no killing. Apparently, the captain had not listened to him.

The tower bell gonged overhead. Laird still demanded an audience, Verl could not convince him otherwise When they found the two guardsmen wounded and dead, Laird had insisted on running up to the belltower so he could alert the city himself as soon as he spotted the Ice Head coming.

The bell gonged and echoed through the halls a second time. Verl covered the guardsman's staring eyes with his bloodied cloak, and went to join the boy-king.

"It's green!" Laird pointed towards the western portico of the bell tower. "And huge!"

The berg was taller than the original berg Arax had chosen. In the long months since Verl and Jere had left the Orliand Ice Islands, that original berg had begun to melt and kept rolling sideways too much to carve it, Arax had written. He had chosen another. The merchant captain had said this berg too had started to melt in the warmer climate. If so, as tall as it was now, Verl wondered how large it once had been, and yet still of a size to be pushed and towed.

It was the same stormy algae-green as the first, and it shone with an eerie brilliance from its center in the morning sun. Arax and his friends had done an amazing job carving it. Sharp angles and deep crags of nose, brow and cheeks around a cavernous tooth-filled laugh became more terrifying as they became more recognizable. It *was* Henrik, the beheaded king, arising out of the sea, coming back to life Even his third tooth on the upper left jaw was

413

missing, a detail remembered in legend that never showed up in coin images or official paintings made during Henrik's lifetime.

Laird gonged the bell a third time. The long bell rope pulled the nine-year-old up into the air and down with it. Verl glanced out the eastern, then southern porticos of the tower, and saw townsmen cresting the cliffs of the city, rushing to the warning of a bell that no one had ever expected to hear ringing. No one, that is, except the boy-king himself. Verl spotted no city nor palace guardsmen yet among the crowd on the hills, but he knew they'd be arriving soon. He and Laird did not have much time left.

Spinning to the western portico, Verl judged the distance over rocks and sand they'd have to run to reach the rowboat left on the beach for them by the merchant captain's men.

"My lord! It's time to go. The people are coming. You want to be the first to challenge that Ice Head and save your city! Hurry, before the guardsmen arrive."

Invisible again, Verl rowed hard towards the cavernous mouth of ice. Already a captain in the royal blue cloak of the palace guard was ordering his men to follow. A half a dozen guardsmen had ridden their horses into the surf as far as they could come. Waves breaking against their mounts' chests, they shot arrows towards the Ice Head--or towards the boy-king, Verl was unsure which. Palace crossbows had limited range, and if the bowmen were indeed aiming at the Ice Head, then Laird and he must be passing into the extent of their range now.

Verl ducked from an arrow and glanced back again. The rest of the guardsmen were running toward the shore, pulling the four other tower rowboats after them. Verl rowed harder.

The Ice Head loomed ahead, rolling in dark green laughter in the deepest center of the cove. Laird stood in the prow of the rowboat, brave and alone on a boat that rowed itself, it would look like. He stood with his heavy king sword raised, challenging the giant head of ice.

A dolphin surfaced beside them, circled their boat, then dropped back beside Verl and, half-rolling on its side, eyed him. It would have no trouble seeing him, his illusion of invisibility could confuse only human minds—

He fooled humans because they saw only what they believed they saw. Twist a man's beliefs, and he twisted his sight! Remembering the awesome effect on himself of touching the god-spot, Verl suddenly understood what his power meant more than he ever had. *Create a god, any god he chose,* Merind's watery voice whispered as he pulled his oar through the wave, *and he could enslave a multitude of believers.*

The dolphin's perpetual smile mimicked the Ice Head's laugh. It squirted sea water at Verl, as if sharing the joke, then dove in the air and raced towards the Ice Head.

He had planned it so long, now he hoped he wouldn't have to do it. He rowed faster, faster.

An arrow whizzed past Verl. He ducked. The boy king did not flinch. He stood sword drawn high at the Ice Head. Through the cry of gulls, the captain of the guardsmen barked an order, and more arrows flew.

Verl glanced behind, saw twenty, thirty guardsmen launching the rowboats, the captain among them. So many of them rowing, they would overtake them long before Verl could reach the Ice Head.

He had no other chance to escape. *Your part in the war ahead,* he heard Merind say.

Verl looked ahead at the giant mouth, then back once more as arrows fell around them. Then he shouted at the giant mouth.

His thought followed his voice as it echoed and grew inside the cave and bounced back. He let it come, then shouted again with it and cast its booming roar towards the crowd of guardsmen and townsmen on the shore.

He reached inside himself and touched the god-spot Merind had shown him, then expanded his sensation as it grew, his overwhelming awe of believing he was in the presence of a god. Then he cast his awe, seeking every presence he could feel behind him, touching every god-spot he could touch. His sensation of awe echoed and grew as he touched one mind to the next, and expanded with it.

415

He floated on air at dizzying heights above himself, above the crowd, seeing forward and backward and under him all at once, the old seasickness of his illusions disorienting him as never before. The dolphin jumped and played black and graceful in front of the green head of ice.

The memory of Laird's frown in the cave flashed inside him. The carved stern brow of ice furrowed into a deeper frown to match it. Verl cast the booming voice, the belief of it into every mind he could touch; and the Ice God spoke.

"Go home," the Ice Head boomed. Its brow rippled and furrowed, its cheeks shone algae-green in their hollows and bright whites along their angled facets, its thin lips opened and curled around the words. "Go home. The War has ended. I have won."

In the prow of the boat, Laird stumbled back a step, lowered his sword a little.

"He lies, my lord," Verl whispered to him. "He's trying to scare you away."

Laird gave a brief nod of thanks and raised his sword again.

Fewer arrows were falling. Verl glanced back, saw the guardsmen and townsmen in disarray. Most bowmen had stopped shooting: only two astride their horses were still in the surf, one was galloping for the hills, the rest had retreated to safety among the crowd. Most of the guardsmen in the rowboats were rowing back ashore too, a few of them had jumped out and were swimming and wading back faster through the beating waves.

But one boat crested onward above a building wave, and from its prow, the captain of the guard in Palace Blue shouted orders to rally his men.

Two boats turned around to follow him and cresting the next wave, the fourth started coming again too.

Verl rowed harder and made the Ice Head speak again.

"Go home! This is my last warning. Go back. While you still can."

The townsmen on the shore panicked. Some stood frozen, shouting, pointing; most were running away. Some of the blue-cloaked guardsmen ran with them, but four boatloads of guardsmen kept coming. Rowing fast, they were gaining on Verl. He could hear the captain's words behind him, not just his voice.

The Ice Head loomed overhead. Verl pulled hard on the oars, waited until they passed under the giant teeth of ice just ahead of the guardsmen.

Then, as they entered the shadowy green glowing mist of the cavernous mouth, as Laird, brave to the end in the face of his nightmare come to life, plunged his great sword into the tongue of ice and shouted defiance, Verl extended his illusion around him and made the boy-king and the rowboat disappear.

The guardsmen back-oared to a splashing stop before entering the mouth of ice. The king's sword glowed green as it rose crookedly out of the tongue of ice.

Verl rowed silently, invisibly away from it and around the hill of the last tooth to a ledge of ice where Arax and two of the merchant shipmen stood waiting. Laird shouted and protested the whole way---stop, stop, go back, get his sword!---but his shouts echoed and echoed around the cave and crashed against themselves, garbling his words and only adding to the effect of his disappearance.

Behind the tooth, out of sight of the guardsmen, Verl dropped his illusion of invisibility so the shipmen could jump on board and seize the boy. Laird's screams for his sword, for help, for his guardsmen, for Verl echoed louder around the mouth of ice, then went muffled, then silent, as the sailors stuffed broadcloth down his throat and bound him inside two burlap sacks.

"Find him!" the captain of the guard shouted, and three boatloads of guardsmen entered the cavernous mouth.

In the eerie green, darkly glowing mist, Arax reached for Verl's hand and pulled him up onto the ledge. Then he grabbed the boy-king from the sailors, and hefting the sack of him over a shoulder, helped the other two men up quickly.

Arax pointed silently. Verl nodded, and followed the two sailors into a dark green crack along the wall that would lead, he'd been told, to another boat tied to the hidden side of the berg. He felt Arax coming behind him, and heard the guardsmen shouting farther behind, finding the empty boat, finding the ledge now maybe.

Verl hurried as fast as he could keep his footing. The ice beneath his boots was slick and hard, and he slid to the narrow walls with every step forward. His breath rose in frozen gasps before him, and his lungs stung with the cold.

He stopped once to catch himself---but then he started sliding again even as he stood. The ice beneath him was moving on its own, rising to one side.

Arax grabbed his shoulder, steadied him under his bear-like grip. "Run now, lad! . She's starting to roll!"

Arax had warned this might happen. No berg was stable, and this one, frozen sea algae trapped in its ice turning it green instead of white, was already upside-down and top-heavy. It had rolled all the way over at least once already, probably when it'd calved. Now if fifteen, twenty guardsmen had discovered their ledge, had added their weight to one side---.

Verl prayed the berg would only bob back and forth in the sea like a cork pulled by a fish, that would be danger enough for him.

He heard a loud crack, and the ice beneath him rose again. Arax pushed past him, the sack of the boy squirming against his shoulder. As he passed, Arax held tight to Verl's arm and pulled him forward with him. An ice shepherd, he wore spikes on his boots, for jumping on and off bergs, securing their nettings, towing them, selling them. Mountain of a man that he was, yet he ran across the ice like he was dancing, and he never let go of Verl's arm, pulling him forward with him, through the green, through the endless cold. Then...there was daylight, blue sky overhead; the boat, the men jumping in, slinging the sack of the boy-king onto the bottom, grabbing the oars, Verl scrambling over its side, when a booming crack sounded louder than before.

The berg lurched up and slapped down, and the rowboat launched into the sea before Verl was halfway in.

Cold water frothed around him. He held onto the side of the boat, but slipped downwards as the water surged upwards, the boat rowing fast away from the berg starting to roll over. Arax grabbed for his hand, started pulling him up, when a wave splashed against him, towered upwards, and pulled him down with it, sending the boat past his flailing reach.

He swirled, down, down, couldn't swim against the tow caused by the berg tipping over.

Saltwater stung his eyes, bit his lips. He tried to swim up, the tow sucked him down.

Through the murky waters, a blackness passed beside him, turned before him, came back. He grabbed for it. Slick as oilcloth, smooth, hard skin, his hand caught against a top fin. He held on and the dolphin glided him to the surface.

He sputtered water as he broke free, coughed for breath, treaded water. The dolphin was gone...if it ever had been there.

The rowboat turned back for him. Arax was pointing at him, calling him. Glancing behind, the Ice Head was turning over more and he heard the screams of men.

Verl took a breath and swam for the rowboat.

Inside, rowed far enough away, visible again—their boat and everyone safe in it—Verl looked back and watched the Ice Head roll completely over into the sea, sending giant waves crashing onto shore against the cliffs. He imagined he heard distant screams. How many townsmen survived, he didn't know, he hoped most. This, his second illusion making a god of terror. The first had killed Jere's mother. This second, making a god of the Ice Head, his grandest illusion of all, had cost him many more lives than Laird was worth.

Verl turned away and rowed harder.

~

"Captain! I want him alive. Release him to me."

The merchant shipmen had the boy-king still struggling in the burlap sack hung upside down from the mast head when Verl had awakened. They were starting to lower the ropes to drag him through the sea for fish bait before Verl stopped them.

The captain jingled the silver Verl had given him. "What could you possibly want of him? He'd kill you, just as likely. Killed his own father. Both casualties of war." He shook his head, handed the silver back to Verl. "We'll take care of him now. If you can't."

"No! I didn't bring him here, through all this today, for you to kill him!" Verl reached into the bottom of his pouch, pulled out the duke's signet ring given to him in a market place over a year ago. He handed it to the captain. "If the silver is not enough, perhaps this is. You do recognize it, don't you?"

The captain took it, looked at it closer, tapped at it, making sure it was genuine. He eyed Verl. "He gave you this?"

"And I give it to you. For the boy."

The captain nodded tersely, then barked an order to his men. "Release the boy. Take him down to the hold, remove the sack but not the ropes." He turned back to Verl and, meeting his eyes, pocketed the duke's ring. "You've bought his life for now. We'll let his uncle decide."

Chapter 34
The Bearman Comes to Town

"So you think you've landed in paradise, do you?"
Crel scratched Jesser behind her left ear as he spoke. Jesser
angled her head, making it easier for him to reach the right
spot, then she rewarded him with a grunt.

In ponderous lazy bear motion, Jesser pawed the
wooden platter of apple chunks closer to her, leaned over to
snuff at them, then clawed a few into her mouth. Then she
stretched her neck back up to Crel for another good scratch.

Plans were to build a gilded cage around her, right
here in the throne room. For now, she was chained to the
foot of a heavy state bureau, surrounded by piles of fresh
hay for bedding and a large royal cushion of blue velvet.
Jesser of course sat squarely on top of the cushion, not on
the hay. A princess already. "Just don't think this means
you'll get apples every day!" Crel warned her.

He ruffled the bear's neck again and listened as
Duke Rayid plotted with Merind a few feet away.

The duke was sitting on his father's throne. As far
as Crel was concerned, Rayid belonged there. But no one,
not even Rayid himself, agreed with him. At least, not
exactly. Whoever sat the throne would be governed by
Rayid as liege lord and pay him tribute, that was the
arrangement. The people of Norgondy had freed
themselves from the tyranny of a false god and a murderous
queen. They had not been conquered by Navarn, they had
only been aided by his army. If the people of Norgondy
could be encouraged to believe that, their debt of gratitude
would last a generation of good will and favorable trade
policies for Navarn merchants. At least that's what the
Norgon traders and farmers would be told, Crel was sure,
when they paid higher tolls at bridges and city gates and
were assessed higher taxes to support their new, much fairer
government.

"Your mother has arrived and will be here any
minute," Rayid said to Merind. "You must decide. Is it

still your intent to hand the crown over to your baby brother?"

Merind paced in front of the duke a moment without answering. Her dog, Avalanche, Ava for short, shadowed her every step. From the stiff determination of her walk, from the rapid darting of her eyes as she thought, from her not taking note of the dog below her, Crel knew her answer. He had gotten used to reading the movement in her eyes and the slight wrinkling of her forehead in the last few months, all he could see of her expression with her tellerwoman veil covering the lower half of her face. All he could see of her face except, that is, in their few private moments these last several weeks when she had lowered her veil to him. She could be as soft then as when he had first met her over a year ago.

She was not soft in her public appearance at all anymore. "What do you suggest?" she said to the duke.

"The people want the Bearman as their king—"

"Now wait—" Crel started.

The duke raised a hand to stop his protest. "Marry him."

Crel was dumbfounded. His fingers froze mid-scratch in Jesser's fur. Merind turned slowly and met his eyes. Her own above her tellerwoman veil stared at him without blinking. In the last few months he may have gotten used to reading her expression through her eyes, but he had no idea what she was thinking now, staring at him like that. Assessing him, he guessed. They had never discussed their relationship. At most, it was a patchwork of unforced, stolen moments together--fond memories, enjoyed by both, he was sure--but never had either asked yet for anything more from the other. There was a lust in those moments, certainly, a lust that dispelled their shared pain and horror and loss of the war around them, and more and more recently, that unexpected softness in her...but was there love? She was a princess. He was a tinker.

Crel broke the spell himself and answered Rayid. "This is my life. I have a say in what I do."

"You do. You can walk out that door to your tinker wagon. And leave the country in war fighting over who shall take the crown, Merind or Henrik's son. Or you could take the crown yourself and, not prepared for it, be a puppet to your counselors. Or you could do what you've been wanting to do for the last several weeks and tell Merind you want to stay with her. Marry her, and give her the power. Make her your queen, through you and through her father, and the war will be over."

Merind spoke slowly. "And if I took the crown in my own name as Henrik's daughter? Without marrying him?"

Rayid looked up past her. Looking quickly in the same direction, Crel saw Ailil had entered the throne room very quietly. "I don't think," Rayid said, "that was ever in your mother's plans to let you do so that easily. Was it, Ailil?"

Merind spun around. Ailil came forward, gave her daughter a perfunctory kiss.

Merind stood stiffer than before. "You tried to kill us all in that avalanche," she said.

Ailil raised a soft hand to her daughter's cheek. "Not you, my dear." She looked past Merind to the duke and to Crel. "It would have been more convenient, though, for Eris to have had fewer rivals. Hello Rayid."

He nodded without taking his eyes off of her.

"And you, tinker." Ailil turned to Crel. " I see you've continued to make up your own answers to the riddle of our cave. You change the rules, change the patterns completely. In the cave," she told Merind, "he wrote 'Damn!' as his only answer. Here outside, this past year, to defeat the power of an unjust god and throne," she raised a hand in mock honor to Crel, "you simply become a more terrifying god yourself."

Crel shook his head, his lips were tight, his cheeks flushing. "Becoming a god was an accident that grew. It was never my intention."

Not wearing her veil, Ailil smiled that same beatific smile she had smiled for him on their way that morning to the cave of the tellerwomen. It was later, after trapping him inside, that she had shown him her real face. How she looked without planting the suggestion in his mind that she was younger, more beautiful. "Becoming a god to the people of this land may not have been your intent, Tinker, but you made use of it. Now the people rejoice in your victory as their avenging god, and they want you for their king."

"I don't want the throne."

Ailil searched his face, nodded. "I never thought you would. Whoever is crowned though, will still need you at his side now."

She turned back to the duke. "So that leaves the two of us, Rayid. I am Eris's mother. I've lived at this court longer than you have now. Your home is in Navarn. Eris is the rightful heir of Norgondy, and until he comes of age, I as his mother claim regency."

"Do you forget, mother, that I am here? I won that war for you---as you sent me to do. Eris is too young. The country is too unstable to unite under him. I'm an heir too. I claim the crown instead, as Henrik's daughter----"

"You're not."

Merind paused. "Not...what?"

"You're not Henrik's daughter. I don't know where you got the idea that you are."

Merind's eyes widened and her hands fell to her sides; she looked suddenly as if she'd been struck by an arrow. Crel felt that way too. "What are you saying? You told me yourself—"

"You must have misheard me, Merind. I do know who your father is. It is not, as you've been claiming to the whole nation, King Henrik. Duke Rayid could have told you the truth anytime."

Merind stared at her mother. " I don't...believe you."

Rayid stood up, went to her. "Merind, you are not my brother's child. Your mother and Henrik and I grew up in this court together, you know that. What you don't know, your mother and I were once," he met Ailil's eyes, "much closer than we are now." He turned back to Merind. "As your father, I couldn't be prouder of a daughter. But your claim to the crown is not through Henrik."

"And, as Henrik's son, Eris is the rightful heir ahead of you, Rayid. And ahead of your daughter. We have come to claim his crown."

"Not so fast, Ailil. It is true your son is an heir to the throne of Norgondy. But he is not king yet." Rayid took a small sack out of his pocket, unwrapped it to reveal a ring with his ducal crest on it. He slid the ring onto his left middle finger.

"Send them in," he said to a guard waiting by the door. Then he turned back to Ailil and Merind. "As you see, the throne is not empty yet."

Escorted by two guardsmen, Verl came walking into the throne room, his right hand resting on the shoulder of a boy dressed in gold brocaded silks who looked to be no older than eight or nine. Crel had never seen the boy-king's face, but from Ailil's quick gasp, the boy must indeed be Laird, boy-king of Norgondy.

Merind spoke first. "Two days before we reached the city, we heard the tales of an Ice God that attacked Norgarth from the sea, and of how King Laird sailed oarless and spellbound straight into its mouth and disappeared. I assumed, Verl, that meant you had taken care of him, as we had said you would."

Verl barely nodded his head to her, then he dropped a brief bow to the duke. "Sir, I have brought your nephew home."

Laird strode forward and stopped in front of Rayid, waiting for him to stand. When the duke stood aside, the boy took the throne.

"Your highness," the duke gave him a brief nod. "You are king still, under my grace and protection. As long as you agree to my terms, we shall be good neighbors. And, as you have agreed already, until you come of age, you are from this day forth under my regency. I shall leave my daughter, the Princess Merind, here in charge to advise you, and with her, her friend, whom your people---and you, yourself, my lord---shall honor always as the Bearman. If you abide by their rules and mine, you shall live long here and well, in their loving guidance."

The boy's young hands clenched the carved arms of the throne as Rayid spoke, and he cast dark looks up and down at Merind when the duke introduced her. But when Rayid introduced Crel as the Bearman, Laird cast him, then his bear, with such a look of hatred that if eyes could shoot arrows, Laird's were doing so. It chilled Crel more than he expected it could. He looked away quickly to meet Verl's eyes.

~

An hour later by the tower bells, Crel stretched back against his padded chair. They had retired to the antechamber behind the throne room to read the agreement Rayid had written and Laird had signed. Merind had finally signed it, and Crel had too.

Ailil was still arguing for concessions. Her son, as Henrik's son, and second in line to the throne, would foster at court from age five to seventeen. Ailil would have rights to visit, but no longer than two months out of each year. Or else Eris could live with her in the Valley of the Capsens and renounce his claim to the throne. The Capsen city of Drespin would be rebuilt by the crown, and the Capsen Valley would be enlarged by two leagues to the north. But Ailil would not be regent when Rayid returned to Navarn, Merind would. And Crel himself too, surprisingly.

The people wanted him in power, the duke had said; and Merind and Ailil both acknowledged it. "Also," the duke had added, "Laird will live longer than the day I leave for Navarn--but only if neither Ailil nor Merind have an unchecked regency over him."

That had silenced both the women for a few tightened minutes, but all Crel could think of was the look of arrows shooting from the young king's eyes.

He glanced at the model map of Norgondy, left in place at the end of the council table by the former queen. Several red and black flags and chess-like pieces dotted it. They included a furred piece with a bearhead that stood beside the duke's crowned piece and a veiled tellerwoman piece. The three were still surrounded by the flags of the queen's forces in Moxie Pass. And all three pieces had red lightning strikes across their chests to their heart, as if still invoking the winged god to destroy them.

Crel took in a tight breath. How would they ever make Laird believe they were no longer his enemies? Simply by signing a sheet of paper? He knew the boy-king must still have supporters in the land. Even traders who claimed the motto Crel himself had once claimed to live by—to be loyal to whoever sat the throne—had hearty arguments and opinions in private they'd never express in front of any guardsman, judge, or client. Laird would sit the throne, Merind would counsel him, and the country would still be divided for years to come. If only Crel could take to the road, leave it all behind him----but then....wasn't he the one responsible now, for every other life around him, believing in him? From the first day he'd let Freyshin say he was, yes, dammit.

Verl stretched in the chair beside Crel, then looked around the room, then quickly into the corner behind them. Crel glanced behind them too. All that stood there watching them was the statue of a king dressed for battle. The crest on its shield that had once identified the statue as that of Henrik had been scratched off and replaced by a painting of the Winged God, Crel had been told. But the sword that had been in the statue's outstretched right hand was gone.

And the boy-king was no longer sitting beside it.

Verl grasped the table, stood up. "Where's Laird? Did anyone see him go--?".

They heard the bear growling in the next room, then she growled again louder.

Crel sprang to his feet and raced back into the throne room. The others followed close behind him.

He stopped when he saw Laird swinging the sword at Jesser.

She stood up in dance position on her hind legs, dropping to her forelegs just in time to duck the sword, then standing up again to bat at the sword's silver flash as it swept past her. She growled again, happily.

"She's playing!" Verl said incredulously.

"Laird isn't" said the Duke.

427

"No. He isn't," Verl answered. "My lord—" He pushed past Crel, ran forward to the boy. "You can't—

Crel ran forward too. "Jesser. Don't—"

Too late. Both of them. At the end of her chain, Jesser lunged her head forward to bite at the flash, and the sword connected to her nose. Blood, black fur spurted; she dropped to the floor and howled.

Laird swung again, lower this time, catching her on the other side of her head.

Jesser rose up, snarling in shock and rage. The left side of her head above her eye had barely been cut open. She lashed out at Laird as Verl caught him and pulled him away.

"Jesser!" Crel shouted. "Down!"

She snarled at Crel, now closest to her, lunging at the end of her chain, slashing her teeth and her claws at him, betrayed and enraged.

"Jesserwiss!" Crel held out his hands, palms open towards her, trying to calm his voice. "Down. Down. Let me see you, help you–"

"It killed my mother!" Laird yelled, struggling to free himself from Verl's arms. "Killed my friends. Took my throne!"

"No, my lord! She didn't!" Verl motioned to the two guardsmen standing nearby to help him.

The bear snarled at the boy, at the guardsmen as they moved, snarled and slashed a claw out towards Crel.

"Wiss!" Crel implored, hoping against hope to reach his former master, if his spirit were, or ever had been, joined inside her. "Wiss, stop her, *stop her!*"

Jesser dropped to her feet, snarled at him. "Jesserwiss, let me look at you. Down, girl."

"Why didn't you stop him?" Verl asked the guardsmen as they helped him wrestle the boy and grab the sword from him.

"He ordered us away–"

"He's the king, sir."

Jesser snarled in their direction, and still wouldn't let Crel near her.

"Jesser." Crel said. Tears wet his cheeks. He bit his lip, turned away from her, and marched towards the boy-king and the guards.

He wrenched the sword from their hands, and carried it back towards Jesser and raised it to swing it hard.

"Crel, no!" Merind shouted. She was behind him, grabbing his arm.

"She attacked him," Crel said. "She won't let us near her again. She'll never trust us. And we can never trust her again. Not now." He jerked himself free of Merind's arms and raised the heavy sword. "I have to."

"No. No, you don't," the duke said. "The bear will stay here. She will be caged, but she will stay here in this throne room, always. If Laird so much as disobeys my orders, or Merind's wishes, in any way, the Beargod will be watching him. Everyday. Seeing him, seeing into his every dream." Rayid turned hard eyes to Laird, and Laird stared back, seething, but silent. He shook himself free of the guardsmen, stood stiff and straight, facing the duke. "That is my order, sir. And it shall be so. That bear ever dies, and you do too."

Chapter 35
Singer of Norgondy

Unlike the drought, quakes, and ashfall of last year, the rains came early this year, and bright days followed. Almond trees, then cherry, apple and chestnut trees scented the air with spring. In the evening breezes from over the sea and down from the hills, wisps of cottonwood and cherry blossoms fluttered through the city streets. Crops in the fields to the north and to the east were sown a month early this summer, and the corn was already as high as a horse's neck, so that it looked like from Hornblower's Hill that riders rode in on a sea of gold. And in every corner, orange poppies, blue heather, red paintbrushes, and the golden meadow starflowers carpeted the land with renewed faith.

Verl could play Dellet the Younger's Song of the Meadowflowers this year---he knew he could. And so easily he could make people see the flowers too. Believe the golden flowers fell upon their heads as they listened to him play. Blue, red, yellow, green lights from the stained glass windows above colored his hands, colored each finger, and each string. Two new regents ruled the land, two new gods blessed the people. A Capsen Springing Tree had been erected in Norgarth Square, and the citizens of all faiths had for months rejoiced and danced under its long silk ribbons at nights. And the gods, the Bear God and the new sea god, with the spirit of their former king in its face, had smiled down from the stars. Verl's fingers tensed as he waited to play.

In the small audience, Eleidice stood waiting too. She had sung at the Springing Tree in the Square last night, and during the dance, she had made Verl promise he would come today to Singerhalle and try again to become a Master Singer.

"No one plays like you," she had said. "No one ever has."

It was two years ago when he had last stood in this hall. Two years ago when he had last listened to the colors fall from the stained glass windows above as candidates for the Chain of Mastery played. When he had last tried to translate his music into the lights he saw. And when he had last tried to make his listeners see exactly what he saw, visions of flowers—and had failed.

He could force the vision on his listeners now, on every mind he could touch. Jere stood in the audience beside Eleidice, holding her hand, and smiling up at him. Verl smiled back, and knew then what he should do.

Verl bowed to the judges as they sat under the dancing lights. "This is a song I promised a friend I would play someday." He met the little boy's eyes, nodded. "I dedicate this song to Jesser the Bear. This is her life."

Verl played notes ponderous and slow at first, remembering. He watched the falling lights on the floor, on his fingers, blue, purple, white, white, blue. He had first met Jesser in the sleep of winter, rescuing Jere from the dragon of Malla. From the corrupt tax collector, corrupt captain, more corrupt mayor, defeating their lies by making their lie of a dragon look real. By making the dragon look like the images of the Winged God, then blaming it. Black, blue, yellow, black, Jesser in dancing position boxed the Winged God, boxed the night air around her. Red, red, red; she charged and killed the captain charging at her, the only enemy she saw.

Then marching, a winter and spring of marching, traders and farmers rising up, wearing masks of fur and teeth, wielding scythes and shepherds' crooks. And in the evening, dancing, laughing, singing the songs of the people that Jere had reminded him how to play. Blue, blue, red, blue, Jesser twirled and boxed and danced with Merind to the farmers' music. Then white, glorious white, the tailed star splashing across the sky. The march again, the call to arms, the march to victory, to the shining bear god splashed high upon a mountainside, to a faith that flowed in colored lights and music through Verl fingers, through his memories, through black dolphins, black bears, boys chasing monkey tails, to nights of falling stars, and beyond.

There was no reaction when Verl laid his hand across his lute and silenced his strings. The judges sat watching him, saying nothing. The audience stared back at him, and even little Jere had lost his smile.

And then, slowly, one by one, they began to clap.

~

Ten years later, Verl stood on the roof of the palace beyond the bright glare in the sun of the observatory and listened to his song being played in the streets below. It had become the March of the Bear of Norgondy, the song of the people's war, and as the band played the national anthem, spectators threw meadow flowers upon the gilded carriage of their new young king. Crel and Merind's son.

Verl gripped the stone wall harder. He, for one, could not feel like celebrating. Could not help wondering if the tales from last year of the two young princes in the tower, King Laird, Prince Eris, killing each other were true.

Or if instead, Merind had arranged it.

He didn't like thinking that. And Jere, now a young apprentice at Singerhalle, would shake his head at him if he knew he were suspecting her again.

Peace reigned now. Verl watched the cascade of flowers falling on the parade. The irony of how his naming dream had played out hurt inside him. Not even Jere, after all he had tried to teach him, was asking questions anymore.

Their war had made a difference. The people under Merind's regency were far better off now than they ever had been under Felain's... Weren't they?

His song in blaring horns and pounding drums and strong proud voices in the streets proclaimed it so.

~

An hour later, Merind, Crel and their young son, the newly crowned King Wissernel, waved to the crowd from the rose balcony. Then with Jesser's young daughter on a chain, they went into the throne room below to accept their new lords' congratulations, and Verl, invited to play at the coronation, hurried down to join them.